Praise for *Swimming Between Worlds*

"A perceptive and powerful story told with generosity and grace. The struggle of its deftly drawn young characters to navigate the monumental changes—cultural and personal—that the civil rights movement brought to the South is rich and compelling."
—*New York Times* bestselling author Charles Frazier

"A smart and tender tale. I was left with admiration for Orr's exquisite prose, along with an awareness of one simple truth: Sometimes it takes living in another culture to better understand your own. A beautiful book."
—*New York Times* bestselling author Diane Chamberlain

"An original and important novel certain to take its place in American literature on race. The narrative unfolds with urgency and power, in graceful prose rich in sensuous detail. [Orr's] finest work to date."
—Angela Davis-Gardner, author of *Plum Wine*

"A blistering story told by a gifted writer. From the moment I began this compelling novel, it followed me around; the riveting plot and real-life characters would not let me go."
—Anna Jean Mayhew, author of *The Dry Grass of August*

"Lush and sensuous. This poignant and triumphant story shows two Americans emerging in a complex time from their own sorrow and displacement to take on political unrest and the turmoils of love."
—Peggy Payne, author of *Sister India*

"A touching love story . . . [and an] intelligently written and vivid evocation of a civil rights struggle that has heartbreaking relevance to the here and now."
—Eleanor Morse, author of *White Dog Fell from the Sky*

"Poignant and agonizing, the novel captures the South the moment before the gun went off, prefiguring our current national trauma around race and society."
—Fenton Johnson, author of *The Man Who Loved Birds*

"A captivating narrative about race, sex, nationality, generations, and romance, Orr's expansive new novel fulfills the promise of her debut tour de force, *A Different Sun*. Her keen sense of historical impact and geographical detail keeps us reading and hoping for a sequel."
—ie Miner, author of *Traveling with Spirits*

Also by Elaine Neil Orr

A DIFFERENT SUN

GODS OF NOONDAY:
A WHITE GIRL'S AFRICAN LIFE

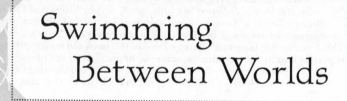

Swimming
Between Worlds

Elaine Neil Orr

BERKLEY
New York

BERKLEY
An imprint of Penguin Random House LLC
375 Hudson Street, New York, New York 10014

Copyright © 2018 by Elaine Neil Orr
Readers Guide copyright © 2018 by Penguin Random House LLC
Excerpt from *A Different Sun* copyright © 2013 by Elaine Neil Orr
Penguin Random House supports copyright. Copyright fuels creativity,
encourages diverse voices, promotes free speech, and creates a vibrant culture.
Thank you for buying an authorized edition of this book and for complying with
copyright laws by not reproducing, scanning, or distributing any part of it in any
form without permission. You are supporting writers and allowing Penguin
Random House to continue to publish books for every reader.

BERKLEY is a registered trademark and the B colophon is a trademark of
Penguin Random House LLC.

Library of Congress Cataloging-in-Publication Data

Names: Orr, Elaine Neil, author.
Title: Swimming between worlds/Elaine Neil Orr.
Description: First edition. | New York: Berkley, 2018.
Identifiers: LCCN 2017024292 (print) | LCCN 2017019831 (ebook) | ISBN
9780425282731 (print) | ISBN 9780698406384 (ebook)
Subjects: LCSH: Race relations—Fiction. | GSAFD: Bildungsromans.
Classification: LCC PS3615.R58843 L63 2018 (ebook) | LCC PS3615.R58843 (print)
| DDC 813/.6—dc23
LC record available at https://lccn.loc.gov/2017024292

First Edition: April 2018

Printed in the United States of America
1 3 5 7 9 10 8 6 4 2

Cover photograph of pool by H. Armstrong Roberts/ClassicStock/Getty Images
Cover design by Sandra Chiu
Book design by Tiffany Estreicher

For Scarlett

And in memory of
Samuel Adegoke Adeniji

ACKNOWLEDGMENTS

I wish to thank all those who helped me and supported me through the writing of this book.

My family—mother, father, sister—for the sweet American year we shared in a foursquare on West End Boulevard. And then again, my mother, who encouraged my writing even as she left this sphere. My husband, Anderson Orr, who was my constant and best consultant on how to fashion this novel.

My fabulous agent and friend, Joelle Delbourgo, who sold the proposal early and then served as the book's best friend as Random House and Penguin merged and we experienced a number of tremors. My wonderful editor, Katherine Pelz, who caught this book on its fourth bounce and "got it" and loved it and told me exactly how to make it better and better. Thanks also to Natalee Rosenstein, Kendra Harpster, and finally and wonderfully Kate Seaver. And everyone else on the Berkley team who enthusiastically ushered my novel into the world.

Those who offered significant research assistance—to them I am profoundly grateful: Yomi Durotoyo, my Yoruba guru; George Williamson, who participated in the Woolworth's sit-in in Winston-Salem; Katherine Foster at the New Winston Museum; my colleague Jason Miller; tour guide Laura Giovanelli; and crucially, Fam Brownlee, renowned Winston-Salem historian, as well as Edwin F. "Abie" Harris, Jr., university architect emeritus, NC State University, who submitted to being interviewed and then read a draft of the book, commented, and offered important insight.

Rebecca Walker and Rachel Harper, who spent an afternoon talking me through my beginnings. Wilton Barnhardt for important early conversation. My friends and early readers Nell Joslin, Angela Davis-Gardner, Virginia Ewing Hudson, Kate Blackwell, Dana Lindquist, Peggy Payne, and Jane Andrews. Later readers Deb Wyrick, Katy Yocom, Molly Beck, Marc Dudley, Nancy McCabe, and Fred Hobson. Tony Harrison, my department head, who championed my writing and offered every assistance possible.

All my friends in the Spalding University low-residency MFA in Writing program, beginning with Sena Jeter Naslund, for their brilliance and cheer and encouragement. They are my writing village, my writing home.

Friends and fellow writers of the North Carolina Writers' Network and the North Carolina Writers Conference.

The Virginia Center for the Creative Arts and the Hambidge Center for Creative Arts and Sciences for significant time to write in beautiful and generous environments. I am also grateful to Cedar Cross Retreat Center for meditative writing time and to Toni and Dave Phillips at urbanpioneer.net for a week in a beautiful, historic quadriplex right on First Street, just around the corner from the foursquare in Winston-Salem.

The "Do you remember Winston when . . . ?" Facebook page for entertaining many historical questions.

Sister and friends who tended my spirit in a time of personal grief: Becky Albritton, Lynn Rhoades, Laura Murphy Frankstone, Nancy Osborne, and Kathryn Milam.

Kathryn Stripling Byer for inspiration, invitation, example, and belief.

The ones I love in their own precious lives: my son, Joel Orr, clear-eyed Scarlett Orr, and her mother and my dear friend, Dominique.

Zachary Lunn and Blair Donahue for assists at the very end.

And finally, thank you, readers, for indulging the liberty I have taken with Hanes Park. To my knowledge, there never was a pool.

Oh, where have you been, my blue-eyed son?
Oh, where have you been, my darling young one?
—Bob Dylan, "A Hard Rain's A-Gonna Fall"

"This is just a geography lesson."
—Toni Morrison, *Song of Solomon*

Swimming Between Worlds

Prologue

January 1958
Ibadan, Nigeria

EARLY MORNINGS ON the university compound were quiet as the dawn of the world. Tacker sipped his coffee. At the first distillation of light, a bird trilled. It was harmattan season and temperatures dipped into the sixties. Tacker pulled on his college sweater, the one his mother had thrown last minute into his duffel bag. He wasn't thinking yet, only feeling the air, the hot cup in his hands. He stepped from the porch into the yard. A woman appeared on the road, and then another, cutting through the compound to the market. Their voices rose like bicycle bells.

He thought about Jill, her long, smooth legs, the way she sat in the grass and later got up and dusted off the back of her skirt, bits of grass and leaf still sticking to the fabric as she walked off unawares. Did his college girlfriend still love him? He didn't miss her. There was too much over here, too much every day pulling him like a magnet, life brighter and fuller than anything back home. He couldn't explain the pull to his mother in letters or to his father the few times he had telephoned. It wasn't like the pull of a girl. It was like a god.

Winston-Salem,
North Carolina

1959

Chapter One

July 1959

TACKER HART CAME home from Nigeria to discover a town he almost knew. The Winston-Salem of his youth was branded by Ardmore Methodist, Reynolds High, and shopping at Davis Department Store on Fourth Street, his youth green with creeks and football fields, turning white in winter with sledding and the Sears Christmas display. And then there was the depot of his father's store, Hart's Grocery, near the intersection of First Street and Hawthorne, right where Peters Creek ran. The grocery existed out of time, smelling of onions and floor wax, blooming with color in fruit displays and on cereal boxes, and sanctified by the community of regulars who stopped by for a special on ham hocks or conversation with Tacker's father or the full week's shopping and a drink from the Coca-Cola machine. Everyone was welcome, or so Tacker had thought.

Almost two years later and the air still carried the high,

sweet smell of tobacco, but there was an expressway through town that nipped at the heels of West End, the neighborhood where he'd grown up, and that occasionally—where an elevated section curved near Hawthorne—threw a car over the guardrails and passengers to their deaths. Thruway Shopping Center had grown up in his absence like a film set temporarily installed, only it wasn't temporary. Tacker's mother drove out there almost every day. Wake Forest College was the new boast of the city, which was fair enough, though Tacker had no investment in it, having studied architecture at State College in Raleigh, flourishing in the competitive atmosphere of design studios housed on a huge courtyard on the north side of campus.

More changed than Winston-Salem was Tacker. He had left home a minor American hero and returned disgraced. The thought of his violent dismissal from an international assignment with the Clintok Corporation hollowed his chest even now, four months after his return.

When Tacker first got home in March, he stayed up late and slept until midmorning. On and off in the night, he woke to a perception of malignant doom, a feeling in his chest like a container filling with terror. There was no escape as the vessel filled, the sensation taking over his entire chest—filling and filling—until he thought it would explode, and then just as the container of his heart was about to burst, it did not. The terror held, containing him rather than he it. He wondered if he was having a heart attack. He would sleep and awaken and the episode would recur, as if he were coming out of nightmare into nightmare. During the day his face felt heavy. He marveled at a blooming red crepe myrtle across the street that appeared at midday to burn like fire, and yet it seemed to him that the inner light of things had dimmed. Perhaps it was merely the contrast with the tropics that he sensed, but Tacker suspected the dimness had more to do with what he had learned. The world was not just and neither God nor any teacher or coach or sponsor was going to save him. Occasionally he felt angry instead of depressed, overcome by righteous indignation. He'd done nothing wrong. But the fire flickered out pretty quickly.

There wasn't anything he wanted to do.

After dinner one evening in July, his father spoke up. "Get your architectural license. I can make a connection for you." They were in the family den. Tacker stood by the mantel, gazing at a picture he had sent from Nigeria, the country of his assignment. He had gone to help design the prototype for a high school to be replicated throughout the country and to establish American goodwill in an African nation on its way to independence.

"I don't want to do architecture right now," he said. In the photograph, he was posed with his Nigerian teammates, ten in all, graduates of Nigeria's first university, in front of a banana tree grove. His hair was below his ears because he hadn't found a barber. Tacker was the tallest, his arms saddled around his best friend, Samuel Ladipo's, shoulders, a smile on his face. A local photographer had taken the picture and sold it to Tacker for a shilling. Tacker marveled that his clothes, and not just his skin, were so much lighter than the others', his figure ghosted. He turned to his parents, neither of whom was looking at him. His father wore a look of pained disapproval.

They were in a quagmire and Tacker had put them there, but he was too sunk to pull anyone out. Even with his father kindly opening a door, he could not walk through it. He left the house for a walk around the block but walked much farther than that, all the way to the tobacco warehouses at the end of Trade Street, where he lay back on an overflowing bag of tobacco leaves, half intoxicated by the scent, and looked up at the stars. Why couldn't he feel proud? He'd stood up for what he'd believed, hadn't he?

But Tacker was accustomed to triumph. An inglorious sacking left a man wholly alone. When he got home after midnight, the lights in the den were out but his mother had waited up for him. She picked up just where he thought he had escaped.

"What are you going to do?" she said, peering through her new wing-tipped glasses. When Tacker was a boy his mother had worn nylon dresses with pearl buttons all the way down the front and he'd thought she was the most beautiful person in the world.

"I don't know."

"You have been home all spring and half the summer. People are beginning to wonder what's wrong." She rose from her seat. "You have to move out and get a job. This is too hard on us."

"Maybe I could work at Hart's." Tacker rubbed the back of his neck. "Maybe I could manage the store."

"I don't know about that." His mother's lips wrenched to one side of her face. "You haven't demonstrated very responsible behavior lately. What happened to you over there?"

Tacker looked at her. "I learned that there's a world outside this town," he said. "That we're not the be-all, end-all of the universe."

"Who's *we*?"

"This country, the way we live."

"How do we live?"

"Superficially."

"Well, Mr. Universe, I'll leave the question of your employment to your father. I don't much like being called superficial. I gave birth to you, in case you've forgotten that particular tidbit." She smacked the door open on her way out of the room.

THE NEXT MORNING, Tacker got up early. He had nowhere but his parents' house to go, no car, no job, but he had a few hundred dollars saved. He walked to a diner at the corner, picked up the

Winston-Salem Journal, went in and ordered breakfast and coffee, opened the paper, and scanned the classifieds for houses to rent. His finger stopped at a house on West End Boulevard. His parents had moved to the newer Buena Vista neighborhood while he was in college and his dad had opened a second grocery, sleeker and more hermetic than the old Hart's. Tacker had eaten half of his breakfast and drunk three cups of coffee when he folded the paper and started walking to the old neighborhood, with the intention of reclaiming his territory. He passed Hanes Park, where he had joyfully suffered four hot summers practicing with the varsity football team, learning how to escape gravity. He had played wide receiver, but this morning he cocked his arm like a quarterback and sent the phantom ball soaring to his younger self on the field, airborne to haul the leather in and press it to his heart. If working at Hart's as a teenager had instilled in Tacker a sense of democracy ("Meet every customer with respect," his father had said, though now Tacker could see that not everyone was actually included), football had taught him fair play, a concept also apparently defunct.

West End was notoriously hilly, and Tacker angled up a side street. The rental house occupied the corner of West End Boulevard and Jarvis Street, an old foursquare, a style popular at the turn of the century, two storied, perfectly square, a mere five blocks from the original Hart's. This one was upright, stately, and composed, and the porch seemed to invite him in. He could see into the spacious sitting room and an adjoining dining room. Another room opened to the right, a music room or library with built-ins. In the backyard, he found a separate wired garage, a perfect place for the motorcycle he dreamed of buying. He'd lusted for one since the days of riding a Schwinn New World as a kid.

Tacker headed to the nearest service station, dropped a dime in the phone, and called the number in the paper.

"Hello. Calloway here."

"I'm calling about the foursquare," Tacker said, giving his name.

"You and your wife?"

"Just me."

"I had in mind renting to a family. It's big for one person."

Did his voice betray his bungled last year? No one knew but his parents, yet Tacker suspected everyone could see through him. But on the phone?

"Might be better if we met," Calloway said.

The man's office sat right where Summit Street wheeled down to converge with West End and Reynolda near the old Daniel Boone marker. Tacker took a seat across from Calloway, who had a washed-out look and round shoulders.

"It's actually my mother's house," he said. "Tied up in a trust. So you understand why I'm particular about it."

"Of course. It's a great house." Tacker felt more confident.

"What did you say your name was?"

"Tacker Hart."

"The football player?"

"Once upon a time."

"So you can catch a ball. How about minor repairs? Can you keep up a yard?"

"I'm pretty handy," Tacker said.

"Thirty-five a month?"

Midmorning, Tacker was in the basement of his parents' house, digging through boxes of college leftovers. He found towels and a few old dishes and kitchen essentials, all of which he stuffed into a laundry basket and hauled up to his room. His mind sped. The cloth he'd brought home from Nigeria—he could see the girl he'd bought it from, under an umbrella, her entire inventory consisting of two bars of soap, one pack of cigarettes, and four yards of indigo-dyed cloth. It could be a curtain.

A week later, on a hot August morning when his mother was out shopping and his father was at work, Tacker wrote a thank-you note and scribbled his new address at the bottom, walked to the bus stop with his suitcase and duffel bag, and waited. It seemed riotously funny that at age twenty-five he was running away from home, but the back side of funny was a welcome feeling of honor. He figured himself a pilgrim out to slay the dragon of his failure.

He spent his first night on the floor.

The next morning he scouted out a secondhand store full up with dressers recently cycled out of Baptist Hospital. They were metal and light. Of the two mattresses he could choose from, he took the one that came from someone's guest room, or so he was told. He picked up the metal dresser, carried it onto a bus, and put it in the house. The mattress was a bigger challenge, especially considering the hills he was going to encounter. For a fee of two dollars, a kid at the store offered to help him walk it to the foursquare twelve blocks away. Tacker didn't relish another night on the floor. At noon and ninety degrees they started out, trying to hold the mattress under their arms. But they kept losing hold of it. Tacker thought of the men he'd seen in Nigeria, pedaling bicycles, balancing mattresses on their heads, uphill and down. How had they done that?

"Let's try it on our heads," he said.

They jousted to get the mattress up and the weight distributed, and off they went. When they met folks on the sidewalk, they were forced to stop or tuck into an alley. Halfway to the foursquare, the kid backed up, not looking where he was stepping, and fell into a ditch. The mattress toppled, landing in the grass with a muffled thud.

"I think I twisted my ankle." The kid stood and tried to put weight on it. "God Almighty," he yelled, slackening back to the ground.

"I'll run back to the store and get someone to come pick you up," Tacker said.

The kid looked like he was going to cry.

"I'll pay you anyway."

The kid wiped at his eyes.

FIFTEEN MINUTES LATER Tacker was alone with his mattress, feeling fortunate to be on a side street. But it was a pitiful fortune, almost sublimely tragic. He used to be good at everything—in that other life when he won high school football games and picked up scholastic and civic awards, then excelled in college, finding himself in his senior year recommended by the department head, Professor Cabera, a dapper Argentinian with a vision that transcended North Carolina, for a choice international assignment with the Clintok Corporation. It had come to him like a perfectly thrown pass, a brilliant opportunity to further his career, though once he got to Nigeria he had found himself much more interested in the place itself, its cacophonous yet serene atmosphere.

He pulled a tall blade of grass from its green sheath and put it in his mouth. A rumble of thunder and a dark cloud encroached in the western sky. Tacker hauled the mattress up and stood it next to a tree. His arm span was just wide enough to match the width of the mattress and grab hold of the sides. He put his head in the middle of the bed and tried to hoist it, but he was too close to the tree. He tried again, and this time he managed to get it up, but the thing slipped from his grasp and slid down his back. Across the street, two women his mother's age stopped to watch. He tried again. The thing wobbled and Tacker had to shift it a little and brace his legs to keep it on his head. When he thought he had it, he took a step. Another. Five steps. He was back on the sidewalk. But the mattress hung in the front and he couldn't see very far ahead. Not only that, it kept snagging on nearby branches. He went slowly. A breeze came and it felt good, but then there was another rumble of thunder. He couldn't turn his head. There was no way but forward.

Turning onto First Street with a mattress on his head, Tacker's vision of himself as heroic pilgrim was pretty well fried. First was precipitously steep and the sidewalk way too narrow. A car horn blared and a DeSoto Firedome glided past, its finlike fenders bright in the sun. Finally he got to West End; only one more block. He swung out right into the center of the street. At the foursquare, he stepped up onto the porch, slid the mattress off his shoulder, and stood it against the front windows, slipping down beside it.

A yellow leaf floated down, harbinger of fall. The rain that had threatened didn't come. Tacker lugged the mattress in, through the front rooms and to the bedroom, where he fell onto it and slept.

The next day he went to Southern Bell and picked up a telephone. In the afternoon when his mother was at her bridge game, he slipped back to his parents' house and returned with his old record player, two dozen LPs, and a fistful of forty-fives. He meant to work up his nerve to call Jill, his college sweetheart, twenty slender miles away in Greensboro. Pat Boone crooned "Ain't That a Shame" as Tacker drank a beer. Back when he was at State College, he'd borrow a friend's car to call on Jill at Meredith College. As far as he knew, she had no idea that he had returned from Nigeria several months ago now. He hadn't written to her all spring because doing so would make the point. Now he needed to explain why he hadn't written, much less called, in all that time. When darkness fell, Tacker stomped out the front door and took a long walk up from First onto Fourth Street and on into downtown. Finally he turned around and came back. He'd call her tomorrow.

A WEEK LATER he called his dad though he still hadn't called Jill. "Come by and see my place."

His dad showed up with da Vinci, Tacker's cat, rescued from a Raleigh alley when he was in college, living in a frat house. Tacker offered his dad the only chair.

"Your mother says you can have the couch we've got in the basement. And the old dinette set. She told me to bring the cat."

"Thanks." Tacker stroked da Vinci's back.

"What are you doing about a bed?"

"Hauled a mattress from a secondhand store."

"I could have helped you with that."

"I managed."

His father was a large-framed, lanky man, his curly hair beginning to gray. If Tacker had to choose one word to describe him, it would be *particular*. "You know, Dad, I'd be happy to help at the grocery. It's just around the corner."

His father straightened himself in the chair. "Well, son, I could give you some hours. I'm not sure it'd be enough to live on."

"I'd like to manage the store."

His father looked at him as if beholding a square object that needed fitting through a round hole. "I'm not so sure about that."

"You know I can do it. I know that store frontwards and backwards."

"You can do it if you set your mind to it. But your mind has been absent of late."

Tacker still didn't know what his parents knew of his sacking;

enough, he guessed, to be reasonably anxious. The dismissal papers included a recommendation for a mental assessment.

"Let me think about it."

"Sure."

"I've got to get back to work."

"Thanks for coming." Tacker dug his hands into his pockets.

IN THE KITCHEN, Tacker opened a can of tuna fish. Da Vinci purred over his bowl, tail curled on the linoleum. Tacker rinsed the tin, the rush of water catching the slant of light through the window. In a sliver of memory he was knee-deep in a Nigerian stream out in the bush, light glinting off the water as he filled a bucket for his evening bath.

A few days later, his father showed up on Tacker's doorstep.

"Frank Tilman's ready to give up managing the store. Told me back in May. He and his wife are retiring to Boone."

He handed Tacker two keys on a ring. "Mind you, I don't want to get in the way of your doing what you really want to when you're ready. Connie's staying as assistant manager. You show her some respect."

Long ago, Tacker had worried that his dad was sweet on Connie, or maybe Tacker was sweet on her when she first started at Hart's, twenty-five years old and not married and Tacker was fourteen. Now she had two kids and a disappeared husband, and chain-smoking had withered her face.

"Don't let me down."

Did he say "again"? Looking back, Tacker couldn't remember. The keys were in his pocket as he conjured Jill a few days later. They seemed tangible evidence that he might belong somewhere. That evening, he checked his reflection in the mirror and dialed her home number. The hall phone was cold in his hand. "Jill?"

"Tacker? You're back," she said. "I thought you were supposed to be here in August. But I haven't heard a word from you." She sounded relieved and at the same time contrite, as if there was something on her side she was holding back. "It's good to hear your voice."

"Been readjusting, I guess"

"I almost drove to Winston to check with your folks. But I thought . . ."

"I should have been in touch. I want to see you."

"Me too. You're staying in Winston?" Her voice took on the barest hint of judgment.

Was he ready to open up to her? He'd suggest a movie. "For now. How about I come down next Saturday? We'll go to a matinee and have dinner." Jill had a funny upper lip, almost a little lopsided. He adored it.

She paused. "What time?"

Was she trying to figure out how to squeeze him in between other appointments? He recalled an evening in Raleigh, a football game. She'd asked why he didn't play college ball. "More important things to do," he'd said. She had gathered his lapels in her hands and raised her mouth to kiss him.

"I'll be there by noon. Think about what you'd like to see. I haven't been paying any attention to the movies."

"Well, you just got back," she said, letting out a breath.

In the silence after the call, he struggled to reassure himself. Of course it would take time for her to warm up. It had been two years.

MONDAY MORNING HE showed up at Hart's an hour early and still his dad beat him there.

"I need to remind you of a few things."

"I know everything, Dad."

"Humor me."

WEDNESDAY TACKER WOKE to the sound of a bee in the room. He pulled on his blue jeans and closed the window and the sound stopped. In the kitchen he poured cornflakes into a bowl and he thought he heard the bee again. The afternoon when he was packed out of Nigeria, all he could hear was the drumming of his ears. Right this minute, he wondered if he was trailing some tropical disease, though he'd always heard it was the eyes that went first. He walked onto the screened back porch, down the stairs, and into the yard. Individual pine needles twenty feet up were clear as day. He whistled and could hear himself fine. Back in the kitchen, staring at his cereal, Tacker recalled Jill's jet-black hair with its perpetual bounce. She probably wore a girdle now like his mother. He wasn't any longer the man she had loved.

He managed to eat his breakfast and get to the store, set up the cash drawers, and put out fresh bread. His mother stopped in around eleven. She said she preferred the old store but Tacker knew why she was there.

"I'm making butternut squash soup," she said, as if that explained everything.

"You look great, Mom," he said.

"So do you, son."

"Thanks." What she probably wanted to say was, *Are you feeling stable? Do you want me to do your laundry? Are you back to normal?*

That evening he rang Jill again.

"Something's come up," he said. "I'll call you again. Soon."

"Tacker?"

"Yes?"

"I missed you for a long time."

"I know." He thought he heard her sigh before she hung up. Jill wasn't prepared to hear about what had happened. Though as a rule he told the truth to a fault, he knew he would lie to her. The sadness he felt was almost a comfort, it was so familiar.

WEST END HAD been Winston's first suburb, designed when streetcars were in use. At the turn of the century, the upper crust had built Victorians and then Craftsman homes with terraced lawns along the neighborhood's hilly, curvilinear streets. It didn't matter to Tacker that the neighborhood was now transitional, at least around the edges. Transitional fit his mood. He bought a porch swing.

He started running the track at the north end of Hanes Park. The third day, he experienced that terrible déjà vu he had had back in the spring, his heart seizing with terror. He bent over from the waist and breathed. That wasn't enough to dispel it. He had to sit down on the grass and hold his head.

IT WAS MARCH in Nigeria, still the dry season. Dust lifted from the roadside and entered the windows, settling onto the men's damp arms as the university van motored up the Ibadan–Osogbo road, delivering Tacker's team to a small mud-and-plaster chalet uphill of the Osun River in the heart of Yoruba land. After a year and a half on the project, they were joining a local contractor and a group of the town's men to lay concrete block for the first classroom building. Auspiciously, it seemed, they would be in town during a week of Osun festivities, Osun—Tacker had learned—being not merely a river, but also the goddess of the river, a divinity whose power lay in her capacity to enhance fertility. Every woman in town, Christian or not, had been to the river. Men too.

That first night in the chalet, Tacker and Samuel and the rest of them stayed up late, talking and drinking palm wine—all but Joshua, who was a teetotaler and read his Bible in the corner by lamplight. The incense of mosquito coils slued the air blue. They used sleeping mats. Near the end of the week, he met Anna Becker, an Austrian woman who had become an African priestess, and he wondered if everything he had ever known was illusion.

Their last morning in the chalet, he woke to someone calling his name. Tacker groped for his shirt, knocking Samuel's shoulder. "Were you calling me?" Samuel turned onto his back just as the curtained door to the room whipped open. Tacker's American supervisor, Mr. Fray, a man he had met only twice, barreled in. "Get up and get dressed," he said.

Samuel was instantly up and at attention, all five feet seven, one hundred thirty-five pounds of him. Tacker pulled on his shirt, getting it inside out in his hurry.

"Please, sir. How can I help you?" Samuel said.

"I'm not here for you. I'm here for him," Fray said, pointing at Tacker. "Get your things." Other men in the corners of the room woke and stretched.

"Where are we going?" Tacker said. "Are my parents okay?" His throat pulsed.

"Your parents are fine."

Outside, smelling the river, Tacker was fully awake. "I'm not going anywhere until you tell me what's going on."

"What's going on is you're coming with me to Ibadan."

"No, I'm not."

Fray lunged, grabbing his shoulder. Tacker jerked free and backed onto the threshold of the house.

"What in the hell is that on your arm?" Fray said.

The day before, Anna Becker had painted Tacker's arm with

henna, her idea, and Tacker had obliged as he might accept a piece of fruitcake from a pretty girl even though he hated fruitcake. Except that with Anna he was probably bewitched.

"It washes off," Tacker said.

"Wetin dey happen?" someone uttered.

"Just come with me," Fray said, his forehead beaded in sweat though the temperature was cool enough that Tacker suddenly remembered he had dreamed of snow. "You're serving here at the will of the Clintok Corporation, in case you've forgotten."

"What's that supposed to mean?"

"'Exemplify American values. Exhibit discipline, leadership, self-control.' Any of that ring a bell with you?"

"Please, sir," Samuel said, slipping past Tacker to face Fray. "Let us have some discussion."

"No discussion," Fray said, sidestepping Samuel, lurching at Tacker a second time.

"Don't touch me. I'll come. But you've got nothing to complain about with me. I've done my job."

"And a little more than your job," Fray said.

"Please," Samuel said to Tacker. "Wait for us to come with you."

"I'll be in Ibadan when you get there," Tacker said. "I'll see you in a few hours."

Fray opened the passenger door. Tacker got in. Fray started the Jeep. Samuel ran next to the vehicle, slapping Tacker's window until Fray picked up speed, though Tacker could still see Samuel in his mind's eye, the man's chest open to the sun as he stopped to catch his breath, his arms by his sides, his neatly trimmed hair and oval face with its broad mouth.

Halfway to Ibadan, it occurred to Tacker that Fray might have thought there was something going on with Samuel. "All we did was drink a little palm wine," he said. "Why are you doing this?"

The man's hair was so short Tacker could see the pink of his scalp. Veins bulged at his temples. "You've been reported more than once," he said.

"For what?"

"For getting tangled up in the culture."

"What do you mean?"

"We'll talk in Ibadan."

Tacker slumped in the seat as the Jeep's speed sliced the green world in two.

DUSK IN WINSTON-SALEM. Tacker on his front porch.

A light went on over a doorway across the street. He heard the strains of a Crickets song coming from somewhere, Buddy Holly. "That'll Be the Day." Buddy Holly, who was dead, fallen from the sky. The memory of bitter quinine came into Tacker's mouth and he wondered if regret had a taste. A breeze came up and the chill went through his shirt and he felt the wound of his heart, but it seemed eased somehow, or dulled. He wasn't sure which.

Chapter Two

EARLY IN OCTOBER Tacker looked up from the customer service desk to see a young woman in an old yard coat, too big for her, standing in the produce section, studying the apples. She put some in a bag and stopped, appearing to weigh her effort against their worth. The store phone rang and he took an order. When he looked back up, the woman was standing on the other side of the counter. She was a flower coming out of the old coat: a slender stem of neck, long mahogany-colored hair, pale skin, large eyes. As he looked at her, she cast her face back toward the produce and Tacker recognized her from high school, though she had been chubby then and wore her hair short. Now she was something else entirely, but her look was a little haunted then and it was a little haunted now. Dimly he recalled that she had been at the center of a sad story. Her father had died in a swimming accident at the coast. Monroe. Tacker couldn't recall her first name. She was one of those girls who seemed to have been born to a higher station in life.

"How can I help you?" he said.

"Kate Monroe," she said, turning her head back. "We were in high school together."

"Tacker Hart. I recognize you."

"That's nice. I guess." She produced a brief smile. "Look. I was wondering if you have a couple of boxes of apples. I remember they used to come in from Mount Airy this time of year."

"Right now all I have is what's out. The crop's running a month late. I can put some aside for you when they come in. We can deliver them." He made a mental note to order two extra boxes. Her face brightened for a moment.

"My parents always kept boxes of apples on the back porch to last through the winter."

"A fine tradition." A grin broadened across Tacker's face. Her chin jutted out just a little and this slight imperfection seemed to match her intensity about apples.

"I'll just pay when you bring them?"

"Don't you have a line of credit? Your family used to . . ." He couldn't finish the sentence. It seemed like maybe her mother had died too, though how could he know that?

"Let's start a new one," she said, "under my name. I like Stayman and Winesap." She put her hand to the back of her head where her hair folded into the coat. "I'll write down the address."

In a moment she was heading out the door; *1229 Glade Street*, she'd written, and her phone number. The note felt warm from her hand and Tacker wanted to keep it warm.

A HEAVY RAIN came mid-October, thunder rumbling for hours. In the morning the sun broke through. Da Vinci rolled onto his back, stretching out his soft white underbelly. Tacker took a last sip of coffee and set the cup down on its saucer, the familiar click of ceramic reassuring. Folks dallied after a rain. A quiet morning at the store would give him time to catch up on inventory. He enjoyed the clean aisles, the symmetry of displays, pyramids of oranges.

He walked out his front door, pulling it to. Every day, he felt sturdier. Still it seemed he was on vacation from the real point of living, a point he could only vaguely have described, though it had something to do with putting oneself at the edge of the world and staying there long enough to imagine something absolutely new. Outside, wind herded a curve of clouds at the far edge of sky and the air smelled of tobacco. The sidewalk was dark from the night's rain and fall leaves lay sleek on the pavement. Here and there morning light fell in dazzling sprees. Tacker felt the key in his pocket, cool and solid against his knuckles. He'd be happy to see Kate Monroe drop by again. She'd seemed as dazed by her present life as he felt about his.

Oaks still held their leaves and a gust of wind sent false rain onto his head. He wished for the cap he had left behind. At West End and First he took a sharp left, heading down the steep decline of First Street. A glint on the sidewalk caught his eye. He stopped and leaned over. At first he'd thought it was a girl's ring but it was only a penny, the burnished edge shining. Standing, he sensed someone behind him. A young Negro stood ten feet away. He wore a trilby hat and a camel-colored jacket. Where had the guy come from? Where had the word *Negro* come from? Since he'd been home, the appellation seemed bizarre. There were *Negroes* and *coloreds* and that South Carolina senator said *niggras* and lots of people said worse. "Morning," Tacker said.

The fellow tipped his hat. "Morning," he said, his eyes looking to the right of Tacker.

Tacker had never seen a Negro man his own age walking in West End. Unless they were working for a white family, Negroes rarely ventured past Church Street except to shop in a few downtown stores that everyone tacitly understood would admit them. Tacker started walking again and the fellow walked behind him. Tacker wanted to strike up a conversation but it was impossible. Why? The question angered him. In Nigeria he walked the lanes with friends all the time. They were garrulous, slapping his back good-naturedly, linking arms. Boys and men even held hands. There was a mellowness to it that he hadn't known before, like the evenings they sat together with kerosene lamps and talked about new countries and farming yam and round houses versus square ones and girls and God and the problem of gaining English but losing your native tongue.

Leaves clogged a storm drain. At the stoplight the Negro stood beside him. Tacker let him take off first and followed. For some reason he was afraid. Since coming back, he'd heard about rabble-rousers, black boys from up north showing up where they weren't welcome and asking for a fight. Across the street, the fellow turned right, walking the length of Hart's Grocery, in front of the advertisements for turkeys and hams and sweet potatoes plastered onto the window fronts, before gaining the parking lot on the other side and turning to approach the entrance. He adjusted his hat before reaching for the door.

"Is there something I can help you with?" Tacker said, stepping up. He pulled out the key.

"Wanted to buy some milk this morning," the man said, a look of surprise on his face.

"I'm Tacker Hart. We open at nine."

The man turned to go.

"You've walked all the way over here. You might as well get your milk," Tacker said, relieved that they were talking. "What's your name?"

The fellow hesitated. "Gaines. Gaines Townson."

"I manage the store for my dad. Go on. Get the milk."

"You sure, now?"

"The meat isn't out."

"All I need is the milk—for my baby sister." Gaines headed down the wrong aisle.

"No," Tacker said. "Let me show you." He started for the far aisle, through the produce, back to the cooler. "What do you like?"

Gaines reached for a quart of skim. "This'll do," he said.

"Take the whole milk. Same price."

"All right."

At the checkout, Gaines handed Tacker a quarter. Tacker tried to catch his eye, but he was looking out the window. For the first time he seemed nervous, as if someone might think he was out of place. As surely they would.

"I thank you," he said, tipping his hat again.

"There's not something else you need?" Nostalgic for Ibadan, Tacker didn't want to lose sight of the man in front of him. Couldn't they talk about where he was from? Though Gaines was taller and more substantial, he reminded Tacker a little of his good friend Samuel, the way he moved his mouth, the column of his throat. But Gaines was out the door, holding the glass bottle cradled against his chest. Sunlight filled the front windows and Tacker lost him in the glare. Seconds later a scream of tires broke the air.

Tacker spun around the counter, running for the door in the same instant.

Outside the light was so bright he had to make a visor of his hands; a tang of rubber and ground metal filled the air; an elderly gentleman walked as fast as he could away from the store; a white woman in a blue suit and matching hat stood on the sidewalk to Tacker's right, her mouth half-open, her hand up shielding her eyes. What Tacker saw next was all wrong. A green Buick pulled at a right angle to the street just in front of the store, two tires up on the sidewalk, the headlights practically kissing the storefront, the rear end sticking out into the street. The driver had swerved across oncoming traffic. Cars were backing up, horns blaring. Tacker stepped off the sidewalk into the street.

"Gaines?" he called, his voice echoing in his ears. He didn't see him anywhere, only his hat in the middle of the road. Two men were getting out of the Buick but Tacker had to get the hat. Where was Gaines? *Dear God, don't let him be sprawled out dead on the other side of the car.* The road was clear. Tacker got down on all fours. Nothing under the car.

Standing, he saw everything he had missed. The men had cornered Gaines at the storefront; they'd swerved to cut him off; Tacker had walked right past when he went to pick up the hat. Cool as a cowboy, the older fellow lassoed Gaines with a belt, pinned his arms, and pressed him against the plate glass of the front windows right below the TURKEYS, 12 CENTS A POUND sign. "Hey," Tacker said, "what are you doing?" The milk bottle was sitting on the window ledge. The younger of the two men looked at him. He was a kid, really, a swath of dark hair cutting across his forehead.

"Teach that nigger a lesson," Tacker heard from somewhere. He scrabbled around the Buick, his heart whapping. The woman in the blue suit backed away. "Cut it out," he yelled, close enough now that he could see the kid's pocked face.

They flipped Gaines around so he was facing the street and the boy kneed Gaines in the groin. He fell like a rag doll onto the sidewalk.

"When a white lady is passing," the older fellow said, "you get off the sidewalk." The man's belly sagged over his belt.

"Let's just cool down," Tacker said, trying to imagine what his father would do.

"Good idea," the kid said. He leaned for the milk, opened the bottle with his teeth, took a gulp, and threw the bottle into the air, a waggle of white soaring for a moment before splattering on the asphalt with a boom, glass shattering like ice.

"Let him go," Tacker said. The kid smiled and kicked Gaines in the side. In the fleeting instant of that kick, Tacker saw himself on the floor of the University College Ibadan dorm room, tackled and bruised.

Everything went into slow motion. A long, sharp whistle came from somewhere. The kid pulled his leg back again. A piece of glass glinted in the sun. Tacker pushed the old geezer away and elbowed the boy hard in the neck. His head went back and the soft white of his throat faced the sky, exposing the faint purple veins, his clavicle, the odd dimple in his chin. His hair fanned out when his leg gave.

"What the hell?" the older fellow said, quietly, as if something holy had occurred. He took a step sideways, almost polite; Gaines remained unmoving, his hands like strung-up doves resting on his back. The woman in the blue suit stood in mock judgment, a gloved hand to her mouth.

"Gaines," Tacker said. "You okay?"

Gaines opened and closed his eyes.

"You some kind of nigger lover?" the old fellow said, but he said it like a revelation. He was still too close to Gaines. Tacker sensed danger in the backs of his legs, like he had known when someone meant to hurt him in a tackle. Then everything sped up. The boy was on his feet, moving like a nervous fighter in a ring.

"You some kind of nigger lover?" he said, mimicking his older friend, maybe his father. He spat on the sidewalk. "You like these fancy niggers tipping their hats and winking at our women? He was taking up the whole sidewalk like a damned cock."

"Look here, now. This boy works for me." Tacker was twisted up pretty tight. Pray to God Gaines wouldn't dispute him.

"Coming out the front of your store? Colored help comes and goes from the back," the old fellow said, switching his toothpick to the side of his mouth.

Tacker glanced at Gaines, still lying on the sidewalk. Without his arms free, he couldn't even shield his head. A truck slowed its way around the Buick.

"He was delivering that milk," Tacker said, sidling over to put himself between Gaines and the others. "You gentlemen have had enough trouble for one morning." His blood surged and he thought his skin would split.

The kid lit a cigarette, took a drag, threw it down, and stubbed it with his toe. "You keep him in line or we'll be back. We'll be looking for him. You hear that, boy?" he said down to Gaines. "We got your number."

Tacker felt his heart clutch. "Shut the hell up. Just shut the hell up."

The kid pivoted. The men shambled to their car. Doors slammed. Tacker's heart pumped hard as the Buick pulled away. The whole scene flashed again: Gaines on the ground, the poison-mouthed men, and the woman in blue playing her part like a queen, gone now.

Gaines groaned and turned onto his side.

"Let me help you," Tacker said. "Careful. You might have a broken rib."

In a back room of the store, Tacker made Gaines lie on the old sofa his father had brought in years back, calling it and a dinged-up coffee table his lounge.

"Easy does it," he said. "I'll get a damp cloth for your face. You've got a scrape there."

"What time is it?" Gaines said.

"Must be eight thirty." He looked at his watch. Only eight fifteen. "Here. Press this against your face. You ought to have some ointment." The store had to be ready to open in forty-five minutes. He tapped Gaines's hat out while Gaines wiped his face. "Almost good as new," Tacker said, setting the hat on one of the armrests. Then he felt like a dolt. Gaines might think he meant he was good as new after a swipe with a washcloth. "Your family got a telephone?" Tacker said. "They might worry you're not back yet."

Gaines looked at him, swung his legs to the floor, and sat up. "You know any colored folks with telephones? In Winston? Where you been, man?" He started to laugh, then caught his side and winced.

"I'll call my father. He'll give you a ride home." Tacker cracked his knuckles.

"Never mind," he said. "I've got to go. Don't worry. I'll leave by the back door this time."

"No. I'll walk you home. The store can wait. No one comes in this early anyway." Tacker felt himself at that intoxicating edge of his known world, as he had with Samuel riding motorcycles in the bush.

"I'll run along."

"I'm going to get you another bottle of milk." Tacker flipped through the swinging doors of the lounge and headed to the cooler. The milk was becoming important to him, the white liquid encased in glass, the cardboard cap: BILTMORE DAIRY FARMS. In the lounge Gaines was bent over, still hugging his abdomen.

"Forgot to lock the door," Tacker said. "I'll be right with you. Wait here." He set the milk bottle down on the table. He hadn't felt this alive since Nigeria, before Fray picked him up that morning, busting everything up, charging him with the massive impropriety of going native. "Let's go." He flapped open the doors into the back room. But Gaines was gone. He'd taken the milk and left the hat. Tacker ran out the delivery entrance and around the corner but didn't see the man anywhere. He almost ran into the street, but a car horn blasted and he swung around like a top. A cool wind pierced the weave of his shirt.

Only when he was back in the store did Tacker see blood on his sleeve. From Gaines's face? Before the lavatory mirror, he discovered a shard of glass in his hair. Removing it he found another. The splinter sliced his finger. He turned on the water and let the finger bleed into the stream of it until he remembered how stupidly American he was being, wasting water. In the mirror his face looked a little warped. Probably the mirror, but he turned from side to side, examining himself. Was he losing hair at his temples? He walked out of the lavatory into the lounge. "Have I got a clean shirt?" he said out loud. Only he didn't quite say it. He mouthed it, as if carving himself out of air.

Suddenly he was back at the Hay-Adams Hotel in D.C., the summer before going abroad, he and a dozen other men, recent college grads, being lectured in the purpose of their assignment. Tacker had roomed with a guy from Tennessee named Seth Hudson. Tacker was out of clean shirts. "Here, take one of mine." Seth had wadded the shirt and thrown it across the room. At dinner the Clintok rep had preached, "Essentially you're going as nonreligious missionaries. Russia has an army of doctors and engineers and teachers spreading communism." Later that evening, Tacker and Seth read from the *Manual for Behavior* that they'd just been handed like a New Testament. Seth couldn't contain himself. "Says here, *Wear Western clothing.* Do they think we're going to show up in a loincloth?" They'd laughed. *"Avoid the local food,"* he went on. *"Always boil your water."*

"Do we have to make our own fire?" Tacker had shot back. "*No swimming except in chlorinated pools.* Hey, get this. *No romantic liaisons or physical involvement with the native population.*"

Even though he was going to be on the other side of the Sahara, Tacker had imagined an Egyptian woman in a white gown, carrying a lantern and a teapot, walking across the desert, looking back to see if he was following.

"Wow," Seth interrupted Tacker's reverie. "This takes the cake. *Do not participate in traditional religious practice.* No voodoo for you, my friend," he'd finished, dusting his thumb against his fingers in a sign of magic.

Six weeks after the Clintok training in D.C., Tacker was in Ibadan. He had a week to settle in before the project began, a week "to acclimate." Samuel, who had picked Tacker up at the airport, introduced him to an open-air market. Raw slabs of meat, covered in flies, hung from the bamboo rafters of stalls. The vegetable stalls were a little better but still the flies were everywhere, landing on the nostrils and lips of sleeping children on mats. But then he spied a yellow pineapple. He bought it on the spot. The seller chopped it up for him, juice spilling out. The taste was sweetly sharp, bearing no resemblance whatever to the pale slices of canned fruit that passed for pineapple in America. His acclimation to Nigeria began with that pineapple. Nigeria, where new banks went up and the old mud structures stayed alongside them, women in bright clothes with babies tied to their backs cooked on open fires right next to a modern department store. Boys hawked bread in the streets while Muslim men opened mats and sent their prayers toward Mecca. Before long it was nothing to see a beautifully dressed girl leave a shoe store and sit on an upturned concrete block enjoying a warm Coca-Cola purchased from a toothless vendor. High-life music floating out of storefronts rendered the world fluid, giving inanimate objects their own life. A mossy water pot set under a tree seemed as alive as the hawk in the air.

After his week of acclimation to Nigeria, the rest of Tacker's team had shown up, Nigerian men who had been selected for their prowess in what they called "maths." Including Samuel, there were ten of them. They spent their days on the University College Ibadan, or UCI, campus, reviewing fundamentals of architecture, practicing conceptual drawing, building models, writing up specifications. Tacker was something like a graduate teaching assistant to the Nigerian engineer who had been hired to lead the project. The windows to the classroom where the team did their draftings stayed open all the time.

Tacker had known since knowing that he was smart. He knew through some internalized moral guide—his mother?—that brains did not constitute goodness. Yet he was not wholly free of the notion that, as a receiver who could catch a ball outside the bounds of the playing field and plant his feet inbounds for the touchdown and regularly show up on the honor roll, he was a little more special than your average Joe. In his first two weeks at UCI, his pride met a corrective. One of their group, a squat man with a broad face, named Abraham, could add six-figure numbers in his head before Tacker could put the first number to paper, and when they made a dash for the dining hall one afternoon, he was lucky to be in the middle of the pack. These Nigerian men were like the Greeks, equally trained in mental and physical exertion. Their capacity sharpened Tacker's desire as nothing ever had. Something mythic seemed afoot in this fermenting African world, something deep beneath the surface of things.

During a break between classes, they strolled down the long lanes of the campus, beneath palm trees and flowering hardwoods, past the Catholic chapel with its decorative cinder-block tower, going as far as the entry to the university where they purchased oranges from young girls practicing to become market women. Their faces spoke a determination Tacker had never seen on a girl, while their thin dresses held the breeze as if the fabric were lined with butterflies. He wondered how the movement of their cloth could be replicated in architecture.

In Winston-Salem, North Carolina, in the back of his father's grocery, Tacker Hart put his sliced finger to the mirror and left his print in blood.

Chapter Three

ON A MID-OCTOBER morning in Winston-Salem, Kate Monroe sat cross-legged on the braided rug in her father's study, her family correspondence spread out around her. Not her parents' correspondence. That she hadn't found, though it must be here somewhere, what with her father's research trips, her mother's visits home to South Carolina, and before that, their courtship. A variety of other dispatches were abundant: for example, a long, spidery letter from an aunt with pictures of Kate's cousins who had grown up in India, their father in the foreign service. The photos were by an amateur. Her cousins frowned into bright sun, their heads cut off at the top. In one, her oldest cousin was entirely decapitated. There were other letters: from Kate herself when she was in camp that summer in South Carolina and learned to canoe. The sensations of it came back to her, the sluicing sound of paddles in water, a rhythmic side-to-side, a silver plane of lake ahead. Kate believed her parents' letters would have a similar but more necessary effect. They would ground her, resolve something.

Kate's father had been dead nearly a decade, drowned at the North Carolina coast, her mother for a year and a half, after terrible suffering with pancreatic cancer. Her mother's death was still too vivid to be bearable if Kate thought about it for long: screaming, an arm slung out. She dwelled on the sweeter parts that had allowed a depth of tenderness she and her mother had not known before the illness.

Kate's mother had been a runner-up for Miss South Carolina in 1937, the first year of the pageant, the year before she married. Even in her mid-thirties, she looked better in a swimming suit than college girls at the beach. Her hair fell in blond tendrils across cheekbones the color of tea rose. Though petite, she was immensely able, doing all the things Kate wasn't interested in: sewing, housekeeping, planning complex meals. She would not have a maid in the house though they could easily afford one. At ten, dark-haired, chubby Kate wondered if she was really her mother's daughter. She took sides with her father, more like her in temperament and appearance. Brian, her younger brother, was blond like their mother, thin and athletic, and Kate thought their mother favored him. At least there was balance: Brian and their mother; she and their father. Then, when her father died, the balance was gone. Her mother started taking painting lessons at the garden club and became very good at it, moving from lilacs and hydrangeas to portraits, even Kate's. The period of that composition was a sweet interlude. Yet when the portrait was hung, Kate and her mother still held out against each other. Only in her mother's dying, when Kate was twenty years old and took off a year from Agnes Scott College, did she feel her mother's dearness, and then she wondered if all along the problem had been hers.

A nurse had come to the family home on Glade Street. But in

the hours that they were alone, Kate was her mother's minister. "You're all I need," her mother whispered as Kate combed her thinning hair. Later, in the hospital, eased by morphine, her mother still smiled in recognition. "Thank you," she said every time Kate offered her apple juice. For the first time in her life, Kate saw her mother naked, her skin still beautiful. Kate was so strengthened by the hospital visits that she began to believe her mother would not die. Balance had returned. All she needed to do was show up and all her mother needed to do was stay. One afternoon in her hospital bed, her mother turned to Kate and said, "Letters . . . no," and she shook her head. Once she looked fiercely at Kate, declaring "not sorry enough" before slumping back on her pillow. When Kate held her hand, she whispered, "Burn." Kate thought she was hot and pulled back the sheet, but her skin was cool to the touch. Kate climbed into the bed, lying curved around her mother's small body, feeling herself a blade. *I am a knife*, she'd thought. *I am steel.*

The next day, her mother was sitting up in bed, looking like a girl grown suddenly old. "Are we all here?" she said. The next day she woke and peered with a confused countenance at Kate, and five minutes later she stopped breathing. Walking out of the hospital into the bright parking lot, her aunt Mildred steering her by the elbow, Kate felt she might blow away. "You'll come stay with us now, you and Brian," Aunt Mildred had said. Aunt Mildred was Kate's father's sister.

The thought of her aunt brought Kate back to the present and the family correspondence and the October morning outside the window. Her foot had fallen asleep. She stretched her leg and flexed her toes, examining the envelope in her hand, one she had sent from South Carolina six years ago. She laid it aside and picked up another, a letter from Kate's mother's great-aunt

Jane, who had left her mother an inheritance. Included in the letter was a recipe for tomato aspic. "Oh my Lord," Kate said aloud as she tossed the recipe into the trash.

THE SPRING AFTER their mother's death, Brian and Kate had lived with their childless aunt and uncle. Brian stopped carrying his books to school. Kate came into the living room to find him watching *Howdy Doody* though he was sixteen years old. Finally someone directed him to a shop class and after that he started working with wood in their aunt's garage.

"You're acting just like Mom," he said to Kate one day.

"How's that?"

"Like you don't feel anything when you really do."

"What do you mean?"

But Brian turned his attention back to a piece of wood whose secret he appeared close to unlocking.

I do feel, she had wanted to say, but a cool lozenge had settled into the right lower chamber of her heart.

There had been talk of Kate's transferring to Wake Forest College to finish her degree before a letter arrived from Dr. Lovingood, urging Kate to return to Agnes Scott and Atlanta. A flowing figure with reddened hair over gray roots, Dr. Lovingood had written her dissertation on Dorothy Wordsworth. Kate had changed her major from music to English because of her, a woman in charge of herself who talked about literature as if it lived and breathed. In her letter to Kate, she asked for something. The Agnes Scott student paper, the *Profile*, needed a photographer. Did Kate think she might do it? Dr. Lovingood would be grateful if she could. Kate saw through the request. It was like Brian's woodworking. They were both being led by the nose. She didn't care. She might find a career in photography. She left Brian with Aunt Mildred and went back for her senior year. The plumpness of her girlhood had fallen away the year before. Now her figure emerged and her hair thickened. For the first time in her life, boys flocked to her. Kate thought it had something to do with the camera, the Argus C3 Dr. Lovingood gave her to use. Oddly enough, the metallic camera warmed her.

"It's called a Brick," said a boy caller when she showed it to him.

He must have seen confusion in her face.

"For its shape," he said. "Didn't you know?"

"No," she said, "but I like it."

She found security in the heavy rectangular camera with its smooth leather case and shoulder strap. It offered a connection with her painter-mother and seemed an extension of life into the future. After a while, she settled on one suitor, a resident at Emory University Hospital. His name was James. He was dark-haired like her father, not as tall—but he had sensitive hands and a powerful mustache that hinted at a deep level of sexual energy in spite of his conservative clothes. He was a heat she needed. Kate let herself melt into his kisses and fantasized the rest. To finish her degree, she had to attend summer school, and when August came, James wanted her to stay in Atlanta.

"I've got to go back to Winston," she said. "At least for a while."

They stood on the back stairs of her dormitory.

"Back to your parents' house?"

"It's my house now. Brian got the beach house. I've told you that."

"But I'm in love with you." It was the first time he had said it. He pressed her against the wall and kissed her and put his hand to her breast. She felt enormously excited and afraid. She wasn't ready to give him everything. He would hurt her if she did. The next morning, she woke feeling the flint of her backbone. She said good-bye to Dr. Lovingood and the next day left for Winston-Salem on the train, the Brick cradled in her lap. Her professor had made a present of it.

From the window of her father's study, Kate heard the crunch of car wheels in the back alley. James had owned a Corvette. It made Kate feel in vogue, but James was a little too proud of it. Since her abrupt departure from Atlanta, he called regularly, sounding remorseful and wounded. She had been tempted to get right back on the train and go to him. But to where exactly, and to live how? Renting a room and working as a secretary while he finished his residency? For now, they'd agreed he would call every Saturday night. She missed the kissing but she also felt shame, for her thoughts were purely carnal. James spoke vaguely of a visit.

Kate nibbled on a piece of toast. Part of the mystery of the letters was their haphazard state. Her father always bundled important correspondence with rubber bands, labeling each bundle with his long, beautiful script. As a girl she had sat with him in his study, watching him write, trying to create a script just like his. Why was she spending all this time searching for letters anyway? Who knew what her mother had meant in her ramblings at the end? *Letters . . . no.* Maybe it was *know. Letters . . . know.* Or *No letters.* Who had she expected would write?

The hall clock chimed eight o'clock. Kate looked out the window. Sun was breaking through. Where had she put her camera? The phone rang.

"Kate?" It was Aunt Mildred.

"Good morning," Kate said, fingertips poised on her father's desk. She was a little sorry she'd picked up so quickly.

"How are you doing over there?"

"I slept like a baby."

"Are you eating?"

"Yes, thank you. I have everything I need." *Except a car,* she thought. It still burned her up how Aunt Mildred had convinced her mother to sell the green Ford when she was in the hospital. With a car Kate could be out shooting pictures. Two of her photographs in the *Profile* had won college-level awards. In one of them a woman holds a young boy back from the street where his sister has just been hit. It turned out the girl was not seriously harmed. Nonetheless it had alarmed Kate how quickly she could pull out the camera and shoot rather than try to help.

"Now, Kate, you know anytime you want to you can come stay with us. It's an awful lot for a young lady to have two parents . . ."

Dead, Kate thought. *Dead is what you call the deceased.* Tacker Hart had stumbled over the same problem in the grocery. *Your family used to . . .*

"You don't want to be living in the past. You're young and beautiful. You have your own life. Don't bury yourself over there."

Bury herself? It was amazing what perverse things people said when they were nervous, and two dead parents did that to people, made them nervous. Kate sat down in her father's chair. "Don't worry. Remember I've got that meeting with the library board coming up. They want me to take Mom's place." Maybe Kate did want to live in the past. Her mother had spent her time cultivating their home, leaving for the garden club and the library board and coming back with old-fashioned roses and books. Her father had been a historian. He taught at Salem College. Kate loved Old Salem, the brick streets and simple, elegant buildings. Painters and writers and historians lived in the past. By the time a photograph was developed, it was the past.

"Where are your friends? Are they in touch?" her aunt said.

Kate noticed a scratch on her father's desk that she hadn't observed before. She ran her finger across it.

"Kate?"

"I'm writing Janet today, my college roommate, remember? She came to Mom's funeral." Buxom blonde Janet had shown up in a cobalt blue dress. Kate had not intended to write but now she would have to. She ought to call James. The last time they talked, she lost her temper when he asked about her plans. "I don't know yet. You can't imagine what it's like, what I have to think about, my brother, my parents." She'd hung up precipitously.

KATE WAS THIRTEEN and Brian still in elementary school that August they went to the Outer Banks for the first time and their father got caught in a riptide. They'd been shell collecting in shallow water, watching the waves draw, the shells tumbling. Kate took a handful up to their towels, leaving Brian with their father. When she looked back, they were farther out. And suddenly their father was carried away. His head went under. Kate ran to grab her brother from the surf. Their father reappeared, trying at first to swim to shore, but he couldn't do it. He turned his head and went out with the tide. It was what they had been taught to do; in a few moments, he would begin swimming parallel with the shore and then come in with the waves.

"He'll be okay," she said, Brian howling, jumping up and down like he was covered in ants. Then they were running down the beach. Their father seemed to wave to reassure them. But they lost sight of him. They searched and searched until someone got a police officer. Brian threw a fit when they tried to put him in the car, and once they were in, he scratched Kate's arms when she tried to hold him.

Kate's mother was at the little white motel, sitting in bed in a summer dress, her back against the wall, and smoking, when Kate and the officer walked into the room to tell her. Her eyes went to Kate and then the officer. "Where's Brian? Oh my God. Where's my boy?" she demanded, not grasping that the news was of her husband. She threw the cigarette to the floor and flew at them, shaking Kate's shoulders. "Where is he?" she cried again. "Don't do this." She pushed Kate aside and ran out the door. "Brian?" she called.

Through the motel window, Kate watched her run barefoot across the gravel to the second police officer and pull Brian out of the car, Brian looking back toward Kate, his body limp.

"Ma'am." Kate heard the officer speak. "It's your husband. He was carried out in a riptide."

Their mother pushed back her hair, still claiming Brian's hand. "Don't say that."

"I'm sorry, ma'am. He's been gone for over an hour and a half. The Coast Guard is still looking. But chances are slim."

"No," she said. "He said he wouldn't leave."

"Believe me, ma'am," the officer said. "I wish I could tell you different."

"Kate!" she called, and Kate ran to her, grateful to be remembered. She threw herself into her mother's arms and the three of them folded down onto a patch of grass. Kate would never forget her mother's dirty feet, the smell of salt and grass.

"We need you to come with us to the station," one of the officers said. "We have to make a report."

Kate's mother raised herself, never letting go of Kate and Brian, and they walked to the officers' car and got in. The station, like the motel, was white and hot, and Kate's legs stuck to the wooden seat. A fan hummed. Brian sucked his thumb. The officer's desktop was littered with water stains. The next morning, one of the same officers came to the motel at five o'clock, just as the sky outside the motel window was beginning to chalk. Brian still slept. Kate heard the officer. "The body was found. We need you to ID it."

Her mother turned and looked Kate in the eyes. She had slept in her dress and now she slipped out in her bare feet, leaving Kate with Brian, foretelling everything, as it turned out.

When she came back her hands shook as she lit a cigarette. Still Brian slept.

"Mama," Kate said. She had never called her mother that and never would again. But her daddy was gone, who had been as steady as a clock all of her life. "Why did you say he wouldn't leave?"

"Oh, Katie," her mother said. "I'm in shock. Can't you tell?"

All Kate could tell was that her mother's yellow dress had a tear at the waist and her feet looked battered. And she could tell that what had happened would never end, not when they were back in their house, not when the welts on her arm were gone, not when she graduated from high school, never. Her mother left the room again with her coin purse and in a little while she was back with three Coca-Colas and cherry fruit pies. She woke Brian and the three of them sat on the bed and ate their breakfast.

Now Brian lived at the coast in the beach cabin their father had purchased long ago and worked on through the years. The cabin was his inheritance, along with stock in Reynolds Tobacco Company, while Kate had the Glade Street house and the remainder of her mother's estate from Great-aunt Jane, who was a Hanes, rich from hosiery. Though he had barely gotten through high school, Brian was now apprenticed to a builder of sailboats and they were beautiful, glossy objects. "Come home anytime you want," she had said when she last saw him.

Kate dropped the last fragment of her toast in the trash can. She resented feeling she must write Janet today. The friends she depended on were Mrs. Bosson, next door, whose husband had divorced her, and Mr. Fitzgerald, who lived across the park and owned an Oldsmobile and would drive Kate anywhere.

In the kitchen, she fixed a second piece of toast, thought of James, and added a dollop of strawberry jam. *I saw one solitary strawberry flower under a hedge,* Dorothy Wordsworth had written one January almost two hundred years ago. Kate suspected a moment of passion. She also knew there was steel in Dorothy Wordsworth's backbone. She gazed onto the backyard. The first morning she woke in the house after leaving James and Atlanta, she had gotten up and gone out to greet everything. She knew where the hyacinth had been in April and the crocus, too, under the dogwood. If she raked the leaves, she could conjure again that sense of connection to this square of earth. Kate pulled her hair up and fashioned a ponytail with a rubber band, making a mental note not to get into a habit of it; split ends. Her father's old twill coat still hung on the hall rack. She'd rescued it from the shed off the patio and wore it for chores as a kind of protective armor. Kate slipped it on over her pajamas. She had always been charmed by the privacy of the backyard, each side buffered by a tall hedge of viburnum, a four-foot fence completing the enclosure along the back where the lot met the alley. One end of the alley emptied onto Forsyth Street and the other came out onto Fourth. The alley was where Kate's father had taught her to ride a bike. *My outside girl,* he'd called her.

The old rake was still in the shed. Gloves Kate didn't find. "Oh well," she said, feeling safe in her father's coat, pleased with herself in the cloistered yard. Of all the books she had read growing up, she loved *The Secret Garden* most. She resolved to rake the leaves out of the monkey grass. Her father had put the plugs in above the retaining wall when she was small. It was one of her earliest memories. Now the clumps were huge. The phone rang in the kitchen. But by the time Kate got to it the caller had hung up. Back in the yard she let out a sigh, thinking of James. Aunt Mildred had been distressed that Kate had left him in the lurch. "A man with a good career. A man who loves you. Why?" *Because I felt an undertow,* she had thought.

The leaves were wet and heavy and there were a lot of them, more than she'd anticipated. Suddenly she was much too warm. Kate pulled herself out of her father's coat and swung it over the picnic table. She caught a whiff of her own perspiration. Like an arrow, a moment from another time came straight through to the present: her physical education class in eighth grade, running laps around the field. As Kate completed the last lap, she'd stumbled to the chain-link fence near the street and held on, catching her breath. The second she lifted her head, her father drove by. He didn't see her and she had the oddest feeling that she didn't know him, or perhaps that he didn't know her. She never spoke of the incident.

A movement at the back of the yard caught her eye. A strong-looking Negro fellow was striding down the alley. Kate clutched the neck of her pajama top. Perhaps he had not heard her, as her raking had ceased, or seen her either, the young Negro fellow in a jacket, carrying a bottle of milk, his head tilted forward as if he wished to avoid contact with the world. The milk bottle gleamed like a huge opal. He must have stolen it. The fellow paused, turned, and looked across the yard at her. Kate put a hand to her mouth. What if he came in her direction? The back fence was low enough to vault. But the man merely lifted the milk bottle to his forehead. Then he pressed an arm forward as if pushing aside a tree limb and disappeared up the alley toward Fourth Street.

Kate sensed a brief thrill of danger and mystery beyond her reach. Her high school friends had grown up with Negro women who were practically their mothers, but she had not. Her father hired white boys to help with the yard. Her parents had expressed no real philosophy about Negroes and Kate had little to go on, so that when she was a freshman in high school and overheard some older girls talking about how a white girl in Durham had been raped by a nigger, she was deeply impressed in the way she might have been to hear a shark was swimming the waters of Crystal Lake. She looked for the story in the newspaper, but in Winston-Salem there was no report of it. She had only learned about sex when she was twelve and it still seemed a remote and clinical operation. The story put her on her guard and the dark man lurked in her consciousness, an abiding danger beneath the surface of her good life. This though she hardly ever saw a Negro boy in Winston. At Agnes Scott the fear was rekindled when she and her classmates were told to travel in groups if they went downtown to Rich's. No reference to the source of danger needed to be given. They knew.

A squirrel jumped out of a tree and Kate yelped, taking a step back toward the door. She had never before considered how close she was to the colored world. Because, after all, Negroes didn't pass this way. She grabbed her father's coat from the picnic table. Inside she turned the deadbolt on the kitchen door. The Negro would turn left on Fourth and go straight until he reached Broad, where he could catch a bus to any Negro part of town. Maids waited to catch the bus all the time. She wanted a confidant. Not Aunt Mildred. Aunt Mildred would say this was just more proof of how unreasonable it was for her to be in her house alone. She could just hear her: *That boy could have forced his way in and how would you have stopped him?* Kate shivered and hugged herself. She would shower and dress and go to the grocery to pick up something for lunch and see if more apples had come in. She locked the door of the upstairs bath. Out of the shower, she dressed quickly. Downstairs, she reclaimed her father's old coat, picked up her purse, and walked out the front door, pulling it tight behind her.

She had been surprised that Tacker Hart remembered her. They hardly knew each other growing up. Two years' age difference was a chasm then. And he was practically a god in high school. She'd first seen him back in the neighborhood three months ago at Summit Street Pharmacy, buying a new razor. He looked somehow more solid but also disheveled, his hair longer than anyone was wearing it around here. His appearance had piqued her interest because he seemed a little dangerous but still attractive, like Heathcliff.

Getting to Hart's was all downhill, and she half ran. This morning Tacker wasn't at the customer service counter. His absence seemed devastating. She needed a sense of connection and she needed it right now. But she rallied herself to gather a few things for lunch—tomato soup, Saltines, and cheese. At the apples display, she stopped and held a lemony Stayman to her nose. If her order wasn't in, she would purchase a few today.

Kate opened a brown bag and began to fill it. About halfway through she stopped and looked out the store's front window. Yellow leaves fell like some heavenly currency. Vaguely she remembered a story from mythology about a runner who threw down golden apples to slow his opponent in a race, a woman whom he wished to love. Kate had not particularly wished to know Tacker in high school after hearing a rumor about how the football team placed bets on who would deflower the class valedictorian, a shy girl with a slight lisp.

The Negro seemed very far off now. Maybe Tacker had not been in on that bet. But he might have been. She had prided herself on never attending a football game in high school. She looked forward to pep rallies because she had the library all to herself. She had consumed *Paradise Lost* in a month of pep rallies three years after her father's death, reading from a rare illustrated copy that couldn't be checked out. When she had left the library to see her classmates released from the assembly, she thought she had a fair sense of the difference between heaven and hell. Hell was the average, the mediocre and predictable. It was popular. *Long is the way / And hard, that out of Hell leads up to Light.*

Heading to the checkout, Kate saw that Tacker had emerged from somewhere and was ringing up a customer who had enough canned goods for a year. She observed his mobile mouth as he talked, his hay-colored hair, still wildish. She was forever looking now as if she were focusing through her camera. The woman who had worked at Hart's forever called from the other register, "Can I help you?"

"Oh," Kate said. "I was going to ask him about a delivery." She motioned toward Tacker and moved a step closer to his register as the woman with the canned goods talked on and on. Recalling the Negro, Kate tapped her foot.

When Tacker was finally free of the canned-goods customer, Kate pressed her cart up to the register. "You're back," he said, his face alert and open.

"I needed a few things for lunch." His eyes were green like sea glass. She set her groceries on the counter and he rang them up.

"I put in your order." He packed her items into a small brown box, then rested a hand at his belt. He had a cut on his finger, a slice like she had once made peeling tomatoes.

"Thanks." She shifted her weight onto one foot, touched by the minor harm to his hand. "I was surprised you remembered me. I wasn't a cheerleader."

"Good for you," he said, grinning, cracking his knuckles. It disturbed the nobler image of him she was beginning to develop.

"What are you doing back here? I heard you'd gone abroad."

For a moment his face went blank. "Yeah, sort of between things at the moment. What about you? You here for a while?"

"For as long as I want. The house is mine now." She felt proud of herself, felt the pride strongly enough to know she could influence him if she wished to in spite of the fact that this was the second time she had come to the store in her father's old coat. She smoothed her hair back. "I've been back since summer started."

His face lit up. "I'm renting a house on West End," he said, coming around from behind the counter. Kate thought he might place a hand on her shoulder or even give her a hug, but he was just moving a cart. It would behoove him to ask her if she'd like to get together.

She slipped out the door clutching her bag. A froth of leaves lifted where the sidewalk turned. Something about Tacker was different. It both vexed and enticed her. A wind whipped up the hill and she considered how James hadn't called in two weeks, and she calculated he might be dating someone new. She felt a stitch in her side. "Remember who you are," she whispered.

In the night, she dreamed of a man in a white coat at the edge of her property, a milkman. He was telling her something but she couldn't hear his voice for the wind. She woke thinking of strawberries.

IN THE MANUAL for the Brick, Kate had found a note on half a sheet of typing paper. It was folded lengthwise and acted as a bookmark. She presumed the note had been made by Dr. Lovingood, but it was typed and she couldn't be sure. It was a passage by László Moholy-Nagy—she'd had to look him up; a Hungarian painter and photographer.

Thus in the photographic camera we have the most reliable aid to a beginning of objective vision. Everyone will be compelled to see that which is optically true . . .

It was the next paragraph that mattered.

We have—through a hundred years of photography . . . been enormously enriched. . . . We may say that we see the world with entirely different eyes. We wish to produce systematically, since it is important for life that we create new relationships.

Kate had found the sentences wonderfully strange. Was optical truth different from other kinds of truth? Would she know something truer of her parents if she discovered old pictures she had never before seen? Would she know James differently if she had pictures of him taken when he was unaware of the camera? In their dorm room, she'd read the passage aloud to Janet. "I wonder what he means by 'produce systematically,'" Janet had said. She was putting her hair up in a beehive. Janet was five feet nine inches tall, and the hairstyle made her even taller. "Maybe photographing the same thing over and over."

"Yes!" Kate said.

"But why do that?" Janet put the last bobby pin in her hair and turned around.

"Because there will be variations," Kate said. "From second to second, light changes. A fly lands on the vase of flowers. Get it? The next day, a petal drops. That means truth changes."

THE DAY AFTER the Negro passed through her alley, Kate sat in the family library and ate a grilled cheese sandwich for breakfast. Her mother's Smithsonian books were still on the coffee table. *Birds of the World, The River Nile.* Until recently, Kate had pitied her mother these unscholarly books, but now she was interested in the photography. She had underestimated her mother, who perhaps had wished to travel, or even escape. Kate had never asked her. She bit into an apple and perused *The River Nile.* It embarrassed her to imagine Tacker understanding her need for him. Once in high school, he had passed her in the tunnel that connected the main campus to the gymnasium. He had stopped and she'd thought he would speak. But he'd only smiled and walked on and she had not known what it meant, though she harbored the thought that in some secret shadow life they were each other's muse.

The subjects of great literature didn't teach Kate anything she didn't already know—that life was sad and lonely, or tragic and lonely, though occasionally relieved by humor and a great love, such as she felt for her father. What the study of literature taught her was that the way to deal with life was through the perfect arrangement of words. A novel contained an ordered world even if the subject was the chaos of war. A sonnet was a world in sixteen lines. Even death was made more complete in literature because it was written and thus ordered. Her father's disappearance was a nothingness, whereas a written account of death was substantiated and could be dealt with. So literature relieved her of absence, and not through abstraction but through detail. Literature was pain organized with the symmetry of a camellia.

Kate looked to her mother's self-portrait above the fireplace. It depicted her seated, knees covered by her skirt, her body at an angle but her face looking straight ahead, her hair more golden than it really was, a bouquet of peonies on the table behind her shoulder. There were so many questions to ask when a person was gone forever. For example: How did you keep those peonies alive long enough to paint the portrait? Did you paint them first? Did you wish to escape? Kate hadn't paid enough attention. She had no memory of her mother bringing peonies into the house. Had she painted them from an illustration? Kate hoped not. She sat for a moment, recalling her mother's words, *the letters . . . no* or *no letters*. Kate's breath rose and fell. Suddenly she heard a series of loud ticks, like a piece of equipment cooling down. She thought of the Negro in the alley and seized *The River Nile* to her chest. Silence. In a few moments, she slipped down the hall to the kitchen and peered into the backyard. It was as peaceful as a church. "Old house," she said.

To prove her mettle she decided to open the attic. Maybe her parents' personal correspondence was up there. If there were no new photographs of her parents, letters certainly existed somewhere. *Burn,* her mother had whispered on her deathbed. She must have been speaking of her pain, but over the months, Kate had held in her mind, like a trinity of stones, her mother's enigmatic words—*know, letters, burn*—hoping to solve the riddle.

The attic was spacious enough for standing, but it would be chilly. Hair tied with a red bandana, she pulled on her father's coat again. The door at the top of the stairs creaked when she opened it and she hastened to pull the light cord. The items before her had been holding their place for years: her grandmother's old trunk, the chifforobe her parents used to store off-season clothes, and an old rocking chair whose origins remained unclear. Dimly she heard the big clock downstairs and sensed the cool lozenge in her heart. She opened the old trunk. An enormous amount of yellowed fabric met her eyes. Her mother's discolored wedding dress. No help at all. The chifforobe complained as she pulled at the doors. A conglomeration of old dishes filled a box on one shelf. Next to the box was the green glass jug her grandmother kept in her refrigerator so she always had cool water. Kate hugged it to her chest and felt momentarily soothed. *Aunt Mildred is right. I need to get out more.* Jug in hand, she descended the attic stairs, glad for the noise of her shoes on the steps. By the time she was in the kitchen, she had decided to call Mr. Fitzgerald. "Could you drop me off at Thalhimers?"

"Doing some shopping?"

"Taking pictures."

"I didn't know you were a photographer now."

"But I am. Give me thirty minutes to get ready."

A WHOOSH OF air swept up the yard as Kate opened the front door. She reached for her umbrella, Mr. Fitzgerald pulled up to the curb, and she skipped down the granite steps of the yard. She'd been cavalier about being a photographer. Yet she was beginning to wonder if she could be a professional. In the car, she leaned over and pecked the man's cheek. He was thin with sharp features and golden eyes, forever sporting a bow tie. Though older than her father, the two had hunted and fished together when Kate was young. She had never known his wife. "What would I do without you?" she said.

"Find a boyfriend?"

"You know you'd rather I call you."

"You're blamed right. Not a boy in this town good enough for you."

He smiled but Kate bristled under the paternalism, thinking of James and the way he rubbed her palm as he drove, as if he were reading braille.

"Give me a ring when you're ready for me to pick you up," Mr. Fitzgerald said, pulling into a parking space.

"Oh no. I'll just take the bus. Mom and I took it all the time."

"If you're sure. But I'd rather fetch you." His eyes were sincere.

"You sweet man. I'll be fine." She sprang from the car.

The department store was housed in a three-story Art Deco

building at the corner of Fourth and Spruce. Winston's women were more faithful in coming to it than to Sunday morning worship. Kate wasn't interested in clothes today. In Atlanta, she had taken a series of photographs of the Fox Theatre for a competition sponsored by the chamber of commerce. One had been featured in the Sunday edition of the *Atlanta Journal-Constitution*. If she wanted to pursue photography in Winston-Salem, she ought to take some pictures of it. She walked up and down the street, glancing skyward at the building. Finally she aimed the camera straight up so that Thalhimers rose in her viewfinder like a cliff. She would not have been surprised to see swallows nesting. She took several shots before bringing the camera down. A man in a yellow Windbreaker stood next to her.

"What do you see up there?" he said.

"Peaks and valleys," she said, refusing to smile. Middle-aged men liked to tease her about the camera. *Well, little lady, what are you lugging that piece of equipment for?* She made her getaway, heading for the Zinzendorf Hotel on Main, built soon before her mother was born and which her mother had loved for its ornate balustrades and parapets. It wasn't in the best part of town now, and the awnings looked a little peaked, but she loved it because they had gone to the Zinzendorf Grill for lunch after shopping expeditions, and on occasion the whole family ate there. The dining room with its recessed ceilings and tables covered in white tablecloths created in her a powerful sense of formal order when she was eight years old. The wind picked up and Kate hugged the Brick close. She had never been into one of the hotel's bedrooms.

She caught sight of the five-story hotel a block away, just as a long shadow fell across the façade. Before the light shifted, she pressed the shutter button at least a dozen times, shifting the camera from vertical to horizontal and back. Briefer than a three-line poem. Snap. Kate couldn't remember when she had last been in the hotel. A portly bellman with a face the color of parchment opened the door. Dark wooden chairs illuminated by globed sconces were clustered in various seating arrangements around the large room, just as she remembered. In her mother's day, high school couples came to the Zinzendorf for dinner before prom. She banished those stiff boys and frilled girls from her imagination. She was interested only in the imprint they may have left, the sag of marbled floors occasioned by a million steps.

"May I help you?" a woman said from behind the registration desk. Her hair was frozen with hair spray.

"If you don't mind, I'd like to take some pictures."

"I don't see any harm in it." The woman flicked ashes from her cigarette.

"Thanks." The hotel smelled as if it had been flooded and hadn't quite dried out. For a moment Kate's heart sank, but she revived herself. If she was serious, she might one day be required to work amid fire. She snapped several shots of the chairs, their seats concave in the center. These she followed by close-ups of the Mission-style arms, the wood bleached light where hundreds of arms had rested. She took the marble staircase—indeed the steps did dip at the center. Coming down she missed a step and spilled onto her knees. Luckily, a rug softened her fall and she was able to hold on to the Brick.

The bellman came rushing in her direction. "Are you all right?"

"I think so."

He extended a hand and she felt a strength in his lift that surprised her.

"Why don't you have a seat for a few minutes? Would you like a drink?"

"Water is fine, thank you." He was short legged and walked like a duck, from side to side.

Kate sat, cradling the Brick, sipping her water. If only the hotel didn't smell like old green beans. She rested her eyes and when she opened them she was captured by the idea of taking a picture from inside looking onto the street. At the window, she brought the camera to her face. The rounded shape of a farm woman, but out of focus, filled the viewfinder. The image was so uncanny she pressed the shutter button before she knew what she was doing. Then she lowered the camera. Across the street stood a Negro woman in a long skirt, clutching a shawl around her shoulders. Kate advanced the film and brought the Argus back to her face. It allowed one-step focusing and yet she worked methodically. It appeared that the woman framed in the viewfinder was staring right back at her, staring into her, into her eyes, into the maze of her interior life, into the right chamber of her heart where the cool lozenge lay, evidence that she was not, all in all, a warm and generous person, and even deeper, into something Kate could not fathom. She lowered her camera and stood motionless, gazing out the window as a little colored boy came out of the shadow of an awning, clutching a sucker—the woman's grandson, perhaps— and then claimed the woman's hand as they walked off.

Had other photographers felt such rebuke? She knew the answer and it was yes. She'd heard of a woman taking pictures of elephants in Asia who had been seized and murdered by villagers because they thought she would report them for poaching.

As she came out of the hotel, the first big raindrops began to splatter on the pavement. She had misplaced her umbrella somewhere along her route. She bent over the Brick, making a tent of her back. Fortunately she didn't have to wait long for the bus. As they headed away from downtown, the world lit up in a great flash followed by a hard rumble of thunder. A second bolt of lightning split the sky right down the center of Second Street.

Chapter Four

EVER SINCE THE incident on the sidewalk, Tacker had been expecting his dad to come by to talk about it. That was his way. When the football team lost in a heartbreaker, his father never tried to talk to him right away. He'd wait and bring it up days later when they were driving to the hardware store or stopping for hot dogs. Would he have waited that day Tacker was sacked in Ibadan?

Leaving Samuel behind in the dust, Fray hadn't driven to UCI but to an old colonial residence in Ibadan, surrounded by a low fence and a garden. Frangipani trees bloomed in profusion and the cool morning air carried their perfume across the yard. Tacker felt his spirits lift. There was some misunderstanding. It would all be worked out in a few minutes. Fray wasn't a bad guy. He was caught in the middle; some bureaucratic hoopla. Inside the house, Tacker followed Fray to a broad open room with a fireplace, of all things.

"Have a seat," the man said. Tacker took one and Fray another. "Tell me how you like your work here."

Tacker looked at Fray, but his face told nothing. "I'm very happy with it. Couldn't we have had this conversation on the drive?"

Fray looked at him impassively. "What do you like especially?"

A steward dressed in the standard white uniform came to the door. "Drinks, sir?"

"Not yet, Fidelis," Fray said.

"What do I especially like?" Tacker said, repeating the question. "Everything. UCI is a terrific place; the guys on the team are superb. The land is phenomenal. People are friendly."

Fray made a steeple of his fingers and placed them at his lips. "You like the nightlife, Mr. Hart?"

"What's the 'Mr. Hart' about? You can call me Tacker. Not sure what you mean by nightlife. I go to the faculty club pretty often."

"Tell me what you think of the country's women," Fray went on. Tacker had lost the sense of reasonable calm he'd felt in the yard.

"The women? That's hard to say. I don't know any that well."

Fray looked suddenly tired, with his tapering fingernails and sun-damaged skin.

"Isn't there a woman you know quite well?"

Did he mean the vice-chancellor's daughter, Rebecca? She'd visited from London the first Christmas Tacker was here. He had walked her home one evening. The vice-chancellor's home was high on a hill above faculty housing. They'd talked about living in two countries. Tacker had joked that he might never go home. Rebecca had lamented that she might never be able to return home. When Tacker had asked why, she'd laughed sadly. "My father. He will want me to be a traditional woman here, many children. Even if I teach, my money will go to my husband. In Great Britain I have more freedom." "You can always come back for a visit," Tacker had said. "And what will my children be," she had said, "the ones born to me abroad?"

Fray cleared his throat. "Mr. Hart, I asked you a question."

"No," Tacker said. "There isn't a Nigerian woman I know well."

"No little postcards to the parents back home reporting on a girl you've been seeing in Osogbo? Let's see . . ."

He pulled a piece of paper from a folder and read. *"Most amazing coincidence . . . a woman who lives by the river and can talk about Picasso . . . makes me wonder if I could stay here . . . what would you think about your son becoming an African?"*

Tacker was dumbstruck. The postcard he'd written to his parents three days ago. Or was it four?

"And by the way, what's this business on your arm?" Fray said.

"Like I said, it's nothing. It'll wash off."

"Dabbling in witchcraft to top it off," Fray said.

"Hardly," Tacker said.

"You were told very clearly in training. No romantic relationships with the locals. Perhaps you don't think a white priestess is a local. I can see how it might be confusing. She is quite beautiful. Oh, don't be surprised. Of course I've been to see her. A very pretty juju priestess." He glanced at Tacker knowingly.

"I haven't done anything to jeopardize the project. I haven't broken a single rule. The last time I checked I had an American girlfriend. But what difference would it make if I had a Nigerian girlfriend?"

Fray rose to his feet and when Tacker looked at him, his face appeared contorted as if pressed against a glass. "It's against the rules," he sputtered. "No one here wants his daughter being disgraced by an American. The publicity would be a stink hole. And the Austrian woman is married to a Nigerian man. You stupid boy. You could be killed." He slumped back into his chair, the bamboo-and-rattan frame chirping against the man's weight. From the folder he pulled a news clipping. "What about this disturbance over the idol burning?"

"You have a folder on me?"

"You work for an American company. You're not in Oklahoma anymore."

"North Carolina."

Fray dug deeper into his folder. "And you felt the need to tell a Shell representative that they shouldn't be drilling for crude oil? They might spoil the jungle? The Nigerian government is collaborating with Shell Oil. They don't particularly like the word *jungle* as a way of describing their country. If you're not willing to write a formal apology for your various indiscretions, you're going to be sent home."

Tacker had forgotten all about the conversation with the Shell Oil man. "Who exactly am I supposed to write to?"

"To me. I'll take care of it from there." Fray started for the door.

Tacker caught up with him on the steps of the veranda. "But I haven't done anything wrong. There are no indiscretions. I've spoken honestly about my opinions. I've worked hard. I have a real feeling for the country." His voice sounded distant and his head felt hot.

"Oh hell. I don't know what I'm doing in this hellhole of a country. I wish I could get sent home," Fray said. "Get in the goddamned Jeep."

Tacker wheeled around the vehicle and ran down the drive.

He had no idea where he was going because he didn't know what part of Ibadan they were in. Out of the yard, he turned left and ran down the side of the road, sidestepping children and vendors and goats. A horn sounded and he looked over his shoulder to see Fray in the Jeep, leaning out of the window.

"Get in this vehicle right this minute. That's an order."

Tacker turned his head forward just in time to see a cooking fire. He hurdled over it. The horn sounded again.

"You've got ten seconds to get into this Jeep," Fray shouted.

Tacker slipped into an alley too narrow for the Jeep. One more honk of the horn. It seemed he ran for hours until he was in a neighborhood of old mud houses squared around a court-yard where children began to trail him, calling out his white-ness. He slowed, and an old man looked at him sternly. Goats, chickens, children, cooking pots, a central shade tree. Tacker leaned over at the waist, his shirt soaked with sweat, then backed up into the shade of a tree and sat down. Some older boys gathered. "Have you got a drink?" Tacker said. "A Fanta?" The largest of them took out a warm Fanta and a bottle opener and waited. Tacker fished in his pocket for a sixpence. He opened the bottle and shared it with the boy.

TACKER'S FATHER CAME in to Hart's early the next week, walking up and down the rows jiggling change in his pocket before heading over to the customer service counter. "Heard there was a little trouble out front the other day."

"It was a misunderstanding, Dad. The guy didn't mean any-thing." Tacker straightened a sheaf of invoices.

"The colored boy, you mean?"

"If that's what you've got to call him. He came to get milk for his baby sister. The dang sun was so bright, no one could have seen anything. If it looked like he was smiling at that woman, he was squinting. I don't understand anyway why cordiality is an affront to people."

"You have a store to run and customers to keep. Things might need some changing, but not too fast. Too fast and we all lose." His father patted the counter flat-handedly like some fathers might a well-loved car or even a horse.

"Look, Dad. You're the one who taught me to treat everyone with respect. Was there a footnote I missed, a list of exceptions?"

"I've always been cordial with Negroes."

"Sometimes cordial isn't enough. If a man's being accosted because he smiled at someone, a fine howdy-do won't help him much."

"You have any idea what he was doing in this part of town?"

Tacker dipped and lifted his head, trying to loosen the suddenly too-close fit of his collar at his neck. "What difference does it make?" he said. Just what he had said to Lionel Fray in response to the Nigerian girlfriend question.

"Don't get too self-righteous, son. I'm just saying your first responsibility is the store."

"I understand that. I don't see a conflict." Tacker sensed that thin edge where the known world ended and another began, like the crest of a wave.

His father turned to take in the aisles of the store, the produce section, the meat counter.

"Sales this month are up over last year this time," Tacker said.

"That's good." His father patted the counter again. "Bass are biting at Kernersville Lake. Let me know if you want to get out there Sunday morning."

THE NEXT DAY, Tacker looked up to see Frances, his family's maid, coming into the store. He hadn't seen her much since moving into the foursquare. She would have come from his parents' house on the bus. She could shop at Hart's precisely because she was a maid. It irked him to be reminded of this unwritten rule. After her shopping, she would take the bus to the Watkins Avenue neighborhood, where she owned a tidy shotgun house.

Frances was stately, six feet tall at least, long, stilt-like legs from her ankles to her skirts. She nodded at him, walking slowly with her neat pocketbook. "Pocketbooks are my weakness," she once said. The handbag she carried today was as blue as a Crisco can. Frances liked to read from the merchandise and she did so aloud. She was in the canned-fruit section and Tacker could see her examining the cranberry sauce. He had never known her age. Once she seemed much older than his mother, but then she seemed to plateau.

"Your daddy set these prices or you?" she said, coming through the checkout.

"Same prices as last week, Frances. But you get your discount as always."

"I know my discount. Why you think I shop here?"

"I'll drive you home."

"Looks like you working. I can't wait. Got a week's ironing waiting for me."

"Connie can take care of the store. One of the part-time boys will be here any minute. I've got Dad's car today." Frances seemed weighted down, more than usual. Tacker was sorry for it because he was beginning to feel in possession of himself, even joyful on the days he saw Kate Monroe, and he didn't want this band of hope scattered.

Frances got into the backseat. Tacker said nothing about it. Maybe she liked it this way. Maybe she would be uncomfortable in the front seat with him. He'd been driving her home since he was sixteen, but now the arrangement felt all wrong. She was chewing gingerroot. In Nigeria, he and the guys had piled into lorries or mammy wagons when they went out to a village for the yam festival or to help thatch a roof. These were trucks converted to rough-riding buses. They toted just about everyone: farmers with hoes, women going to market, tradesmen traveling to Lagos, and on top of the vehicle, chickens in baskets, bags of cocoa, firewood, and mangos. The fruity smell wafted through open windows, mixing with sweat and hair pomade and starched fabric. These vehicles boasted fabulous signs—YOUR TIME IS NOT YET and SAFE JOURNEY—though the lorry was swinging wildly from side to side. There was always room for one more in a mammy wagon, or if the distance was short, a man might simply hop onto the back runner and hold on for dear life.

Watkins Avenue was a pocket neighborhood, one of those developed to house Negroes who served white families and establishments. Frances had never had children, and her husband, who had died with complications from diabetes, was only a vague memory in Tacker's mind. At the first stoplight, he glanced back at her through the rearview mirror. Her eyes were on him.

"What?" he said.

"Why don't you hire you a colored boy to help in that store?" she said. "Plenty of them need a job this time of year." Before the light turned green, she broke her gaze.

"Not a bad idea," he said. "You got someone in mind?"

"Might have. I don't know what you go to Africa for and come back here same as always."

Did she think he should have fought to stay? Besides his parents, Frances was the only person in Winston-Salem who knew he'd been forced out. He tightened his grip on the steering wheel. How long had she waited to speak to him? Had she planned her shopping knowing he had the car? "My mother thinks I'm not the same as before," he said. "She thinks I've lost my ambition." It had crossed his mind that maybe his mother had inquired, had someone send the full report of his dismissal. He'd only skimmed it and it almost took the top of his head off. *Liaison with married woman, interference with federal government business, native ritual, violent inclinations, homosexual tendencies.* The last was followed by a question mark.

"I know she's worried," Frances said, moving the gingerroot around in her mouth. "But change can be good."

"I guess you mean that all the way around, for her and for me." Tacker thought his mother might relax a little, have more faith in him.

There was hardly any traffic but Tacker drove so he would hit every light, giving Frances time to rest. Stopped at the corner next to a Baptist church, he spotted a group of white women at the side door, apparently coming out from a meeting. Every one of them wore a little hat. They gazed at the car, taking him in and then Frances in the backseat, and then they were happy enough to go on talking. He caught a glimpse of Frances in the rearview mirror. She was looking out the window, deep creases at the edges of her mouth.

"Are you too warm?" He rolled his window down.

"That fresh air smells good," she said.

He parked in front of her house and jumped out to open her door. But she already had her feet on the ground, those long legs ending in heeled lace-up shoes that reminded him of his grandmother. He offered her his hand. She took it. At the steps of the inclined yard, she placed her hand on his arm and leaned into him. Brown-tipped chrysanthemums filled the brick planters on either side of the galvanized-pipe railing. Frances took one step at a time. He wished he'd picked up some extra things for her.

"You go on in," he said at the door. "I'll get the groceries."

Some oranges. He could have grabbed some citrus.

"Back here," she said when he stepped into the house.

The living room was shaded but light came down the narrow hall. There was her father, Old Daddy, in the chair asleep. And a little girl next to him on the floor, coloring by the window. She glanced at Tacker and then focused again on her work. Tacker hadn't been here for more than two years. "Here you are," he said when he reached the kitchen.

Frances was at the sink, washing her hands.

"Set that box on the table there. You want some coffee?"

A thrum of vibration filled the air. Must be the heater in the basement.

"Sure," he said, visualizing Connie back at the store, a line of customers likely forming. He looked at his watch.

"Anything I can do for you before I leave?" he said.

"You just have a seat."

Tacker had never sat at Frances's table and he wondered if he had blundered in some way. He pulled out a spindle chair and sat down. She was rinsing the coffeepot. It would take a little while to percolate. From where he sat, he could see into the next room. A shelf ran high across the wall and along its length were bottles of all sorts—blue glass, deep green, red, and brown. When he glanced back in her direction, Frances had turned around and was leaning against the sink with her eyes closed, her fingers linked and resting on her tidy stomach. The light from the window lit the outline of her form and she seemed to shimmer. The coffee began to percolate and with the thrumming of the house created the illusion of a thin brown veil levitating over them. The ginger smell was back. Tacker recalled an afternoon in Ibadan, the brown curtains in the dormitory lifting in a breeze, and then the memory hitched on to Kate in that old brown coat, a slight down above her lip.

Frances said something.

"What?" Tacker said. "I'm sorry. I didn't hear you."

"My nephew over here from Nashville," she said, her eyes still closed. "His mama, my baby sister, Gwendolyn, had her chest carved out from the cancer, can't work for some while. She got a baby girl. My nephew back to aid his mama. Take care of that child. He and I sharing the task. He could use a job in your store. He's smart. Starting his last year at Fisk before this come up."

Tacker fidgeted with the zipper pull on his jacket. Something besides coffee was percolating.

"How you take your coffee? Maybe you changed that too," Frances said.

"Black," he said. "I did change that. Used to take sugar and cream." He jittered his brain sideways. Where was the father of the baby? To Frances, who was pouring his coffee, he said, "Okay. Your nephew. He needs a job. What's his name? Where is he?"

"In the next room," she said.

A pause like Tacker knew on the field, just before the snap.

"Gaines," she said.

A cool ripple ran up Tacker's spine. The same Gaines? Did she know what had happened? Tacker had to be careful not to hurt the next minutes, not to foul it up. Frances still had her back to the sink. She shifted a hip.

Everything was timing. Even architecture. The time the eye takes to comprehend the foundation, the rising wall, the shape of the portico, the heartbeat of windows, the rise of the roofline, the surging back-and-forth of the brain's receptors comprehending, achieving finally the vault of sky.

"I think I know him," he said.

"You know what?" Frances said.

"Gaines." Tacker sat forward in his chair.

"Gaines!" she called.

The air buckled.

There was Gaines in the doorframe of the room with the colored glass, the scrape on his face beginning to heal. Tacker had that slow-motion sense again. "Are you okay?"

"I'm fine."

"So what do you think?"

"About what?"

"Working at the grocery." Surely Gaines was going to say something about how Tacker had saved him before he was hurt worse.

"Could be helpful."

"You're not worried? You know. About those guys? Coming back to the store?"

"Of course I am. But what are you going to do? Be afraid forever?"

Tacker got why Frances had come to him; his dad would not do well with a Negro this frank and self-possessed. He glanced at her. She looked tired and he regretted his earlier impatience. Maybe a new way of speaking was emerging. He and Gaines were trying out for parts in a play no one had written yet. He got excited. "Wrong place at the wrong time?" Tacker said. "I know a little about that myself."

Gaines knuckled one hand and pressed it against the flat of his other palm. "The job would help my mother out, and my baby sister," he said, his tone softening.

"How old is she?"

"Five."

Tacker had imagined a baby. This was the girl with the coloring book. And then she slipped into the kitchen. She must have been listening from the hall. A thin girl, determined-looking, brown velvet cheekbones, her hair plaited on top of her head.

"Valentine, meet Mr. Tacker," Frances said.

"Hello, Valentine," Tacker said, offering his hand for her to shake.

TACKER GOT BACK to the store to find Connie smoking out front.

"Been out here only a second, boss," she said, ribbing him. "A little hectic. One of the freezers is on the blink. Started leaking." She stubbed out the cigarette. "A kid was back there stomping in the water. Got it cordoned off now."

"Have you called an electrician?"

"Not yet. Turned off the water main and got everything moved to a freezer in the back."

A rivulet of water had moved past the fresh meat counter and into the aisle where hams were displayed on a long table. "Sorry, folks," he said to shoppers who stopped like voyeurs at a car wreck to see if anything more disturbing was going to happen. "We'll have this cleaned up right away." The crowd dispersed and he started mopping. Before long, he sensed someone watching. Billy from high school—once a second-stringer on the football team—stood beside the hams, one hand resting on a particularly large ham, as if he were taking possession of the goods. Tacker had not considered Billy Cyrus's existence in half a dozen years, until he ran into him at Krispy Kreme recently and Billy had boasted of being promoted to assistant branch manager at Wachovia.

"We've had an accident back here." Billy's appearance was so sudden that it was impossible for Tacker to mask the disdain he felt.

"So you're the janitor, too," Billy said.

Billy had not changed much since high school except that he was now sausaged into a suit. Five feet ten, so fair-skinned his eyelashes were blond and his face perpetually pink. When he had gotten into a football game, which was rare, he was always jumping the snap and getting called for offsides.

"Is there something I can help you find?" Tacker said, determined to keep his cool.

"I told Connie I'd give you a hand." Billy started clapping, walking forward, closing the gap between them. "By the way," he said conspiratorially, "you ever think about squeezing her?"

"Have you got no decency?" The guy was an ass.

"Hey, I'm just passing the time with an old friend. Remember? From football days when you told Coach not to put me into the championship game."

Tacker stopped mopping. "Are you still living in high school?"

Billy ignored the question. "You meet Tarzan in Africa?"

"What's your beef?"

"You kept me out of that game."

"I never did any such thing. Coach would have had me sidelined if I'd told him how to do his job."

"So you say, but I heard about it. You were a regular heller, weren't you? How the mighty have fallen."

When Tacker had gone to Nigeria, he'd imagined teaching benighted young men the basics of architecture. Turned out no one at UCI was benighted.

Billy's bubblegum pink face blurred like a bad television screen. Tacker spun back to that day in Ibadan, running from Fray, collapsing in the brown compound, drinking the Fanta. Finally getting himself up. "UCI," he'd said to the taxi driver.

Samuel wasn't yet back from Osogbo. Tacker fell onto his friend's dormitory bed. He must have slept. The next thing he knew Fray was in the room. He'd brought enforcement, two Americans. Tacker scrambled to get up. His mouth was dry and when he tried to speak his voice came out in a whisper. Fray had something white tucked under his arm.

"What?" Tacker said.

"You're being sent home," Fray said. "This afternoon."

Tacker's brain raced. Out the window, a student strode by on his way to class, almost floating in his casual, confident walk. For the first time, Tacker wished he was a Nigerian. "I am home," he said.

"You're losing it," Fray said, unfolding the white fabric. The long arms fell out. A straitjacket. Tacker bolted for the window but a tackle sent him to the floor, the cool tile smacking the left side of his face. Two weeks later the bruise would still be blooming. One of the men sat on top of him.

"Leave me alone," Tacker said. "I'll cooperate."

"You've missed that particular opportunity," Fray said.

Tacker managed to flip himself over, the drumbeat of his own ears all he could hear as he thrashed against the two men. They were stronger than they looked. What was the question that demanded an answer? He couldn't remember. They lifted him and threw him facedown onto the bed.

Anna's blond hair in the sun. Swimming in the Osun. The boy with the Fanta. The man burning the family gods, moaning on the ground. Talking with the Shell Oil rep at the Ibadan swimming pool. Samuel. He ceased to fight. The men slipped one arm and then the other into the long sleeves of the jacket, then turned him and stood him up on his bare feet like a toy soldier. There was a terrible wrenching in his shoulders when Fray tightened the sashes. They took him out by the door at the end of the hall, where the Jeep waited, already running, a driver at the wheel.

Tacker heard nothing but a dull roar as he was led from the Jeep to a prop plane at the Ibadan Airport. He was surprised to see he had shoes on his feet. In Lagos he was transferred to the international airport and put on a Nigeria Airways flight for

London. After takeoff a Nigerian stewardess shook his shoulder to wake him but he couldn't hear her voice. In a while she came back with water in a glass and held it for him to drink. Twice she did this and Tacker remembered the question. "Do you have a Nigerian girlfriend?"

When the plane landed in London, he was allowed out of the straitjacket but not before he was told he would be given a tranquilizer if he tried anything. He was accompanied to his next flight. In the air he slept, and always he was running but he had lost his arms and he fell over and over off of the bridge, out of the sky, into the dark water below.

He had not been able to tell the story to his parents and it would never be possible to explain the injustice. He still didn't think he'd done anything wrong. But he was labeled: *a stumblebum, a wacko, a queer.* It pissed him off and flattened him all at once. *You aren't a respectable American. You haven't got the backbone.* Which really meant: *You're not a man.*

He never asked his parents if they got the postcard.

Billy's puffy pink face reassembled itself.

"That game happened years ago." Tacker got back to mopping. Out of the corner of his eye, he saw Billy pick something up from a shelf and set it back down. Finally he heard the *flump* of the man's shoes as he headed in the other direction, out of the store. Tacker emptied the bucket and rinsed out the mop, washed his hands and put on a clean shirt. *He's not worth your time,* he said to himself, *farabale,* "calm down" in Yoruba. He headed up to the registers. "You want a Coke?" he said to Connie.

"A Nehi grape," she said. "Thanks, boss."

The Coca-Cola machine stood in a corner between an old onion crate and the ice-cream freezer. Though Tacker had a key, he dropped the coins in and purchased Connie's Nehi and a root beer for himself. He glanced at the calendar his father kept on the wall above the machine: October 24, dedication day for the Nigerian high school he had gone to build and left unfinished. A cool hand seemed to brush against the back of his neck. He wheeled around, suspecting Billy, but no one was there.

ON HIS EARLY-MORNING runs, Tacker kept an eye on the new construction at the south end of Hanes Park. It was enclosed by temporary fencing and a sign announced a pool opening the following summer. Work was stalled. Reynolds High already had an indoor pool and there was Crystal Lake four miles out of town, where he'd gone to swim growing up. Tacker wondered who had cooked this up and wasn't sure he liked it. If he were a kid, sure. But he liked the grassy southern field the way it always had been, without a pool.

Heading back from the park one morning, he caught sight of a motorcycle for sale on Jersey Avenue. It sat back against the owner's yellow-brick porch like an animal in its latent power, the machine cocked in the middle so the headlamp pointed toward the street like a face. A piece of cardboard painted with a FOR SALE legend tilted against the front wheel. Tacker gazed at it. Had to be ten years old but it was a stunner: ocean blue, oversize fenders, brown leather seat tacked neatly around the edges, an Indian Chief. A friend from high school had owned a Chief and it seemed to Tacker at the time the smoothest thing going. He climbed the yard to get a closer look and placed his hand on the seat, then examined the front tire, white-rimmed, the spikes glittering silver, a flat chrome luggage rack that could nicely hold a box of groceries. He could almost hear the cat purr of the machine, remembering that other world, the excitement of it that this bike might bring back.

In Nigeria he'd ridden with Samuel, whose pastor owned two Mustang Ponies purchased from an American missionary going on leave. They were slender, thin-wheeled machines, perfect for African pathways. Samuel borrowed them for evangelical runs to villages on Wednesday afternoons, just as the sun began its downward tilt. When Tacker first arrived, Joshua, the teetotaler, was riding with Samuel on these trips, but then Samuel asked Tacker to go and they'd ride out every week. He and Samuel mounted the cycles. Joshua watched them take off, wiping his forehead with a white handkerchief. And Tacker felt bad about it, but not bad enough to give up the ride.

Grasses slapped against their arms; flocks of guinea fowl lifted as they approached and cataracted off en masse. The Ponies had a tendency to backfire, and long before Samuel and Tacker were within view of walkers, they had taken to safety on the side of the path, women with firewood on their heads, their necks rotating in perfect synchronicity as the bikes passed, faces inscrutable. Nearing a creek, Tacker felt the sudden rush of cool air. Then they were back to the afternoon heat, the smell of fire somewhere. The brown path sped past just inches from his sandaled feet. Curtains of bamboo slid away. Their motion stirred white strips of cloth hanging from limbs of baobabs. Onward they ranged past large cultivated fields until they were back in forest. Finally the path ended in a brown yard. Samuel brought his bike to an idle. Tacker stopped alongside, the bikes making little nickering noises as they cut the engines. Within seconds waves of children came running to form a single broad line five feet from where the bikes stopped, even toddlers. Elders sat in the shade of trees or a pergola roofed in blooming red hibiscus. Here and there were those who did not farm or trade: heavily pregnant women, a potter, a tailor with his sewing machine on an elevated veranda under the eave of his house, or a drum maker who would show Tacker a thing or two about how to hold the roped sides of the talking drum in order to change the sound and the message. For the next few hours Tacker was blessed by the floating hands of children: on his blond hair, against his pale legs.

On Jersey Avenue in Winston-Salem, morning light sparkled on the Indian's gas tank. A screen door creaked and slammed back into its frame. An older fellow ambled out from behind a stand of overgrown azaleas flanking his porch. He favored one leg as he walked.

"She's a good one," the man said. "You interested?"

"Who wouldn't be? This bike's a beaut."

"Bought her new over in Charlotte before we moved. No one's owned that bike but me, myself, and I. Ride it out to Greensboro on occasion. Took her to Raleigh a few times. Mostly I like to ride up into Virginia in the fall. Now, that's the thing. Leaning into those curves."

The man mimed the action of holding the handgrips and pitching against the turn.

"You got a girlfriend?" he said. "Offered to put the passenger seat on for my wife, but she didn't take to the idea. Matter of fact, I got an extra seat. Just never installed it. I could trade that luggage rack out for it."

Tacker avoided the girlfriend question.

"She'll get you there in good time and in style. Twin engine, three-speed transmission. A 'forty-eight. Good, solid machine. Real fine Stewart Warner speedometer. New battery. Headlamp replaced but all the original chrome."

Tacker knew a little about cars and figured he could learn how to tinker with a motorcycle. Riding an Indian said something. *I may follow the rules, but I've got plays you never dreamed of.*

"I'd be happy to put that passenger seat on for you. Wouldn't take much time."

Tacker thought of Kate showing up at Hart's, the secret of her

wrist disappearing into her sleeve, her lovely face, her resistance—
she still had it—and it was why he remembered her. In high
school, she'd worn earmuffs during a required assembly to honor
the football team. Way back then he'd wanted to know her but
he'd gotten distracted by the pretty girls who were more exciting
in a different way.

"What are you asking for it?" Tacker said, cracking his
knuckles.

"I've doted on this bike. That's a fact. But it sat in the garage
all summer. This bum leg isn't getting any better. How does four
hundred sound?"

Tacker let out a low whistle and palmed his face. "Not sure I
have that kind of change."

"Maybe we can work something out. You're the kind of boy
I'd like to see owning it. You live close by?"

"Just down on West End. I manage Hart's Grocery. Belongs
to my dad."

"You're Hart's boy? Why didn't you say so? Harris here." He
held out a hand. "What can you afford a month?"

Tacker dug a heel into the grass.

"Tell you what. You take her for a ride. See what you can
figure."

HIGHWAY 158. PALE fields spread to the horizon and the road
was a dream. A pond dimpled the middle of a pasture and a blue
heron sailed overhead. White cows clustered on a muddy hill.
Browned fields held skeletons of tobacco stalks—he could smell
the dusky hulks; barns glowed silver in the sun. But mostly it
was the air, fierce as a demon, whipping up his hair, pressing his
lips against his teeth. Tacker thought of Samuel and how he
would love this bike. Sam had written four times. Haunted by

fear, Tacker hadn't opened a single letter. He slowed the bike and brought it to idle on the side of the road. Even out here in the broad country, he felt himself shrinking into his jacket thinking about his carelessness. What if Samuel had been sacked on Tacker's account? Or something worse? He remembered how Samuel had come into the classroom one day with a brown package and he and the other men made Tacker open it—a Yoruba man's gown and loose trousers. They required him to put it on right then, over his short-sleeved shirt and seersucker shorts, and everyone had clapped. A thickness gathered in his throat and he shook his head, revved the bike, and started to pull onto the road. A horn blared and a truck passed so close he felt the heat of the exhaust on his face.

Back in Harris's yard, he pumped the Indian onto its stand. The man was reclined on his porch. Tacker took the steps up to him. Harris pushed himself to standing.

"I can give you three hundred. Fifteen a month until it's paid off," Tacker said.

"You're hard on an old man," Harris said, rolling back on his heels. He laughed softly, rubbing his belly with both hands. Tacker saw half a finger was missing.

The man dipped his head as if he had to think privately. A pair of towhees fretted around the azaleas. "All right. I'll take your offer." Harris hitched up his britches. "I do like knowing she'll be close by. You want me to put that passenger seat on?"

"Sure," Tacker said.

"That's what I thought. Good-looking boy like you. Come back in the morning. She'll be ready."

He held out his hand and they shook on it.

Tacker felt the shift, down in his bones. He'd found something he needed without looking, like Gaines and Kate, something new shoring up against the ruins.

IN THE WEEK after buying the Indian, Tacker found himself surprised by the lightness of his legs, the way they felt in his trousers, like waking animals. The whole city—the entire state—opened to him. He could pack his gear and head out for an overnight at the beach if he wanted or go west into the mountains. He worked late, preparing orders for fresh Thanksgiving turkeys. Someone—his dad?—had slipped an A&P flyer into this work stack. A&P was the worst with price wars. Tacker tossed the advertisement into the trash. Finally the next morning a shipment of apples arrived. He found Kate Monroe's address and phone number stuck to the bulletin board behind the customer counter.

"Hello?" she said.

"It's me. Tacker. From Hart's."

"Of course it's you," she said, a slender authority in her voice.

"Your order finally came in."

"It's nice of you to let me know."

"I suppose I shouldn't mix business with pleasure."

"I don't see why not."

"I could drop the apples off and we could get supper at the Toddle House."

"When?"

"Tonight."

"Yes," she said.

"How do you feel about riding on the back of a motorcycle?"

"I feel like it's going to be awfully damaging to my hairstyle," she said.

"I didn't think about that," he said.

"I'm kidding. I'd like to go."

Tacker hadn't kissed a woman in a good while. It was a grave thought, and at the edge of it was the scent of rain.

Chapter Five

TACKER SHOWED UP with two boxes of apples strapped to the back of a mammoth blue motorcycle. Kate watched him leaping up the granite yard steps, with first one and then the other, and he was just as swift and sure with the second box as with the first. She felt suddenly vulnerable to the breadth of his shoulders and the breadth of his stride and searched hard for some intellectual question to stump him with over dinner at the Toddle House. Twilight descended as they headed up Glade on the Indian, she snug in wool pants and a wool coat that fell to midcalf and a pair of boots that came up past her ankles. She had to hold her cap on her head with one hand and pull herself tight against Tacker with the other. Was this why men owned motorcycles? The headlamp traced a finger of light up ahead of them. She thought of James and the way he kissed her mouth with great curiosity, and she felt she must make clear to Tacker how things stood with her even though the fact of the matter was that in spite of recommencing phone conversations, she and

James still fought and the time he invited her down to Atlanta for the weekend—explaining that she could stay with one of his cousins in Decatur—she'd turned him down because she was afraid he would try to seduce her and afraid she would let him. And the thought of a strange bedroom—or, worse, a motel room—frightened her.

The Toddle House was packed and they had to wait, choosing to stand outside under a great bare oak. She smelled the hamburgers cooking. "Why do you think it is that little boys walk up and down the street whacking at the bushes with sticks?" she said. It was a spontaneous question, only subtly intellectual.

"Do they?" Tacker said.

"I saw a couple of them today from my front porch. The younger one couldn't have been three years old. His brother may have been five. They just whacked away at everything. Does someone teach them to do that?"

"I have no idea. I don't remember doing it."

"Good," she said, restraining a smile. "I'm starving."

"Maybe they were hunters and gatherers. The boys."

"If they did that in the springtime, it would upset birds' nests."

"Good point. Let me check to see where we are on the list," Tacker said.

"I can do it." Kate rushed in, leaving Tacker out on the sidewalk so it wouldn't seem so much like they were on a date.

"Are you against chivalry?" he said when she returned.

"On the contrary. My story about the boys indicates just how much I am for it. No tree whacking. We're third down on the list."

When they were seated, Tacker ordered chili and two hot dogs and Kate ordered a burger with French fries. "So tell me again where you went and what you did," she said.

"I don't think I told you the first time. Nigeria. On the west coast of Africa." He took a napkin and drew Africa and filled in

Nigeria. "I was helping design a high school. It was going to be duplicated around the country, the south primarily."

Kate smoothed the napkin. "They have a south like we do?"

"Actually, yes."

She dipped a French fry into her ketchup. "What was your biggest surprise?"

"In Nigeria?" Tacker rubbed his chin. "I guess I'd say how serene and self-confident people are, even kids, like every one of them is going to inherit the earth."

It wasn't what she expected. "What do you mean?"

"People just seemed sure of their place. It sounds trite. Don't get me wrong. I was pretty shocked when I first got there. A lot of people are poor, living in mud houses and doing their wash in the river. But even little kids act like they own the world."

"Were you happy being there?"

"Maybe too happy," Tacker said.

He had that funny look she'd first noticed at Hart's weeks back when they spoke for the first time, and then he seemed to recover.

"How about you?"

She finished the last bite of her burger and touched her napkin to her lips.

"Long story, short version. After my mom died, I went back to Agnes Scott to finish college. I had to stay through the summer to get all my courses in. Then I came back here and ran into you. My story's less glamorous."

"What do you think you'll do now?"

"I'm considering photography."

He put down his half-eaten second hot dog and looked at her. "As a hobby?"

"As a career. What do you think?"

His eyes were clear and bright. "I think you can do anything."

All through the meal, she tried to find a way to bring James up but she couldn't, and besides, Tacker wasn't acting a bit romantic. He was just being himself and she was a little miffed. But then they left and Tacker drove them through downtown and it was beautiful and calm and she wasn't miffed as they passed the Carolina Theatre where *Journey to the Center of the Earth* was showing, and then they headed to Old Salem, clackering along a cobblestone street, and finally Tacker turned around and they headed back. His hand glanced hers as they got off the bike but he did not hold her hand or put an arm around her. They walked up the stairs and he waited for her to find her key.

"Thanks," she said. "That was fun."

"I'm glad you enjoyed it. So did I."

He put a hand to the back of his neck and for a moment Kate thought he would lean in and kiss her. She waited a heartbeat. His eyes scanned her door.

"So I'll see you around," he said.

She walked into her house alone and turned the deadbolt and in a little bit she heard the bike start up again. In the library, she switched on the light and sat down in front of her mother's portrait. The cool lozenge in the lower chamber of her heart seemed to pulse. She was too withdrawn, too aloof, perhaps because she was afraid that any man she loved would end up dead. In a little bit, she got up and moved to the downstairs bedroom that her mother had transformed into a studio, turned on a light, and looked around. She might make it into a darkroom.

KATE HAD LEARNED to develop film in the darkroom adjacent to the student paper offices at Agnes Scott a year ago. She'd been taught by an art professor who was also the faculty adviser to the *Profile*. His name was Mr. Lancaster.

"If you're going to be a photographer, Miss Monroe," Lancaster had said, pushing back his glasses, "you should have the experience of developing your own film. I don't mind showing you if you can stop by on Saturday."

"Saturday afternoon?" she said. "I have a paper I need to finish Saturday morning."

"That will do fine. Shall we say three o'clock? Meet me at the side door. I'll have to let us in. Shoot a roll of film you don't care much about. It may get ruined."

On Saturday she was there as promised.

"Go ahead and rewind your film," Lancaster said once they were upstairs.

She did.

"Very well. Open your camera and hand me the roll."

The camera clicked open nicely.

"Once we enter the darkroom, you will have to accomplish these first steps blind." He paused. "Miss Monroe, the building is locked. You may set your camera on the counter. You won't be needing it."

Yes, Lancaster had used the key to open the building, but somehow Kate had not thought until now about being locked in with him. "Of course." They walked toward the back of the classroom, Mr. Lancaster's head to one side as he talked.

"When we go in the red light will be on. That's the safe light. But as I said, we must turn it off at the beginning. Just a moment of light and your pictures will be ruined."

Mr. Lancaster was a serious old man, but suddenly she was afraid he might touch her. The year Kate was home with her mother, she was walking down a neighborhood street and a man passed and she smiled at him and in the same instant felt his hand on her bottom, and she ran. Lancaster pulled a small instrument from his white jacket pocket. It looked like a bottle opener. "The first thing you do is pry off the lid."

"Yes," she said. Mr. Lancaster's hands were large.

"Before we turn off the light, I'll show you the film reel and the metal container. Once the canister is open, you must pull out the film, holding it just so." He demonstrated with his thumb and forefinger. "The roll is going to snake out. If you feel something against your leg, do not scream and drop your film."

"Of course." She would scream if he touched her.

"You must line up the film to the reel so that it catches on the teeth and then start rolling. I'll talk you through." He pulled out a handkerchief and coughed and replaced the handkerchief. "You'll put the film reel into the black box and place the lid on top. Only then can we turn on the safe light."

"I believe I can do that." *Just don't even breathe on me.*

"I believe you can too, Miss Monroe. You have steady hands. Now, follow me."

Lancaster led her to a funny-looking door. He backed into it; it swirled around, making a mechanical sound and emitting a red light, and for a moment Kate thought he had wound himself into the film reel. The door padded shut. "Are you coming, Miss Monroe?"

She pushed forward through the revolving door. It breathed the same mechanical sound and padded shut behind her. She was in the center of a red jewel. A chemical smell filled her lungs and three rectangular basins met her eye, full of liquid like witches' brew. Her fear of Lancaster was gone.

He showed her the film reel and the metal box and explained the stop bath and the fixer. "Now," he said. "Are you ready?" He handed her the bottle opener.

"Yes." The red light went off and the dark rushed into Kate's eyes. She placed the opener against the canister, feeling for the lip, turned the canister, and kept pressing. At last the canister sighed and the lid popped off.

"Now, that's fine," Mr. Lancaster said. "Take hold of the top of the film—we'll call it the tongue—and let the film spool out. Put the canister on the tabletop to your left."

She obeyed.

"Now find the reel with your other hand and picture in your mind getting the perforations to slide onto the teeth."

Kate felt her way. So this was what it was like to be blind: a life of touching, of smell, of loving through touching. "I got it," she said, pressing hard on the reel.

"Start turning."

Kate had the loaded reel in the box and the top in place when Mr. Lancaster turned on the red light. She was almost sorry. The chemical dark had become a book in which she was reading the world new. Lancaster poured in the developer and they turned the box several times, then poured the developer out. Then came the stop bath and then the fixer. Finally they poured water into the box. When Kate lifted the film out, she felt a rush of mastery, as if she were creating the realest of worlds. They flipped themselves back through the revolving door into the disorienting white light of the office.

"Here, Miss Monroe," Mr. Lancaster said, showing her a kind of closet where she would hang the film. He looked at his watch. "It will need to dry for a good hour and a half. Do you have errands to run?"

"Not really. I brought a book to read."

An hour later, she was cutting the long reel of film into strips of five images each and entering each into a plastic sleeve. At the light table, Mr. Lancaster's breath had gone to peppermint. Using a magnifying loop, Kate discovered a mysterious world of light and dark turned to opposites. She circled every image. Then they were back in the red jewel of the darkroom, putting the first set of images onto an object like a pancake and sliding it into the enlarger, slipping paper into the bottom of the machine, the paper thick enough that she could imagine its treeness. Lancaster set a timer.

"Light in the machine for fifteen seconds," he said.

Was it like this at the beginning of the universe? Light off. Paper out. Kate slid the thick sheet into the developer pan. The images coalesced like ghosts becoming people, ghosts becoming buildings. One thing became something else. At last she held a photograph. She submerged it into the stop bath, into the fixer, then rinsed in water and rinsed again, squeegeed off the water, and put the photograph on a dry rack.

On that day in Decatur as Kate walked out into the late afternoon, carrying with her the smells of the developer, the stop bath, the fixer, her pictures in an envelope held tight to her heart, the breeze lifting her skirt, she thought of James and the house she had inherited back in Winston, and nothing compared to what she was holding.

Southwestern Nigeria

1957

Chapter Six

TACKER STARTED SKETCHING in an eighth-grade art class. He was fascinated by perspective. The summer after tenth grade, he worked for a surveying company in Winston. Mostly it was a matter of lugging equipment and cutting weeds. The next summer, he worked for an architect, running errands and learning to do renderings. He had an uncanny knack for drawing. When a friend went off to North Carolina State College, School of Design, and came home at Christmas talking about his teachers, Tacker was hooked. "You should see this one prof," the friend said. "He makes his shoes out of old tires!" The friend switched to forestry and Tacker applied to the School of Design. When he got to those reused barracks on that huge courtyard, he'd found his niche. His pals were as competitive as football players, but they were kooky, some of them, and smart. Working over his table, twelve other fellows in the room, books puddled everywhere, was like summer camp for nerds except that snow swirled outside. Tacker loved it.

In the afternoons he played intramural football. He was too good and people got mad at him, so he switched to basketball, which he wasn't nearly as good at. He joined a fraternity, and his second year, he started dating Jill. There were summers at the beach and the years cycled one after the other until his fifth year, when he found himself chosen for the Clintok assignment.

A week before Tacker was to take the train to New York to board a freighter headed for West Africa, he got a phone call telling him that his partner in the two-year assignment, Seth Hudson, whom he'd roomed with in D.C., had come down with mono and couldn't go. "Spend a year here doing an internship. Apply to Clintok again next year. You'll be a shoo-in. I don't want you going alone," his mother said.

"No, Mom. They're counting on me." As soon as he said it, he regretted his conviction. No one knew where Nigeria was, and when he told them, they looked alarmed, as if he were going to the heart of darkness. All the shots he'd taken wouldn't protect him from snakes and he'd almost certainly get malaria regardless of the medicine he'd be taking weekly. There was some horrible illness called elephantiasis carried by the tsetse fly.

His mother sat on the edge of her chair in the breakfast room. His father held back. He'd always told Tacker to finish what he started. "I can always come home early if something happens," Tacker said—prophetically as it turned out.

His father ended up taking the train with him to New York, where they spent the night at the Ritz Tower on Park Avenue. The next morning at the dock, the freighter's black hull loomed titanic and Tacker might have backed out if his father hadn't been there shaking his hand, pressing his duffel bag into his arms, telling him to write. The trip was tedious. There were only eighteen passengers and Tacker was seasick for the first few days. Once he gained his sea legs, he played deck golf with a Norwegian, but they could hardly communicate. The sailors chipped incessantly with hammers and chisels at the rust that constantly bloomed under the hull paint. Multitudes of porpoises swam alongside the ship.

In Liverpool, an Englishwoman and her daughter boarded. She was joining her husband, who worked for an aluminum company headquartered in Lagos. The girl did correspondence school in the morning. In the afternoon she and her mother walked on the deck and had tea. They invited Tacker to join them. An African steward appeared with a tray carrying a silver teapot and a bed of butter cookies.

"I had no idea they'd be this well supplied," Tacker said.

"Oh, these are my things," the mother said, waving the steward off with her handkerchief.

The girl was good at checkers. Tacker wondered who her playmates would be in Nigeria. At night he walked on deck and brooded over what he had gotten himself into. He was probably going to die. Three and a half weeks after departing New York, the ship docked in Monrovia and from there it picked its way down the west coast of Africa. Finally they reached Takoradi. An official representative of Clintok, Charles Robinson, came on board to help Tacker clear customs.

Africa smelled like an enormous green organism on fire, a pungent soup of salt water, smoke, and enough growth for an eighth continent. They offloaded onto an enormous canoe. Astonishingly, they found themselves within a marketplace of canoes: women selling umbrellas and flip-flops and banana leaves that held some native dish. "Don't eat a thing," Robinson said. "And don't buy anything either. It only encourages them." Onshore, Tacker focused on Robinson's back until they reached his Renault. They would drive along the coast to Accra, where Tacker would catch a Nigeria Airways flight to Lagos. As he came out of a disorienting slumber, his eyes met an enormous structure jutting out into the ocean. Peach colored and colossal against blue sky. He sat up in his seat and wiped his eyes.

"Wow," he said. "What's that?"

"Elmina Castle," Robinson said. "Built by the Portuguese. Fourteen eighty-two."

"Amazing," Tacker said, straining his neck to see better.

"An important stop on the slave-trade route," Robinson said casually. "Thirty thousand slaves a year through the door of no return."

Dazed, Tacker closed his eyes, his teeth set against a rising tide of nausea.

A PETITE NIGERIAN man in a starched white shirt grasped Tacker's hand. "Come, my friend. I am Samuel Ladipo, here to fetch you for the university." Tacker had just deplaned at the Lagos airport, a structure not much larger than a good-size barn flanked with corridors. Samuel had three upward-slanting scars on his cheeks, deeply drawn. Had to have been with a knife. Or a razor. A nerve-tingling jolt ran through Tacker's groin. Miraculously, Samuel seemed to know exactly which were Tacker's suitcases, and before Tacker knew what was happening, two boys not much larger than the luggage were carrying the bags out the door into broad daylight. Everything smelled of deep wells and machine oil.

Tacker tried to watch his bags. The boys zigzagged this way and that, around carts with root vegetables and vehicles parked at every angle and displays of blue cloth and women with babies who had set up thatch booths for selling cigarettes and watches and tomatoes. They were in a pinball machine, and only by some mad happenchance was Tacker ever going to see his bags again. Samuel chuckled, loping along, his brown sandals clacking. Around a low building, and there was a beige Volkswagen van, the luggage already loaded, an older man standing at the driver's door. He wore a kind of gown over trousers. The boys stood at the back of the van, their hands resting on the bags, legs lightened by dust.

Samuel offered each a small octagonal brass coin. The boys shook their heads and laughed. One motioned to Tacker in a way that seemed to say, *Come*.

"They are not satisfied with the dash," Samuel said. "What do you say in your country? The tip? They want American money."

Samuel's English was impeccable, but Tacker couldn't identify the accent. It wasn't British. He fished in his pocket for the nickels and dimes he still possessed. The boys extended their hands.

"Thank you, sah," they said ceremoniously. "You are welcome," they also said.

Then they were off like low-flying birds.

SAMUEL DELIVERED TACKER to a hostel on Victoria Island, not far from where the ships docked out past the lagoon, and prepared to leave him for the night. In the morning, they would drive upcountry.

"Aren't you staying with me?" Tacker said.

"Ah. Independence has not registered yet," Samuel said.

What? Tacker wondered. Maybe there was a special meaning to *register* that he didn't grasp. When dinner was served, he understood. The hostel was full of white Americans and Europeans. Nigerian men in fitted white jackets with brass buttons waited on them with great ceremony. At the end of the meal they were served blocks of ice cream on plates.

In the morning he waited for Samuel downstairs in the fenced yard surrounding the hostel. A light haze floated above the ground and the temperature was pleasant. Tacker was surprised by tall evergreens along the avenue. He caught a whiff of something that smelled like homemade rolls baking. Across the street were two-story buildings with large open windows, and in them he could see men dressed in shirts and ties, moving about, working at typewriters. He wondered if he was observing a bank building or a newspaper. Elderly men strolled along in their long robes as men on bicycles wove in and out among taxis and cars and the occasional Mercedes-Benz. A boy carried a whole flock of chickens in a basket and a man on a bike balanced mattresses on his head as he cycled. Scores of kids in blue uniforms skipped by, laughing and calling out. Women walked barefoot, carrying stacks of tinned goods or huge vegetables Tacker thought might be yams.

A church occupied the lot just next to the hostel, Episcopalian perhaps. Its soaring windows arched and the nave suggested a capacity of three hundred. The square vestibule, ornamented with a single round window, rose to an imposing tower. Tacker wondered if anyone had ever slept there. Enormous carved doors against cloud-colored masonry walls in a setting of coconut palms and flocking white birds and a wafting ocean breeze gave the building an ethereal composure. It seemed a church in paradise.

Samuel arrived in the van for the trip upcountry to Ibadan. Loading his things into the vehicle, Tacker asked about the church.

"Everything for constructing that church was sent here by boat after your civil war," Samuel said. "Even the bell."

"Episcopalian?"

"No, my friend. Baptist. Those people are very enterprising," he said. "It's good, no?"

"It's fantastic," Tacker said. He was surprised to find such a fine expression of late-nineteenth-century architecture on this side of the Atlantic. After the fear of death he'd felt on the ship, he was reassured by Samuel's warm welcome. This morning he had wakened and brushed his teeth as always—though with filtered water delivered in a thermos—and eaten breakfast and listened to the news on the radio. Now he sensed a current of opportunity waiting for him in this country, sure and clear as an underground river. Lagos wasn't Paris. But for that very reason he would do something important here. This was why he'd won the Clintok appointment. He was destined.

Within a mile, they entered a congested market area. Buses and goats and bicycles and boys and women moved about according to their own code, though there was plenty of yelling and honking and pleading and somehow no one was getting hit. Market stalls reached out in every direction as the VW van turtled along.

"My country," Samuel said, grinning. "The drive to Ibadan may take three hours. How do you say it? More or less." He used his hands to indicate *more* and *less*.

At last they were out of the city and into marshland. The one-lane road required they pull over onto grassy shoulders to avoid oncoming traffic. Eventually they wound through dense forest, gentle hills rising, clusters of enormous palms where streams ran. Crossing a bridge, they were offered glimpses of women and children bathing and doing their wash. Women's naked breasts, long and tapering. In training, he'd been told to expect more exposure but he hadn't quite expected it this morning. Among the women were girls whose breasts sat firmly on their chests like inverted teacups. He felt their influence and was glad to be sitting.

All up and down the road women and girls carried pots and

basins and firewood on their heads. When children caught sight of Tacker, they yelled and waved. "What are they saying?"

"Oyinbo," Samuel said. "White man."

"Oh, right," Tacker said. He'd been apprised of the word but it hadn't been pronounced as the children said it: *oh-yeeen-bow*, with the second syllable stressed. Nor had he been told that children would run through the streets calling his whiteness out with such enthusiasm. Since leaving the hostel, he hadn't seen another white person.

Samuel carried on as if all of it was normal, this enormous country, a boy offering to sell them a "grasscutter"—a terrifically large rat, newly dead and swinging on a pole—the dense heat, two gentlemen walking single file, carrying ancient rifles, long-horned cattle that suddenly appeared as they rounded a curve, and then the van stopped and no one rolled up the windows as the herd passed by, though any of those humped beasts could easily send a long horn straight into Tacker's skull.

UNIVERSITY COLLEGE IBADAN, or UCI, was their home base, where Tacker's team would design the high school, going and coming from the field as need be. The lead architect was a Yoruba man who had attended MIT. Someone at Clintok had recruited him, since UCI had no faculty in design or architecture. One goal of the project was to inaugurate a program in architecture at the college. Tacker was housed with some Israelis in an unoccupied faculty residence on campus. Samuel and the other Nigerian men on his team lived in a dormitory named Tedder Hall. Tacker expected that the arrangement was akin to the Lagos hostel, separation based on skin color. He didn't ask.

Samuel was team captain, which was why he had come to Lagos to pick Tacker up. The first day the group met, the Nigerian men were dressed in suits and ties. Tacker arrived in trousers and a short-sleeved shirt. The dress code relaxed the following day, but Tacker's teammates always dressed smartly. Recent graduates of UCI, they would receive a certificate in architecture for their participation. Tacker was getting a stipend, gaining a nice line on his résumé, and maybe shaving a year off the time it would take to get licensed when he got home. The Israelis, it turned out, were in charge of the Western Region's waterworks. Tacker had never worked with concrete block or considered what sort of roofing was appropriate for equatorial Africa or how to keep termites from destroying a building before the foundation was finished. But he knew the European and American architects whose work had inspired the modernist buildings of UCI and he knew how they had achieved it. It would be in this intersection of knowledge and opportunity that he would make his mark.

The second week, Tacker contracted diarrhea. The toilet in the faculty residence was temporarily out of service and one night he found himself stumbling to a latrine. The stench wasn't as bad as he had expected, but the occupation of emptying his bowels into a great cavity of excrement along with the wrenching in his belly and the sweating faintness that followed this evacuation caused his African ambition to dim. What delusion, that he or anyone could achieve something of significance in a country without reliable toilets. He heard a rustle outside the latrine and bolted, tripping and finding himself on his hands and knees in the darkest night he had ever known. For the first time since landing in Lagos, he doubted his capacity merely to endure.

A light came bobbing down the path. Samuel with his flashlight, which he called his torch. "My friend," he said, helping Tacker up. Tacker wondered how Samuel happened to be there just when he needed him, but back in bed he fell into a deep sleep and the next day his memory of the episode ribboned away like a dream.

One weekend in late September, Samuel had to go to Lagos to pick up supplies and Tacker was at loose ends. So when Joshua invited him to his village for a "tremendous event," Tacker accepted. Joshua's father owned a modest compound and an impressive yam farm. Unlike Joshua, who was rotund and round-shouldered, his father was thin and regal. His mother had the look of a young woman who had aged twenty years overnight. Her skin was still supple but the color was ashen and her lips tight. Tacker sensed that Joshua's father had judged the world and found it wanting, including his wife.

Sunday morning early Tacker was wakened by the sound of bicycles. By the time he found Joshua in the compound, a crowd was gathered, men sitting under trees, women and children at the house fronts. At the center of the compound stood a contrite-looking man in an outfit of worn shorts and a shirt transparent from age. He held a soft hat in his hands and kept his head lowered. At his feet was arranged an assortment of carved figures on a pyre of sticks. Tacker caught a whiff of gasoline.

Joshua was suddenly beside him. "You're just in time."

"Why didn't you get me up?" Tacker felt disoriented. "What's happening?"

"The man you see is my mother's brother. He is a recent convert. This morning he will burn his family gods. My father has decreed it."

"Why?"

"So they will have no more power for him."

Tacker shook his head. "But if he's a convert, the gods already don't have power."

"You don't understand."

Just then Joshua's father stepped out of the shadow of his veranda, wearing a tall red cap and a heavily embroidered robe. The poor man at the center of this tremendous event seemed to shudder. "Are you sure your uncle wants to do this?" Tacker had the awful feeling that the man would light the fire and leap in with his gods.

"He has no choice."

"I just want to ask him." Tacker took off toward the center of the compound and reached the poor man at the same time as Joshua's father. The idols were wondrously, frightfully carved, with bulging stomachs and huge foreheads and blank, all-seeing eyes. The farmer's eyes were red.

"Yes?" Joshua's father addressed Tacker.

"Look. Your brother-in-law. Is this what he wants? These carvings could go into a museum. Why burn them?"

"Who are you to meddle here? If you were not my son's friend, I should ask you to leave my compound."

"Ask him." Tacker pointed to the poor man, who took the opportunity to fall to his knees and wail. A high screech filled the air. Tacker turned to see a woman in a blue dress, holding a burning stick, running across the yard. She lit the pyre. Tacker reached for the nearest god. A jolt like an electric shock ran through his arm, and he dropped it. The man fell to his side, still wailing, while the woman, perhaps his wife, retired to her children.

Back at UCI, Tacker was interviewed about the experience, and it was written up in the student paper, the *Herald*. "The man seemed pained," Tacker was quoted as saying.

Interviewer: You are new to our country. By what authority
    do you judge our goings-on?

Mr. Hart: I'm here to collaborate. I was trying to be helpful.

Interviewer: Perhaps you prefer for Africans to remain un-
enlightened. You can write to your friends about our native ways.

Mr. Hart: That's not true.

Interviewer: You believe you know better than the town elders.

The story might have caused Tacker significant hardship on
campus, but a boxing match between Nigeria's two greatest ri-
vals was scheduled the day after the story ran, and by the next
week the tale of his interference in the tremendous event of the
burning gods was pretty much forgotten, or so he thought.

By mid-October, Tacker was leaving the faculty house and
the Israelis most evenings to join the guys at the faculty club. A
few women always showed up. High-life music filled the air,
a brassy, swinging sound that compelled dancing. The night
Tacker showed up with Elvis Presley's "All Shook Up," things
turned in his direction. Within seconds, everyone stopped to
listen, as if a new gospel was being proclaimed. As soon as the
song ended, they demanded that it be played again. The women
giggled under their bright headdresses while the men took the
floor, pumping their elbows out. "All shook up" became a slogan. "Tacker, my friend. All shook up!"

Only Joshua held out against Elvis Presley. "The devil plays
fine, fine music," he said one morning when he crossed paths
with Tacker in an open courtyard. "Otherwise, why would so
many people follow him?"

"You think Elvis Presley is the devil?" Tacker said.

"One of his emissaries," Joshua said.

Tacker expected that his visit to Joshua's compound had
caused him some difficulty with his father, so he didn't argue.
He felt sorry for Joshua.

On an aerogram, a thin blue piece of foldable and gummed paper, he wrote to his parents in Winston—

> *I'll send a package soon with film to develop. You'll*
> *see a picture of me washing out my shirts in a bucket.*
> *A determined old man comes by to press them, using a*
> *flatiron he heats on charcoal in a clay pot. There are*
> *others of me playing soccer (it's called football here)*
> *with some kids and one of me with my friend Samuel*
> *at a local Esso station.*
>
> *The heat takes getting used to. Americans and*
> *Europeans take naps. But I'm trying to gain my*
> *African legs so I drink black coffee after lunch,*
> *Nescafé instant. Except for open corridors in the*
> *classroom blocks and all the palms and the bougain-*
> *villea hedges, the campus is a lot like one back home.*
> *The Nigerian guys on the project include me in*
> *everything.*

Tacker had never encountered anyone like Samuel. His modesty almost hid his keen mind, his skin was darker than that of Negroes back home, and his crossed ankles looked delicate. But he could brush his teeth with a chewing stick and juggle a ball with his feet for five minutes at a time and outlast Tacker on the playing field any day of the week. He went to church for three hours every Sunday morning and read his Bible daily, though he didn't seem rabid about it.

One evening as he was cleaning his leather sandals, Samuel asked Tacker about his faith.

"I've been Methodist all my life," Tacker said. "I guess I was born into it."

"Faith is the silken thread that brings power to the cloth,"

Samuel said, spitting onto a rag and applying it to his sandal. "If the thread is removed, the fabric falls apart." Trancelike, the man seemed almost to address his sandals rather than Tacker. "My forefathers believed that divinities rest in trees, at the crossroads, all about." Without taking his eyes from his work, Samuel waved his arm in an arc. "That is why it is not hard for us to believe that Jesus walks with us everywhere. Why should I be surprised? I am not surprised."

Another day over lunch, Samuel described the round houses of his mother's village to Tacker. "Further north, north of Ilorin," he said. "My father married a Nupe woman from a wealthy family. The houses are round." He formed an O in the air. "Like a mother's womb." Often Samuel wore the traditional men's gown. The cloth fanned out in the breeze so that the simple act of walking was a spectacle. The first time he came up behind Tacker and claimed his hand, Tacker swallowed wrong and started hiccuping.

"I have startled you," Samuel said. He laughed but didn't let go, and they kept walking to the cafeteria.

Later that day Tacker pulled out his wallet and looked at his North Carolina driver's license, surprised by how distant he felt from the reflection of himself in his own world. What had his ambition been before he came to Nigeria? Something else seemed to call him now, something more than architecture, some mystery he still hadn't glimpsed. The silken thread with that other world seemed very thin.

FOUR MONTHS AFTER his arrival, Tacker and his team had perfected initial sketches for the high school. They drove upcountry to Osogbo to visit the property seventy miles north, where the first high school would be built. It was early November, the day clear and warm. The van gained a hillier terrain and entered wooded savannah. After a sudden cloudburst, the sun was out again. Palm shacks with food vendors appeared along the highway. The driver pulled over and everyone spilled out to buy some tidbit—skewers of grilled meat and boiled yams with palm oil for dipping. Tacker couldn't imagine how the women and children got here so far from town. For a moment he had a vision of his father's grocery invaded by Nigerian women traders coming in to barter with their bananas and individual cigarettes and groundnuts packaged neatly in funneled cups made from newspaper. He purchased his first *eko*, a corn-based starch wrapped in banana leaves. It tasted a little like cold grits and he managed to eat most of it though the sauce was some sort of hot he'd never dreamed of.

Back in the van, Tacker dozed but snapped awake when they took a sudden turn onto a bad road. The van lurched up a hill and down the other side before the driver pulled in under a stand of mango trees and applied the brakes in a spasm of authority, and then the quiet man who had said not a word the entire trip announced that they would pray. He took off his cap and held it as he thanked God for safe travel, for God's eye on the road and his hand on the steering wheel, and for sending Jesu Kristi to save them.

"Amen," the driver and Samuel and all the other men said in unison.

"Amen," Tacker said, half a second later.

"Come," Samuel said.

Out they went.

"Is this the land for the school?" Tacker said. They lunged through grass as high as their chests, someone in front beating it back with a cutlass. *Chow-ow, chow-ow.*

"Not yet," Samuel said. "We are giving you an initiation."

Tacker thought of a knife and his face surely showed it.

"Don't worry. We don't require blood," Samuel said, the

planes of his cheeks lit by sun. Then an amazed laugh as if life was too brilliant to bear.

They began a decline and Tacker had to be careful not to slip. Most of the time his high-top sneakers were adequate, but the Nigerian men were finding better purchase with their sandals. Tacker couldn't see anything for the undergrowth and overhead canopy.

"Watch," Samuel said.

Tacker was about to step on a huge black snake. He leapt forward, colliding with Samuel, who managed to keep them upright. Tacker turned to look back and saw a tree root.

"I thought it was a snake," he said.

"Not so deadly," Samuel said, slapping him on the back.

Abraham, the team member with an adding machine for a brain, turned around. "Tacker, I think you are all shook up." Everyone laughed.

At last they looked out to see a brown river below. Here and there gray stones jutted up like humped backs of great turtles, the current rippling around them. Shortly they reached an open clearing and a swinging bridge high above the river.

"We're crossing over," Samuel said.

Tacker felt a wave of energy pass through him. He recalled the days aboard ship, crossing the Atlantic, the fear, followed by Sam's warm welcome, then the odd normalcy of a world so unlike his own. Yet he was constantly being surprised as if he were living in a story that was being written every day. There wasn't an ending yet. If he could just keep his balance. The wood-and-rope contraption swung just enough to make his head swim. *Look straight ahead.* On the other side, they continued, single file. Feeling victorious, Tacker wondered if he might stay in Nigeria longer than two years, maybe three. Why not longer?

A switchback in the path took them downward again, and

Tacker scrabbled for roots and saplings. There was the river. White-faced, white-chested monkeys chattered in the trees along the opposite bank. Tacker slid down the final hill.

"Welcome to River Osun," Samuel said. He slipped off his sandals, his feet imprinting the brown earth.

They had come to a lagoon where the river broadened. Some of the men squatted onshore, filling cupped hands and releasing river water over their heads. It flowed in glistening streams down their dark curly hair and over their faces like mercury. Only Joshua sat out, appearing to brood. Tacker wondered if he was self-conscious because of his rotundness.

"Please join us," Samuel said to Tacker.

"What if I just put my feet in?" Tacker said, heeling off his sneakers. He'd already risked eating that *eko*.

"It's not like that," Samuel said. "Osun is a sacred river. It will bring you good health. It will also bless your mother in America."

"It will make you potent," Abraham said, grinning, pointing to his groin.

Tacker had promised his mother he wouldn't swim in an African river. He'd also been warned by the State Department and the Clintok Corporation to steer clear of all rivers and lagoons except for salt water. He couldn't remember the name of the disease. It started with an *s*. Well, here he was. Maybe it was best just to pour a few drops over his head. Refusing would be like turning down a gift from a local king. Maybe this was where faith came in, though Tacker felt only foreboding. He would die, only the death wouldn't be quick. Some gruesome parasite would eat him inside out.

Samuel joined the others and Tacker followed because waiting was worse. He squatted and dipped his hand into the water. One douse and he wiped his eyes.

"It's not enough," one of the men said. "Come again."

Tacker figured he'd already taken the risk. He poured water over his head several more times and wiped his face.

"Now you are baptized into Nigeria," Samuel said.

Abraham and the others were in the river, naked, swimming. Everything in the world was brown and green. Tacker had never gone swimming with black people, certainly not naked.

"How do you know what's below the surface?" Tacker said. He couldn't see one inch into the water.

"I don't," Samuel said, launching himself chest first into the Osun.

Tacker slipped out of his shirt and trousers, his underwear, his skin so white he looked like the albino lizard in Samuel's dorm room. The floor of the river felt good, a little silty but solid. When he was thigh-deep, Tacker raised his hands into a V and dove. Fantastically, he knew he would not be ill. Not that he disbelieved in parasites. Rather he believed that Nigeria was an entirely plausible country.

WHEN THEY GOT back to Ibadan, it was late. The driver dropped Tacker at the faculty residency. Dinner had been saved for him on the dining table, covered with a napkin—two chicken legs, spinach, potato fries, and sliced pawpaw. Everything was cold. But he was hungry and ate. The Israeli men took up the adjoining living room. Being in the midst of some debate, they hardly acknowledged him. They talked in Hebrew, so it was only when a city or political leader or country was named that Tacker knew the subject. These men were not as animated as Samuel, but they were more intense and Tacker hadn't been able to figure out if they ever joked.

He wished someone would ask about the trip. There was no crack in the wall of their conversation. With all the mentions of

Jerusalem and Palestine, they weren't talking waterworks. Tacker had tried to extract from Rafael, the one who seemed most favorable to him, what Israel's interest in Nigeria was. The answer had been brief. "Nigeria's advancement."

Tacker was weary of being left out. "Hey, guys," he said.

No one turned in his direction.

"Hey!" He clapped his hands. Finally he picked up his chair and brought it down hard on the tiled floor. "For the record, my day was fine. I hope yours was too."

They looked at him. Rafael gave him a wave. "Thank you for the report," he said.

"I'm going to bed," Tacker said, and as he left the room he sensed the pocket of air he had taken up closing behind him.

"I still don't get it," Tacker said. He, Samuel, and Abraham were eating in the cafeteria.

"You're all Christians but you think the Osun River is sacred. Wouldn't that be . . ."

"Pagan?" Joshua said, suddenly beside Tacker, sliding his tray onto the table.

"It's a reasonable question," Samuel said. "The Nigerian is like one of those large pottery vessels made everywhere by women. In Ilorin especially. The pottery is made of clay. Yet even some little bit of goat dropping may go into it. Some ash from the fire." Samuel rubbed his thumb against his fingers. "Some bit of trash from the bottom of your shoe. But once the clay is mixed and formed and the pot is fired, then the vessel can carry clean water. That is the Nigerian. It is especially the Yoruba man. He is made of many things, like the clay. Yet he can carry the true word. So we don't throw out the old part or what some may consider the impure part. To do so would be to spring a leak in the vessel. No. We use all of it to carry the word of God."

Joshua swung his great head in disagreement and peeled a mango. "Then I am not a Yoruba man," he said. "I am a new man in Christ."

Abraham guffawed. "You are a Yoruba man. You have the stomach."

Joshua made a loud cluck with his tongue. "Please, brother. Don't talk of my stomach. You satisfy your appetite with women and palm wine." He devoured the mango.

A MONTH LATER the *Daily Times* announced that Nigeria would hold its first national election in 1959. All in preparation for the country's independence from Britain the next year. The news was cause for intense debate among Tacker's friends: the queen would still be the titular head, the northern part of the country was too backward, or the North would use any means to dominate. Tacker, whose awareness of polarity was limited to the North and the South in the American Civil War—and that was ancient history—was over his head in these debates since Nigeria had three major regions and apparently hundreds of smaller tribes and languages within each of those regions, and all of these territories were in play at the present moment like matter swirling in outer space. It reminded Tacker of the inconclusive science of physics, in which he had not excelled. He did, however, enjoy his friends' passion, especially since the ferocious discussions were generally followed by a soccer game and jovial reconciliations and then libations. One evening they planned an excursion into the city proper, where they would eat at a new Lebanese restaurant. A fellow from Osogbo was joining them. He had graduated a year before Samuel and already owned his own business, installing corrugated roofs on mud houses that had formerly depended on thatch. His name was Chukwu. He arrived on campus dressed in starched trousers pressed like blades, a gray button-up shirt with long sleeves, and pale Italian-looking shoes. A slender paperback fit neatly into his shirt pocket. Tacker could make out *Langston Hughes*, a name he didn't recognize, though it seemed that he should. Chukwu brushed past Tacker to climb into the front seat of the van.

The restaurant occupied the second floor of a building that housed a CMS bookstore beneath it. Awnings sheltered tables on the spacious upstairs porch. Several tables were already oc-cupied by Europeans, the largest gathering of white folks Tacker had seen since arriving in Nigeria. Entering, they were met by a woman with sable brown hair.

"I think we will like a table in the front," Samuel said.

"I'm sorry," the woman said. "They're reserved. Please come this way."

Tacker was happy to follow her nicely curved figure. He imag-ined how her breasts would gentle down when she undressed.

"What are we doing?" Chukwu said. "We are fine taking those tables there," he said, pointing to a table on the porch that was free.

"Those tables are already occupied," the woman said.

Chukwu laughed, but this was not a pleasant laugh. "By ghosts?"

"Please follow me," the woman said. She tilted her head in the direction she meant, causing her breasts to tilt too. She led them toward the back of the restaurant where the tables were set in one long row. The men began to fan out and Tacker straddled a bench.

"Why have you brought us here?" Chukwu said, blocking the woman's passage to the front. "As yet, there is room on the veranda. This table is for children."

"Come along," Samuel said. "It's cooler here. We won't be feeding the flies."

The Lebanese woman managed to slip by Chukwu. Tacker was sorry to see her go.

"This is my own country. No?" Chukwu said. "Who is this woman to seat the *oyinbo* in the choice spot and leave us for this area? Is this her country? Even the British are leaving."

Tacker sat down and swung his leg around.

"See?" Samuel said, sitting down. "This American is happy to eat in this place."

"My brother," Chukwu said. "Are we pushing off Britain only to embrace her sister country? America is not my country. Those are savage people, you know. Very violent. They will not allow us—if we visit there—to eat at the same table with Tacker. They will beat you if you cross the line into their districts. You should educate yourself to the United States of America. It is worse than Great Britain."

Tacker looked into the man's face. It was dark in the dim light of the room, but his eyes were bright.

"Ask this man. My friend"—he pressed a finger into Tacker's shoulder—"tell us. If we come to visit your country, will I sit at the table with you?"

Tacker couldn't think of a good answer. He doubted if Chukwu and Samuel would be allowed to sit with him in a Winston-Salem restaurant, but he'd never thought about it. They were Africans, not Negroes. But folks at home would not see a difference.

Chukwu laughed. "See. His mouth hangs open like a baby's. He cannot answer. Let us leave the American to use this table. I will sit in the front." He left in his Italian shoes.

The rest of the group stayed with Tacker. Soon they were

amusing one another with talk of Awolowo and Azikiwe and Balewa—Tacker couldn't keep the Nigerian leaders straight, though his teammates knew about Eisenhower and Nixon and U.S. secretary of state John Dulles, and more about World War II than he did. Their fathers and uncles had fought for England. Some had died in the East Africa campaign. Tacker itched to master their discourse. Why hadn't he developed a brain that could house such details? He knew all the U.S. states and capitals. But those were permanent. These men seemed capable of storing knowledge that slipped and spun and changed like currents in a stream.

Back on campus, he asked Samuel about Chukwu.

"He's an Igbo," Samuel said. "A very serious Igbo."

"What does that have to do with anything?"

"He is critical of everything. Very direct. He thinks of himself as principled," Samuel said, poking Tacker in the shoulder the way Chukwu had.

"Why?"

"He is a Marxist Igbo."

"You're pulling my leg."

"Not at all. The Soviet Union wants to make friends with Nigeria as well," Samuel said. "I'm sure you know that." He clapped his hands, then stood at attention. "All of history is the struggle of class warfare," he intoned, wagging his finger.

"So Chukwu's an atheist?" Aside from a general notion about the evil of Soviet Russia, the only thing Tacker knew about communism was its godlessness.

"Don't be crazy," Samuel said. "Every African believes in God. Don't let Chukwu worry you."

"Who is Langston Hughes? That book he was carrying."

"Ah! You don't know? He is an American poet. From your

own country. He has one poem, 'Youth.' We love that poem. I'm surprised you haven't heard of him. He writes about Negroes in America."

How could he explain that coming to Nigeria had nothing to do with Negroes?

"Why not sleep in the dormitory tonight?" Samuel said. "You don't want to climb that hill to the faculty house this late. Those Israelis are asleep by now. You will wake the night watchman. He doesn't like his sleep interrupted."

It was a joke they all shared—the sleeping night watchman.

"You don't even have your torch."

Tacker had a momentary vision of his bedroom at home—his desk facing a window, a lamp glowing pleasantly, a State College Wolfpack pennant on his wall, the double bed with the maple headboard, the bedspread folded back.

He was happy for the invitation.

"But where will I sleep?"

"Just here," Samuel said, indicating his bed.

"What about you?"

"Don't worry. I'm an African. I can sleep on the floor. I prefer it."

Winston-Salem, North Carolina

....

Late Fall 1959, into 1960

Chapter Seven

KATE WAS ALONE with Aunt Mildred and Uncle John for Thanksgiving because Brian had not come as promised, and during the meal she kept looking at his chair, feeling guilty that she had ever begrudged him their mother's affection. When she got home late in the afternoon with nothing to do, she wandered into her mother's studio. It still smelled of oils and turpentine and easels, and stretched canvases were still scattered around. Kate had made no progress on a darkroom.

She squeezed watercolors onto a palette, filled a jar with water, found a pad of watercolor paper, and selected a brush. Her bids at watercolor as a girl were not especially successful. Kate dipped the brush into the water and then into the paints and ran the brush in a wavy line across the paper. The colors bled nicely, the image continuing to bloom for five or six seconds until the color was absorbed. She tried again, another wavy line. Again the colors bloomed and settled. That brief uncertainty followed by the staying of the image reminded Kate of developing film.

She wished for someone to share this small revelation with. If she had invited him, James would have come for the holiday. Why did she refuse his company? Was she punishing herself for something?

Kate made a supper of butter sandwiches and at eight o'clock she went to bed. The next morning she walked to the drugstore down from Hart's and bought a pack of Lucky Strikes and a Christmas card. She'd smoked occasionally with her roommate, Janet, never by herself. Back at the house, she settled at the kitchen table, where she pulled the card from the paper bag and slipped the cigarettes into her pocket. She wasn't sure how to begin. Finally, in a mad flourish, she dispensed with the salutation and below the card's standard greeting wrote, *Thinking of you as Christmas approaches. With memories of last year, Love, Kate.* She slipped the card into the envelope, sealed it, and addressed it to James. She walked back through the house, drew a stamp from the stationery drawer in the library, picked up her key, shut the door, and walked to the nearest mailbox, where she dropped the envelope in the slot before she could change her mind.

Early the next week, Kate saw Tacker at the K&W. She was out with Aunt Mildred. Tacker was leaving and it appeared he had eaten alone. Kate felt an odd conflict in seeing him: attraction mixed with annoyance. He hadn't called since their outing. She had thought she needed to explain that she wasn't free, but it appeared he wasn't interested anyway. Last December, before Kate came home to Aunt Mildred's for Christmas break, she and James had gone to the Sky Room at the Atlanta airport for dinner and eaten oysters. She'd never had oysters before and she swallowed them whole and drank wine and got slightly tipsy, and James called Janet to meet them at the door and whisk her back to their dorm room without Kate's condition being detected. It gave her a shiver to think about it: the salty, cold oysters and wine and the ride back to Agnes Scott with the windows of the Corvette down, the freezing air on her face.

"Kate?" her aunt said.

"Yes, ma'am."

"You're eating with your mouth open. What's wrong with you?"

"I was distracted for a moment; I thought I saw an old friend but I was mistaken."

In the evening, she sat in her mother's upholstered Queen Anne chair in the library and opened the pack of Lucky Strikes. She bit the cellophane, releasing the smell of tobacco. The first match went out before she got the cigarette lit. She succeeded with the second and inhaled. The back of her throat burned and she coughed like mad. When she had herself under control, she drew again on the cigarette, more carefully this time. She'd forgotten an ashtray, so she moved to the fireplace, sitting on the hearth, tapping the cigarette against the brass andirons. A cigarette was a little bit like a companion, a rhythm, a give-and-take.

On the first Saturday of December the radio announcer proclaimed midday temperatures in the seventies. After a walk-about in the garden and a visit to the early-blooming camellia, Kate threw open the back door. She would clean out her mother's pantry. Kate carried a trash can from the side of the house to the back patio. How pleasant to keep the door open, clear shelves, and throw things out. Kate had reached the top shelf when she found the old Saltine tin her mother had kept from who knows when and periodically refilled with new sleeves of crackers. The tin had yellowed, but the word *PREMIUM* in blue still slanted across the front. *Nabisco*, in red, filled the left corner. When she was a girl, Kate would place a cracker on her tongue, absorb the salt first, letting the cracker turn to mush, and then swallow. Later, when she was confirmed and took her first communion, she thought of Saltines as the bread of life. A sense of well-being stole over her. She wanted the tin, a sign from her mother.

On the patio, Kate forced open the old lid, turned the tin upside down, and emptied the contents into the trash can. What fell out was not crackers but a bundle of letters held by a rubber band. Kate's heart leapt. She leaned into the can to retrieve them, and on the threshold of the back door, she curved forward and sat down. The first letter was addressed in her father's script. Her hands began to tremble as she leafed one end of the envelopes like a deck of cards. They clicked in complaint and the rubber band snapped. All of the letters had been written by her father to her mother, all in the aqua blue ink of his fountain pen. The exact dates on some envelopes had faded, but the year was 1951. Opening the first letter, she scanned the date—June 14. She remembered the summer right away. She had volunteered in the children's ward at Baptist Hospital, after her seventh-grade year. That was the summer she started wearing a bra, though it always rode up over her little buds. About her father she vaguely remembered that he had spent that summer doing research at the Smithsonian in D.C. Her mother had made simpler meals: pigs in a blanket, macaroni and cheese, and ham sandwiches. Brian had loved it, but Kate had missed her father. It was a summer of imbalance.

The first letter was two pages long, onionskin so thin she could almost see through it. The most interesting tidbit was a mention of President Truman eating at a Woolworth's one day, an entourage of Secret Service men with him. The rest of the letter reported on the predictables: where her father was staying, where he took his meals, how the buses ran. Yet this banal reporting created a tide of images so vivid it seemed Kate had shadowed her father that summer: her father in gray trousers and a burgundy Windbreaker, the slight folds of flesh over the far edge of each eye.

Kate held the letter to her chest. She took her time.

A second letter detailed his first full week and gave the outline of his days. Breakfast in a café on the street. A mile's walk to the Smithsonian, the sidewalk skirting a city rose garden. Kate conjured just the way his thin hair lifted in the breeze. Mornings in the library stacks, working in his carrel. Lunch with other fellows in a common room. Each Friday someone presented his research. Her father's topic was the use of conscription during the Civil War.

In the third letter, he mentioned someone named Louise. Kate was surprised, never having considered that a woman might be working alongside her father at the Smithsonian. She thought perhaps she should know who this was—a family friend, a distant cousin?

> Louise Martin and I have been selected to have
> monographs published at the end of the summer. She's
> the only woman here and not surprisingly, a little
> nervous. I offered to read her draft when she's ready.
> She reminds me of you and causes me to miss you,
> my love.

The romantic touch gave Kate a jolt. Though her parents were devoted to each other, her father had never used terms of endearment. *My love?* Kate felt like a voyeur. These letters were not for her. But she couldn't stop herself.

In every letter her father asked about Kate and Brian and sent his love. Kate could not remember her mother sharing these sentiments, though she must have. In fact, Kate couldn't remember ever seeing the letters, but that was because she was volunteering at Baptist Hospital and her mother had received them during the day. They must have sustained her through that long summer of separation. Kate worried she might arrive at a paragraph that carried too private a message, but at the same time she was avid for it. But by the middle of the stack no such paragraph had appeared, though in every one her father began, *My dearest Virginia.*

Louise's name popped up now and then, along with Joe Clarke, a fellow from Colorado, whose research was in Civil War medicine. The three of them had gone out for Chinese food. Kate formed a picture of Louise: middle-aged with tie-up shoes and a haircut like Mamie Eisenhower, beautifully bland—until she arrived at the second-to-last letter.

> *It's only fair to tell you, Virginia. I have strong*
> *feelings for Louise. I have not broken our vows. But I*
> *am torn. Louise and I have been working together all*
> *summer. Whatever happens, I will always love you*
> *and the children.*

The children? She and Brian were now the generic children? Kate set the letter down. A sickening feeling spread through her like poison. She tore the letter in half, made wads of each half, and threw the malignant paper into the trash can before stalking into the yard and picking up the rake—it was still there after all these days—and hitting the long handle against the tree. Her arms rang with the effort.

Just there was the back fence her father had put up; they had painted it white together. Briefly she remembered the Negro with the milk bottle. Then the back of her father's head appeared in her mind's eye. There was one letter more. Kate ran to the patio and ripped it open.

I understand if you prefer I not come home. I can rent
a room in a house near the college and send for the
things I'll need. Louise has been offered a research
position at Duke for a year.

Louise was no longer a plain-looking woman. She was Grace Kelly with blond hair and long legs, wearing a pale green skirt and matching summer sweater, dark glasses, her feet shod in leopard-dotted heels, a slip of white scarf around her neck.

The universe became unmoored.

Kate's mother had sat right here at the picnic table on the patio and opened the letter, and her heart had broken as the white pages fell to the ground. How could her father have betrayed them? How had Kate not known? She retrieved the torn letter from the trash can. At the kitchen counter she smoothed the pieces back into alignment so she could reread it, but there was nothing she had missed, no hint of family loyalty above all. Her father had fallen in love with Louise, had suggested he might take lodging near his work, and in the last letter he did not mention Kate by name. She folded each letter and inserted it into its corresponding envelope. When she was through, she stacked all of the letters and set them on the breakfast table, wondering if a match could be set to them without harm to the table, for she never wished to touch them again.

She sought to recall any detail she could from that August. There had never been a break in her parents' marriage. She remembered finishing her volunteer job at Baptist Hospital, receiving a blue autograph book as a parting gift—full of heart shapes and *X*s for kisses. Otherwise her memory was blank. She sat down again at the threshold of the door, hand resting on the warm brick of the stoop, looking out at her father's garden. She closed her eyes. A little later, she lay back on the cool kitchen floor and turned her head sideways. From here she could see under the kitchen cabinets. All manner of dirt and dust and who knew what else was under there. Why had no one in a million years cleaned under those cabinets? For a moment she almost forgot the letters, gazing absentmindedly at the detritus, and then her father's words hit her again and she turned on her side.

She fingered the collar of her shirt and recalled how her mother had sewn her dresses with waistbands and pockets and round collars. The summer her father was gone, she went on a sewing spree, cutting patterns on the dining table for days on end so that they ate all their meals in the kitchen. She had her sewing machine installed in the dining room too. Fabric and patterns covered every surface. Once the dresses were sewn, Kate had to stand on a stool in front of the window where the light was best and turn in a circle while her mother turned up each hem and pinned it. She recalled a particular dress she had loved, short-sleeved, low-waisted, with a pleated skirt. It had a V-neck and a large square collar down the back and a knotted ribbon in front so that it looked nautical, sailor-like. She'd worn it when they went to the beach.

And just like that she remembered what had happened when her father returned from that summer in D.C. They had gone to Ocracoke and he had drowned. Kate sat up. Had he done it on purpose? Viperous thought. She drew her legs to her chest and held them.

Moments later, she found herself opening the kitchen cabinet and rummaging around for the cooking sherry. She held her nose and took a sip. Then, comprehending that she must eat, she took two pieces of bread out of the bread box, tore one slice into four pieces, and ate. She took another sip of sherry, this one warmer, and her head swam a little as she ate the rest of the bread. Another good sip of the sherry and she put the bottle down. The tiles of the backsplash went as fuzzy as caterpillars. Kate took one more swig of sherry and felt a peeling sensation, as if someone had pulled a tight swim cap from her head. The floor seemed as good a place as any to rest.

KATE DOZED, HER head pillowed by her bent arm. She woke and turned onto her back, staring at the ceiling. How could she stay in this house and how could she not? The past was ruined. The doorbell rang. She burped and felt the sour heat of sherry in the back of her throat. The person at the door must go away. Why had her mother kept the letters? Perhaps because even so awful a reminder was an indissoluble bond. She saw her mother's fine hands blurred with paint, her father's gold wedding band, heard the click of her father's briefcase opening, the snap of her mother's compact closing, saw the waves at Ocracoke bleached white.

The clock chimed and Kate wondered mildly if Aunt Mildred—if that was who it was—would come around to the back door and find it open and her splayed out on the floor. The doorbell rang again.

Oh. It might be Tacker. Kate sat up, her hands going to her breasts.

Don't leave. I'm coming.

She could see Tacker through the beveled glass at the side of the front door, only it was about four Tackers, the way the glass multiplied him: several sets of legs and arms and torsos and heads. *Don't leave!* Racing down the hall, Kate wiped her face and plumed her hair. She yanked the door open.

Chapter Eight

TACKER WAS OFF for the afternoon and had a hankering to see Kate. Why he'd waited so long, he couldn't say, except that he didn't want to hex his future again by acting precipitously. As he had with Anna Becker. Still, he went without calling. But Kate didn't appear to be home. He had just turned to leave when the door flew open.

"You're here," Kate said.

She wore Keds and old jeans, her hair falling out of a ponytail.

"Are you okay?"

"Better now," she said. A smile ticked briefly on her lips as she showed him into a room to the left of the foyer and pointed to a butter-colored sofa next to an ornate chair. "I've got a headache. I'll be right back."

She padded off. He could hear a cabinet open and shut and water running and shutting off. In a moment she was back with a glass of water and aspirin. She placed the tablets on her tongue and drank, her throat tilted up.

"Oh," she said. "I forgot to offer you something."

"I'm okay," he said.

"Can you stay?"

"Sure," he said, his chest unlocking. "You left these on the table the night we went to the Toddle House." He reached into his coat pocket and brought out a pair of gloves. "I'm sorry it's taken me so long to get them to you. I'd put them in the handlebar bag on my bike and forgot all about them."

"I wondered where those were," she said. "Thanks."

She went off and blew her nose. Then she was back in her sock feet, her hair still up in its uncombed mass. She settled on the other end of the sofa and tucked her legs under. On the coffee table sat a large glossy book about Greece.

"Have you been?" Tacker said, gesturing toward the book.

"That was my mother's." Kate tilted her face to one side.

"I've come at a bad time," he said.

"Oh no," she said. Yet she sat within her own circle, composed in whatever it was she was managing.

"I always liked your yellow hair," she said finally.

"Thank you," he said, touching his hair. Had she been drinking?

Kate unfolded herself and stood, moved to a wingback chair—that must have been her father's chair; the ornate one had belonged to her mother. Kate lifted an afghan, swirled it around her until she was papoosed. Then she came to where he sat, lifted his hands, sat beside him, and leaned into his chest.

"Hold me," she said.

Tacker brought his arms down around her.

If he had not been to Nigeria this would be odd, sitting in a house he had never before entered with a girl he knew but didn't really know. But it was not odd because of all those mammy wagon rides where complete strangers—men, women, and children—fell asleep against him. Mothers gave him babies to hold while they rearranged their layered outfits. When floorboards were wedged full of chicken baskets and yams, people found any kind of way to accommodate their legs, sometimes in Tacker's lap.

Kate's repose made more sense than most things that had happened in the past year. Tacker studied the room. Two walls had built-ins, full of books and artifacts. In Nigeria it would be library enough for a high school. Over the fireplace hung an oil painting of a woman who must be Kate's mother, though Tacker didn't remember her well enough to know. The head was too large but the mouth was mobile and full and the skirt of her red dress seemed to move out of the canvas into the room. The hearth was granite, maybe from right around Winston. But the mantel was pink marble, carved to reveal an image of a tree branch in bloom. It was a surprising combination in a Craftsman house and Tacker felt he had seen into the family's character, observing this point.

His stomach growled. Kate shifted her position.

He gazed at the open door to the left of the fireplace. He could make out a rattan chair and a curtained window. He thought of the bottle-lined room at Frances's house, the thrumming sound he took for the furnace, how he had gazed into the room and seen everything but Gaines. How Gaines had then walked into the kitchen, how the house itself seemed to breathe, the smell of coffee, how that house was brown and narrow and this one light and spacious. Tacker's father had agreed to let him hire Gaines on a trial basis. Kate's head settled onto his lap. As he breathed, it rose and fell, wisps of dark hair hovering around her face. A crease settled on her forehead. He smoothed her hair, thinking of Valentine, Gaines's little sister, born on Valentine's Day.

Kate opened her eyes.

"Sorry," Tacker said, pulling his hand back.

"Don't stop," she said. She put her hands to her face and pulled her tucked legs closer.

"What's wrong?"

"Oh," she said. She pushed herself up and turned so her breasts met the back of the sofa.

"Hey," Tacker said. "What's up?"

Her eyes welled with tears.

"Here," he said, handing her his handkerchief.

"My parents," she said, taking the handkerchief, wiping her eyes.

"I know."

"No, you don't."

She maneuvered until she was sitting forward, her legs crossed, looking at the painting.

"That's my mother's self-portrait," she said.

"Amazing."

"I know. She took painting lessons when I was in high school. Have you got a cigarette?"

"Ah, no," Tacker said. She smoked? He hadn't expected it.

They sat. She all inwardness. Tacker with his hands on his knees, looking at the mother's portrait.

"Some things should not be opened," she said.

"Like Pandora's box," he said.

They laughed together at how quickly he said it.

She sobered. "Too bad someone didn't remind me when I went looking for old letters."

"Sorry."

"It was a stupid accident that I found them, even though I was looking. I could have missed them altogether."

She told him how her mother had whispered about letters in the hospital, how she had searched, exhausting every possibility. "Then this morning I decided to clean out the pantry. She always kept an old Saltines can. I figured the crackers were stale so I opened the tin to throw them out. Bingo."

Tacker thought again about how he hadn't read Samuel's letters. Every passing day worsened the crime of omission. Yet he feared—what? Some requirement or request he could not honor? Some news to prove again his unworthiness? Kate was quiet again.

"You'll think awful things about my family."

I'm thinking them about myself. "You don't have to tell me," Tacker said.

"I need to tell someone."

She looked at him. He nodded. It was good to be able to listen to someone else, help ease another's troubles for a change.

"My dad had an affair. He wrote to confess to my mom." She pulled her hair loose and combed through it with her fingers. "I really wish I had a cigarette."

Tacker had a vague recollection of her father, eccentric in the store, his coat open, hat tipped back, oldish-looking. Who would be tempted by him? "Can I help you with supper?"

Kate looked at him, that quick tick of smile again. "I'm not very hungry." She brooded. "You know how he died," she said.

Was that a question?

"He drowned," she said. "Now I wonder if he meant to."

"That seems a stretch," he said, though his mind churned at the thought.

"You hardly knew him."

Tacker recalled her father again in his loose-fitting coat. Some element of his bearing affirmed his stolidity. "I could make a fire," he said.

"That would be nice."

"Things will look different in the morning."

TACKER WOKE TO the smell of bacon and the sound of pots banging in the kitchen. Kate had gone to bed and asked him to stay. He'd slept on the sofa. It was still dark outside. His mouth was dry as a shoe. He turned on a lamp. "Hello?" he called.

"The bathroom is down the hall on the right," she said.

In the kitchen she'd set out plates, bacon already on them. She was scrambling eggs, still in her jeans but now in an over-size sweater. When she looked at him her eyes appeared violet and he thought of the rose stained-glass window in the Cathedral of Saint John the Divine that he had seen on his three-night stopover in London on the way to Nigeria.

"You got hungry," he said, still waking, observing the well-preserved house with its pedestal columns and dark wood accents. He figured the time before looking at his watch. Maybe four a.m. He was right on the money.

"I'm starving," she said. "You're working today?"

"Yeah."

"I shouldn't have asked you to stay—I hope you know I don't usually do things like that. And you probably didn't sleep well."

"I slept fine. You mean you don't usually ask for company when you're sad?"

She tilted her head. A habit, Tacker thought, something like the maneuver of an animal wishing not to be sighted. "I guess I've learned not to."

He waited for her to say more.

"My roommate, Janet, used to say I'm a loner. Except with

her. She'd drag me to this bar down by Emory. We'd take a taxi, and then she'd fight off the boys—they were after her, you understand, not me—and we'd sit there and drink a beer and leave alone.

"So, what brought you back to Winston?" she said, spooning eggs onto the plates. "Sounds like you had the world in front of you. You know all about me now."

I know almost nothing about you, he thought. The evening at the Toddle House had been all surface, like skating on ice. Where had this direct-talking, vulnerable girl come from? Tacker considered the house again. Maybe her folks had money. Maybe money made girls confident. Maybe Atlanta did that. Or having your parents dead. Was it the artificial light or were the walls of the house pale pink? He wondered if Kate was a virgin, and this possibility as well as its opposite intensified his impression of pink.

"There's a lot to tell," he said.

Maybe she read his face.

"Let's eat first."

A few embers still burned in the fireplace, and after breakfast it didn't take much for Tacker to rekindle it. They kept drinking coffee and Kate listened as he told her about Samuel and the Ponies and the mammy wagons, Marxist Chukwu and the intellectual Israelis, UCI and the Osun festivities. He left out Anna Becker, who had gone native and painted his arm with henna and maybe gotten him fired. He glossed the dismissal.

"It's a shame you didn't get to stay to the end," she said. "But it sounds like you had a great experience. Just think how few people ever do anything like that."

The way she put it made what had happened sound wonderfully positive. Tacker wanted to kiss her in gratitude.

"But was it odd at all being with all those black people?"

"For about five minutes. It was odder coming back to all these white people." He grinned at her but couldn't tell if she understood.

"But wasn't it primitive?"

"If you mean are there bathrooms when you're traveling, there aren't. And villages don't have running water. But everything kind of works. The cities are a little crazy because there's not much traffic control. I got used to it in a hurry. I liked it. That was the problem."

Outside the balance of light and dark shifted and Tacker could see the first faint outline of trees.

"Do you have pictures?" Kate said.

"Plenty."

"I'd love to see them."

"Sure," he said, his blood whirring from too much coffee. "You'll be okay today?"

"I'll be okay."

"You need a plan."

"Like what?"

"Come help me put up Christmas decorations at the store."

"Maybe. I'll call you. All right. I'll come."

"Thanks for breakfast," he said, standing, shaking out his arms.

On the street, jacket collar up, he turned the cycle and rolled down Glade. He parked in front of the foursquare and leapt up the stairs. As if Samuel was calling but he was running from him. Because if he fell hard for Kate, he might forget Nigeria. He didn't want to forget.

He slammed the door behind him. Da Vinci looked up from the couch, yawned, and stretched. "Hey, sorry, kiddo. Let me get you something to eat." He threw his jacket onto the couch. The cat rose to all fours, stretched his spine, and resettled on the jacket.

"Well, looky here," Tacker said. A dead vole lay neatly at the threshold to the kitchen. Da Vinci could get in and out of the house. Tacker would have to find the hole and patch it. He'd been plugging holes for months, holes ominous and dreamlike, dark as night, abysses like the end of the world, which was why he hadn't read Samuel's letters. He had time right now, thirty minutes, to read one at least. After feeding the cat, he walked to the bedroom and pulled out the tackle box he'd made in Boy Scouts. The letters lay in order and he lifted the top one from the stack.

Chapter Nine

KATE LAY ON the sofa, pulling up the afghan Tacker had used, recalling the tents she and Brian had created over the dining table on rainy days. Their mother fixed jelly sandwiches and they camped and read and colored for hours on end. But her father's letters came back, a rosary heavy on her heart. Then her head was hot with shame that she had opened herself to Tacker. Where was her solid backbone, the blade she had felt and counted on that night she'd held her mother? Janet always said that a man would interpret weakness as willingness in a girl. Asking someone to spend the night might fit the bill. She focused on the glowing embers in the fireplace until she felt cross-eyed.

In her dream she was in junior high attending a family reunion. Brian wasn't there. A cousin brought his fiancée to meet her family. Kate and her parents sat in a living room in front of a coffee table. The cousin stood on the sidelines, but the fresh-faced bride-to-be came directly into the circle and made herself comfortable. On the floor next to the sofa was a baby all by it-self, untended. Kate woke to light pouring through the dining room window. She pressed the afghan to her face and smelled the faint scent of Tacker Hart's aftershave. All at once she was violently thirsty. In the kitchen she drank straight from the fau-cet. The sulfurous smell took her to the summer following her father's drowning. Kate's reduced family of three had headed toward the mountains with Aunt Mildred, as far from the beach as they could get, their mother driving the Chrysler and smok-ing like a sailor. Every water fountain they had drunk from smelled just so.

Kate stood at the sink and looked out at the bank of monkey grass, the white fence. On that very trip, her mother had won-dered if her husband's drowning had been on purpose, though Kate had thought the idea preposterous, and Aunt Mildred had assured her it was only grief talking. Kate had forgotten until just this minute smelling the faucet.

Brian had slept while Kate gazed out the window of the backseat, dozing on and off. After a while she heard her moth-er's voice. "At some point it may be too hard to come back. He'd already left in a way," she had said. "Watch what you're saying," Aunt Mildred had said. Kate kept her eyes closed and listened. "Maybe he didn't have the strength or will for it," her mother said. Kate had felt her scalp prickle and had to clasp the armrest to keep quiet. "It's not that hard to imagine letting yourself go. From so far out, the shore must seem insignificant. Poor man." "Hush, just hush now," Aunt Mildred had said.

Kate was fourteen at the time. Her mother or Aunt Mildred, one had flipped on the radio. There was static and then some-thing that sounded like what her mother called "that abomina-ble hoedown music." Quickly the static returned and then a voice came into the car that sounded like molten silver, a voice singing about a blue moon: "*. . . blue moon of Kentucky . . . Shine on the one that's gone and left me blue.*"

"I don't know if I like that song or not," her mother had said. The static came back and suddenly they were in the middle of the old hymn "Farther Along." *Farther along we'll know more about it. Farther along we'll understand why.* Her mother sang with the radio, gleefully, a gospel song they would never sing in the Episcopal church they attended. Her voice rose and the car climbed the mountain. She did the soprano and Aunt Mildred came in on alto. As soon as the song was over, Kate pretended to waken. Right that moment the sun came out and her mother picked her sunglasses up off the seat and slipped them on. Kate peered out the window at the valley below, the sheer fall. Would she ever jump? Would their mother drive off the cliff? "Mom?" she had said. "Why, I thought you were asleep. Did I wake you? My grandfather loved that song. I haven't heard it in so long. There's a way station up ahead. Let's stop and eat our sandwiches." "That sounds like a good idea," Aunt Mildred had said.

Kate noticed a sign for a motel in Pineola up ahead. Her mother held the steering wheel firmly. "Brian, wake up," her mother said. "We're about to pull over. Don't you just love it up here?" she said to everyone. "Those mountains put everything in perspective."

Are we all here?

At the way station, Aunt Mildred pulled Kate aside. "If you overheard anything, I just want you to know that it's your mother's grief that's talking—you hear me? Strong men drown. It happens all the time. Your father loved you better than the earth. Now, there." She had shaken Kate's shoulders slightly as if to see if she was solid enough.

Last night, Tacker had almost talked her out of the idea that her father's drowning was purposeful. Now, this morning, it rose like an evil plant in the garden, crowding out everything else.

The clock struck eleven a.m., and Kate remembered her three o'clock appointment with the chair of the library board. What a relief. She had to dress and go somewhere and act normal. She called Tacker. "I can't come by the store," she said. "I have a meeting at the library. I forgot." She didn't explain.

"Too bad. I mean, good luck with the meeting," he said.

"Thanks."

"I'll give you a call later, check up on you."

"You're very kind," she said, which was true and could hardly be misconstrued as romantic, except maybe in a Jane Austen novel.

For her meeting with Mrs. McCall to talk about taking her mother's place on the board, Kate selected a soft gray dress. Rather than wear a hat, she put her hair up in a loose chignon and at the last minute selected a pair of her mother's earrings, small garnets set in gold.

The bus was only half full.

In the lobby of Main Library, she asked for directions to Conference Room A. It was on the second floor. She could see Mrs. McCall through the glass windows as she came close. A square woman with a freckled face, sandy blond hair, and a permanent tan, Mrs. McCall could have been a physical education teacher.

"Kate!" she said. "Don't you look splendid! It's so good to see you."

"Thank you," Kate said.

Mrs. McCall was thoughtful enough not to go on too long about how lonely and heartbroken Kate must be. Instead she invited her to sit and then she interlocked her fingers and rested them on the table in front of her.

"Our primary mission is to make the library the best resource it can be for the community. I'm sure you know that. We raise money and we decide how to spend money and we decide on future directions for development. A bright mind like yours will be an asset for next year's campaign. It will be a new decade and we've been batting around ideas for a slogan."

Kate leaned forward to take a look at a mimeographed sheet of paper Mrs. McCall had placed in front of her.

LAUNCH THE FUTURE WITH BOOKS

"What do you think?" Mrs. McCall said.

"Like the space satellites," Kate said. The concept seemed chilly. To Kate's mind, reading was a warm activity, undertaken in comfortable environments. Reading wasn't going outward. It was going inward. "I can see how it could appeal to some people," she said, not wishing to offend. "I wonder if I can think more about it."

"Yes, of course," Mrs. McCall said. "I knew you were the right person to enlist. I don't like it myself." And she laughed, throwing her head back, a large laugh. When she composed herself, pulling her lapels back into place, Mrs. McCall turned to Kate, who could now see that the woman's eyes didn't quite match. One was a little sleepy, and immediately Kate felt endeared to her, not only because she didn't like launching into books but also because she was marked by a flaw that she had likely carried all of her life. What one loved about literature was all of the flaws, not in the writing, but in the characters.

When Kate got home she had a letter from James.

Hello darling,

Your card arrived today and nothing could have made me happier. I think about you up in Winston and it seems half a world away. Still, early in the morning when I'm leaving the hospital so sleepy I can hardly stay on my feet, I know I could drive eight hours to see you for ten minutes if I knew you wanted me to. I hope you get whatever it is you need to do there taken care of so we can be together. I long for you.

Love,
James

Kate clutched the card and threw herself across the couch in the library. She was reassured and newly fearful. She'd been home almost six months and still she didn't know what it was she needed to get "taken care of," nor how long it would take. James was reignited in his desire for her and she was responsible, but did she really want that, want him, a life with him in Atlanta? Who would she be? She wondered if the cool lozenge in her heart had made her fickle and ruined her for love. Maybe she was the one who should move to another country, and not to Europe but someplace more distant, as Tacker Hart had, a place where she could feel everything again as she once had felt it in the backyard with her father when the world was whole.

Chapter Ten

TACKER ENDED UP reading all of Samuel's letters sitting on his parents' old couch in the foursquare. What froze him was learning—in the last letter he read but the first Samuel had written—about Joshua. Joshua who had invited him to his compound and believed Elvis Presley was an emissary of the devil, who eschewed even the mildest palm wine and didn't douse himself with the waters of the Osun. He stared at the letter blankly.

The week the team was in Osogbo laying concrete block for the high school, the week Anna painted his arm with henna and showed Tacker her surreal sculptures in the forest by the Osun, Joshua had offered to mail a postcard Tacker had written to his parents. He'd read the card and then taken it upon himself to place a call to Lionel Fray. He'd reported that Tacker had gotten himself involved with a pagan priestess who happened to be European but was married to a Nigerian and it was going to cause big trouble for the project. Apparently, Joshua had been an eager reporter of Tacker's misdeeds, including his moving out of the faculty house, taking Samuel's bed and forcing him to sleep on the floor, challenging local authorities on matters of religion, even drinking beer with local high school students.

Tacker's head reeled. Someone—was it Abraham?—had offered him a Star beer when they were sitting under a tree on the high school grounds one evening after the day's work was done. The best thing about the beer was that for once it was actually chilled and the bottle felt good in his hands. He hadn't shared it with anyone.

Samuel had defended Tacker when he learned of the allegations—after Tacker had been put on the plane in Lagos. The other fellows agreed with him. But Joshua was somehow related to a higher-up at the U.S. embassy in Lagos and Fray took his word over the others'. Plus there was actual evidence—the postcard and the student paper interview. Tacker knew he'd been accused of practicing "native witchcraft," along with a bunch of other things, some worse, in the report he had skimmed on the plane coming back, after which he had vomited into one of those little bags. The woman next to him had blanched. He'd had to crawl over her and go to the bathroom, and then he spent the rest of the flight to New York facing the window, hollow as a tin man.

What he had not known until he read Samuel's letter was that Joshua had betrayed him. He leaned against the back of the sofa and howled, an enraged laugh that startled da Vinci, sending him off in a low dash for the kitchen. The whole episode of that morning with Fray ran through Tacker's brain one more time. A hot brew of anger and disbelief filled his chest. Why had Joshua twisted it all up? What had he ever done to Joshua? He might have believed such a betrayal coming from Chukwu, who had little affection for him.

So maybe he had been naïve, stepping into situations he knew nothing about, like idol burning. Doubtless he had been a know-it-all talking with the Shell Oil man. But he had experienced something close to conversion. He had been ready to stay in the country, even give his life to it. Or at least now that the opportunity was gone, it seemed that way.

Dazed, Tacker read the rest of the letter. Samuel's brother had lost a leg after a bad accident with a hatchet led to infection. All of this months ago. Guilt settled over the anger and shame as Tacker thought of Samuel and how he hadn't written back and how his silence misconstrued his own feelings.

In one letter, Tacker learned that Samuel had been hired by Godwin and Hopwood Architects and moved to Lagos. He described himself as a "small boy" in the firm, but Tacker knew he'd work his way up.

He stepped into a cold shower. "Shake it off," he whispered to himself, lathering up, rinsing off, jumping out, and toweling off. "Shake it off. Shake it off." But a cool blue anger mastered all other feeling, and he rode the anger into the store and it was just as well Kate couldn't come in. The butcher was late, not arriving until afternoon.

"Nice of you to show up," Tacker said.

"I always do," the man said.

"Hell, is everyone out to ruin me?"

"I had to leave my car at the shop."

"So drop it off in time to get here when you're supposed to."

"Dear God in heaven," the butcher said, pulling off his white apron, walking toward the door.

Tacker had to follow him down First and beg him to come back. The man was built like a barrel; he had a huge beard that he covered with a net while he worked. He'd served in World

War II and was no one to mess with. "I've got plenty of work and I don't need a boy lecturing me," he said to Tacker, looking him in the eye.

"I understand and I apologize," Tacker said. "I was angry about something else. We can't run this store without you."

"I won't come back next time."

TWO DAYS LATER, Kate dropped by for a loaf of bread. She was quick with a smile but that was it. On Sunday afternoon he rode the Indian east toward Kernersville, hooking off and onto country roads, down a stretch beside an old wood fence. He smelled a section of pinewood before he saw it. At dusk he circled the bike around and sat. He heard an owl. It sounded to be right above him and it was, sitting out on a dead branch, blinking its huge eyes. A cold mist hung in the air like a fine screen so that it seemed to Tacker he was immersed in the place and partitioned from it all at once. What the hell had he done to Joshua? His anger at Fray had been nicely focused. Now it bled in more than one direction.

Back home, he rolled the bike into the garage and set it back on its stand. Inside, he started a fire in the fireplace. He opened a can of pork and beans, emptied them into an old pot, then held the pot over the flame, heating the beans as if he were in Nigeria, where fireplaces were built into an indention in the mud wall but without chimneys so the smoke hung around the ceiling and glided out the open windows. He tried to put himself in Joshua's place. The guy was overweight. Maybe his dad gave him a hard time, demanded too much, was overly critical; Joshua could never do anything well enough to please him. Maybe he'd been bullied. Tacker ate straight from the blackened pot. The beans tasted better cooked this way, smoky and dense.

The truth was he thought himself superior to Joshua if not the other members of the team, and the man knew it and had gotten even, and maybe Tacker did deserve some payback, but not sacking, not in a straitjacket.

Tacker still had some blue aerograms in the zippered lining of his suitcase. He pulled them out, the sheets permanently contoured. The paper crackled as Tacker's hand made its way across the page.

Dear Samuel,

Please forgive me for not writing sooner. I'm very sorry to hear about your brother's accident. In a separate envelope, I'm sending ten dollars to help pay for whatever he needs right now and I'll send more later. Thanks for explaining about Joshua. It doesn't add up for me. Besides the incident at his father's compound, do you know if there's anything I did against him? Don't try to spare my feelings. It would help to know.

I never got to thank you for everything you did for me. I was afraid that what had happened to me might have made things hard on you. I'm glad to know it didn't. Great to hear you've been hired by Godwin and Hopwood. I expect you to be famous before long. How's life in Lagos?

Tacker needed to get his own career back on track. He thought about the swimming pool in Hanes Park. It would need a bathhouse. Maybe he could moonlight with an architectural firm, do some renderings, and get in on a nice assignment like that. He'd always excelled in drawing.

On Saturday he called Kate. She didn't answer. Days passed and he didn't see her.

A SLEET CAME mid-December but it thawed by noon and he opened the store. He had a steady stream of customers and was glad to have Gaines. Around three o'clock, Tacker found him on aisle two, shelving cereal. The man had a knack for organizing and Tacker let him experiment. His presence hadn't caused a ripple in the store. From the first day, Gaines displayed a comfortable adaptability and Tacker wondered where he'd learned it.

"What were you studying at Fisk?"

"History," Gaines said.

"What did you plan to do?"

"Still planning to do it. Plan to finish my degree as soon as I can. Teach."

After three days in the store, Gaines had claimed management of the baseball card display near the checkout, pairing Cracker Jack boxes with the cards. "Every boy's dream," he'd said. "Who's your favorite player?" Tacker had said. "You have to ask?" Gaines answered. Tacker sold more baseball cards that week than in the previous two months.

Tacker's father gave Gaines two weeks to acclimate before he came in, pretending to be a customer. He drifted down the aisle where Gaines was unloading boxes of paper goods. Tacker overheard his father ask where the maraschino cherries were.

"My baby sister loves those things," Gaines's voice sang out. "Have to hide them from her at home. Right this way, sir."

"That's a good boy," his father said at the service counter. "I like him."

"He's Frances's nephew."

"Why didn't you tell me?"

"I thought it was fairer for you to see for yourself. No prejudice." The word wobbled out of Tacker's mouth before he could stop it.

On a Wednesday evening when store traffic was light, Kate came in just before closing, purchased a bottle of vanilla, and asked if Tacker would see her home. Her fingers traveled up and down her scarf. Connie was closing out her register. Gaines had left.

"Happy to," he said, a little irritated that she'd disappeared and was suddenly back asking something of him. Was he her lackey? "We'll have to walk. Left the cycle at home today."

"I'll just mosey around." Eventually she returned and leaned against the front windows, looking out onto the darkened street, still bundled up as he locked everything away.

It was cold out and gusty and they leaned into the wind, heading uphill.

"I got the spot on the city library board," Kate said. "I'm working with Mrs. McCall two days a week and Saturday morning. One of my neighbors drives me."

That explained Saturday when he called and she didn't pick up. "That's great," he said. "You seemed to have disappeared."

"If I had my mom's car . . ."

"What?"

"I'd do what men do. I'd leave."

Tacker left that alone. They veered left onto West End, not right as Tacker would, going to the foursquare. An untrimmed holly bulged over the sidewalk and they had to step into the street. Tacker trotted to Kate's right and held her arm until they were back on the sidewalk.

"At least the job keeps Aunt Mildred out of my hair," she said.

"Aunt Mildred?"

"My dad's sister. She thinks I should come live with her."

Good glory, no, Tacker thought, conjuring Kate's pink walls, the marble mantel, the library where he assumed they were going right now. Pursuing Kate under an aunt's supervision sounded dismal. Not that he knew for sure he was going to pursue her. She was lovely. But she also seemed like a handful. They'd arrived at her front door. Indoors, she showed him into the parlor. It housed a white-brick fireplace that had never seen a fire and two short, stiff settees facing each other over an empty coffee table.

"I'll be just a minute," Kate said. She returned with a silver tray laden with a teapot, china cups, cream and sugar, and little sandwiches you might throw to the birds. When she was seated opposite him, Tacker had the sense he was going to be interviewed.

"I wanted to thank you for the other night," she said.

"You don't need to thank me," he said.

"It was an unusual situation."

What was she talking about? "You were distraught."

"Yes. But I don't usually act that way."

She wanted out of any obligation. Fine. Still, his hands felt suddenly empty. "I was happy to keep you company," he said.

"I don't want you to misunderstand."

"About what?" He heard the impatience in his tone. She would too. Good.

"This is harder than it should be," she said.

"Listen. Come find me someday when you know what you want to say." In a minute he was really going to be steamed.

"You're making this difficult."

"No, I'm not. You are. I like you but you're wearing me out."

"I'm a little confused." She sheeted her hair over her shoulder and flipped it back.

"Let's get out of this room," he said.

THEY PLAYED SCRABBLE at the breakfast table, feasting on apples and pecans. Tacker drew five vowels, an *R*, and a *J*. In the end, Kate had played her *Q* and her *Z*. It wasn't a rout, but she beat him. "Chinese checkers next time," he said, patting the table with both hands. "Let's go up to the Toddle House and get some real supper. I'm starving after that squirrel food. I'll get my cycle."

"It's freezing out there."

"It'll make us hardy," he said. "Get a hat and scarf. I'll be right back."

She was waiting on her porch when he pulled around ten minutes later.

"I can't believe we're doing this," she said, climbing on behind him, the pressure of her breasts against him bringing Nigeria back, the girls' breasts, Joshua, who, for some reason he now felt tender about, and Samuel, whose brother had lost a leg, and now Gaines, whose face softened when he looked at Valentine. Everything was connected, but figuring out which part of his life was his to direct and what he most wanted and how to get it—that was still shaky.

FRIDAY DURING HIS lunch break, Tacker walked the long block from Hart's to Hanes Park, cutting through the lot where a new elementary school was being built, facing Peters Creek. He couldn't believe the city was putting a school right in front of the creek. Some boy would throw his shoes down there just so he'd have to go get them. Then another kid would do it the next day, and on and on. Were they going to build bridges across it? He thought of the swinging bridge in Osogbo. At the park, he headed for the south field. He wanted a feeling for the land, a sense of where a bathhouse might be located. On his second circling of the perimeter of the pool construction, he nearly bumped into a woman bundled in hat, gloves, and a heavy coat. It was Kate.

"What are you doing out here?" he said, almost cross at the interruption. He'd come at lunch to avoid all the kids from Reynolds who would be running around once school was out.

"Well, it's not your private park, Mr. Hart."

She picked at a piece of lint on her coat. "I'm on my way to Mr. Fitzgerald's. He's the one who chauffeurs me around. I go over Friday afternoons to keep him company. He reads the paper to me—stories he's saved through the week—and we eat popcorn." She lifted her eyes.

"Sorry to sound short-tempered. I was just thinking."

"Don't worry. You think it's odd? It just seems like a nice thing to do. He gets lonely."

He did think it was odd. "I think it's nice of you." Her eyes were violet in the sun and Tacker recalled the pale pink walls of her house.

"Well, I'm relying on him. I could take the bus but it's a lot easier when he picks me up. He's like an uncle, since he and my dad were such good friends."

"So you've got it all worked out, then," Tacker said. "No westward ho?"

"I wouldn't say that."

"You mean you haven't got it all worked out or you might still leave?"

"Both."

"I'll walk with you." Almost violently Tacker needed Kate to stay in Winston. She was as lost as he was, but something in her was deep, way down in another dimension, and made him feel alive. He'd started to worry that there was another man in her life. There had to be.

"I remember how the football team practiced in the park in

the summer," she said. "I could climb a tree in the backyard and see the field."

"I thought you weren't interested in football." He meant to be playful, spark some happiness in her.

"Summers can be long. And I loved climbing that tree. I always took a book with me. But I'd look out and there you all were. Like toy soldiers."

A man with a dog came from the other direction and passed them. At a fork in the path, they slowed and Kate stopped. She took a deep breath. "I keep trying to understand about my dad."

"You said you didn't think anything really happened."

"I did?"

"You said your dad came home."

Kate took off her close-fitting cap and her hair sprang out. "Still, he hurt my mom. He made it sound like he loved that woman. And I still wonder—you know—about the drowning."

"Your dad didn't drown himself."

"How can you be sure?"

"Sometimes you just have to choose what to believe."

A cache of late leaves from a pin oak. A shadow along the ground. Above them a cry of blackbirds driving away a hawk. Samuel had once slain a hawk with a slingshot. Kate held her cap out in the breeze, as if she were going to toss it, as if its landing would foretell her fortune, whether for good or ill. She turned back and looked at him, her lips slightly parted, concentration on her face.

"Would you say your dad was an optimist or a pessimist?" Tacker said. It was all he could think of.

"Oh, an optimist. Absolutely."

"So there's your answer."

She looked at the cap in her hands and after a moment she put it back on her head. "I've got to run."

She turned, one gloved hand trailing behind her like a ballerina leaving the stage.

He should have kissed her. He should have leaned in and kissed her when she held her cap out and waited. His timing was off. Though when he glanced at his watch, he still had fifteen minutes to look at the lay of the land in the south field. His timing wasn't off. He'd lost confidence. He squeezed his eyes shut and ran his hands up and down his arms.

That night he dreamed part of it. Fray comes into the two-bedroom chalet in Osogbo, perched above the Osun River, only it's not a hill they're on; it's a cliff. And even though it's five in the morning and still dark and he's lying inside, next to Sam on a mat—they're all on mats on the floor and he's looking up at the ceiling—still, he can see the river streaming past in silver and hear the monkeys chattering and screeching. In the dream, Fray grunts. He's a monkey. He's a baboon. His arms are hairy. Samuel jumps up from the mat and tightens his sleeping cloth around his waist. "Please, sir. How can I help you?" he says. And Fray's head thrusts itself out toward Tacker, his short, low brow gorilla-like. "I'm not here for you. I'm here for him." Though there aren't words, only monkey sounds. Tacker puts his shirt on inside out. "What is it? Are my parents okay?" he says. The top of the hut lifts off and Tacker is in the Jeep with Fray, Fray's monkey hands on the wheel. And Samuel is running beside the vehicle, slapping the door. "I beg you," Samuel says over and over.

Chapter Eleven

ON THE AFTERNOONS she didn't work, Kate bundled up and took long walks with the camera. This was her solace, randomly photographing abandoned birds' nests in crepe myrtles, cushions of moss in an empty lot, raised root systems at the bases of oaks. She asked Mr. Fitzgerald to take her to the airport and she took pictures of Piedmont planes coming and going. Another letter arrived from James.

Dear Kate,

My current rotation has me at the hospital eight nights in a row. It's tough going. Especially since I don't sleep well during the day. I've decided becoming a doctor is more about physical stamina than brains. I remember last winter walking around the Decatur courthouse at night, freezing to death, but we didn't want to let go

*of each other. I miss you, more than I'm going to tell
you about—*

Love,
James

*P.S. I can't get away for Christmas. I'm working
straight through. Maybe soon after, in the new year,
I could come up to see you?*

The self-portrait James offered the public was of a determined man, focused, moored, a marathon runner. But his writing of their snowy night in downtown Decatur also disclosed a capacity for tenderness. Still, it startled her to think of him in Winston-Salem. This wasn't his territory. She'd meant to put Tacker off and instead she'd let the friendship deepen. James would not understand. Tacker was just different, more different than ever now that he had been overseas and back and didn't seem worried that he was working in a grocery, as if money and station were not what he was after but something else, something less tangible. Perhaps it was because he still had his parents that he could be so cavalier about such essentials as a career and owning a house and laying plans. Kate's dreams had become populated with the oddest assortment of men, a high school teacher she had fantasized about mildly, the Negro with the milk bottle who kept sending silent messages across her backyard, the fellow from Georgia Tech who told her she had a Brick. In her dream, the Georgia Tech boy was in her classroom, which made no sense; Agnes Scott was a women's college. But he was there and she needed protection and in the dream she wanted him to kiss her. He was almost her lover but not quite.

He was aloof, superior, older. She longed for him much more than he longed for her. She would probably never have him.

The next morning she had three stops to make on her rounds. First the photography store, where she'd left two rolls of film for developing, then the notions store to buy buttons to finish the shirt she was making for Brian, and finally Hart's to get ingredients for the chocolate pie she was planning for Christmas dinner at Aunt Mildred's. She wished she and Brian had an alternative. The pictures at her aunt's house were hung too high and Kate always had the feeling she was in a scene from *Alice in Wonderland*. Some things too big, others too small, the clock ticking off the wall. She knew, or supposed she knew, that this sense of oddity came from spending several months with her aunt after her mother's death. She would not tell Brian about their father's letters over Christmas; perhaps she never would.

It was misty outside, and she pulled a clear rain cap out of her pocket, tucked her hair in, and tied the cap at her chin. Among the pictures she would pick up this morning were shots of the Summit Street Pharmacy, the Sears building, and Modern Chevrolet. She would force herself to wait until she got home to look through them.

SHE WAS AT Hart's, wandering up and down the aisles, expecting to come upon Tacker, when she saw the Negro who had walked down the alley behind her house. She knew him immediately by his profile, the shape of his shoulders, the way he wore his clothes. She stopped and watched him pull canned tomatoes from a box and stack them on a shelf. She wished for her camera, though of course it would be vastly inappropriate to take his picture. Still, it was amazing how such ordinary activity appeared sanctified when imagined through a lens. He lifted a can with his left hand, transferred it to his right, set it precisely on the shelf while with the left he was capturing another tin. And then he stopped midmotion as if the electricity had been cut off, and he looked at her. "Good morning," he said. He didn't look quite at her but in her direction. "Am I in your way?" He scooted the box closer to the shelf. "Help you with something?"

"No," she said. But she didn't move around him. She waited. In a moment, he looked back toward her.

"You sure I can't help you find something?"

"I know you," she said.

"I don't remember that we've met," he said.

"Not exactly." She considered how to say it. "Maybe a month ago. I was in my backyard. You were walking in the alley, carrying a bottle of milk."

He put down the can he was holding, lifted his white apron, and wiped his forehead.

"I hope I didn't cause you any alarm."

"Not at all," she lied. "I didn't know you were working here. I'm Kate Monroe, a friend of Tacker's, Mr. Hart's."

"Gaines," he said, looking at her frankly. It startled her.

"You turned and lifted your milk bottle," she said.

He shifted his gaze to the back of the store.

"I'm glad to see you," she said, and she was, because now she was safe. He was in just such a place as she could imagine him, not visiting her in dreams or causing her to look behind her back when she was out in the yard.

"Likewise," he said.

Gaines seemed to steady himself and Kate found herself embarrassed to have expressed such feeling. She had to compose herself in front of the spices before heading to the checkout with the items she needed for her pie.

"That Negro boy," she said to Tacker at the checkout.

"Gaines? You know him?"

"Sort of. I'll tell you later."

"Sounds intriguing," he said.

"I just picked up some pictures I had developed. I thought you might like to see them." Maybe he would say no. She had not intended to invite him over, but seeing Gaines in the store made her feel her world might have a pattern, and besides, she craved an audience. She'd always had her teachers to tell her how talented she was and before that her parents.

"Do you accept criticism or only praise?" he said.

What did that mean? Could he read her mind? She blushed.

"I'm kidding. Yeah. I'll come over."

KATE SPREAD HER best pictures on the dining table. Tacker knocked on her door at seven fifteen, freshly showered and smelling like English Leather and exhaust fumes.

"Follow me," she said.

In the dining room, she flourished a hand. "The up-and-coming city of Winston-Salem, destination of hundreds flocking from tobacco fields and turkey farms."

Tacker grinned. "What are you practicing for? A travel agent?"

"No. An avant-garde photographer."

"That's impressive." Tacker leaned over the table. He examined the pictures one at a time. "I didn't know you were interested in architecture."

"We're trying to lure people here," she said, "get ourselves noticed."

"I like that idea better than you leaving for somewhere else. Let's take these to the library." He scooped up the photographs and moved in front of her down the hall, taking her father's chair, leaning forward with his elbows on his knees. He was an impressive man to look at. Kate sat on the edge of the sofa. Tacker stopped at the picture of Modern Chevrolet and Kate thought of the Negro woman she had seen in front of Wachovia Bank.

"Oh," she said. "About the colored fellow at the store."

"Gaines?"

"I saw him in my yard one morning, maybe the week before Thanksgiving. It kind of frightened me."

"In your yard?"

"In the alley behind the yard. He was carrying a bottle of milk."

"Huh," Tacker said, and he sat back in the chair, rubbing his jaw, the photograph of Modern Chevrolet still in his hand. "What time was it?"

"About nine. What do you think he was doing?"

"Going home."

"Through this neighborhood?"

Tacker glanced at his watch and set her picture down. "Something happened that morning. He came in early to get milk for his kid sister and when he left a couple of losers beat him up."

A needle of guilt rested in Kate's throat. She had misjudged. But how could she have known?

"What for?" she said.

"For nothing."

"He must have provoked someone," she said.

"Not necessarily," Tacker said, frowning.

"Did you see it happen?"

"I ran outside when I heard car tires screeching."

"What did you do?"

"I broke it up."

"Why haven't I seen him at your store before?" She expected Tacker to be concerned for her. The least he could do was admit that Gaines's presence was puzzling.

"He's in the back room a lot of the time pricing new inventory. And he works in the mornings. I don't know why you haven't run into him. He's a great worker."

Tacker sat with his hands at his sides. In the dim light of the room, his eyes seemed deeper set and he looked older. Kate remembered the cut on his finger that morning when she had gone into the grocery.

"You know a lot about him."

"His aunt is our family maid. I've known her all my life."

So much could shift on small sentences, just a word, just the verb tense. *Is* our family maid. There *is* a family. The slightest of breezes came down Kate's stairway and touched her photographs. It carried a scent reminiscent of her mother and Kate wondered when it would be—when in human history the time would come—that a woman could say plainly what she wanted.

Gaines frightened me. I'm confused by you. I know you're a man accustomed to attention but I'd like to talk with you about my boyfriend and see what you think. Do you really like the photographs? Tell me again and remember that I am a serious person. My backbone is a blade. Is it possible for a woman to live alone for some years until the ground firms up and she knows what she wants?

At the door, leaving, Tacker patted her on the shoulder. So she was his little sister, amusing. Kate called Janet. She was probably sitting in her bedroom in her house robe, her blond hair up in a towel, reading *Time* magazine and painting her toenails. But Janet didn't answer. In the library, Kate picked up Dorothy Wordsworth. *The quietness and still seclusion of the valley affected me even to producing the deepest melancholy. I forced myself from it.* She ran her hand across the sofa cushion. Her father had bungled his last year. Her mother had not confided it to Kate. Both parents were cast in doubt. She thought of László Moholy-Nagy, whose mysterious words, copied down by Dr. Lovingood, she had read aloud to Janet: *the photographic camera . . . a beginning of objective vision . . . we wish to produce systematically.* Yet Kate had concluded that systematic production meant truth would change. The truth about her father had changed—based on paper evidence. Kate didn't trust her feelings for James. Tacker was a little too self-interested.

She would wrestle to the ground this paradox of systematic production and objective truth. On a Saturday morning—the busiest day downtown, she selected a spot outside Thalhimers, this time across the street. For ten minutes, she would photograph everyone who walked in. Twice she had to stop to reload. In the end, she had shot forty-eight pictures. Three people had walked in and come right back out. She caught them coming and going. It was lunchtime and she was hungry but she was too excited about her work to wait, so she went immediately to a nearby camera shop and offered to pay extra to have the film developed as soon as possible. Monday morning she had her pictures. In her mother's studio on the large table that had once been used for wintering over begonias, Kate spread out her photographs. She took out the three that were duplicates. That left forty-five pictures, arranged in order taken. Almost without thinking, Kate picked out the photographs of men (nine), leaving thirty-six of women. Of those, five women had children in tow. Kate selected them out. Now she had thirty-one women on the table, all headed into Thalhimers alone to make a purchase on Saturday morning. Of the thirty-one women, thirty wore skirts. One woman was dressed in slacks.

One variation among thirty-one. What did it mean? Kate couldn't say. Her method wasn't very scientific.

In the kitchen she fixed a cup of black tea. Back in her mother's studio, she picked up the photograph of the woman in slacks and suddenly she wasn't sure it was a woman. How could she know absolutely? The picture was taken from behind. The character wore a kind of French-looking cap and carried no visible pocketbook. Her shoes were flat and her coat came to her knees. Kate had assumed it was a woman. Why? The implied movement of her figure?

The picture could not prove the assumption. It was neither one thing nor the other absolutely. If her image was the objective vision Moholy-Nagy alluded to, then objective vision was not absolute. Or objective vision could not determine the truth. Or the truth was not objective.

SUNDAY AFTER CHURCH, Kate turned down dinner with Aunt Mildred—she would be there later in the week for Christmas— and came home to cottage cheese and canned peaches. The phone rang. It was Tacker.

"Want to come over for hot chocolate tonight? You haven't seen my place."

She should say no. But she had finished Brian's shirt and didn't want to read. She said yes.

"I'll pick you up at five thirty," he said.

Tacker's place was sparsely decorated but attractive. A couch in front of the fireplace, a triangular side table with a turquoise lamp and a sketch pad, and over the fireplace two African carvings, silhouettes of a woman and a man, from Nigeria she assumed, along with some beautifully woven shallow baskets. The music room included a built-in and it was full of books about architecture as well as Tacker's record collection and a turntable. A dinette set was pushed against a large picture window in the dining room and at the center of the table Tacker had placed a vase of nandina berries. A new radio sat solidly on the kitchen counter. Yet the sum of these few artifacts was greater than they suggested individually, as if he had captured the essence of himself in small appointments and was content not to have more.

Tacker had the milk warmed and he stirred in the cocoa mix. "Let's sit in front of the fire," he said.

"Oh, I like the table with the nandina," she said.

"My only Christmas decoration. In Nigeria we had poinsettias that grew up twelve feet next to houses. But they weren't thought of as Christmas decorations."

"What do people there decorate with?" Kate said.

"The same things we do," he said, "artificial trees and Christmas balls and Nativity sets."

It didn't sound very exotic and Tacker seemed to have little more to say on the subject. This evening his eyes were green and bright. Kate pulled out a chair and sat down. Tacker did the same, a sweet, inscrutable smile on his face.

"If I lived here," she said, needing to fill the silence, "I'd sit and watch people walk by and take their pictures. I think I'm becoming a voyeur." A normal couple would not be meeting for hot chocolate on a Sunday night. They would be at a Christmas pageant, which sounded horrible, but it would be normal. She and Tacker weren't a couple. He hadn't tried to kiss her. He felt just as she did, that they were friends, old acquaintances from high school. This probability was a bit of a letdown.

"Kids walk by on the way to school," Tacker said.

Kate had to think back to what she had last said. A large cat strode in like a panther. "Who's this?"

"Da Vinci."

The cat leapt into her lap. He stood and arched before settling. She petted his back with one hand and sipped her hot chocolate with the other. Tacker turned his head sideways and looked out the window.

"Kate," he said.

"Yes?" Don't let him say what she had been meaning to say all along. *I don't want to lead you on.*

"About Gaines."

"You don't believe me?"

"Of course I do. I just wonder. You said he frightened you. He got beaten up by two fellows who thought he was being fresh with a white lady. I just wonder what you think."

"About what?"

"How should he act when he's walking down the street?"

"I don't know. I was just surprised to see him so close by. Actually, since you're asking, I thought he might have stolen the milk he was carrying. But then he kind of signaled to me and I felt like everything was fine. Did you invite me over for a lecture?"

"Sorry," Tacker said, taking her hand and pressing it. "There's a lot to figure out. I just want to get it . . ."

Kate felt a silence roll between them.

"Get it what?"

"Get it right. I just want to get it right."

Tacker leaned back in the smallish aluminum chair so his legs were stretched out in front of him and he latched his fingers behind his head.

"I suppose I mean I want to get the big things right."

For example? Marry the right person? Choose the right career? Raise your children well? Make the world better? He sure was smug. "You sound like a preacher."

"Oh God," he said and laughed. "I don't want to save anyone. I couldn't. Look at me. I'm lost myself."

In a heartbeat, he had gone from apparent smugness to being the most charming man she had ever met. "You don't appear lost." She stopped petting da Vinci.

"Well, I am. Or I was."

The cat complained with a *meow* and she got back to scratching his head. "Then I guess we're lost together," she said. "Except you said you *were* lost."

"Well, you're here," he said.

Tacker drove her home. On the second set of yard steps, he found her hand and took it in his and she let him, and on the porch, he opened her hand and touched the four points of her palm and then closed it, and she remembered seeing him at Summit Street Pharmacy months ago, how she wondered whether they would ever speak, and now she knew his smell but not his mouth. In silence, she found her key and let herself in.

Chapter Twelve

Two DAYS BEFORE Christmas the grocery was a madhouse. It was just as well. Tacker was falling in love with Kate, perhaps because of the darkness in her. Or maybe it was his darkness and she mirrored it. He suspected she was comfortable with a *Negroes in their place* mentality and that angered him. But he wanted her. So he argued with himself: *She should know better. She could be brought to know better.* His yearning won out and he called her on Christmas Eve.

"Hello," he said. "It's been crazy at the store."

"I figured," she said, a little guarded maybe.

He forged on. "In Nigeria we celebrated Boxing Day. It's a British holiday; I don't even know what it's about. Over there it meant lots of music and drinking. If it's not too cold, I thought we could ride up to Pilot Mountain. What do you think?"

"You just delivered me from taking down Aunt Mildred's Christmas tree," she said.

"Dress warm," he said.

❧

TACKER PULLED OUT his letter jacket for the first time since he'd come home.

"I have on my leotards," Kate said, exposing the ankle of one blue-jeaned leg when he picked her up. They hopped on the bike and headed toward Mount Airy, taking Highway 52, rolls of hay in pastures, horses looking up with their curious, coffee brown eyes. The sky was Carolina blue, the air like fingers of ice against their faces. Halfway up Pilot Mountain, past the wintered pool and dance pavilion, Tacker parked the Indian and they started out on a trail. Kate found herself a walking stick. Out of nowhere she began talking about her last year of college. She'd considered going on to get a master's degree in English.

"I thought I might teach in a college." She trimmed a small branch from her stick. "Like my dad," she added.

"You could still do the master's," he said.

"Oh, sure," she said, but she seemed to be thinking of something else.

"There was this guy," she said, trimming another branch.

Not at all what Tacker wished to hear.

Kate described a resident at Emory. He sounded like stiff competition, though Kate seemed detached as she talked about him, as if it were in the past. "He loved to play golf but he didn't like the woods. He worried about ticks."

Tacker ran a hand through his hair.

"What's wrong?" Kate said.

"Nothing." *Everything.*

"Your hair." She lifted a hand to smooth it, her fingertips warm on his forehead.

Tacker would have been content to linger there. But she slipped away.

"Let's explore," she said.

They walked single file, for the path would not allow otherwise.

"You ever go camping?" she said over her shoulder.

"Sure. My dad and I camped in the Smokies when I was in junior high. My favorite part was reading in the tent at night. Well, that and jumping naked into whatever water was close by."

Kate slowed down. She covered her face in her hands, then threw her head back. "God," she said.

"A bad topic?"

She laughed and half sobbed.

She was awfully skittish this morning. Did she think he was going to jump on her?

"My brother was always swimming naked in the lake," she said at last. "He didn't show up yesterday for Christmas at Aunt Mildred's even though he promised after missing Thanksgiving. He called at the last minute to say he was having dinner with some family at the coast." She paused. "It's like he's turning into my dad or something, disappearing."

"Have you told him about the letters?"

"Not yet. It almost feels like he can tell there's something bad and he's staying away."

They meandered along, light glinting on the path.

"I had a horrible dream that the house flooded. The big oak in the front yard was uprooted and all you could see was red clay all the way down the hill," Kate said.

They continued to walk, startling a blue jay to flight.

"Ever try throwing stones at a target?" Tacker said. "It's best if they're tin cans and you can hear them clatter."

"No. But it sounds like a great idea." She bent for a thumb-size stone. "See there?" she said, pointing to a knot on an old pine.

She threw like a girl and missed.

"Here," Tacker said. "First widen your stance. Okay, now make your arm into an L." He adjusted her arm upward so her elbow was shoulder high and then placed a stone in her palm. "Now lay your wrist back and snap it forward when you release."

She tried again. Her form was better but she still missed.

"More follow-through," he said, demonstrating.

"We're not leaving until I get this," she said.

Once she achieved her aim, she didn't want to stop. She took her coat off.

"Hold this," she said, and she half slid downhill to gather more ammunition.

She was a girl who would keep at something until she mastered it.

Back in Winston they stopped at Staley's, sitting in the restaurant a long time watching kids from Reynolds High cruise by in their parents' cars. He put his arm around Kate's shoulder and she settled back. At her door, he reserved the kiss he had meant to give her before hearing about the boyfriend. He had more than enough pride remaining not to lay himself at her feet.

SINCE COMING BACK to Winston, Tacker listened religiously to WAAA on the radio, a Negro station playing R&B. The show was produced in a glass booth in a restaurant near Winston Lake, the Negro part of town. It came on at three in the afternoon and Tacker planned his lunch break during that half hour, sitting in the lounge, his feet on the coffee table. Rather than the jitter of "Rockin' Robin" and the syrup of "This Magic Moment," he could listen to James Brown's "Try Me" and Fats Domino's "Walking to New Orleans." This music was how he imagined the Mississippi River, dark and deep and long. The DJ called himself Daddy-Oh. "Daddy-Oh on the patio. The black spot on your dial."

Tacker purchased his first album by a Negro musician, Ray Charles's *Yes Indeed!* The sound of the title song was less river and more fountain, bursts of liquid energy filling the room. He had the album on two nights after Pilot Mountain, when he found himself sketching in an old drafting pad from college. He sat before the fire, legs akimbo, cocooned by lamplight, listening to Ray. He didn't know what he was sketching at first. Loops, circles overlapping at the edges. It looked a little like segments of a caterpillar. He added a rectangle, wondering if whatever this was might have a veranda. He added another circle larger than the others and for some reason it occurred to him that the rectangular bit might cantilever out—over what? A lagoon? There were no lagoons in Winston. Over a lake? He thought of the booth where Daddy-Oh broadcast his program, the DJ sitting up in the glass box, Negro kids gathered in their cars in the parking lot after school. He and his friends used to drive by in the afternoon just to hear one song and Daddy-Oh would shout out, *There go my white boys!*

Lagoon wouldn't leave his head. *Lagoon.* Where? Tacker stroked da Vinci's head, set the pad down, and headed to the kitchen for a cold beer. He popped it open using a bottle opener mounted on the frame of the back door, opened the door, and walked onto the porch and from the porch onto the steps leading into the backyard. The night was damp and the temperature had risen with the moisture, fog shrouding the bare hardwoods gauzelike. He pitched his shoulders up and then relaxed them. In a wet dawn in Nigeria, palm trees were so bathed in mist, a person could almost walk into one before he knew it was there. Lagoon, moon, monsoon. The Lagos lagoon, of course. It was the only lagoon he knew. And how did he know the lagoon and who had planned to erect a house on a plot of land overlooking it? Alan Vaughan-Richards, who had married a Nigerian woman and agreed to share her name—thus Vaughan-Richards—and who had come to lecture at UCI several times and shown Tacker's team the plans for the house he was going to build on the Lagos lagoon.

A Brit, Vaughan-Richards consistently applied curvilinear geometries in his designs, sometimes as adornment but often as integral elements of walls and rooms. Modular designs were his staple, initially from blocks and roof sheeting, and then from timber framing. The design for his house was a series of overlapping circles, rooms annexed one to another like a set of beads: bedrooms, office, kitchen, living and dining rooms.

Tacker pulled open the screen door to the porch and it clattered shut behind him. In the living room, he retrieved his sketch. Vaughan-Richards's face might as well have been looking back at him. The caterpillar design was his, somehow channeled through Tacker's brain on a winter's night in Winston-Salem, North Carolina. Memory was funny, how it slipped up on you. The southwest monsoon of the rainy season began on the Nigerian coast. Tacker had been in Lagos on a shopping trip two years ago when the first rain came in. They'd had to stop the van and wait it out. And even after the rain lifted, the fog was so dense, Abraham had gotten out of the bus with his torch and walked beside the driver to help him along the road.

The fire was down to embers. Tacker threw in another log. Stroking da Vinci, the sketch tilted against his chest, he stared into the flame, wondering what it was all about, this lapping of shores one against the other: the Atlantic shore in Nigeria, the Atlantic shore of North Carolina. These rooms lapping one against the other. He conjured Kate's mouth, her breasts. When he couldn't keep his eyes open any longer, he switched off the lamp, stretched out on the couch, and fell asleep. In the morning, it came to him instantly that the sketch was inspired by the swimming pool in Hanes Park and the possibility of a bathhouse he might help design. He was half-awake, and the notion stirred him deeply, like the dream of a woman in the most intimate gesture imaginable.

After a shower and cold cereal and two cups of coffee, he sobered up.

He was hungry to build something. But not like that. He would get laughed out of town. He turned the design over on the couch. Later he'd start again on something more reasonable, something Craftsman-like, for example.

JANUARY EVENINGS WERE slow at Hart's. Five o'clock it was nearly dark. Customers thinned out. Gaines came up aisle five and cut over to Tacker at the register. "I'm heading out," he said. "Unless there's anything else you need." He purchased eggs and two oranges.

"No. We're fine," Tacker said. "Wish I had a car to give you a lift."

"A friend's picking me up," Gaines said. "Meeting me out back," he added.

Tacker wondered who was meeting him and was surprised by the envy he felt, watching Gaines saunter down the aisle and knock open the swinging doors, then a minute later hearing the slam of the car door. The loss of Nigeria poured through him and he bent over the counter.

SOME DAYS, TACKER still woke expecting to see palms out the window, the sound of Samuel's radio coming through the screen. Flipping through stations on the radio early the next morning, he picked up the English accent of the BBC. He tried to listen once a week, to see what news he could gain about Nigeria. Da Vinci jumped into his lap and he rubbed the cat's head as he sipped his coffee. Tacker had to hear about the British economy and fluctuations in the pound, as well as news from Germany, France, and Italy, before he was rewarded with a story from West Africa.

A recent report on the higher training of Nigerians advocates an expansion of educational facilities not only in the southern regions, but in the North, the region slower to develop in this regard . . . would cost the federal and regional governments nearly fifty percent of their recurring budget . . . crucial for training citizens of a modern nation-state. The country's independence . . . October 1. Hopes high for a country often called the giant of Africa.

In other news from Africa, Patrice Lumumba, president of the Congolese National Movement . . . serving a sixty-nine-month sentence in Brussels for inciting an anticolonial riot in Stanleyville.

Tacker looked at the clock. He stood; the cat leapt; Tacker rinsed out his coffee cup. Marxist Chukwu had admired Patrice Lumumba for his black nationalism. *He will never kowtow to any colonial power,* Chukwu had said. *Not that man. He is a true African.* Tacker could see Chukwu now, standing in an open corridor along the Science Building at UCI wearing a black beret as he spoke, a Bic pen resting on an ear. *Lumumba may be killed one of these days. He will not stand down.* Tacker's thoughts shifted to Samuel and the proliferation of schools in Nigeria. How many secondary schools? Hundreds? Thousands? How many would use their design?

By the time Tacker pulled his coat on, the broadcaster had moved to news from Asia.

TWILIGHT OF ANOTHER day. Uninvited, Tacker stopped by Kate's house after work. She opened her front door, holding a cooking spatula. He'd come with a few of his Nigeria pictures stuffed in his jacket pocket. It seemed she was returning his affection, but he wasn't sure and he meant to proceed as he imagined a scout would move into unexplored territory.

"Come on back to the kitchen," she said.

She wiped her hands against an old floral apron, the kind a grandmother might wear, tied at the waist, with pockets for handkerchiefs.

"I brought some of my pictures," he said.

"Oh goody."

They stood in front of the counter as he handed them to her one by one.

"How is one woman going to sell that many peppers?" she said.

"I don't know."

"Look at this little girl. She wants to be in the front. She's got her notebook to write down sales," Kate said.

Tacker had feared Kate wouldn't care for the pictures or would call them primitive. But she was right there with him. He wanted to touch her—every part of her, starting with her hair and going down.

"Oh, this river! Look at the monkeys. Do they bite?"

"They're treated so well they're tame. In fact, they'll go sit in the road and the traffic stops or goes around them. They're sacred."

Even that she didn't judge.

Three times she went back to the picture taken the day the foundation stone was laid for the high school. Tacker and Samuel stood before an open field, a passel of chickens and goats in the foreground.

"I like this one best," she said.

"Why?"

"Because it's so like you."

"You can have it," he said, his heart flooded.

"Are you sure?"

"Yeah."

She propped it against the windowpane.

Kate rinsed the spatula in the sink along with the mixing bowl and cup measures. She'd placed a recently baked cake on a pedestaled dish on the kitchen table. Maybe the resident had called. They were getting back together. He was probably already driving up here in a fancy new car and the cake was for him. Tacker ducked his head to look out the window, into the backyard. A post light revealed the structure of a garden.

"Tell me more about Nigeria," Kate said.

He turned to look at her, surprised. "What do you want to know?"

"I don't know. I was thinking maybe I should go somewhere."

"You mean a vacation? I wouldn't recommend Nigeria for that. But it would be a great place for taking pictures."

"Why's that?"

"It's hard to describe. Everything is so, I don't know, vivid. Not picture-perfect at all. But maybe because it's at the equator, the light seems brighter and the trees are mammoth. There's just so much going on. It's kind of like a carnival all the time. Well, not at the college. UCI wasn't that different from a college here."

"Maybe I could go teach in one of your schools," she said.

Tacker stared at the thumb-size indention where the bones of her clavicle met.

"Want some cake?"

So the resident wasn't coming.

"Yes." It was a minty chocolate cake with white icing. "Wow. Great cake," he said.

Kate sliced a paper-thin piece of cake and ate it with her fingers.

Every time Tacker imagined he might reach out and pull her close or lift his hand to her face and kiss her, he lost his nerve.

At the door as he was leaving, Kate called his name. Maybe he had left something. But she just leaned across the threshold, though he was halfway across the porch. "Listen," she said. "I'm giving a small birthday party for Brian next week. That's why I'm practicing my cake baking. Want to come?"

"I guess so," he said, glad for the invitation, wondering if his face looked as puzzled as he felt.

"Friday night around seven," she said. "Thanks for bringing the pictures." On the bike riding home Tacker thought again about how he'd lost his instinct for timing even though he seemed preternaturally aware of time, as if he might run out of it. He wanted to go back and leap up Kate's steps and knock on her door and push his way into the house, possessing her.

Chapter Thirteen

FIRST OF FEBRUARY. Tacker and his folks sat at the dining table. He'd come over to help his dad hook up a new washing machine and stayed for spaghetti supper. It was so much easier to visit them now that he had at least the outline of his life back. He thought he might mention Kate if the right moment showed itself. The television was turned to the news. It was a new ritual with Tacker's parents to watch the news during dinner. Their stainless flatware clinked against the everyday plates. His mother refilled their water glasses. David Brinkley's face with its slightly tilted mouth filled the screen. He was talking about North Carolina. In a moment, shifting images of a lunch counter came into focus. A gaggle of angry people. And then four Negroes were in the spotlight, a reporter talking with one of them. "What do you hope to accomplish?" The four men were dressed in coats and ties, but other than that they looked so different from one another, it was difficult to comprehend what the story was about. "We want to sit down at the counter and pay for a cup of coffee and a plate of food," one said. Another of the men leaned toward the microphone. "We come in and make our purchases. The cashier takes our money. But if we get hungry, we can't order our food and sit down to eat. We have to go all the way back home to eat or stand in the street. It's not fair."

The footage of the four men cut off and the screen switched back to David Brinkley in the studio. Tacker was still hearing the second man who had spoken. *We have to go all the way back home to eat.* He placed his hands on the table as a wave of excitement and doubt swept over him.

His parents didn't say a word. The plates clanked loudly as Tacker's mother stacked them. She washed and his father dried. Tacker leaned against the doorway. At last his mother said, "I don't know why they want to stir things up."

Tacker was gathering his words when she turned and looked at him.

"What do you think, son? I suppose you agree with them." Tacker had the sense that his family was on television.

"Pure logic would say they're right. The store sells to them. Why can't they order and sit down to eat lunch?"

"Of course you're right. You're always right about things like this. I guess I'm behind on the times." Her tone was angry and hurt. Tacker didn't mention Kate.

A COUPLE OF evenings later, Tacker was closing the cash drawers when Gaines asked about the back room. "Some folks. We need a place to meet," he said as he sifted copies of news magazines into racks at the checkout lanes. Vice President Nixon's face dominated the cover.

Tacker was trying to close the store. Why had Gaines waited so late to bring this up? He was due at Kate's for her brother's birthday party.

"Is Nixon running for president?" Tacker said.

"You're asking me?"

"Look at the story," Tacker said.

"Says he's considering it," Gaines said. "That means yes."

Tacker should take something over to Kate's, but he hadn't had time to think about what it might be.

"Wonder if we could use the back of the store," Gaines said. "Tonight. I can lock up."

A prayer meeting maybe? On a Friday night? "What are you meeting about?"

"Might call it an information session," Gaines said.

Wasn't there a church or school near Frances's house where they could meet? "I don't know," Tacker said.

"Just a few people," Gaines said. "My friend's car can hold us."

"What exactly are you doing?"

"You hear about what's happened in Greensboro at Woolworth's earlier this week?"

"You mean those four college boys at the counter?"

"Yeah. We're talking about doing it here."

Tacker sensed he was on the edge of something vast, poised at the threshold of a continental divide.

"Here in Winston?" he said.

"Yeah," Gaines said. "In Winston."

Tacker recalled the swinging bridge in Osogbo. Before he crossed he was still American. After he crossed, he was something else. And later still, in Ibadan, there had been that incident with Chukwu refusing to sit at the less desirable tables when he had asked for the veranda. "It's my dad's store, not mine," he said, torn between asking if he could stay and join the meeting and going to Kate's.

"We'll be cool, man," Gaines said.

The language took Tacker by surprise and he smiled goofily. "I'm trusting you."

A HUGE MOON hung in the sky. Tacker revved the Indian, heading out the parking lot onto First, up the hill a couple of turns, and he was looping around to Kate's house. Every window shone with light. He pulled into the driveway, maneuvered the bike onto its stand, and took the steps two at a time.

Brian answered the door. He looked like Kate but his hair was lighter and his skin darker. Tall and lanky and good-looking in the way guys at the beach are. Young. His eyes translucent gray, almost wise, or maybe lost. He wore a beaded shell necklace like Tacker imagined he might see in California.

"Hey, man," Brian said. "You must be Tacker. You don't remember me. I was just a squirt when Kate was in high school."

"Nice to see you. Glad you're here," Tacker said. Kate was in the dining room, wearing a purple skirt with a silver belt, and it reminded Tacker of Anna Becker's belted dress at the Osun. He had a premonition that there was more at stake here than he'd expected. Kate glanced up and nodded and went back to talking with the older woman next to her, doubtless Aunt Mildred. The woman raised her head and she looked at Tacker and then she came to him across the room.

"My, my, my," she said, and gave him a hug, just like that. "I loved to watch you play ball. You come right on in. Brian, get this man a Co'-Cola."

Brian was back with the drink, another man following behind him. The contrast between them was great. Brian in his beachwear, this fellow in tailored dark pants, casual but perfectly fitted.

"Hey," Brian said. "This here is James from Atlanta."

Tacker looked at Brian and then at James, who was holding out his hand; Tacker shook it.

"Good to meet you," James said. "Kate's been telling me what a good friend you've been. Hear you two grew up together. I surprised her driving up at the last minute."

"We were in the same high school. I guess you could say we knew each other growing up." Tacker had not reciprocated the initial greeting, but it was too late now and he certainly was not happy to meet this apparently well-to-do, not-bad-looking rival. Kate was keeping her distance, selecting dishes and silverware and glasses. Brian had his head tilted down, one hand on the back of his neck. He must understand the dilemma even if James did not. This was not a football game, but Tacker was going to play it like one because that was what he knew how to do and in the game there was no time to get nervous. You went for the object of desire.

"Kate, let me help you out," he announced, cutting through Brian and James and heading for her lavender skirt. He walked straight to her and kissed her cheek.

"I'll fill the glasses. What are you serving?" he said.

She looked at him and he saw that signature crease in her forehead. Well, what did she expect? Had she been writing to this guy? A bright anger flashed through his brain. *Cut it out,* he told himself. *You've never even kissed her.*

"Pizza pie and Jell-O salad," she said. "And cake."

"Coke, then. I'll put ice in the glasses."

Kate looked up. "Thank you," she said. "I didn't know he was coming."

"Right," Tacker said.

James might have been five eleven if he was lucky, and he was slender. Still he took up room, pacing back and forth from the kitchen to the library as Kate and Tacker finished preparing the meal. As if he was expected in surgery. Tacker caught himself looking at the man's polished fingernails. Everything about him was pressed and neat. Tacker wondered what kind of car he was driving. Even when they sat at the table, James positioned himself sideways so that he took up more than one place.

Brian ate with eager determination.

"Kate tells me you spent time in Africa volunteering," James said.

"Africa is a big place. The continent has actual countries," Tacker said.

"Not that any of them is particularly different from the others," James said. His face was set on Kate.

"Actually, they're as different as Germany and China," Tacker said. The word *volunteering* stuck in his mind. As if he had been away doing Boy Scouts. "I went with the Clintok Corporation."

"If I were going to travel, I'd start with France," James said, unfazed. "Italy. Spain."

Tacker watched Kate to see if she gave any response to the suggestions of these countries, but she was tackling a particularly jiggly mound of green Jell-O.

"I always wanted to go to Egypt," Aunt Mildred said. "Did you know the pharaohs were buried with their cats? So they would have them in the afterlife. What about you, Kate?"

"I think my mother wanted to go there. But I'd rather go somewhere, I don't know, messier. Maybe India. All of those temples and the Ganges."

"Lands, Kate," Aunt Mildred said. "Isn't there a lot of disease there? James, tell her."

"Of course there is, but shots and antimalarials will take care of most things. Water is the real danger," he said. "Still, it isn't the first place I'd want Kate to go."

"Why not?" Kate said.

"You'd certainly need a chaperone," Aunt Mildred said.

"It's halfway around the world," James said. "What about London?"

"I thought we were dreaming," Kate said. "I don't mean I've bought tickets."

"You'd get some great photographs," Tacker said, sensing an opening.

"I'll go with you," Brian said, grinning. "We could boat down the Ganges."

"You row and I'll shoot pictures," Kate said, smiling at her brother.

"Don't you two get started, now," Aunt Mildred said.

"Leave room for cake and ice cream," Kate said, brushing off the conversation. In a moment, she laid her napkin aside and pushed back her chair.

"I'll help you," Tacker said, rising so quickly his legs came up against the table and the dishes and glasses sang and spun for a moment, though nothing spilled.

"Easy, tiger," James said.

Tacker wondered how much damage could be done to a man with a dinner knife.

He stood close to Kate in the kitchen. She did not look at him. What should he say? *I'm in love with you. Declare yourself.*

"Give the first piece to Brian," she said. When she raised her face, her eyes looked moist. He hoped she was good and sorry for putting him through this ordeal. Tacker stacked several plates of red velvet cake with ice cream on his arm the way he had seen waiters do. And he almost made it, had delivered all but the last slice, the one for James, when he gave his arm the slightest turn. The cake landed in the man's lap.

"Jesus Christ." James scooted his chair back and stood as the plate fell to the floor; bell ring of broken china, cake and ice cream smearing the front of his dark slacks.

"Wow," Brian said. Tacker thought he caught a confidential smirk on the kid's face. On the other side of the table, Kate half stood and sat back down, her mouth a round O.

"My lands," Aunt Mildred said, hands raised in a gesture of surrender.

"Jesus Christ," James said again, dipping his napkin into his water glass and dabbing at his pants.

Kate rose again.

"Have a seat, honey. I'll take care of it," Tacker said. He held her gaze even when her eyes widened.

"Honey?" James said. He looked at Kate and then at his tie, satisfying himself that it wasn't permanently damaged before glancing up again.

Tacker imagined the satisfaction of flipping the tie into James's face.

"Kate darling, get the broom," Aunt Mildred said. "It's Brian's birthday. Now, you boys settle down." She smoothed the tablecloth.

Kate slipped out and came back with a damp cloth and a dustpan.

James was seated again, his legs sprawled out, one foot to either side of the mess. "Kate, oh, Kate," he said.

Tacker took the implements from her. "I'll do it." Halfway into a squat, he caught the amusement and disdain on James's face and stood back up. "Look," he said. "Go sit somewhere else. I need to get under your chair."

"You're resourceful. Work around me."

"Oh, James. For heaven's sake. Just move back," Kate said.

"Boys," Aunt Mildred said again.

"He made the mess; he can clean it up," James said.

For an instant, Tacker saw Fray's face that morning he showed up in Osogbo, spitting his words: *I'm here for him.* He shoved James in the shoulder. "Now, go sit somewhere else." He made a first sweep of the floor when he saw James's fist. It glanced off his cheek. Tacker felt something deep and primary, a huge bird lifting in his chest.

"James, stop!" Kate cried.

The only point of reference was her voice. The rest of the room was a submarine glow. A disconnected flash of a milk bottle thrown into the air before it burst onto the pavement. Tacker fisted his hands, straightened, and glowered at his opponent. If he had something better than a damp cloth, he would already have thrown it. "Lucky you're not better with your swing."

James drifted out of the room, down the hall, and into the library.

"I could try to fix it for you," Tacker said to Kate, holding the broken china plate, suddenly tender for her.

But she had slipped like a moon behind clouds. "Don't worry. I have too much china."

Tacker looked around. "How about a second piece of cake, Brian?"

"Sure," Brian said.

"Sorry about the ruckus," Tacker said when he delivered it.

"No big deal," Brian said.

"Sorry," Tacker said to Kate, who had retaken her seat. "I'll be saying good night. And before I forget. You look beautiful."

She opened her mouth again and her eyes lit up.

"Man," Brian said. A goofy smile covered his face and Tacker remembered how young he was even if he was built like a full-grown man.

"Oh, I almost forgot," Tacker said. He jogged down the hall, ignoring James, out to the Indian, where he retrieved a tin from a leather satchel.

"Peanut brittle," Brian said. "Thanks."

Tacker angled around the table, kissing Aunt Mildred on the cheek. He tipped his head in Kate's direction.

HE RODE THE Indian out of town toward Mount Airy, the way he had gone with Kate, dwelling on the silver belt around her waist, her lavender eyes, and then he let the anger burn from the backs of his hands up his arms to his shoulders until it consumed his chest.

He got far enough away from Winston-Salem to see the sky. The bike purred in idle. Pressing his hands into his pockets, he discovered the Life Savers he had meant to give Gaines for Valentine. He opened the roll and put one in his mouth, conjuring Gaines and his friends in the grocery.

It was amazing what he could see by moonlight. Pinecones in the trees. Frozen cornstalks in the field, looking like failed men. And beyond the field, long hedges of trees, a darkening to the woods, an uprise where a hill met the sky, the sky itself a lighter color than the distant land. All of this so vast and cold; yet he felt a fire inside.

Chapter Fourteen

AUNT MILDRED REFUSED to leave, even after Brian went to bed. There wasn't a thing Kate could do about it. Eventually James got up and stretched. The spot on his pants was still glossy from the icing. At the moment, Kate felt little affection for Tacker or James either. She felt only miserable. Recently she'd not been able to recall the sound of her father's voice.

"I've got a room at the Howard Johnson's," James said. "I'll have to leave first thing in the morning."

Kate walked him to the door.

"I was hoping we could talk," he whispered, on edge. "I've been offered a post-residency fellowship in Sweden. I want you to come with me."

"What do you mean? I can't come with you. We're not married."

"We can get married. Listen. Have you got feelings for him?"

Was that a proposal? "I told you. I don't know what got into him."

"I can give you time, Kate, if you'll just give me something to hold on to." He handed her a slip of paper. "Here's the number at the motel. Call me when she leaves, and I'll come back. I'll make you a proper proposal."

Kate pressed her lips together. Though her feelings for Tacker were a jumble, he had more gradations of illumination and darkness than the man before her, who seemed too predictable, an obvious choice for her, which went against her sense of independence.

"Let me come back and take you for a drive, then."

"It's late."

"Kate." His look was stern.

"Okay. Just move your car; park down the hill. I'll get Aunt Mildred out of here and then I'll come out."

No sooner had James left than Aunt Mildred was talking about the lateness of the hour and how she must get home. Once Kate saw her taillights pulling away, she flickered the front porch lights, pulled on her coat, and waited until she saw the Corvette.

James drove like a wild man, speeding through town, taking turns so fast Kate had to hold on to her seat. She was too frightened to speak and hardly even noticed which way they headed out of town. He sped down a hill and up another, choosing at the last moment to take a left onto a dirt road and then suddenly pulling over to park the car. Neither spoke. Kate felt her insides tighten and turn. After what seemed an eternity, James hit the steering wheel twice. Then he pressed the horn a good half a minute, though it seemed like hours.

"My God, Kate," he said at last, "he's just a friend? You expect me to believe that?"

She said nothing.

"Silence isn't saving you."

Suddenly he was all over her, kissing her hard, pushing her against the seat. She kissed him back, strangely and terribly thrilled by his heat and anger. He unbuttoned her coat and her blouse, still kissing her, and pressed her bra down, exposing a breast to his hand. He pinched her there, softly at first, then harder, and she felt a deep flood of desire. His mouth was on her breast and then her shoulder and he reached behind to undo her bra until her entire chest was open to the moonlight and to his mouth and hands; he was nearly on top of her. Kate had never felt such need. His hands moved under her skirt and she felt herself let her legs go. It was almost as though she was watching it happen. His fingers sought her out and then he was there, pressing her open. She moaned and it seemed to her now that she was not looking down on herself but that instead she was underwater, looking up, watching the last bubbles of air surface above her. Why fight it? She was drowning and it seemed easy to drown. But then she saw that someone was in the water with her. It was Brian, young Brian. He was holding her hand. She pulled herself upright, or tried to, but James had her pinned down. Something bubbled out of her. "Stop it," she said.

"Oh, Kate," James said. "Come on, honey."

The heat was gone. She felt ice-cold. "Stop it. Get off of me." She gathered all her force to push him away. "Take me home." James looked at her, then straightened up, gazing out the driver's window as she buttoned her blouse.

"Damn," he said.

When they got back to Glade Street, she opened the door before James brought the car to a complete stop.

"Don't be an idiot," he said.

"Don't call me," she said, pulling her coat together and running up her steps. From the safety of the library window, she watched as the little Corvette made a U-turn and headed down

Glade toward Hawthorne. She'd almost forgotten about Brian, upstairs sleeping. Recalling him, her shame deepened. At least she couldn't be pregnant. Turning off the kitchen lights, she glimpsed Tacker's picture, the one of him with his friend Samuel. She hadn't even thought to hide it when James arrived. Now she picked it up. Tacker looked entirely at home with the goats and chickens and a cleared field and beyond that what appeared to be a farm. Did the picture tell the truth? Or did their history together influence how she felt about his image? She lay the picture facedown on the windowsill.

In the morning she and Brian visited their parents' graves in Salem Cemetery. For Kate, it seemed a somber duty that might cleanse her of what had happened with James, the way she had let it happen, as if she deserved it. The morning was cold enough to cloud her breath. Brian called for a cab. The small gesture of care chimed like a clear note in her heart and at once she wished her brother would stay with her. She had always been the older sister but now they could be equal.

"The cab's here," he said. He wore the shirt she had made for him.

Kate pulled a wool cap over her head and they stepped onto the porch, Brian supporting her elbow down the steps. He had never done such a thing and she wondered if he had a girlfriend and these gentlemanly forms had been learned for her.

The cemetery was planted in hollies and magnolias so even in winter it was beautiful. They stepped through an iron gate. Mockingbirds skittered from holly to holly. Old headstones, weathered and lichen covered, attested to BELOVED WIFE, DEAREST DAUGHTER, DEVOTED FATHER. Kate reached for Brian's hand as they neared their parents' plot. A stone angel the size of a child, with large wings and folded hands, stood in a corner of the fencing, seeming to belong to all of the departed congregants equally. Kate had laid a wreath at Christmas, keeping her visit brief. It had been a rainy day and cold, and the wind seemed to blow right through her. Today it was just as cold but sunny and calm, and she took off her cap and shook out her hair. Brian had not mentioned the fracas at the dinner table and she had not spoken of their father's letters. Squatted between the headstones, Brian ran his fingers over their parents' names. His shoulders stretched the coat across his back and she saw how he had come to his manhood.

"What happened to that book Dad was writing?" he said.

"What book?"

"About the Civil War."

He remembered?

"It wasn't really a book. More like a monograph."

"It was going to be published."

"The Smithsonian may have a copy of the manuscript. They didn't publish it because he wasn't able to revise it."

"You think there's a copy in the house?"

"Why?"

"I always thought it might tell me something about him that I never had a chance to know."

"Like what?"

"I don't know. That's the point."

We're both searching through remnants. "What would you ask him if you could?"

"Why he left," Brian said, standing. He turned to Kate and she saw his silent tears.

"He drowned," she said softly.

"He left us," Brian said.

"What do you mean?" Her throat was thick and her head was suddenly freezing. She pulled the cap back down over her hair.

"You don't know? Mom never told you?"

"Told me what?"

"He loved someone else." Brian wiped his eyes with the back of a hand. "I still love him. I forgave him a long time ago. I had to."

"When did she tell you this?"

"Way back. You didn't know?"

"How far back?"

"When you went off to college. That's why I thought you knew. I figured she waited so you didn't have to hear about it again."

"You never said anything."

"What's to say?"

"Do you think he drowned on purpose?" Kate said.

"I don't know. I hope not. I'm sorry I brought it up."

Kate looked up at the sky wheeling by—bright clouds, a mockingbird.

Farther along we'll know more about it. Probably not, Kate thought.

Back at the house, she recommended searching but now with Brian's help. She was not going to tell him about the letters. He already knew, and why add painful details to painful knowledge? There were many places where she knew the manuscript would not be found—all the places she had already searched. What if it was planted in plain sight like the purloined letter? She headed to the library. Brian was there ahead of her.

"Oak leaves," he said, pulling out folded sheets of waxed paper.

"Did you do those?" Kate said.

"Mom and I did."

In the interlude of Kate's imagining her mother and Brian collecting leaves, the memory of James and last night surfaced and she shivered in a mixture of disgust and fear.

"You cold?" Brian said.

"One of those weird momentary chills. I'm glad you're here."

By three in the afternoon they had discovered a poem by Kate in the *K* volume of *Encyclopedia Britannica*, a sketch by their father that was not discernable at first until Brian turned it sideways and they saw it was a design for the backyard gardens. They found numerous four-leaf clovers tucked in volumes that had nothing else in common except as storage for the family talisman, a recipe for Cottage Cheese Bake serving as a bookmark in a volume on the rudiments of still life painting, and Monopoly money folded inside a book about South America.

"I put that there," Brian said.

"Why?"

"I was cheating. I kept the money there and when I was behind with Mom, I'd pretend I needed to go to the bathroom and sneak in here and replenish my funds."

"You think Mom knew?"

"Nah. She was too preoccupied." Brian put the money back and returned the book to its place on the bookcase. "I can stay another night," he said.

"Thanks," Kate said.

They made a dinner of birthday party leftovers and a bottle of wine. In her bedroom, later, Kate listened to the sounds her brother made. He ran the water in the faucet brushing his teeth. Then he went back downstairs and returned soon after. She heard his steps in the hallway, coming and going. She could not hear but imagined the gentle sigh of the mattress as he lay down and the rustle of sheets. After turning out her light, she opened the curtains to the moonlight, casting the garden in blue. She had drunk one glass of wine beyond what she should have, and rather than make her sleepy it had brought her to wakefulness.

She thought of James and wondered if she would regret her last words to him: *Don't call me.* James would want a new house in the Atlanta suburbs. Even if he embraced her family friends— and he would, because they were the right people—still, they would be defined by his profession; she would have to join the Junior League instead of serve on a library board. Though bereft of parents, she belonged in Winston-Salem, quixotic in her ways but well thought of by the likes of Mrs. McCall, welcomed by those a generation above her who were relations of relations, as her mother had been with the Hanes family. Kate's orphaned status allowed for her oddities. She might go years and not marry and no one would judge her. The straight and narrow would not be required of her, or if the straight at least not the narrow. No, presently, she did not regret her good-bye.

THE NEXT MORNING was overcast and Kate required Brian to adorn himself with a variety of scarves and hats and sit for her as she took his photograph in the library, in the backyard, on the front porch, exploiting the soft light of these locations. Finally, he threw down his hat.

"Enough. I want to run to the hardware store. There's time before my bus leaves."

"I'll go with you."

They decided to walk to town and then Kate would take the bus home and Brian would walk to the Greyhound station. Kate had a funny sense they might run into James. As they were headed up Fourth, as they came up to Broad—at any moment, the Corvette might pull up. It was a fearful hope or an exciting dread. She touched her fingertips to her cheekbones. The self-assurance she had felt the night before about her ability to live alone, guiding the ship of the Glade Street house, was dissipating quickly. She considered again the Negro woman who saw into her secret heart. On the street, she was surprised at how many people greeted Brian, but then again he had lived here all of his life until just recently.

"Miss Monroe," an elderly gentleman said as they slipped into Brown Rogers Dixson Hardware.

"How do you do?" she replied.

"Who was that?" she said, pulling on Brian's coat sleeve.

"I don't remember, but I love this place," he said. "We bought skates here, remember?"

"Not really." She gazed at a large assortment of hand drills.

What she wanted was a certain amplitude in life but enough security to keep her level. Were those levels she was looking at now? Perhaps she should purchase one.

"Hey, I'm ready to check out," Brian said.

"Go ahead," she said, lifting a level and tilting it this way and that, watching the bubble in the tube of liquid as it moved one way and then the other.

Back on the street, Brian handed her a paper bag.

"What?" she said.

"I noticed you needed some new light bulbs."

"Thanks," she said, almost tearing up.

"Thanks for the party. You've got some interesting suitors." He grinned.

"Tacker's not really a suitor."

"Keep telling yourself that. Hey. I've got to go." He gave her a hug and with nothing more than a slender satchel over his shoulder and his recent purchase, he headed down the street.

"Get something to eat," she said, but he didn't reply or turn his head as her voice was taken up by the wind into the moist wintered air over the town.

AT HOME, KATE fixed a pimento cheese sandwich and drank the last of the wine from the previous night. She settled in the library and picked up *The River Nile*. In a condition of puzzled nostalgia, she examined the photographs and read the captions and bits of narrative.

Wholly Arabic in character, Omdurman is a city of the desert. Gliding like white shadows, draped women stroll in the city. One gown, or tob, unfurls a colorful embroidered hem.

The women's backs were to the photographer so Kate couldn't see their faces, but one of them raised her arm expressively and they walked with intent, the lower portion of their legs exposed.

Following the text with his hand, a Zanzibar merchant reads the Koran in front of his shop. Most Zanzibaris are Sunni Moslems, the most numerous of Islamic sects. Islam means "surrender to God's will."

The man in the photograph was barefoot.

Kate wished she had a photograph of her father that last time at the beach. His face would tell her everything. She thought about the woman in trousers going into Thalhimers—if it was a woman. And she wondered if the women in white could tell off their suitors or postpone marriage. She expected not.

Chapter Fifteen

A SWARM OF crows gathered among the trash cans at the back of Hart's, calling to the morning as if they had never seen one as good. Tacker watched as one flew off, and then another, and soon they were gone, every one, in a great gathering of wings. He looked in the direction they had flown. There was Billy Cyrus, standing in the parking lot. Yet the store was not due to open for an hour. "What do you need?" Tacker called.

"Saw some Negroes leaving out of here couple of nights ago. Round ten o'clock," Billy said.

"Is that right?"

"Three of them."

"You generally keep a watch on my store?"

"Your dad's store. I happened to be driving by."

"You've got some keen eyes."

"I pulled into the lot. Asked them what they were doing. One of them said he works for you. Showed me the key he'd locked up with."

"Well, there you have it." Tacker was already irritated, having slept poorly since the night of Kate's party.

"What I'm trying to figure is why he had his friends with him."

"That matters to you?"

"Ought to matter to you."

"Thanks for the neighborly concern. I'm not a bit worried."

"What happened to you?"

"I'm not sure what you mean. I've got work to do."

Tacker entered the lounge. He'd had Saturday off and hadn't been in Sunday. The place was cleaner than usual. Newspapers stacked. Coffee cups washed and put up. Floor swept. Even the cushions on the couch were plumped up. It was almost eerie—as if mysteriously he had awakened after his death into a more perfect rendering of life, or as if he had dreamed his life and was finally waking into it.

Gaines stepped in.

"Thanks for cleaning things up," Tacker said. "How'd the meeting go?"

"Went fine. If it's all right with you, I need to take off today from eleven to noon. I can come back and stay later than usual."

Later Tacker would marvel at his lack of discernment about Gaines's behavior, given the trail of clues the man had offered up. But Tacker was preoccupied with Kate and Billy and with his father, who had received an inconclusive result on a medical test after his annual physical revealed that his white blood cell count was way up. Tacker had learned about it from his mother after Sunday dinner.

"If there's no way around it," he said. "But I have to be able to count on you."

He didn't like being a boss, telling people what to do. It made him feel old.

Gaines was gone close to three hours, but Tacker was checking inventory when he got back and didn't have time to speak with him. He'd spent most of the day trying to decide how to act if Kate came in, but she didn't come in. And no word from her.

At the foursquare that evening, Tacker made up a handsome blaze in the fireplace. He cooked a steak, drank a Pabst Blue Ribbon, and let da Vinci sit in his lap as he ate. The fire he felt for Kate shifted back and forth from anger to lust and there was not much difference in the feeling one way or the other. He had another beer and thought about his own parents. How in all those years had they maintained their composure? He reran Brian's birthday party and drank another beer, imagining Kate in her bedroom, sitting at the window, looking out, waiting for him.

He woke on the couch, the fire long dead, da Vinci asleep on his feet. He had overslept.

Gaines was waiting for him at the store, dressed neatly in black slacks and a gray denim shirt.

"I went ahead and mopped. Made coffee."

Tacker touched his day-old beard and glanced down at the flannel trousers he had worn yesterday.

"You're early."

"Might need to take off again around noon."

"Is everything all right? Frances and Valentine?"

"They're fine."

"What's so dang important you have to be gone again?" Tacker's head hurt. "You're not moonlighting, are you?" He spread a hand out, half expecting his fingernails to look as ill-kempt as he felt. But his hands looked perfectly sound and reliable.

Gaines handed him a newspaper folded to display the legend: *Students from Winston-Salem State Stage Lunch Counter Sit-in at Kress.* Tacker stared at the grainy photograph just beneath the legend. Gaines went off to the produce section. Tacker took a sip of coffee and picked up the paper a second time. It wasn't a newspaper he knew. Maybe it was a Negro newspaper. One of the men in the picture was Gaines. Of course. Like what happened in Greensboro. Tacker fidgeted with his shirt cuffs, feeling loopy and unprepared. Across the store, Gaines was moving his hands expertly over the citrus.

"What are you doing?" Tacker said, coming up beside him.

"Clearing out overripe fruit like you told me," Gaines said.

"No. In the paper. What are you doing?"

"Demanding my right to be served a club sandwich, just like you."

Tacker put a hand to the back of his neck. "How many were there?"

"At the sit-in? Fifteen. Students from Winston-Salem State and Atkins High."

"How did you get involved?"

"I've been involved," Gaines said, looking at Tacker as level as a crossbeam.

Tacker shaved in the back of the store and put on one of the clean shirts he'd learned to keep on hand. He got to work with the butcher, filling the meat case. He'd see what happened. His father wouldn't come across a Negro paper. Thinking about what Gaines was up to was a welcome diversion. He thought again of Chukwu and wondered what kind of ruckus he was kicking up in Ibadan these days.

Gaines returned at two o'clock, an hour late, his collar turned inward.

"Sorry," he said. "A little rougher today." He pulled the collar out to expose the tear. "Someone tried to jerk me out of my seat." He tucked the collar back in.

The store wasn't busy and Gaines's tardiness wasn't an inconvenience, but the torn collar brought back that October morning when the man had come in for milk and ended up on the sidewalk along with the shattered glass. Someone might hurt him worse than that. Gaines was squatted in the canned-fruit section, restocking the bottom shelf.

"You can't keep this up," Tacker said. "The store's not a carousel you can get on and off of."

"We're making history," Gaines said, not looking up. "You ought to come with me."

"What?" Tacker said. A skim of dust dulled the cans on the shelf in front of him and he took out a handkerchief and began to wipe.

"We close down enough lunch counters, it gets too costly for the stores."

"What do you mean close them down?" Tacker scanned Hart's to see if anyone could hear before he squatted next to Gaines.

"We sit down, they close the counter. They don't sell any hot dogs. We go to the next five-and-dime and they close down that lunch counter. Put up signs: CLOSED FOR PUBLIC SAFETY. The longer we sit, the longer they don't sell. Some folks get arrested and that clogs the system more. Reverend King called it nonviolent civil disobedience when he spoke over in Durham at White Rock Baptist."

"You were there?"

"Mid-February."

"I've heard mixed stories about King," Tacker said, picking up a can of orange juice, wiping the tin top and setting it back down.

"Of course you have. You think white people are going to paint him pretty?"

"It just seems risky to me," Tacker said.

"Ha!" Gaines said. "You *want* risky. I know about you. You

wanted to do something important going to Africa. This grocery ain't it."

"Hey," Tacker said. "What right have you got?" He straightened back up.

"To do what? Tell you what I think?" Gaines stood. "What right have I got to talk back to a white boy? Same right as you've got to talk to me."

The butcher at the meat case shot them a look. "Hey, hold it down," Tacker said, unease filling his chest. "I saved you from getting beaten up a lot worse," he said.

"Thank you, sir," Gaines said under his breath. "Nice playing Jesus, ain't it?"

Tacker's hands felt heavy. "What do you want from me?"

"Help us out," Gaines said. "You could make a difference for us."

Tacker gazed at the stacks of fruit juice. A faint whirring noise came from the fan at the back of the store. "We'll talk later. School's out. The parking lot's getting full."

"You tell me when," Gaines said.

IN THE BACK room after closing, listening to Gaines talk, Tacker saw the kaleidoscope of the past weeks turn and shift and he puzzled out that the man had come to the store for more reasons than extra money for his mother. A grocery had meeting space. An owner might be willing to give away a few cans of ravioli to folks working for a cause—if he was sympathetic.

"Students from Wake Forest College are joining us tomorrow at Woolworth's. We're walking in together," Gaines said.

"You're not afraid?"

"Are you?"

Tacker felt a wave of vertigo, as he did when he took mountain curves fast on the Indian. You had to know the exact angle and when to let up on the gas and allow the momentum to carry you. Something in his life was connecting. He better pay attention.

"Going to jail seems like a bad career move," he said.

"I feel for you," Gaines said sarcastically, but he smiled.

It was hard to know whether fear or excitement trundled up from Tacker's center.

Tangled up in the culture. Fray's accusation.

"Okay. Hold on. One thing at a time. I can go for an hour tomorrow. That's it. We're leaving before anyone gets arrested."

Gaines just kept smiling.

Tacker's vague discontent with his homeland suddenly snapped into sharper focus.

HE LEFT CONNIE in charge of the store. Midday it was cold and clear, the sky a thin white. Tacker had never done anything political that he could think of. The frigid air and the roiling in his belly made him think of a story he'd once heard about an army air corpsman in World War II who'd plugged in the top of his flight suit but not the bottom, so half of him was freezing and the other half roasting. They took off on the Indian, Tacker figuring to go by way of Old Salem. A white fellow and a black one sharing a motorcycle wasn't an everyday sight in this town. He hooked through alleys and side roads, aiming for Academy Street. Tall, uncut swirls of wintered rosebushes fell across fences. Within the lanes, the bike's sound was muffled and soothing. Obliquely Tacker sensed a country in which streets were throughways and not borders. From Academy he went left onto Main, then left onto Fifth. He'd forgotten the stiff upgrade at Fifth and Liberty and he had to gun the cycle to keep it from rolling back. Just a block and he took a left onto Liberty and there was Woolworth's. Tacker brought the bike to an idle. Gaines leapt off; Tacker cut the engine and kicked the bike back onto the stand.

"Follow me," Gaines said.

"Hold on," Tacker said, tipping the bike's front wheel against the sidewalk.

"Hurry up, man. We're late."

Gaines walked on the right side of the road, a sign for MARY JANE SHOES looming above him.

"We're meeting the others up this way," Gaines said. "Filing in together."

They walked four blocks, cars slowing to observe them. They didn't find the convocation of protestors Gaines was expecting. "We were supposed to meet them here," he said. "We were going to pair up, a white student and a Negro student. We must have missed them." They turned in unison and hurried back to Woolworth's. Tacker shouldered his way into the store, giddy with expectation. Yet everything appeared normal as day, the usual noon crowd, the store smelling of popcorn and the grill. A woman working the candy counter looked up. Tacker smiled at her. She smiled back. Then her face seemed to contort, and Tacker knew she had seen Gaines come in behind him.

In a corner, a few high school boys, cutting class no doubt, huddled together like outcasts from the drama club. Dozens of regular customers filled the long line of vinyl counter stools. With the avenue of overhead lights and the red-and-white Pepsi-Cola sign, the scene appeared like a stage set, familiar and odd.

"I don't get it," Gaines said in half whisper. "They're not here."

"What do we do?" Tacker said.

"I'm here; you're here. What do you think?"

How do you know what's below the surface? His question to Samuel at the Osun. *I don't.* Samuel's reply. "Let's do it," Tacker said, the urge to act irrepressible.

There were two seats down at the far end. Before he knew it, Gaines was in front of him, heading toward the lunch counter.

Tacker caught a glimpse of a bespectacled man with the look of a professor, standing under the Pepsi-Cola sign, rolling up and down on the balls of his feet. He stepped back as Gaines passed, as if he had expected him and was making way. As Gaines took a seat, Tacker strode down and took the one beside him. Nothing happened. It was as if the game hadn't started. Tacker had been here a hundred times. The place was his, like the practice field at Hanes Park. He could walk onto it and wait for the snap and run with casual confidence toward the uprights. He would turn and see the ball at the apex of its flight and it would come to him like a trained bird. When he scored it would be as if he hadn't really meant to.

He was intoxicated, filled with a mad hilarity that such an astonishing thing was happening. Sliced apple pie filled a glass dome so close he could reach out and touch it. The man beside him pulled out his wallet and left two dollars at his plate though he hadn't finished his sandwich. Tacker avoided looking down the line at the other customers. He surveyed the staff behind the counter: two women and one man, the grill cook, and the waitresses, one of them a Negro. The white waitress was closest and she met his gaze. Tacker swiveled side to side, catching a glimpse of Gaines. There seemed an inevitable quality in the air. "Ma'am," he said, "I'd love a piece of that pie."

She didn't speak as she lifted the glass dome, selected a plated piece of pie, and set it before Tacker. She brought him a fork.

"Thank you."

"Coffee?"

"Yes. Black is fine." He was astonished by how easy it was. Amazed by his intelligence. *Black is fine.*

The woman's eyes moved to Gaines. "We don't serve coloreds," she said.

"Yes, ma'am. I'll sit here anyway."

Suddenly all the seats to Tacker's left were emptying.

"There's a nigger down there," someone said.

In a single motion of delicious precision, Tacker slid the pie and coffee mug in front of Gaines.

"Get that nigger out of here."

"Have some pie," Tacker said.

Gaines picked up the fork as if it were a serpent. He raised a small piece of pie to his lips, his shoulders dipping as he leaned forward.

"You with him?" the waitress said to Tacker, her face waxy.

"I am." Tacker felt his chest expand.

"We don't serve coloreds," the woman said, her lips tight.

She whisked the pie away before Gaines had a chance at another bite, throwing the dish into the trash can with the pie. She poured the coffee into a sink before throwing out the cup.

Do as you like, Tacker thought; *we're not moving.* All he might have said to Fray came to him now. *What's the point of coming here if you're not going to live with people and eat the food and figure out what makes folks tick and learn something from them? You're the one who should be sorry. You never really made it into this country.*

"Ever feel like you'd die for a cigarette?" Gaines said.

"Right this minute."

"Monkey see, monkey do." A voice spoke behind them. "Get on back to nigger town and you can smoke all you like."

Tacker turned around but Gaines did not.

One of the high school slackers he had seen earlier stood a foot from their counter stools, two others behind him. His hair was dirty blond, eyes slightly protuberant.

"Don't worry with them," Gaines said. "Face forward."

Tacker didn't like the feeling of turning his back.

"Hey, nigger," the boy said. "I'm talking to you."

Gaines didn't respond. His face was a mask.

"Hey, nigger."

Tacker turned again. The boy pulsed up and down. Behind him, customers who had now risen from their seats stood in a semicircle like Romans gathered for a gladiator contest. The front door seemed miles away.

"Ignore him," Gaines said, looking straight ahead.

"What?" How did you ignore a mob?

"We don't fight."

Out of the corner of his eye, Tacker saw the boy lean forward and spit on Gaines's neck. His partners squealed with delight.

Tacker leaned over the counter and grabbed a bunch of paper napkins. Gaines wiped his neck.

"A fag and his nigger," the boy said.

Tacker looked down at the counter before him and saw reflected in the polished Formica the silhouette of his head, a form both absent and present. Anger, simple and hard, rose in him, and his arms shook in the swaddling of his coat.

"Don't," Gaines said, placing a cautionary two fingers at Tacker's wrist.

"What'd I tell you? A fag and his nigger," the boy repeated gleefully.

Tacker looked at the Negro waitress, who had not moved since they sat down. More than the Atlantic Ocean separated her from the Nigerian women he had seen who sent taxi drivers packing when they pulled too close to their market stalls. Nigerian women took up the entire avenue with their dancing, traffic control be damned.

Gaines began to whistle "Go Tell It on the Mountain." The Negro waitress shifted her stance.

"Shut that nigger up," someone yelled.

Over the hills and everywhere, Tacker imagined the words. Many a time he'd heard Gaines singing in the back room as he unpacked merchandise, the tune relieving the tedium of the day. At the moment in Woolworth's, the crowd quieted and Tacker had again the eerie feeling he'd had that morning at the store when everything was tidied up—that he had passed to the other side of some mystical boundary.

And as if the play had reached its climax, someone called, "Police." Tacker looked toward the entrance of the store. In came a dozen officers. His heart flapped as the walls of the store leaned in.

"Over there," a woman said, pointing toward Tacker and Gaines.

The officer glanced in their direction. He turned toward another officer and conferred. No one moved toward them.

"What's going on?" Tacker said.

"I have no idea," Gaines said.

The crowd buzzed, everyone moving toward the front windows.

"They're here," Gaines said.

"What do you mean?"

"The students from Winston-Salem State and Wake Forest College. They're just now getting here. They must have gotten held up."

The doors opened and in they came, two by two, black and white, women and men, a black girl who couldn't be out of high school yet. The crowd separated. And then like a lasso dropped from the sky, the police surrounded the students before they could make it to the lunch counter.

Gaines was grinning ear to ear. "Man, we're the hottest show in town." He spoke like a jive man, full of street poetry, a musician playing for change who had hit the jackpot. "This is the point. This is the whole point. See now. We're making them hustle."

Tacker watched, slack-jawed.

"My name is Chief Waller," one of the officers said, his voice like a chainsaw. "You are trespassing. You have one minute to leave this store or you will be arrested."

Another of the police officers pointed back to Gaines and Tacker in their seats. Waller cut them a glance before turning back to the students.

"Let's go," Tacker said.

But Gaines was whistling again under his breath.

"The side entrance is right over there." Tacker gestured with a head tilt. "We can slip out." Ordering pie and passing it over to Gaines was one thing. Resisting the urge to torpedo the blond kid was hard but doable. Getting arrested was inviting dark water to close over his head. He looked at the clock behind the counter. It seemed they had been here an hour. It had been less than fifteen minutes. "Hey. We've got to go," he said. But Gaines wasn't moving.

No one was moving. The students stood like a tableau. Chief Waller gripped his nightstick. Tacker caught the eye of a beautiful chestnut-haired girl from Wake Forest College. She looked like Joan of Arc.

"Men. Arrest these people," Chief Waller said. Tacker heard clicking. Every one of them was being handcuffed.

Again the second officer motioned toward Tacker and Gaines. Waller started in their direction, the soles of his shoes complaining against the floor. It seemed to take forever for him to reach them. He stopped three feet from Tacker. "You part of this group?"

"No, sir," Tacker said.

"Yes, sir," Gaines said.

"This some game with you?" he said to Tacker.

"No, sir. We got here first," Tacker said.

Waller looked back at the students thirty feet away, then back at Tacker. He gazed at him a minute. "I seem to remember you," he said.

"May be," Tacker said.

"I believe I do know you, and I know your father. I don't think he would be proud of you pulling a stunt like this. Get on out of here," Waller said.

Tacker felt Gaines's hand at his elbow.

They sidled toward the small secondary entrance, a handprint on the wall near the door that Tacker would never forget, like the sign of some forlorn prisoner long ago. The door seemed stuck. Tacker pushed hard and it leapt open and they tumbled out. He thought of the whale spitting out Jonah. Fourth Street was full of people, but everyone was looking at the paddy wagons as the students were loaded up, blacks in one, whites in another, to go to their separate but equal jails. The Pepper Building wheeled in front of them.

"Don't walk too fast," Gaines said.

The crowd stayed riveted on the bigger show, their taunts aimed at the students.

"You're a disgrace to your race."

"Kill that nigger."

"Lock 'em up and throw away the key."

Tacker and Gaines reached the Indian a block away.

"Man oh man," Gaines said.

Tacker turned the bike and they headed up to Fifth, the sky opening to blue, Winston-Salem larger than Tacker had ever known it, and more dangerous. He felt Gaines's chest expand and contract as they wove their way back to Hart's.

❧

THAT EVENING TACKER caught Gaines on his way out the door, after the store had closed and they'd cleaned up for the next day. "What did you mean when you said you've been involved?"

"At Fisk. We were planning a sit-in in Nashville. Then I had to come take care of my mom."

"So you got involved here."

"I couldn't let it go. I found this fellow, Carl Matthews. He's at the center of the action here in Winston."

"What makes you want to risk it?"

"There are a thousand reasons, but one of them alone is enough. You ever hear of Emmett Till?"

Something about the name seemed prophetic. They sat on the floor, their backs up against the checkout counter while Gaines told the story.

TACKER'S HEAD REELED. A boy in Mississippi buying candy. Maybe he winks at a white woman. A couple of days later he's abducted in the night, taken to a barn. An eye gouged out. An ear nipped with shears. Tacker felt sick to his stomach. Skull shattered. Gunshot to the head. Ribbons of barbed wire used to tie a cotton gin fan to his neck before his body is thrown into the river. A crucifixion. Tacker's throat constricted. His left hand trembled involuntarily. And Gaines that first day in front of Hart's. It was too close. It was way too close.

SUNSET. TACKER WALKED his usual route into Hanes Park, aware of each footstep. There was no moon. Emmett Till's fistful of candy kept interrupting his thoughts, then the eye, the ribbons of wire. Winston telephone lines were humming, the story of the arrests growing by leaps and bounds. Someone he knew besides Waller had doubtless seen him at Woolworth's. A cotton gin fan weighing seventy pounds. He wandered from the path, blank and stunned, the metallic sound of handcuffs in his ears. His own flesh seemed too soft a thing to endure. He walked alongside Peters Creek. It had been a favorite haunt in his childhood, clear and sandy, deeply etched in the land so that the drop from bank to water was ten or twelve feet in some places. On one of the bridges that crossed the waterway he had once painted his initials. He thought he might remember which bridge, and he picked up speed, hoping to get there before dark. But either the initials were gone or he had not remembered correctly. He headed for a curve in the creek where someone long ago had stacked rock to create a pool. It was hedged by a stand of hollies. He and his friends had caught minnows here, skipped stones, even submersed themselves in summers.

Hardly thinking what he was doing, Tacker took off his jacket and laid it on the bank. He pulled off his shoes and socks, balancing on one foot at a time. In a single motion he pulled off his undershirt and sweater together, folded them, and set them on the shoes. He pulled off trousers and underwear. The night air moved against his arms and legs and he thought briefly of how, as a boy, he had imagined Indians living beside the creek, their chests painted. A dark bird flew low across the field. Tacker rubbed his hands together. It surprised him that he didn't feel colder than he did. Descending a set of steep steps—who had fashioned these?—he wondered if he could be arrested for this. The creek was shockingly cold. Even before sitting, he felt himself shrivel. He lowered his backside and yelled, the sound swallowed by the creek's basin. Tacker lengthened his legs in front of him. His feet were still browned from the Nigerian sun. Though he pushed against both of them, Kate and Samuel filled his mind. And then he thought of Gaines's two fingers on his wrist. Tacker looked at his hands and closed his eyes.

His back hitting the water made a splash like a large bird makes in rising. The sting of cold was deadly, but he stayed, his abdomen bobbing up, his skull half-frozen. He counted to one hundred. When he sat up he rubbed his limbs, his neck and face. Out of the creek and up the bank, he dried himself with his undershirt, rubbing his skin again with his sweater. His body felt as keen as birth. He dried his feet with his socks and put on his shoes without them.

"Don't fight," he said aloud, poised in a squat, suddenly starving, laughing out loud, delirious. There was nothing but the night, and what light there was in it issued from the trees themselves and the grass, mirroring the stars.

"Yeah, I went," Tacker said to his father.

"What for, son?"

"To see what's going on in my hometown."

"I don't like it much."

"You don't dislike it that much," Tacker said. "Gaines and I were gone less than an hour. We didn't get arrested. We're talking about getting a sandwich at a lunch counter. That's a nice store, by the way. New swivel chairs. I guess I hadn't been in there since coming home."

Tacker eyed his father, trying to gauge his response. But in his plaid, button-up oxford, he was hard to read. "The woman behind the counter said she couldn't serve me if I was with coloreds," Tacker said. "Imagine if you were hungry and tired and couldn't sit down."

His father rubbed his chin. "We have a long tradition of being separate. It's how we've managed to stay civil. You might think about this store I've entrusted to your care."

"Every month since I've been here we've outpaced last year. But we haven't stayed civil, Dad."

"What do you mean?"

"I mean a Negro can get spit on for sitting at a lunch counter; he can be beaten up for walking down the street in front of your store, killed for speaking to a white woman."

His father lifted his hat and scratched around in his graying hair.

"You're the one who said small changes. A sandwich is pretty small when you figure it," Tacker said.

"I don't know whether to blame your mother or me for this streak in you," his father said, his brow knotted.

"Both of you," Tacker said. "Let your conscience be your guide. You said that."

His father put his hat back on.

FOUR DAYS AFTER Woolworth's, Kate came into Hart's wearing a pink fitted coat buttoned up the front. Tacker thought about everything that was under it. But he was still angry with her about James and a useful irritation came into the back of his neck and warmed him and he did not move to greet her. He was even annoyed with her for not knowing what had been going on with him even though he'd made no effort to communicate. He focused on checking out customers and hoped to make his lack of interest as clear as a pistol shot. Kate's hand placed a single Forelle pear on the counter, yellow-green with a cloud of pink on its upper side.

"Is that all?" he said before looking up.

"No," she said. "I'm sorry about Brian's dinner party. I didn't know James was coming."

"That's your business."

"I said I was sorry."

"For what?"

"For making you feel bad."

Tacker gazed at her. "Who said I felt bad? Look, I can't talk right now." He was about to crack his knuckles when he thought better of it and placed both hands down on the counter.

"I didn't have time to tell you."

No time for a phone call? Tacker imagined the resident with his precious necktie. He looked beyond Kate as if something else had fetched his eye.

"Call me later, okay?" she said.

"I'll see what I can do," he said. But he did not call her.

Chapter Sixteen

KATE HAD NOT heard from James or Tacker in a week. She didn't want to hear from James, except perhaps to hear how sorry he was. Her considerations of Tacker were more complicated. Any thought of him necessarily brought to mind his hands resting at his lean hips and his well-formed chest and the compelling column of his neck.

She had a call from the photography store that her last set of pictures was ready for pickup and she left the house to fetch them. The man behind the counter looked wan and his collar was loose at the neck. She hoped photography would not have a wasting effect on her. At home, she selected six of her best photographs to send to the *Winston-Salem Journal*. A large envelope came back several days later. *We're using your photograph of Modern Chevrolet in Sunday's paper. Enclosed find your remaining photographs and a check for $10.00. Please consider us when you have other pictures that might be of interest to our readers.*

She turned a circle on her porch. Inside, she called Mr. Fitzgerald and Mrs. McCall to tell them her news. She wanted to call

Tacker and she dialed the first numbers before she put the handset back into the cradle. She did the same a few minutes later before heading out with her camera. It lay solid upon her chest like a heavy locket, though its effect was not to cause heart weariness but rather to speed her step.

The very next day, Mrs. McCall phoned, asking Kate to take some shots of the library for the upcoming campaign. "We want pictures of our patrons," she said.

"I'll be there in the morning," Kate said.

The media room of Main Library was full of elderly gentlemen reading the newspapers: the *New York Times*, the *Washington Post*, the *Journal*. She walked upstairs to locate Mrs. McCall, who had said to call her Nancy, though the transition was proving difficult for Kate. Nancy seemed too familiar a name for such a formidable presence as Mrs. McCall. When she couldn't find her, she asked a librarian at the card catalog.

"Oh yes. She had to go to a meeting. She said to tell you to go ahead. Just ask before you take anyone's picture." She smiled briefly before looking back to the drawer into which she was entering cards for new books. Each card made a little snap as it fastened in place.

Kate felt relief and trepidation. It could be awkward to work with someone like Nancy McCall standing by waiting for her to finish, and yet now she had to approach all of these strangers. She should go back to the gentlemen with the dailies before they shuttled home for lunch. The room was still full, but now she must decide whether to approach each one individually or claim their attention all at once. The room was quiet save the rustling of papers. Kate made her way to one side. "Excuse me," she said to a silver-haired man in tortoiseshell glasses whose diminutive comeliness made him seem the most approachable. "The library has asked me to snap some pictures. Do you mind?"

He looked up at the camera and then at Kate.

"Why, not at all." He straightened his eyeglasses.

"Do you think you could . . ."

"Ask the others? Yes. Of course."

He stood and she saw he was a little stoop shouldered. He rolled his paper and slapped it against his hand. "See here," he said, his voice precise and authoritative. Most of the men looked in their direction. A few poked at others who had not heard. "See here, this young lady has been asked to take our picture. What's your name?"

"Kate Monroe."

"Miss Monroe," he repeated.

One man rose slowly, returned his paper to the wooden rack, and ambled out of the room. The rest of them looked at Kate.

"Please just keep reading," she said. "Pretend I'm not here."

It took them a moment to settle back to reading. Kate slipped her shoes off and walked in stocking feet. Occasionally one of the men would look up to see if she was still in the room. They seemed a gentle agglomeration of elders who in bygone times would have gathered at the general store, eating chunks of cheese and surrounded by the odor of tobacco, while the most erudite among them read aloud from a single paper. The image in her head of that earlier era seemed truer than the present moment she was about to capture on film. There was no smell here save a faint whiff of open books. The shutter button made a sweet light sound each time she pressed it. Kate took at least twenty shots, some close-up, others angled to capture the magazine racks, some over a reader's shoulder to capture a headline. She slipped her loafers back on.

"Thank you," she said to the silver-haired gentleman.

He took his eyeglasses off. "You're welcome, Miss Monroe. I knew your father, you know."

"Oh?"

"I was dean at Salem College for many years. I believe I remember you playing hopscotch in front of the main building. I wasn't sure until you said your name. Well, he would be proud of you now."

"Thank you," she said.

"I'm here most every day. Drop by again," he said and shook out his paper.

"I will." Her chest swelled with pleasure until she was halfway across the room, when she realized she'd forgotten to ask his name. The cool lozenge in her heart was still there. Quickened by conscience, she made a point to ask the names of the mothers in the children's book section and helped finger-comb their offspring's hair. She and Brian spent time in the library when their mother was running errands. Brian wasn't good at sitting still so Kate would sneak in a bag of Sugar Babies and find a hidden nook where she could feed him one after another. "Suck on it. That one has to last five minutes." He would sit with his book open, his mouth tight in concentration, and she would read as much of *Wuthering Heights* as she could before she had to give him another candy. He was like a little bird and she was the mother. Kate finished her second roll of film.

In special collections she found two women poring over an old copy of the *Woman's Club Year Book* of 1930–31. They wore their hair in nets and looked like sisters with their well-corseted midsections and aged-to-transparency skin.

"Yes, yes, dear, go ahead," the shorter one said, waving a handkerchief.

Kate took several shots before the same woman looked up and said, "We want to take your picture."

"Oh, thank you. That's not necessary."

"No. We want to, don't we, Annie?"

The other nodded. Apparently the shorter one spoke for both of them on a regular basis, the royal *we*.

"Only one person can take a picture at a time," Kate said, as if speaking to a child.

They stood before her unfazed.

"I'll have to show you," Kate said, reluctant. "Who wants to go first?"

"Annie does. She'll do it for both of us," said the taller woman, finally finding her voice.

The women smelled slightly of mothballs.

"Let's slip the shoulder strap over your neck," Katie said. Annie was so short, the camera landed well below her belly. But her hands were dexterous and steady, her fingers long.

"Turn this knob until your subject is in focus," Kate said. "This is the shutter button. Just push it when you're ready."

"Go stand over in front of those books," Annie said. "No, don't look at me. Study the books."

Kate heard the slight click of the camera.

"Now pick out a book," Annie said. Again the soft click.

"Now turn around and pretend you're reading it. Now look at me."

Kate heard the click and blinked. "That must be enough, don't you think?"

"One more."

Kate complied.

"Oh yes. You're going to like those. Now sister and I have to get back to our work," she said, as if Kate had requested her portrait be made, not the other way around.

"Thank you," Kate said, relieving Annie of the Brick.

KATE DEVELOPED THE film herself at the photography shop, where she'd arranged for the privilege in exchange for assisting, on occasion, with in-studio photography sessions with brides-to-be. The girls fidgeted and moaned about their hair and cried and giggled, and their mothers were worse.

Methodically Kate worked through the long streamers of film. It was always miraculous to watch an image come up on a shiny white piece of paper. Some of the pictures of the media room were overexposed; in several the composition was ruined by shadow. But she had at least three that would make a worthy offering to Nancy McCall, along with four good ones of the children. The pictures of Annie and her sister were disappointing. The women looked washed-out in their pale dresses against the busy background of wall maps.

She almost threw away the five frames of herself without developing them, but then she thought she might be humored to see what Annie had wrought. Three images were so ill focused she hardly recognized herself. But in the last, she was faced with an image of herself moving forward, rows of books behind her creating the illusion of a tunnel, her face bent forward in a strobe of light, one shoulder in front of the other, a flicker of recognition on her face as if she were moving toward something she had been looking for, for a long time. Gazing upon the image was like looking at herself in a dream in which she knew where she was headed and who waited for her, and she wondered what the photograph would reveal to someone who didn't know her.

She felt dizzy and dug into her purse for a package of Nabs. Her camera seemed to know more than she did. It was a little frightening to consider what it might reveal next.

Chapter Seventeen

TACKER GAVE IN and called Kate. She made him feel alive and he wanted her. It was as simple as that. "Wonder if I could drop over tonight?"

He knocked rather than ringing the bell. In a moment, he could see Kate come into the hallway.

"Tacker?"

"Yes."

She wore a man's flannel shirt over slacks. Tacker had never thought about Kate wearing makeup but she must because her face was scrubbed clean and he saw the difference. She was still pretty but younger-looking, her face rounder than he had thought.

"I was reading," she said.

He followed her into the library. A book was turned over to keep the place. It looked like one of her mother's tourist books, but he didn't ask. He took a seat in one of the chairs and looked again at Kate's mother's portrait. Kate sat on the green sofa next to him. She looked small. Neither of them spoke.

"What about James?" he said when it was clear she was waiting on him.

"James is going to Sweden for some fellowship," she said.

"Some fellowship? I expect you know the name of it."

"Really I don't. It's a post-residency fellowship."

"How long?"

"A year."

"He asked you to go with him?"

"Yes."

"What did you tell him?"

"No."

Tacker liked her having to answer him. "Have you been writing to him?"

She looked at her hands. "I sent him a Christmas card."

Tacker thought about their drive up Pilot Mountain on the Indian. He would like to undress her. He would also like to walk out on her.

"You're mad at me," she said. "I knew you were."

"I don't like being jerked around."

Tacker stood and went to the mantel, his back to Kate. He was so close to the mother's portrait that the red skirt now appeared like a burning range of hills. He had a wild urge to touch the painted surface. Kate cleared her throat. Tacker turned around. She was tossing her hair up with her hand and the sleeve of the shirt fell open, exposing the pale underside of her arm. He wondered if she would wear an ankle bracelet. It was a nice thought. "What do you want from me?"

"That's an odd question," she said.

"No, it isn't," he said. "We've been spending time together. You invite me over for your brother's birthday. An old boyfriend shows up. What do you want, Kate?"

"I've missed you," she said.

Tacker looked into the hallway. "Yeah. Well, I've missed you too. And I don't want to keep missing you. Are you coming or going? Which is it?"

"I like being with you," she said.

"Tonight? Longer than tonight? I don't know, Kate. You're all over the place. With your parents and your dad and all that, I get it. I'm just not interested in being on call when you need me and dropped off when you don't."

"It's not like that," she said.

"Yes, it is," he said. Why was he saying these things? He should be kissing her.

Kate started crying. He felt unjustly persecuted. "Hey," he said finally, moving toward her, sitting back on his haunches in front of her. He ran his index finger down the pale flesh of her arm. Then he pulled her arm forward so her wrist was exposed and he made circles where her veins ran. "I guess your aunt Mildred wonders about the men you attract."

"She said James was arrogant," Kate said.

Tacker let that comment enjoy some room.

She wore a necklace at her throat and as he ran his hand over her arm, she held and twisted the small jewel. Tacker thought of all her hinged places. She was beautiful in the pale light and he had to keep his anger kindled to talk to her rather than pull her with him onto the rug. "I don't like being the last man available," he said.

"I'm just afraid. After learning about my dad," she said.

Her face suddenly looked very young, like tenth grade. She had secrets he didn't know. And the other way around. Tacker stretched his legs out in front of him and leaned back on his arms. He was aware that his feeling for the girl in front of him was intensified by James's prior claim. It wasn't something to be proud of.

"You're really good with people," she said. "I'm not."

Tacker considered her comment. It wasn't what he had dreamed of a girl saying. But her unshielded face was exactly what he imagined. He looked at her unsocked feet, her ankle, the arch of her foot implied in her flat shoes, the architecture of her Achilles tendon. He moved to circle her ankle with his thumb and middle finger. Immediately she went still. He stayed just so, feeling his heartbeat, registering her tension, imagining her head bent down looking at him.

"Please stay right here," he said.

"If that's what you want," she said.

Her ankle was firm and tender at once. He rubbed it, then stopped and just held it. "I really like you," he said. He pressed into the soft area between her ankle and the tendon.

"I'm glad," she said.

He let go of her foot, stood all at once, reached for her hands and pulled her up. Her head tilted back, and she looked up at him. He bent to her mouth, and she kissed him for a long time.

"I NEED SOME water," Kate said at last.

She held his hand and he followed her, barefoot, to the kitchen. She pulled the lever back on an ice tray, took one square of frozen water, picked up her hair, and wiped the back of her neck with it. Then she put the slip of ice into Tacker's mouth.

She reached into the refrigerator and brought out the Forelle pear and they stood next to the sink as she fed him lopsided half-moons of the fruit, sliced from the skin to the center, leaving only the core. Tacker left Kate's house enormously grateful for Sweden, which, with any luck, would swallow James whole.

TACKER'S MOTHER WANTED him to go with her to hear the Reverend Bobby Ransom at First Baptist on Sunday night. "Next month he's going on a world tour. He's going to Nigeria, that town where you were."

"Ibadan, Mom. It's a city. Where did you hear about this?" Tacker took the last bite of his mother's chicken potpie. "We're not Baptist." He wondered if she hoped to curb his political activity.

"There might be a chance to talk. You could tell him about the college there. Some of your friends might go see him."

"Mr. Ransom's not going to want to talk to me."

"Reverend Ransom. Well, I wish you would go with me," she said. "Your father won't."

So she wasn't trying to redirect his extracurricular activities. She just wanted company. "I've been wanting you to meet a girl," he said. "I'll bring her. Satisfied?"

Her eyes sparkled.

TACKER HELD KATE'S hand. His mother walked on his other side with her hand looped through his arm. The church was lit up like a ship. People streamed in from every direction.

"Goodness," Kate said.

Tacker had no idea this guy was so popular.

"I told you we should have left earlier," his mother said. "I hope there's a spot left in the balcony."

"We'll be fine," Tacker said.

THE ORGAN STARTED up and the space took on an amber glow. Tacker thought of First Baptist, Lagos, Samuel explaining: *Everything for constructing that church was sent here by boat after your civil war.* Would Bobby Ransom be preaching there? Maybe even staying in the hostel next door, the whites-only hostel? Independence still had not come. That would be October, eight months away. Tacker could imagine the pomp and circumstance of independence: flags unfurling, chiefs and traditional rulers in voluminous robes, grade school children bearing flowers, youths in sunglasses riding their bicycles in parades of their own making. He felt the nagging guilt he always felt when he remembered Samuel. He hadn't heard back from him yet.

The organist stopped. A man in the row behind them cleared his throat. Tacker looked at Kate's hands in her lap. Someone was playing the piano. Reverend Ransom was going to Nigeria. Samuel might indeed hear him. Suddenly Ransom mounted the steps to the pulpit. The piano music reached a crescendo. When the well-known preacher reached his seat behind the pulpit and turned to look out on the congregation, a huge smile across his face, Tacker was surprised at how tall and handsome he was. Ransom looked like Charlton Heston, with his jutting chin, tanned face, and enormous white teeth. The music minister lifted his arms and they stood to sing "All Hail the Power of Jesus' Name." Reverend Ransom seemed to grow taller. Tacker let his hand graze Kate's skirt. He felt as he did before a football game when someone sang "The Star-Spangled Banner." After the hymn and a prayer, they all sat, including Ransom, while the minister of First Baptist extended a welcome. Ransom strode to the pulpit.

Tacker heard the man's cadence more than the words, though certain passages seemed to fire the preacher up. "My friends, I am going out as Paul taught us . . . So many in darkness . . . childhood to old age . . . never hear of Jesus."

Reverend Ransom came to the end of his sermon. He was returning to his seat behind the pulpit when a man in the third row stood.

"Reverend Ransom, if I may."

The music minister stood for the last hymn but the man persevered.

"Reverend Ransom, surely you will allow me a question.

You're going to be gone several months. There are things here that press on us."

The movie star preacher moved back toward the pulpit. "Yes, go ahead," he said.

"Reverend Ransom. What should we do about the Negro problem? All this activity going on here; sit-ins and such. What do you think about it?"

"Well, that's a good question," Ransom said. "I've gone to God about it. After all, I'm getting ready to go to Africa. Folks may ask me about this very thing. We're hearing some demands from our colored brethren about rights. The right to sit at lunch counters. To gain employment in white-owned establishments. There's talk of desegregating public amusements. I respect Negro people for their desire to better their lives. But we have a special situation in this country. We have learned to get along in our separate communities. Negroes have created some fine colleges. Certainly colored folks have their own beautiful churches that preach the word of God. But in social situations, I don't condone integration, especially where young people are concerned. I see a lot of danger there." He paused as if he were waiting on God for an update. "I'll be praying with you about all of this on my travels. I'll carry it with me." Reverend Ransom lifted his head so that his gaze seemed to depart the church and aim straight at heaven.

"Thank you," the man in the third row said.

A collective sigh went up from the congregation. Tacker felt a chill at the back of his throat. His mother was turning to a page in the hymnal. He stood.

"If I may," Tacker said, projecting his voice from the balcony.

"Now, we can't keep the reverend here all night," the minister said.

"It's all right," Reverend Ransom said. "One of your fine young men here wants to say something."

Someone—was it Kate or his mother?—was tugging on the back of Tacker's jacket.

"I've been to Nigeria, sir, for a year and a half, on a building project. I was welcomed there like a brother. I've never known smarter, more industrious, or kinder people."

"What a witness," Reverend Ransom said. "I appreciate that word from you."

"My point, Reverend Ransom, is that Nigerians treated me as they treat one another, or better. I am not a Bible scholar as you are. But I do know the Bible tells us to love our neighbor as ourselves. Why doesn't that include Negroes? Why not show them the courtesy of sitting next to you at a lunch counter? Jesus ate with everyone. I remember that from Sunday school."

"My Lord," a lady to Tacker's left said.

Tacker's hands were shaking and he put them on the pew in front of him and held tight.

"Son," Reverend Ransom said, "there is a time for every season under heaven. But as a man who seeks to know the will of God in all things, I must tell you that what is good is also complex and getting there is more complex. The ultimate good is to lead people to salvation. I'm sure you can agree with me on that. God bless you."

As they bowed their heads for the prayer, Tacker kept his eyes open. Reverend Ransom was intoning the prayer, full of high-flown phrases. As the evangelist reached a high point, Tacker let go of the pew in front of him and looked at his palms, turning his hands over. He observed his skin and considered it as he never had before, not even in Nigeria. What did skin mean really? What was the difference?

Tacker's mother nudged him. He was still standing while those about him had sat down. The offering plates were passed, a love offering for Reverend Ransom. Tacker's mother put in a five-dollar bill. Then there was the call to join the church or rededicate your life and half the church went forward. Fortunately Kate did not.

On the way down the balcony stairs, Tacker took Kate's hand. He hadn't looked at her or she at him. Tacker's mother made a point to speak with several people she knew.

"I didn't know you felt so strongly about the sit-ins," Kate said when he dropped her off at her house.

"You do know that Wake Forest students went to one of those sit-ins, right?"

"It could be dangerous," she said.

"Don't you want a man to stand up for what he believes?"

"Yes," she said. "I just don't want to lose what we have."

"What do you think we'll lose?"

"A lot of people are angry, Tacker. They might not come to your store. People are angry enough to cause damage."

"I went to the sit-in the day those students were arrested. The officer let me off. Another time and he might not. I think I know what I'm dealing with."

"Why didn't you tell me?"

"I thought you might not be ready to think about it."

"What if I'm not?"

TACKER WOKE AT two in the morning, the room seeming to tilt sideways. The "social situations" to which Reverend Ransom referred would include swimming pools, of course. He felt certain that swimming pools would be the worst place to integrate according to the preacher and most of the good white folks of Winston-Salem. He recalled Vaughan-Richards's plan for his house on the Lagos lagoon, the jutting veranda attached to circular rooms, the cornerstone of the Nigerian high school, goats in the field, Samuel's face with its three lines on each cheek. The plans they drew on the large tables in the classroom block, the pink and blue pencils they purchased at UTC in downtown Ibadan, the Ponies he and Samuel rode to get there, the clatter of rain in a sudden storm. He saw himself with his mother in the library checking out books, pictures of the Roman aqueducts they studied together, his Schwinn New World, the windmill they constructed in the garden. The classrooms in college. Long blackboards, scrolls of paper like a highway, working late into the night on his senior design: a solarium for the new NC State arboretum. The design got him hired by Clintok. And then there was Kate. Tacker searched for his headboard to bring the world back to order. He couldn't find it. He'd fallen out of bed.

It was five o'clock. He showered. In his living room, he pulled out the Vaughan-Richards–inspired sketch he'd done and almost tore it in two. Then he thought better of it and slipped it into an envelope and stuck it in a book. He needed to get on with an architectural firm, do some renderings like he'd meant to do earlier. Now was the time. He got out the Yellow Pages and made a list and then he wrote five identical letters:

Dear Sirs,

Allow me to introduce myself. I finished the five-year degree in architecture, School of Design, State College, in 1957. Among other honors, I was selected by the Clintok Corporation for a project in Nigeria, serving in the capacity of a graduate teaching assistant to produce a prototype for high schools to be built all across the country. For family reasons, I am currently employed as manager of my father's store, Hart's

Grocery, on First Street. My intention is to seek
licensure as soon as I can, and to that end I would
welcome an opportunity to work with your firm
producing renderings on a part-time basis. Please see
my résumé attached and let me know if it would be
suitable for me to call your office for an appointment.
If you contact my references, I believe you'll learn
that I'm good with a pencil. Being a Winston-Salem
native, nothing would please me more than to be
working as an architect in this city.

Cordially,

The letter was true if the truth was slightly bent; his languor following his "release" by Clintok was the reason he was working at his father's store. He just had to hope no one would feel a need to dig too deep into those lost months.

At lunchtime he took the Indian to the post office and dropped the letters off.

Chapter Eighteen

THE SECOND WEEK of March, Kate heard the mailman on her front porch and when she opened the mailbox, two envelopes gleamed within like slender gloves full of fireflies. She pulled them out to discover the most beautiful Swedish stamps. Kate steeled herself, thinking of her last time with James, his anger, her initial willingness, his aggression. She felt bound to him yet filled with dread. Inside, she placed the unopened envelopes on her mother's dressing table. What might they offer, or not offer? Whatever secret they held, they would not redirect her course since she was not moving to Sweden. She was in Winston-Salem and she must find her way here. Furthermore, she wasn't about to abandon Brian. Tonight she had a date with Tacker.

Out of nowhere, Kate wondered if her mother had had a fling after her father died. Because of her inheritance, she had not had to work even when she was widowed. She had stayed at home all those years while her children were in school. Their mother could have seen someone. In this very bedroom. The phone rang in the hallway and she picked it up before the third ring. It was Tacker.

"I may be a few minutes late," he said. "We were really busy this afternoon."

"All right," she said.

"Where do you want to go?"

"Why don't we just fix hot dogs here," she said, feeling the need of sturdy walls around her. She stretched the phone cord so it reached into her mother's room, opened the dressing table drawer, and slid the letters in among white and flowered handkerchiefs.

"Can I bring anything?"

"Nope."

In the backyard, the crocuses were coming up, the purple before the yellow. She walked up and down the flagstones in the diminishing light. Finally it was too chilly. She plucked a single purple crocus. It seemed to shiver as she plucked it and she took it immediately to her nose to smell the life of it, smelling not the blossom but the broken base, where it was wet and open from the breakage. It smelled of green water and deep pools of rock beneath water. She went into the kitchen, selecting a slender clear vase with a small mouth, filled it with water, and slipped the crocus into it. And now she inhaled the blossom's scent, but it was not nearly so urgent as the broken stem. Kate turned on the oven, got out the buns and hot dogs, decided on Boston baked beans, and pulled open a bag of potato chips. Part of her was still on the flagstones, among the trees and the green cold world of rocks under cascades of water.

She looked up and Tacker was at the threshold of the kitchen door. "You left your front door open," he said. "Anyone could come in. It's dark outside."

"Oh," she said. She had forgotten because of James's letters.

"Hey. I didn't mean to scold," Tacker said. "Just looking out for you."

What was on her face?

They fixed supper and she saw Tacker there in his wholeness, his rough blond hair rushed up like it used to be, his face just a bit off-kilter. His hands on his hips, his beautiful fingers that had circled her ankle and held her face, the fingers of a man who could build things, but also draw a finger decidedly down the center of the book to hold it open.

AFTER DINNER, THEY sat in the library on the sofa. Tacker seemed happier than she had seen him all winter, talking of Gaines and the sit-ins and students getting arrested. It might take all spring, into summer, before something changed at the Woolworth's or any other lunch counter.

This was why Tacker was so complete in himself when he came into the kitchen as though spurred by some divine force. It was all about Gaines, how he had learned civil disobedience at Fisk, how Reverend King had written a book teaching people about nonviolence. She thought of the white patrons of Main Library. Well, what could she do? She was trying to find her own ground. "This is all rather sudden for me. You know I've had a lot of changes all on my own, without a whole national movement to think about," she said.

"I get it," Tacker said. "I'm just telling you about something I find important. I want to share it with you."

Her mind shifted to James's letters glowing in her mother's dressing table drawer, breathing their own life. She pounced to smother the thought of them.

"There must be a law or something," she said. "Or why did those students get arrested?" She was more flippant than she might have been if she hadn't been so confused by Tacker's exhilaration. He was different than he had been when she first saw him back in the fall.

She stood and moved to the bookcase, running her fingers along the book spines. "What if you did get arrested?" she said, shifting to look at him, imagining the cost of such a turn to her own well-being if Mrs. McCall found out or other family friends who expected social niceties from her.

"Everyone here who got arrested was out by afternoon. No one got kicked out of college. It's brilliant. Peaceful protests can get so many people arrested it breaks the system."

Kate had heard about the sit-ins, first in Greensboro and then in Winston, but only vaguely. Tacker knew much more. For once she was understudied on a subject. She was not as good a person as she had been in high school and college, when she had been fully aware of the armistice that ended the Korean War and had followed Eisenhower versus Stevenson; even the Little Rock Nine, integrating that high school. She had admired those Negro students. Education was important. But she didn't know lunch counter sit-ins. Right this minute, she didn't want to know them. She felt like a bird in a hot attic, a small bird, brittle boned. "I thought there were lunch counters in town where Negroes could get a sandwich," she said, aware again and again and again of how different her life would be if she had her father, who would have thought all these things out with her. Instead she had had to endure that loss and then her mother's death, and how could Tacker not see that as apparently privileged as she was, she was a captain of a ship without a crew?

"Those are counters where everyone stands up," Tacker said. "Sitting is about dignity."

"It's about Gaines," she said, taking a step sideways. She liked the library of books behind her.

"What do you mean?" Tacker said.

"You're letting him take advantage of you. Mr. Fitzgerald told me Gaines has been to college. He's probably smarter than most of them. But he's not from around here."

"What do you mean he's smarter than most?" Tacker said.

"I mean he's smart."

"But you said 'smarter than most of them.'"

"I just meant he'd been to college."

"It didn't sound that way. Gaines's family is from around here even if he grew up in Pennsylvania. His aunt took care of me when I was growing up. She was our maid."

Tacker held his hands up as he made his point.

"But don't you see? You're asking something of me that I'm not prepared for. You didn't tell me." She felt her voice getting shrill and she hated herself.

"My dad put in a separate toilet for her off of our carport," Tacker said, looking at his open palms. "She still uses it. It's freezing out there in the winter." He looked pained and she wished she had it in her to soothe him.

But Kate had never questioned the half baths on all of her friend's carports and back porches that existed for the very same reason. Tacker was making her think of things she didn't want to consider. The net was tighter, her bones even more brittle. For some reason, she was immensely aware of her breasts, pin-pricks of desire and fear mixed together.

"Can we talk about something else?" she said, running a hand down her arm.

He looked up, impassive, from the sofa. "No," he said. "Not yet."

What exactly was he feeling? She believed she knew Tacker but his eyes seemed closed to her now and she wanted to hit him. He wasn't being sensitive to her needs. It dawned on her that in her fantasy, Tacker was going to make a professional move. He was going to buy a car and get a new suit and some beautiful wing-tip shoes. Before long he was going to be a junior partner in a firm. He was going to build things. Of course his designs would be different and brilliant, modern and sleek. That's what would make him so perfect.

"I can't believe you care so much about these sit-ins," she said. She marched out of the room. In the kitchen she picked up the supper plates and ran water and rattled the silverware.

"I'm worried for you. If you get mixed up in that stuff, you're going to get hurt," she threw back at him.

Tacker laughed.

"I don't see what exactly all of this has got to do with you," she said. "I think you should give it up."

"Of course it's about me. It's about all of us. And I won't give it up." In her peripheral vision, she saw him coming through the dining room. His voice told her he was feeling loose now. He had made his point. He had won. He was in charge.

"What if there were places you couldn't go into?" he said.

She glanced at his form in the doorway, his hands on the doorframe as he leaned in, his body perfectly calm and whole and magnificent. "There probably are," she said, viciously washing the pot that had held nothing but water for boiling hot dogs.

"Like where?"

"I don't know. Okay. Like a strip joint." She pressed her hair back and looked at him hard. If only she could talk about what was really bothering her. She hadn't even had a chance to tell him about the *Journal* paying for her photograph and inviting more.

"Honestly, Kate. You don't want to go to a strip joint," Tacker said, smiling.

"How do you know? I might want to take pictures. It might be exactly what I want to do, to learn something about men," she said. The net was so tight she was going to be strangled.

"A girl like you could go into a strip joint," Tacker said, sobering. "But a Negro woman couldn't, except to clean up the mess early in the morning after everyone left."

"How do you know? Have you ever been to one?"

"Yes," he said. "Once."

The lid to the pot was in her hand and then she was slinging it at the doorway where Tacker stood. It clattered off the wall. Kate was mortified. She could hardly breathe.

"I don't want to hear any more about sit-ins or any of this," she said.

"I'm sorry you feel that way," Tacker said, running his hands through his hair. "I thought you would understand." He was in the hallway, pulling on his jacket.

"What are you doing?" She followed him. "I'm sorry I lost my temper. I just don't see the need for everyone to congregate together. We're so different. They have their colleges, their own churches. They like it that way."

"Of course they do," Tacker said. He stood at the door now, one hand on the doorknob, the other on his hip. "They like their churches because they can tell the truth there. The lunch counter at Woolworth's should be integrated. And people should be free to walk on the sidewalks however they like."

"I never said they shouldn't."

Tacker cracked his knuckles. "I've got to go," he said.

He opened the door, checked to be sure it would lock, and closed it behind him. She heard him cross the porch. And then the Indian started up and she listened until the sound faded.

———

"WHAT IF WE stop at the drugstore for coffee and a doughnut?" she said when Mr. Fitzgerald picked her up from the library on a cold, rainy afternoon. "My treat."

It was an old store, narrow, smelling of sugar candies and dust and coffee and with a beautiful punched-tin ceiling. Kate ordered two doughnuts and two coffees, with cream and sugar for Mr. Fitzgerald. As she turned to fold her coat over the back of the chair, she saw two silhouettes at the window. She knew they were colored boys because of their hair, because of the way they held themselves. Traveling to South Carolina one summer when she was seven and it was a thousand degrees in the car, her family stopped at a motel outside Spartanburg. It had a blue swimming pool not much bigger than Kate's front porch, but it was water, and she and Brian ran for that pool as if it were the fountain of life. Her parents got in too. A fist of black children stood at the encompassing fence and watched them and that was just how the world was. Kate's chin tilted toward her coffee. She breathed on the dark liquid to cool it. She'd first learned to drink coffee at Agnes Scott, staying up with Janet to study for exams. Every once in a while Janet would intone the Latin phrase *Miserere mei, Deus*. Have mercy on me, God. In the mirror behind the soda fountain, Kate saw her reflection.

"What do you think about the sit-ins, Mr. Fitzgerald?"

"Oh, I don't know that we should get into that."

"Why not?"

"Kate, you're a bold young woman. I expect you will find your opinions evolving. In my day, we were debating how many Jews could be admitted to UNC."

"Not really."

"Oh yes. There was the case of this one boy who met all the requirements but accepting him would break the ten percent rule."

"The ten percent rule?"

"No more than ten percent of the student body could be Jewish."

Kate felt a tug at her sleeve. It was one of the Negro boys who had been looking through the glass of the window.

"You the lady that works at the library?"

"I'm one of them," she said.

"You go in on Saturday?"

"I do."

"I've seen you," he said. "I was with my brother. He shines shoes on Saturday."

"I see. Well, what can I do for you?" The other boy was still outside.

"Would you like for me to buy you a doughnut to take with you?" Mr. Fitzgerald chimed in.

"No, sir, but thank you. My name is Arthur." He looked back at Kate. "You have a nice car. I was wondering. Could you bring out a book for me to read?"

Suddenly an older Negro girl entered the store.

"Arthur, come here. Don't you bother that nice woman."

Kate looked at the boy, his eyes burning into her. "Please," he said, as he swung around and followed the girl out of the drugstore.

At home Kate could find no comfort. Desperate, she opened James's letters. In his first he apologized for his "passion." But didn't she know that he was "crazy for her"? From there he went on writing about his days and the weather and the beautiful streets with very small cars. In the second letter, he asked if she would consider a visit in the summer. Now she must ponder how to answer, though the idea of being with him in a country he had come to know and where she was a complete stranger did not sound safe or inviting. She would be happy to lend the Negro boy some of her own girlhood books. But how would she ever find him? And couldn't someone take him to the East

Winston branch in the Negro part of town to get books? As she was falling asleep, she thought for some reason of the picture Annie had taken of her in the library. Perhaps it was not a man she was waiting for but her own self. In the night, she woke with the troubling awareness that, of course, any boy would prefer to go to Main Library to get all the books he wanted forever.

Chapter Nineteen

FOR SEVERAL NIGHTS in a row, Tacker tossed and turned, waking to remember Kate's clean girl face, her stubborn resistance, the impossibility of her claim and Gaines's claim and his own heart like a wheel running on two tracks. Finally a letter arrived from Samuel. He'd gotten the ten dollars and wrote expansively about Tacker's generosity. He went on to say that a missionary doctor at a nearby Baptist Hospital had donated a wheelchair to his brother, who now had a shop on one of the main throughways of an Ibadan market. The brother was making lots of money selling radios from Japan and Kodak film and English tea towels. Samuel went on to account for Joshua's treachery.

> Joshua has been following a charlatan preacher in
> Ibadan. The preacher lectures against all of our
> traditional ways and promises abundant financial
> well-being to those who join his church and follow his

teachings. He has made Joshua one of his deacons. Joshua is not a stable man. He will follow whoever makes him promises. A man so unsure of himself will try to bring other men down. I hope it does not trouble you so much. Do you think you might travel back to Nigeria? I will be very happy if you can come.

In another paragraph he reported on the high school. *The building is a great success, all of the students in their uniforms. We have running water and electric. I will take pictures and send them to you.*

In closing, Samuel reported that Chukwu had gone to England to study architecture and that everyone expected him to come back and be a professor at UCI. Tacker felt a burst of pleasure, thinking of Chukwu and of Samuel and the mere suggestion that he might go back.

That night he slept dreamlessly.

Way too early, someone knocked on his back door. It was a Negro fellow he didn't know holding a used envelope. Composed on the back in longhand: *Death in the family, Gaines.* Must be Old Daddy. Tacker had time to ride over, give Frances a hug, offer to send a ham, and still get back to open the store. The Indian gave a kick starting up, like a hound ready to leap. At Frances's house, Tacker bounded up the stairs, knocked twice, and let himself in. The front room smelled heavily of cloves. Several elderly ladies sat on the couch, their legs tidily resting beneath their skirts, their pocketbooks in their laps. They bobbed their heads briefly at Tacker, who started down the hall to the kitchen. Gaines sat at the table with Valentine, and some woman Tacker had never seen before was fixing their breakfast.

"I got here as soon as I could," Tacker said.

Gaines half stood and then sat back down. "Man. I can't believe it. I just can't believe it. My mom, you know. That I could believe. But not Aunt Frances."

"What about your aunt?" Tacker said. A cold hand seemed to cup his skull.

"Left my mom's house early this morning, dropped Valentine by here. Aunt Frances always makes breakfast. Ran an errand. When I got back she wasn't in the kitchen and Valentine was sitting in here all by herself sucking her thumb."

"I was not sucking my thumb," Valentine said.

Gaines picked up his coffee but his hand shook and he set the cup down on the tablecloth. "I figured Aunt Frances had overslept. Knocked before I went into her room. She was still in bed. I'd never seen her in bed in my whole life. Went over to rouse her, you know. Called her name. Then I sort of shook her. Man. She was just gone. Gone. Maybe a heart attack. I never knew her to be sick a day in my life. Now Old Daddy is in his bed and I don't know if we'll ever rouse him."

As Gaines talked, the woman cooking breakfast started to hum.

This isn't right, Tacker thought. *I'm in a dream and in a minute I'll wake up and have to run to the grocery.* But then Valentine looked straight into his eyes, none of that looking sideways most Negroes have learned by the time they're eight.

"You take your motorcycle and ride real fast and you might catch up with my aunt," she said. "She's lying in her bed but she's not really there. She's flying but still low to the ground. You could catch her feet and pull her back."

The woman turning the bacon hummed louder.

Tacker turned to the wall and crossed his arms, leaning his head there. A cry came up from his center. In a moment, he felt Valentine against him. "You can have my chair," she said and tugged at him until he followed her instructions. Tacker had forgotten his handkerchief and Valentine handed him her napkin. On the other side of the table Gaines leaned back in his chair, his head tilted forward.

"I guess she took care of you just about as much as anyone in this world," he said, but he didn't sound happy about it.

TACKER DROVE HIS parents to the funeral at Rising Ebenezer Baptist in Happy Hill. He wanted somehow to make amends, for the outdoor bathroom, for calling an elder "Frances," for never considering—until Gaines made him aware—that she could not rest at a table and order a sandwich in Winston-Salem's downtown. Rising Ebenezer was as brown as First Baptist was white. Gloved ushers shepherded folks through the main entrance and side doors. From the vestibule looking into the sanctuary, Tacker could make out Gaines's head, way up front. An elderly man with a rose on his lapel—perhaps a deacon—found them some seats.

Tacker sat between his parents. His mother clenched a handkerchief in her lap. When Tacker had called from the grocery to tell her Frances was dead, she had said, "It can't be," and handed the phone to his father. "Fifty-four years old," his father had said. "That's mighty young. I thought that woman was solid as a rock."

For the first time, Tacker knew her age.

Then he remembered how she was that day he drove her home before Thanksgiving, taking her time on the stairs, letting him help her. She was already weak.

There were lilies everywhere, infusing the air with a violently sweet aroma. Standing room only. Tacker wondered how many people would come to his own funeral. The service began with a prayer that competed with a Nigerian one for length.

People called out, back and forth with the preacher. The choir swayed as it sang. Tacker thought about what he would say to Valentine and Gaines when he saw them after the service. He conjured Kate and his desire for her outstripped his body and he knew he would forgive her anything—thrown pot lids, conventional wisdom, her likely two-timing him—if she would turn in his direction. He put his arm around his mother's shoulders. The minister began the eulogy. Like the prayer, it went on a good long time. Tacker learned that Frances had graduated from high school with honors. Her favorite subject was science and she had wanted to be a nurse. But "our plans are not God's plans," the preacher said, "and instead Mrs. Douglass gave her life to her community in different ways." She had been a regular volunteer for a program to feed the housebound and she was an officer in the Winston-Salem Chapter of the Links, a Negro women's organization committed to youth education. Tacker had never heard any of this.

At the end of the eulogy, Tacker realized that the Frances he knew was not spoken of at all. Nothing in the service alluded to her working for his parents. Mrs. Douglass had been another person altogether. He felt full of straw and remembered a fragment of verse: *for now we see through a glass, darkly.* The preacher took his seat. Two boys lit candles surrounding the casket.

The viewing began. The line was long and the wait was longer. Finally Tacker and his parents were there, in front of Frances, a woman they had never seen recline in a comfortable chair. Her face was tranquil, her skin smooth, palely glowing in the candlelight. She was dressed in a pink suit with a blue blouse, her hands folded at her waist. Arranged at her elbow was a black pocketbook with a silver snap clasp. Except for her hands, which looked swollen in their white gloves, she seemed perfectly natural, and Tacker bent toward her—because he had to say something. But he could not find the words. A stream of tears started down his face.

Before they got back to their seats, a woman from the choir stood and began to sing "I'll Fly Away," softly at first, so softly, she seemed at moments to go into a trance. And then, as from the bottom of a well, her voice came back and grew stronger. She stretched her arms out and held a note like she was waiting for God. She must have seen him, because she shook her arms and began to turn counterclockwise. A second time around and the congregation began to shout. She sang, a cry of desperation, a plea for mercy. A deep hum rose from the choir. The woman shifted into a minor key.

Some bright morning when this life is over
I'll fly away

Tacker was in Nigeria. It wasn't the lyrics but the minor key and the particular dance that transported him, the dancer turning with exquisite precision in a small circle of earth, head bowed, until she gained momentum and threw her head back, and her mouth opened with a click and her voice erupted in exuberant sadness. Tacker wasn't sure then and he wasn't sure now if he believed in God. He believed in the woman.

Eight pallbearers processed down the center aisle. The casket was closed, and a sharp cry pierced the air. For a few moments there was only the sigh of benches, the wither of fans. Until someone called *Praise God Almighty* and an answering flood of *Amen*s resounded.

The service was over. Tacker searched for Frances's family. But Gaines and Valentine and Old Daddy were already in the black limo by the time he and his parents got downstairs and out the big front doors. A familiar gray veil filled Tacker's consciousness and clung to his shoulders. He was the outsider. Outside in Nigeria, outside in Winston, outside of Gaines's circle.

If he had not said good-bye to Frances yet, it was too late. She was gone. Her black tie-up shoes were gone, her turquoise pocketbook against her black coat, her capable hands with the feather duster that had once held his hand as he crossed the street. Gone. Also gone was her corn bread, her banana pudding, her fig preserves. Her ginger smell was gone. Her lean arms as she held the white sheets to hang on the line in the backyard. They were gone. Her frankness was gone. He remembered when he had told her he was going to Nigeria, almost three years ago now. She was ironing but she had set the iron down and patted her cheek. She half laughed. "I always wanted to go to Africa." Tacker had had no answer for her and she had picked the iron back up and kept pressing.

Osogbo, Nigeria

1959

Chapter Twenty

TACKER MET ANNA Becker during that early-March week in '59. His team was in Osogbo, where, at the tail end of their stay, Fray would show himself, flipping up the curtain into the room where Tacker had been sleeping. They had finished the foundational wall of the high school. Now they were staying the weekend because Saturday happened to be a festival day for the Osun River. This wasn't the largest of the yearly festivals but it coincided with the beginning of the rains. So it was a transitional moment, like fall festivals in North Carolina. Hundreds, maybe thousands, of seekers in white, men, women, and children, would come to pay respects and ask Osun for everything from babies to bountiful harvests to money.

Friday morning, Tacker's mates went into town to pick up fixings for the evening meal. Tacker chose to stay by the river. The day before, Joshua had made a joke about Tacker's whiteness. "Your friend's face does not show in the mirror. I think he is a ghost," he had said. "Ah," Samuel had replied, "when you approach the mirror it cracks because it cannot hold your stomach." The interaction was typical Yoruba ribbing. But Tacker felt chilled, as if he were clinging to the glassy edge of a world he could see into but never fully enter. He felt almost homesick.

So he was alone when he saw a white woman with short blond hair on the other side of the river, passing among the newly greened trees. She wore a white dress with a broad belt and moved as if she were in her natural place. Then she was gone, like smoke, and Tacker thought he had imagined her. He waited for her to show up again. But she didn't return. Still, his mood had improved. He forgot how foreign he had felt just an hour earlier.

He walked back to the chalet and there she was, the girl with the cropped blond hair, as short as a boy's, only now she was also wearing a broad-brimmed woven hat. The dress was cut up at the sides to give her freedom to walk, and her legs were brown and strong. Her arms were completely bare except for multiple silver bangles. She rested one hand on each hip, her fingers long but her hands as worn as a farmer's. She wore native sandals, her feet daintier than her hands.

The woman's beauty was new to him: her figure slender yet round, a beautiful boy face with piercing brown eyes, high cheekbones, full, broad lips, and a regal nose that lifted just at the end, sending her beauty slightly in the direction of playfulness. But the perfection of these parts was not her beauty. Her beauty was her self-possession, as with the Yoruba.

"*Ek aaro,*" she said. It meant good morning.

Tacker had been in the country eighteen months and not once heard a white person begin with a Yoruba greeting. His own Yoruba was far less musical than hers and he was embarrassed to try it, especially with this girl-woman who looked like Peter Pan.

"Good morning," he said.

"So I'll talk with you in English, then," she said. "I'm Anna Becker. Where are your friends?"

Her voice was now distinctly European, as if a radio channel had been changed.

"Tacker Hart," he said. "They went into town to shop for dinner."

"And you could not pull yourself away from Osun, Mr. Hart?" she said. She smiled as she said "Osun," as if she were referring to a lover.

"It reminds me a little of home," he said. "Well, not really. It's not anything like the Yadkin River in North Carolina except that it's brown. I learned to drink coffee sitting in a duck blind with my father."

"A duck blind? In America?" she said.

"A shelter for hunters waiting for ducks. To shoot."

"That's too bad," she said.

"Samuel and the other guys will be back soon." He had said too much of the wrong thing already.

"I suspect not soon," Anna said. "They'll take their time."

Tacker felt his arms dangle awkwardly. "Is there something I can help you with?"

"Not really. Only give them my greetings."

She turned to go and then called over her shoulder.

"Would you like to come to my house for tea?"

ANNA BECKER'S HOUSE was a house proper, not a hut or a chalet, up on a hill with a view of the river, built of mud but nicely plastered, roofed with rich thatch overhanging the veranda to create a broad, deep shade. She led him up the steps and into the front room. A Nigerian woman sat next to a window braiding a girl's hair. Two other children sat on a low settee, watching and waiting their turn. They were unperturbed by Tacker's presence.

"Wetin?" one said.

"A new friend," Anna said.

She made tea and served it in small pottery cups.

"What brings you here?" she said.

"I'm with an American organization, stationed in Ibadan, at the university. We're building a secondary school. You probably already know about it since you know my friends. What about you?"

"I didn't know about the American link." She brushed her hair back. "I came with my husband from Germany," she said, laughing. "The husband didn't last. Oh, he's still here, teaching at UCI. Once I found the river and the sacred forest of Osun, I had to live in Osogbo."

A thousand questions came to Tacker: *Who supports you? You live here alone? What do you do all day?*

"I've become a devotee," she said.

"Of what?" he said.

"Everything. The river, the forest, Yoruba life."

The children were switching places. One's hair finished, another's begun. The one whose hair was complete came over to Anna to have it inspected. Anna spoke to her in Yoruba, cradling the child's head in her lap, stroking her neck. Then she must have given her some instruction because the child lifted herself and marched off importantly.

"Whose children?" Tacker said.

"Mine. I adopted them," Anna said. "If you're finished with your tea, I'll show you my work."

Her work was outside, along the riverbank and in the forest, upstream from the chalet where he was staying with his friends. Enormous sculptures in mud and plaster, arched and winding, portions of wall marked by animal shapes, freestanding stone forms—part human, part abstraction—clustered on green hillocks. Squat sculptures of women with children. Wood reliefs filled with drummers. Tacker didn't know much about art, but it looked modernist to him. Like Picasso except the dimensions had been opened up and made life-size, so he was in the art, not viewing it in a museum. They passed through an archway, the crown resembling two abstracted heads joined in a posture of love. Anna ran her hand along the smooth pier, the base resembling tree roots so that the arch appeared to rise out of the ground. Some of the sculptures seemed like gigantic replicas of the body's interior. They passed into a mud-and-plaster tunnel, the walls swirled like a metal coupler, and came out at an eddy in the river. Tacker wondered if he had just walked through the birth canal.

"Amazing," he said.

"You like it?" Anna said.

"*Like* may not be the word. It's sort of unreal."

"What do you mean?"

"Oh. American slang for exceptional."

"Excellent," Anna said, clapping her hands. "Most Americans don't like it."

"Why is that?"

"Oh, they're mostly missionaries. They don't like our revival of Yoruba traditional religion."

"So that's what your sculpture is about?"

"The mystical dimension exists everywhere, don't you think? But I must go see to the evening meal."

"Oh. Sure. I didn't mean to hold you up."

"Not at all. Perhaps I will see you on Saturday."

BY THE TIME Tacker got back to the house, the VW van was parked under the mango trees. At the outdoor kitchen, he found his friends unpacking their goods. They hadn't purchased meat and vegetables as Tacker had imagined they would. Instead they had brought with them a woman and her enormous earthenware pot, in which apparently resided a stew she had begun to cook early that morning so that by now the flavors were, in Samuel's words, "well developed." She sat on a stone near an open fire, occasionally checking the contents and grinding pepper on another stone.

"What's in there?" Tacker said.

"Na monkey," Joshua said. "Proper proper."

"Comot!" Tacker said. He'd finally learned to spar with Joshua in pidgin English.

"Ignore him. Only chicken," Samuel said.

"That sounds better. Got a minute?"

"Of course."

They walked to the front of the house, to the van under the mangos. Tacker leaned against the driver's door. "I just met Anna Becker."

"Ah. I was going to surprise you," Samuel said.

"What do you mean?"

"By introducing you to her. She is a very unusual *oyinbo*, no?" Samuel said.

"I'll say."

"I think you may like to settle down next to Osun yourself. Ha! I can see I am right."

ON SATURDAY A steady stream of people, all dressed in white, paraded past the chalet on their way to the river, most on foot, a few on bicycles, a man riding a bike with a woman perched on the crossbar. Tacker didn't catch sight of Anna all day. On Sunday he went looking for her. She was working on a painting in an open building not far from her house, wearing a sleeveless, diagonally striped dress, with the same belt as before. It appeared that the entire canvas would be shades of blue.

"So. Mr. Tacker Hart. It's an unusual name. You are back."

"We're leaving tomorrow."

"Back to UCI to complete your design."

"I'll be in Nigeria four more months."

"You must return to visit Osun." Her dark eyes sparkled as she spoke.

"We probably will."

"Let me give you something to take with you," she said.

She turned aside, opened a large cabinet, picked things up, and discarded them. At last, clutching brush and bottle, she closed the cabinet, selected a bowl, and dipped it into a water barrel.

"Come," she said.

Tacker followed her out into the brown yard.

"Have a seat," she said, pointing to a large log clearly employed as outdoor seating.

Tacker half expected her to say *close your eyes* and then she was going to put a frog or maybe a snake in his palm. Instead she readied herself to paint.

"You don't have a canvas," he said.

"I will paint your palms. It's my gift to you."

"No. You're kidding."

She gazed at him with a firm clarity.

"How about my arm?" he said.

"Whatever you like," she said.

One of the children sauntered down. "Mah," she said. "My stomach is light."

Was she speaking English for his benefit?

Anna kissed the child's forehead. "You may have biscuit. Share with your sister. You understand?"

"Yes, mah." The girl was already skipping off.

Anna squatted beside him. "Hold the inkpot," she said.

"Wait," Tacker said. "Will this stuff come off?"

"It's henna. In a few days."

She had already begun the first stroke down the interior of his arm, the brush on his flesh an exquisite torture. A slight tickle, the sensation rode up his arm, into his chest, up to his brain, cupping his skull like a vise of feathers, then descended his backbone, filled his abdomen, slipped down around his backside, and rose into his groin.

When she finished, she did not say good-bye in Yoruba or English. She rose and walked away and was lost in the forest. Tacker sat for an hour, looking at his arm and out at the trees, listening to the river. Finally he went back to the chalet.

"Ah, brother!" Samuel said. "I thought you were lost."

"I went to visit Anna," Tacker said. He showed Samuel his arm and Samuel sucked on his teeth.

"Ahh," he said.

"I thought you liked her. What's wrong?"

"Only." He paused. "Someone may misunderstand."

"I hope your thing does not fall off," Joshua declared from across the room. "Let me see it." The other men in the room laughed uproariously. When the glee had subsided, Joshua made his pronouncement. "Ah. It's very bad. A witch. You can see here."

He showed Tacker the form.

"It looks more like a praying mantis," Tacker said.

His mates prepared dinner. Tacker looked out the window. He wished he had had his photograph made with Anna. As she bent over him in her work, he could see the cleavage of her breasts but it was her rough hands that cast a spell on him.

Winston-Salem,
North Carolina

....

1960

Chapter Twenty-one

◠◠ MID-MARCH BROUGHT SLEET. "Must be nice staying home all day," Tacker mumbled as he fed the cat. There was no way he could get in a run that morning. "At least Pops is okay, right?" He scratched da Vinci's neck and put on the coffeepot. His father's tests had come back negative, but things with Kate had chilled to a standstill, making the cold days even colder. Tacker was handing over two boxes of groceries to Gaines every week, some of the donation, such as canned spaghetti and tuna fish, coming out of his paycheck, but perishables, like bread and fruit, would have been thrown away, so they cost nothing. The groceries were for full-time activists Tacker had never met and likely would not. He didn't feel especially noble about it. Just the opposite. He wished he could be more openly involved. Negro students were still showing up where they weren't welcome regardless of the weather and in spite of Winston's mayor, who had appointed a committee of Negroes and whites to study the issue, hoping to avoid the negative press that Greensboro was drawing. Tacker had been to another sit-in, this time at Kress. Nothing much happened. But he was aware of how slowly time moved when he was being served nothing but dirty looks, and he left with a muddy pool of emotion in his gut. Without Kate to lift his heart, he couldn't tell that he had made much real progress since coming home. He was still in limbo.

In the icy morning, Tacker set out on foot rather than taking the Indian, wearing the letter jacket, a thick knit cap, gloves, and his old boots. He had loafers at the store to change into. He did enjoy walking in the silence, the only sound the crunch of his boots. This was as close to prayer as Tacker got.

No sign of traffic until he got to the red light on First, and even then all he saw were a couple of cars on Hawthorne Street. Maybe a lane had been cleared. No one would be in for hours. Coming into the parking lot, he glanced up at the entrance. The glass door was iced up and something—a box?—was pressed against it. A delivery? Tacker looked at the sky. A solid blue-gray. He fumbled with the key and it fell into the sleet. As he retrieved it, nearer the entrance, his vision corrected itself. The glass door was shattered. What he had mistaken for a box was a message. Crudely lettered. Black ink. On a neatly cut rectangle of plywood.

WE DON'T WANT NO INTEGRATION
SEND THESE NIGGERS BACK TO AFRICA

Tacker stared at the message until the silence was broken by a faint sigh followed by a crack. He wheeled around. A large pine limb lay fallen in the parking lot. Tacker turned back to the door, observed the entrance, no footprints but his own, damage perpetrated before the sleet. He walked back to the street, looked both ways. No one anywhere. His knees felt weak as he retraced his steps. The cold key slipped easily into the lock. Broken glass inside. No rock. A baseball bat? Or a stone swaddled in a sheet, slung against the door. Some means more personal than a rock thrown from a distance. Up close. To leave the sign, too.

Tacker was glad for his boots, but still he tried to avoid the glass. He took off his coat to test the air. Not too cold. *Back out. Close the door. Lock it. Go around to the back entrance. Call the police. Don't sweep. Wait.*

THE POLICE WERE there in twenty minutes. He didn't hear them from the register where he was filling the cash drawer but suddenly two officers were standing just inside the door, observing the damage. They must have parked down on Hawthorne. One young and willowy, the other one gray-haired and broad, carrying an air of experience. Tacker didn't recognize either of them.

"Officer Lunsford," the gray-haired cop said, extending his hand to Tacker.

The young cop lit a cigarette. "Not likely to get anyone on this," he said. "Don't see much vandalism in this part of town." He exhaled a spiral of smoke. "You got any ideas? Why anybody would break your door? Leave a sign like this?" His eyes narrowed as if he were practicing for *Dragnet.*

"It's my dad's store."

"I know that," Officer Lundsford said.

"What do you fellas think?" Tacker said, dodging. "We've been here for years. My whole life."

"I'm asking you the question," Lundsford said. "That's the way. Think it over. Any reason for this?"

Tacker cracked his knuckles.

"You nervous?"

"Do you think I should be?" Probably, almost certainly, the broken door was pushback against the sit-ins. Someone had seen him and waited and planned. Tacker stuffed his hands in his pockets. His chest felt cold. The breaking pine bough had sounded like bone.

"You have a place for us to sit?" Lundsford said.

The young willowy cop was out front making notes.

"Sure. In the back. But can you tell your partner not to let anyone in?"

"No one's coming in. Streets are too bad. Still, you might want to turn that sign against the wall."

They sat on the couch in the lounge.

"There is one thing," Tacker said, feeling safer with Lundsford in the familiar space.

"What's that?"

"I went to two of the sit-ins. Woolworth's and Kress."

"You bet I know. Hadn't seen you to remember, though. You sympathetic with colored folks?"

Here we go. Guilty of sympathy. Tacker's mind darted. "Went with a family friend."

"This friend. He's from Wake Forest College?"

Of course he would think that. A white friend. A good college boy. "Actually, a fellow who works for me, a Negro." He probably said that a bit too saucily.

"You said a friend."

"His aunt works for my mother, or she did. She died recently. "

"Sorry to hear that," Lundsford said, his lips a straight line. "Your friend's name?"

"Why do you need it? He didn't do anything."

Tacker considered Billy the banker, once second-string footballer who had seen Gaines leaving the store that night. But Billy wouldn't risk his precious bank job doing something like this. The thugs who beat up Gaines, maybe. He told that story, as briefly as possible.

"And you've seen them again?" Lundsford said. He seemed

bored now, ready to move on, get back to the station, put his feet up, eat a doughnut.

"No, sir."

"You didn't get their license plate by chance?"

"No." Tacker could still see the Buick pulling away, the woman in the blue suit, Gaines on the ground holding his stomach.

"There's no telling. Though if it's only your business that's been harmed, someone's got a score to settle."

Why not give Lundsford a little more to think on? "There's one more thing. I spoke up when Reverend Ransom preached here recently. All I said was that it seemed more Christian to me to allow Negroes to sit at lunch counters than not to."

"So maybe someone from the church?"

"Really? You think that's possible? White church folks go around vandalizing? Wow. I wouldn't have thought." Tacker hoped his sarcasm wasn't lost on Lundsford.

"Anything's possible nowadays," he said, standing, signaling that he was through. But halfway down the center aisle he stopped. "I could help you wrap that door," he said, turning around. "Keep the cold out. Got some butcher paper? Tape?"

"Yeah. Let me take a look," Tacker said.

He found an old tarp and some twine. Lundsford was a pro at wrapping a door, his face softened as he folded and tucked.

"Hey, thanks," Tacker said when they were finished.

"Doing my job," Lunsford said, back to his stern face. The younger fellow had hardly met Tacker's eyes.

"What about tonight?" Tacker said.

"We can have someone drive by," Lunsford said. He pulled out a handkerchief, blew his nose, refolded the handkerchief, and put it back in his pocket. "I'd advise you to stay away from those protests. The mayor is working on that thing. Give it time. Hate to see a good boy like you get hurt."

They left and Tacker stood looking out the raft of windows onto the street. The taste of brine came into his mouth as it had on deck crossing the Atlantic. He waited for the cold in his chest to thaw. The Osun. The heat. Kate. Gaines's face like the sun when the arrests began. *I've been involved.*

CONNIE SHOWED UP. A few customers arrived. His father stopped by in the afternoon. Tacker watched the way he opened the broken door, took his hat off, rubbed an eyebrow, replaced the hat, walked into the store, picked up the board behind the customer counter, looked at it, and turned it back against the wall.

"Dad," Tacker said, coming down an aisle to greet him. "I'm mighty sorry," he said.

"Son, we have to talk."

"I'll pay for the door."

"Things are getting out of hand, son. You're trying to do too many things at once. You've got that nice girl, Kate, you're interested in. You can't be in the middle of this lunch counter protest and meet your obligations here."

"It's not that much really, Dad. I can handle it."

"Son, you've got your rent, that cycle. This sit-in business isn't a game."

"I know that."

"Think about your future. I don't know any profession where reputation isn't paramount."

"Dad, Wake Forest students have been at the sit-ins. They came from their ethics courses. The professors are behind them."

"They're four years younger than you are. And they haven't already had their hats handed to them."

His father looked as if it pained him to speak. "You've got to focus on this store and your future. You're going to get arrested.

It just won't work. You might think about my reputation and not just yours. The grocery business is our livelihood."

"You might as well know," Tacker said. "I'm not seeing Kate right now. I guess she agrees with you and Mom."

His father put a hand over his eyes, then removed it. "I'm sorry to hear that. I'll let you tell your mother. I'll call a glass man to come fix the door. Insurance will cover it."

"What about Gaines?"

His father looked haggard and Tacker thought about his health scare.

"You're the manager here. You decide." He put his hat on, picked up a Milky Way on his way out, and left a dime on the counter.

GAINES CAME INTO the store around noon.

"Sorry I'm late."

"No sweat."

"What happened to the door?"

"A prankster."

"It's the movement."

"Nothing changes," Tacker said. "You've still got a job."

"You sure?"

"I'm sure."

"Things could get worse."

"We're cool," Tacker said, though he felt he needed to get away, slow everything down. What was he trying to prove? The silken thread Samuel talked about, the one that held everything together. It used to be excelling at everything. Now he wasn't sure what it was.

Chapter Twenty-two

AND THEN TACKER got a letter from Thomas Driskell Architects. Tom had been a senior in State's School of Design when Tacker was a freshman. He opened it at the table in his dining room. *I wondered what had happened to you. Great to hear you're in town. I'm doing a lot of residential work. You ever hear from Howard Makino, our old prof?* At the bottom of the letter, below the signature: *Come on out to my house, 720 Pine Valley Road. My studio is in the back—just follow the path. Give me until the first of April—finishing a big project right now.*

"Thank you, Jesus."

Tacker felt an acute desire to share his joy with someone other than his parents. He recalled Kate's ankle, its firm tenderness, their first long kiss. They hadn't spoken since before Frances died. He still felt an itch of anger and he headed down to the Indian in the garage. For some while he'd needed to change the oil. He rolled the machine outside. Using a coffee tin, he drained the old oil, then punctured a new can and sent fresh oil through the funnel. He screwed the lid in place and polished the engine with a rag.

He could see his reflection in the glaze of the fender. "Hell," he said. "You're going to call her. Go ahead and do it." He was surprised to hear Kate pick up on the second ring. "Hello," he said.

"Hi," she said.

Did he detect a chastened tone?

"How have you been?"

"Okay, I guess. Pretty busy with the library." She paused. "I felt like an idiot after I threw that pot lid. I've never done anything like that."

"Good thing your aim's not better," he said, relieved by the familiarity of her voice.

"Yes. Still." She paused and he thought he could hear her breathing. "I'm doing some work for the *Journal*."

"That's fantastic."

"Thanks. I'm not on retainer or anything. More like project to project."

"We should celebrate. Tomorrow night. I know a great barbecue place."

THE SUN WAS setting when they pulled into the parking lot of Hill's Lexington Barbecue. They sat at a small table and Kate ordered a sandwich; Tacker got the barbecue plate. He loaded it up with hot sauce.

"My goodness," Kate said.

"I picked up a taste for hot food in Nigeria," he said. "Want to try a bite?"

"I don't know," she said.

"Come on," he said, offering her a fork-load of pulled pork.

Kate gamely took the offer. She chewed for a moment and stopped; her eyes widened and she grabbed her drink. The glass was full and she spilled Coca-Cola on her plate and her lap but she kept drinking. "I'm on fire," she said, tears forming in her eyes.

"Here," Tacker said, half laughing, offering her his glass.

She drank more, and then suddenly she was spewing the Coca-Cola back out, waving her hand. "Oh my God," she said. "It went down wrong."

"Bread," Tacker said. "Eat some of your bun."

Kate tore the top of her bun in half and started in on it. "What have you done to me?" Finally she calmed down, blowing her nose into her napkin. "Okay, now we're even." She refolded the napkin. "I have a wonderful talent for embarrassing myself with you."

"It was my fault. We can move straight to ice-cream sundaes." He reached across the counter and pushed a wayward strand of hair from her forehead. She pressed her face into his cupped hand and he could feel the lift and release of her breath. They stayed so until Kate lifted her head.

"Go ahead and eat. I'll nibble." She picked up a French fry. "I didn't mean to hit you with that pot lid. In the split second that I threw it, I made myself miss."

"I don't know if that should make me feel better or worse," Tacker said, setting his fork aside. "Hey, I might be freelancing, doing renderings for Tom Driskell."

"Do I know him?"

"He was ahead of me at State. He's got his own firm now."

"I wondered," Kate said.

"What?"

"When you were going to get back to architecture."

"It sure is good to see you," he said, smiling.

Over coffee, he told her about Frances. He didn't tell her about the broken door or the sign left at Hart's or the donations of ravioli. She needed time, he rationalized. So did he. How much time he wasn't sure.

Chapter Twenty-three

IN KATE'S DREAM, she walked out the front door and there was her father. He looked ten years younger than she last remembered him and his face shone. Through a communication that was not speech, she asked why he was here and he told her he might apply to teach at Wake Forest College. He wore a hat with a yellow feather in the band that didn't seem quite appropriate for a job search. Clay pots lined the front porch, filled with red blooming geraniums and she knew he had brought them. She also knew that her mother was in the house and they would work things out between them. Though she stood right beside him and the door was open, her father rang the doorbell.

It was her phone in the middle of the night.

"Kate?"

"Hello?" Her heart was in her throat. Who was dead now? Brian?

"Kate, it's me, James."

"You scared me to death. Where are you?"

"In Stockholm. You know where I am."

She was silent, waiting for her heart to calm down.

"Did you get my letters? I've been worried about you."

"Yes. I did. I'm sorry I didn't write." She wasn't sorry. He'd left after that night of angry driving when he pressed her too far and she did not regret the ocean between them. "I've been awfully busy. How are you doing?"

"I'm doing fine. Sweden is charming and elegant. It's like you."

She didn't have an answer.

"Katie? Come on. Talk to me. Is there a chance?"

"Look."

"I'm listening."

Kate had no experience letting a man down. "It's just that we haven't really done much but fight over the phone since last August. We're not moving in the same direction anymore."

"Are you dating your old flame from the grocery? Is that it?"

"He's not an old flame."

"But you're in love with him."

"I didn't say that. No. Please don't call me in the middle of the night again."

"Can you just tell me what's so attractive about staying in a tobacco town where you grew up with the people you knew when you were eight? There's a big world out here, Katie."

"I'm well aware of that. But did it ever occur to you that when a woman's had her parents stolen from her, she might need to spend some time dwelling in familiar territory? I like it here. I'm at home. It's what I need right now."

"I hope you don't settle for less than what you deserve."

"I'm trying not to."

"Well, that's just fine. Don't let me cause you any more trouble."

Kate heard the dial tone. He'd hung up.

There was no point in trying to sleep. Her mind skipped from one thought to the next. What if Tacker never got past working at Hart's? Just because he hadn't talked about it at Hill's didn't mean he wasn't still involved with the sit-ins. She revisited the question of her father's death, his betrayal, and what it meant. She'd promised the *Journal* she'd get some casual shots of the Reynolds High prom for the evening edition. To be taken seriously, she'd have to make her pictures stand out and she'd need to keep plying the editor with more serious photographs he hadn't asked for. She recalled the boy asking for a book—far more important to him than a treat from a drugstore. She needed a car.

At nine a.m., she went to the bank and made arrangements for a withdrawal from her mother's trust fund. At noon, she called Mr. Fitzgerald. "Do you have time to help me look for a car today?" He picked her up an hour later and they went straight to Hull/Dobbs Ford downtown, where Kate's father had purchased his cars and Mr. Fitzgerald knew the manager. As soon as they pulled onto the lot, Kate saw what she wanted and she didn't drive another car. By two o'clock, she was the owner of a green-and-white secondhand Nash Metropolitan. It was a stick shift and the clutch was a little slippery, but James had taught her to drive on a stick shift when she was at Agnes Scott. A cloak of joy descended on her shoulders as she drove the car out of the lot, waving back at Mr. Fitzgerald.

Chapter Twenty-four

FIRST WEEK OF April. Tacker hoped to make a good impression on Tom Driskell. He tightened the knot of the tie around his neck. From a shelf in the music room, he retrieved a copy of his résumé, slipping it into his jacket pocket: high school, State College, all of the achievements, then Clintok—he couldn't leave that out, a little over a year and a half of his life, though the reminder still opened a hole in his chest. Sometimes Tacker thought he would never get over it. Impossible to explain. Not his fault; or was it? He had moved out of the faculty house and into Samuel's room, had eaten Nigerian food and started speaking pidgin English. He had spent his spare time sketching Nigerian architecture, including structures in the far north city of Kano, where Muslim influences were evident: the central dome of the emir's palace flanked by smaller minaret-like cones, a surrounding wall that repeated the minaret-like cones, and an arched entryway. He had argued against burning the old gods.

Argued against Shell Oil. A woman painted his arm in henna—a woman he had never spoken of to anyone at home.

The Winston-Salem day was overcast and the smell of tobacco thick. Tacker backed the Indian out of the garage. Since early March, he'd kept his ear to the ground for news of city projects other than a bathhouse. The cleared lot near Arbor Road was destined for a fire station. Maybe Tom knew something about it. Stucco could be effective in that location, with arched bays and a clay tile roof.

Tacker knocked at the door of the studio and Tom answered. He looked familiar but different too, a little heavier, and he was definitely losing some hair.

"Tacker Hart," Tom announced. "Come on in."

The room was large and airy, walls of unfinished pine, gangly philodendron plants sitting atop bookcases. A drafting table faced a glassed wall and beyond the glass appeared a goldfish pond. On a long table in the center of the room, designs were anchored with smooth stones. The man might be losing a little hair, but he bore an electric energy.

"So how have you been?" Tom said.

"Great. Itching to get back into architecture."

"Said in your letter you've been working for your father."

"Yeah. He needed me for a while. But I've got time to work on renderings—until I can get back to architecture full-time and follow up with my license. Sounds like you've been going gangbusters."

"Lots of residential building going on," Tom said. "Have a seat."

Tacker took a chair that looked handcrafted, made with canvas on wood, and he relaxed into it.

"Tell me about this Clintok assignment," Tom said, taking the chair behind his desk.

Tacker interlaced his fingers, remembering just in time not to crack his knuckles. His face felt hot. "The big thing was a design for national high schools, or secondary schools. They were going to be built all over the place. I don't know how many—hundreds." He leaned forward in his seat. "We wrote all the construction documents, built a model, so it could be implemented anywhere. My team shepherded the first one, did the hiring, even helped lay the foundation. Part of the point was to train Nigerians in architecture. There's not a college in the country that offers degrees in practical sciences." He took a deep breath.

"So you worked on it start to finish."

Right here was the big, huge, stinking problem.

"That was the assignment," Tacker managed. "Learned a lot about concrete footings." He tried to smile.

"Interesting," Tom said. "So how did you find Africa?"

"Well, it's hot," Tacker said. "I liked it. I learned a lot."

"What besides footings?"

"How to improvise, for one. Electricity's unreliable, so we chose a building site at the bottom of a hill and erected water cisterns uphill. Concrete makes a great decorative wall that looks almost weightless. Scaffolding was bamboo. When we started the first classroom building, we had beams in place but the roofing didn't arrive. Rainy season was on the way and we couldn't take a chance, so the town rallied and put up a temporary thatch roof. The rains came twice and not a drop of water got through. I couldn't believe it."

"The weather sounds like Florida."

"Florida squared," Tacker said, relaxing again.

"In your letter you mentioned an interest in public buildings."

"Won the civics award in high school. I guess I can't escape it," Tacker said. "What could be better than buildings that are going to last? Like Reynolds High?"

Tom swiveled in his chair. "I hear you," he said. "Winston's at a turning point the way it's growing. We can retain its character and change at the same time—if we plan well."

Tacker thought of Nigerian cities: a Barclays Bank next to the old king's palace with its long whitewashed wall. He thought about integrating lunch counters. That seemed like a great change that would improve character.

"You drink tea?" Tom said.

"No, thanks."

Tom plugged in a squat electric teapot. "You hear of Hammond and Smith Architects? They've got new office space on North Cherry Street. They've asked me to join their firm. Meanwhile I've got plenty I can offer you. And if it works out, maybe you can come on board when you're ready."

Had he heard the man correctly? Could he really have skated past the Clintok debacle that easily? "Sounds great."

Tom steeped his tea and stirred in two teaspoons of sugar.

"I'll take you on a tour of the house in a minute."

Tacker wasn't sure he could bear this much success in a man not yet thirty years old who had the same background he did.

Tom sipped his hot brew. "The only public building we're bidding on right now is an addition to a branch library on Fairlawn. I've got my foot in the door with General Electric. They're putting in a new plant on Reynolda Road. Of course there are lots of houses if you want residential. Did you do schematic designs in . . . I'm forgetting. Where were you with the Clintok assignment?

"Nigeria. Schematic drawings, models, you name it. We had an MIT fellow leading the project, a Nigerian," Tacker said.

"Is that right?" Tom blew on his tea. "Oh, I almost forgot. I just took on a Firestone franchise coming in on Fifth, not far from you."

"Tell me about it," Tacker said.

"A showroom with a fold-plate roof and a deep overhang, big aluminum-frame windows." He began to sift through folders. "If I remember correctly, the seven bays are flat roofed. A stone-veneered end wall. I've got the paperwork here somewhere."

"Sounds interesting."

Tom found the folder. "Take a look at their specifications. Go to the site. Let me know if you have questions." He handed Tacker the folder. "Let's take a look at the house."

"Sure thing," Tacker said. Buoyed by his success, he could bear to look at the man's house. Tom carried his teacup through every room. It was a great place, with lots of windows, a beamed, slanted ceiling in the living room, and a slate foyer and four bedrooms; so they were planning on children, though there was no evidence of any yet. Tom had made the hallways nice and wide. But it wasn't a foursquare and it wasn't a house Tacker envied. The teak dining table maybe. They walked out onto the back patio. Tacker looked at his watch. "So, when would you like for me to have something for you?"

"A week or two? We'll go from there."

They walked toward the Indian. "Nice bike," Tom said. "By the way, I heard you were at one of those protests."

Tacker was so surprised he almost laughed. "Yes, I was," he said.

"Interesting," Tom said. "Hey, I've got to get back to work. Call me when you have the rendering."

So that was it.

GAINES WAS WORKING mysteriously with the movement two or three nights a week. He'd moved out of his mom's house so she wouldn't be a target—"If anyone wanted to try something funny with me," Gaines explained. It rattled Tacker but he wasn't going to change his course. He'd given the man his word that his job was safe. He offered to keep Valentine at the store while Gaines was elsewhere. Around eight, Gaines picked her up and took her to his mom's house before going wherever it was he had found a bed. While Tacker finished up paperwork and put in orders, Valentine drew pictures and made paper chains. When they got hungry they made supper out of beanie weenies straight from the can and circles of pineapple. Pretty quickly Tacker tired of the suppers and decided he would take Valentine to the foursquare for a hot meal. He parked in front of the house and they walked next door to meet the neighbor, Miss Smith, an older woman who appeared never to have married. Tacker had made a habit of taking her paper up to her porch and more than once he'd picked up fallen limbs in her backyard.

"Good evening, Miss Smith," he said when she answered the door. "I want you to meet Valentine. I'm going to have her with me now and again. She's the niece of my family's maid, who died recently. Her older brother will stop by from time to time to pick her up. If you see any other neighbors, feel free to mention it." He smiled largely.

Miss Smith looked down at Valentine and back at Tacker.

"Well, she looks as clean as any child I ever saw," she said.

"Valentine, say hello to Miss Smith."

"Hello, Miss Smith," Valentine said.

"Now, isn't she well-behaved. I've got my gravy simmering, Mr. Hart. Thank you for coming by." Miss Smith squinted and patted Valentine on the head.

"That wasn't so bad, was it?" Tacker said to Valentine as they crossed back into his yard.

"She smelled funny," Valentine said.

Tacker stifled a laugh. "I'm glad you kept that to yourself," he said.

After that evening, he kept Valentine at his house rather than the store and Gaines would show up at the back door, his friend's car idling on Jarvis Street. One evening, opening his pantry, Tacker got an idea. "Valentine, I've got a little repair work to do," he said. "Will you help me out?"

"Okay," she said.

Months back Tacker had discovered that da Vinci was escaping through a hole at the back of the pantry; it led to the porch where the screen was loose on a couple of windows. "See there," he said as Valentine peered into the closet. "Da Vinci is getting out on his own whenever I leave this door open. I'm afraid he might get hurt. Stay right here. I'll be back."

Tacker had kept the plywood board with the vile message that had been left in front of Hart's. He retrieved it, careful to keep the lettered side away from Valentine's eye. It fit handily between the two studs where he'd discovered the opening. "Looky there. Perfect fit," he said. "Now I need you to hand me those nails I set on the counter."

Valentine did as he asked, but the old studs were hard with age and the box nails he was using weren't making much of a dent. The unexpected challenge was sobering and Tacker had the ominous feeling that there were other things lurking in hidden corners that he had not reckoned with yet. Fifteen minutes later, he'd done an adequate job.

"Someone left that board at the grocery, wanting to be mean," he said, standing to stretch his legs. "But we've turned it around and made it work for us." He pulled out a handkerchief and wiped his forehead.

She nodded her head, serious as rain, and Tacker wondered if already she sensed ominous things lurking in corners.

A FEW DAYS later, Gaines showed up at the back door of the foursquare. "Put it right here," he said, coming into the kitchen where Tacker and Valentine were washing up dishes.

Tacker slid his palm across Gaines's.

"What's up?" Tacker said.

"Wait for it." Gaines breathed in and his chest expanded. "We have founded the Student Nonviolent Coordinating Committee. Over in Raleigh. At Shaw University. Yes, sir. We're moving. This thing is rolling, man."

"You were over in Raleigh tonight? How'd you make it there and back?"

"One of the other men went. He called to tell us."

Valentine spoke. "What's moving?"

"We are, sister, but not out of Winston. We're moving out of oppression."

"What's that?" Valentine said.

"When someone tells you to get up and help yourself then throws you down and puts his foot on your back. Tells you to run but straps a big weight on your shoulders."

"I don't want any foot on my back," Valentine said.

"Won't ever happen if I can help it," Gaines said.

Tacker thought of Joshua and wondered who had stepped on his back, and he looked at Valentine, strong and fragile at the same time, like a dandelion—until someone did step on her back, which would happen in this country, and then she would be bent and nothing would make her that strong again, or that straight.

THE NEXT EVENING Tacker waited until dark before riding the Indian to the empty lot on Fifth, designated for the Firestone. With Samuel, he'd learned the art of viewing land by moonlight, when a person could better detect small rises and falls in the land. The lot was marked by a slight copse on the right-hand side, and a lone dogwood, just leafing, stood in the center of it. It seemed a good omen. He took some notes and thought about Kate. Their courtship had been so intermittent and almost monastic that he often imagined her a lover in another country who could not be reached by letter or telegram or telephone, this though she was only five blocks away, and he wondered if his love for her would be lessened if he ever attained it.

Chapter Twenty-five

KATE FOUND GREAT pleasure in taking her new car to the service station, standing next to the driver's side door, getting the tank filled and the oil checked, and watching the attendant. She'd kept on the lookout for a shoe-shine boy and a younger brother near the library but with no luck. The *Journal* had purchased several more of her photographs and she had met the editor who'd purchased her first picture. He was a short man with a cigar and round glasses and a bald head. "Well, aren't you the cat's eye," he said when she walked in. "I don't know what that means," she said. "I'm not sure I do either," he said. "My old man used to say it to all the ladies on Sunday." He looked at her pictures, puffed on his cigar, tapped a single index finger on his desktop, and took a deep, almost desperate sigh. "You're on to something," he said finally. She adored him immediately. "I tell you what," he said. "Keep comin' by. I can't offer you a job right now, but I'll print some of your pictures." "Thank you. I will," she said. "Get yourself down to Trade and snap some pictures of those tobacco men. And go to the ladies' shindigs, too, you know, the Junior League and what all." "I will," she said.

SUNDAY AFTERNOON SHE made a surprise visit to Tacker's foursquare. He was unlike any other man she knew. Off-puttingly casual about his career, off-puttingly pious about his moral vision, yet enormously attractive for the risks he took and—she would be lying to herself if she didn't admit it—enormously attractive period.

A slender Negro girl came to the door, outfitted in a pink dress with a white pinafore, white socks, and brown shoes. She held Tacker's cat.

"Hello," she said. "We can't let da Vinci out."

"Is Tacker here?" Kate said, leaning toward the girl, stroking the cat's fur. Da Vinci was shedding and reams of hair followed her hand and held for a moment in the air before settling on Tacker's wood floor.

"Yes, ma'am. This is his house," the girl said.

"I'm Miss Kate. What's your name?"

"Valentine," she said. "Mr. Tacker and I were working on his motorcycle. Now he's getting cleaned up. Then he's taking me home on his big bike. But I guess you can stay." Something about the way the girl held her head reminded Kate of the boy who wanted a book.

Kate heard the hiss of the radiator and then there was Tacker, entering from beyond the stairway where Kate knew his bedroom to be though she had not seen it. He was barefoot, wearing blue jeans and a white T-shirt, towel drying his hair, his movement like an overflow of energy. Kate was still standing slightly to the right of the door. Valentine had settled on a rug—a new purchase?—in front of Tacker's fireplace, singing to the cat.

"Kate," he said. He let the towel fall loose at his side and looked at her, inscrutable, and then his forehead relaxed and a smile lifted his face.

"Hi," she said. The moment was overfull, like a glass of water that would spill if she picked it up, and Kate knew it was one of only a few such perfect moments she would ever be allowed. She breathed deeply and closed her eyes. Tacker was still standing in front of her, still smiling, when she opened them.

"Just a minute. I'll be right back," he said.

He returned in a blue shirt, buttoned up but not tucked in, and crossed the space between them. When he reached her, he put his palm to the side of her face and kissed her. He turned to the little girl and gestured in her direction.

"You meet Valentine? She's Gaines's little sister."

"Yes. She's a very capable young lady," Kate said.

"I need to get her home. Do you have time to stay?"

"Oh, sure. I can wait. Or we can take my new car. I got it a few days ago, a secondhand Nash Metropolitan." She rushed her words, feeling herself in a tumble.

Tacker looked befuddled, as he had that first day in Hart's when she asked what he had been doing since he'd gotten back home. But he regained himself quickly. "What do you think, Valentine? Want to take a drive in Miss Kate's new car?"

"Okay. But you haven't got your shoes on. Can I have some Life Savers?"

"Yes," Tacker said, and she skipped off to the kitchen while Tacker put on his shoes.

"You drive, Tacker." Kate handed him the keys.

Valentine sat between them in the front seat, her legs straight out in front of her.

BACK AT THE foursquare Tacker parked in the back.

"Great little car," he said, patting the hood.

They walked up the slanted yard. By the light of the back porch, a bed of late-blooming daffodils glowed.

"May I pick some?" Kate said.

"Fine with me," Tacker said.

Kate pushed dead leaves aside, getting to the base of the stems. "I was depending on Mr. Fitzgerald too much. I needed a car so I could get out to take pictures."

"I'm all for it," he said.

"And to get to the coast to see Brian," she said, wondering why she was defending her purchase when he'd given her no reason. In the kitchen, Tacker produced a glass and filled it with water. She released the stems into it.

"Want to split a beer?" he said.

"Yes."

He poured the beer into two jelly glasses and handed one to her. Kate felt a cooling breeze waft over her face from the screened porch they had passed through. The wind picked up, overturning a cardboard box. Tacker closed the door and picked up the vase of daffodils, and they found themselves sitting in the dining room, the flowers on the table before the window of fading light.

"How's Brian?" he said.

"Fine, I think. Some other fellow is renting a room in the house so he's not alone."

"Tell me what you've been up to," he said.

"I'm now formally on the library board," she said.

He seemed to make a calculation. "A toast," he said and they clinked glasses.

"What's wrong?" she said.

"Nothing," he said. "You've got good news. When we first got together, we were both pretty bleak. I'm just wondering."

"Wondering what?"

"If we could be a real couple."

He was looking at his hands, not her face.

"Why do you say that?"

"We've been on different tracks," he said.

"With lunch counters?"

"We've always been on different tracks," he said. "It's why I like you and sometimes think it would be easier to tame a peacock than keep constant with you."

"Why?" she said, humored by his poetry.

"About different tracks or keeping constant?"

"You can start with one and move on to the other," she said.

"My family's in the grocery store business. Your mom's family is from old Winston stock. Even when I get my license, I won't be from good Winston stock." She couldn't tell if he was teasing. "Though I suppose that chasm can be breached"—he was ribbing her—"since you appear to find my mind subtle enough. You wouldn't converse with a dull man."

"That last is true," she said, meaning it but also pretending haughtiness.

"You've been woven into the city's governing class since you were born."

"That's an overstatement and you know it," she said, slapping at his hand.

"It's not a bad thing," Tacker said. "Sometimes I envy you."

His face bore a look of loneliness Kate had not seen before. She caught a whiff of the daffodils. The greening, molting smell of living stems, and she recalled the day last fall when she combed leaves from the monkey grass. The press of leaves, the smell the earth produced in fall and spring, opposite seasons threaded on wet leaves, green or brown, turned in her like a dial.

"It's hard to believe anyone is envious of me," she said, and it was true. What she remembered from childhood was the privilege of being her father's daughter, the light in his eyes when she walked in the room. And she had lost that. Also true was her sense of Tacker's confoundedness. Secretly she reveled in his athleticism though she could not celebrate it since she had molded her identity in part by shunning whatever was popular. He had passed her in worldliness by living in Nigeria but he needed to stop hobbying in these Negro campaigns. Still she admired his conscience and so she was caught. She could not imagine stepping out of her social world, which meant, of course, she was not as free as Tacker. And she was a woman, so anything she did would be easier to fault and more dangerous, too.

The long beam of a car's headlamps on Jarvis illuminated the darkening window. Da Vinci jumped onto the table, upsetting the daffodils; the glass tilted and the stems spilled onto the floor.

Tacker placed a hand over hers. "I'll get them," he said.

When he had the flowers back in water, he took her hand and led her to the living room. Without a word, they settled onto the couch. "I want to kiss you," he said and he did. They made a good deal of sound in the quiet house. He ran his hands down her sides and she twisted around this way and that. He held gobs of her hair in his hands and kissed her harder. After one particularly long kiss, they stopped to look at each other. Her hair was damp. She lifted an arm to raise the mass from her neck and he kissed the place she exposed. He pressed himself upon her and she pressed herself into him, her shoulders fitting perfectly into his cupped hands.

Kate pictured them in a river. By turns each was drowning and being saved. Tacker swiveled on one arm so they were side by side and then he pulled Kate so she was on top of him, astride him. He pushed her up and Kate looked at him and watched as his hands went to her breasts. Then he pulled her over him like a sheet and she felt his mouth on her clothed breast and was glad for the thinness of her garments and the warmth of his mouth. He stopped and held her tight.

THEY SAT ON the rug, their backs to the couch, cradling bowls of ice cream.

"It makes me hungry," Kate said.

"What?" Tacker said.

"Kissing like that. It makes me so hungry." She leaned over her bowl.

"I hope that's good," Tacker said, laughing.

"Don't let me have any more," she said, licking the spoon. "Here." She handed the bowl to Tacker.

"What have you been up to?" she said.

"I've been hired to do my first rendering for Tom Driskell Architects," he said, smiling, kissing her forehead. "I'm charging a hundred and fifty bucks for every one I do."

"Why didn't you tell me sooner?"

"And mess up that good kissing? Your doubts about me make me more alluring, or didn't you know that?"

"I thought you were jealous of my car," she said.

"I thought you were going to ditch me because of the protests."

"Are you still going?"

"I'm taking care of Valentine instead, started a couple of weeks ago."

"A Negro boy asked me for a book," she said.

"What did you say to him?"

"He had to leave before I could answer."

"If you'd had time what would you have said?"

"I'd have offered him some of my own. I still have all my childhood books."

"If he had access to Main Library, he could have books for the rest of his life."

"I already thought about that," Kate said.

She rested her head in his lap and he told her about Samuel's letters. He told her about Joshua and his betrayal. She thought he was going to say something else but he stopped.

Chapter Twenty-six

THE NEXT NIGHT, Tacker took his initial sketches for the Firestone building and sat down with paper and pen in the dining room. He'd decided on an angled view that allowed him to sketch in the dogwood but also open the skyline behind the building. He studied the plans one more time before committing himself to the central portion of the design. The roofline was the most interesting part. Because he was drawing from ground level, the shadowed underside of each peak accentuated the gentle upward thrust, like a series of waves frozen in eternity. The next morning he was up early to finish the sketch. That evening, he added some embellishments, using colored pencils. The dogwood gained a green blush in its crown. A pink-and-orange sunset brought the sketch into greater relief. He added three metal benches to the right side of the building, facing away from the glass windows, a nice accessory, Tacker imagined, for a customer waiting for his tires to be rotated. Lightly he sketched in existing buildings. Tacker drank a beer and admired his work before laying it carefully on a shelf in the music room.

Thursday during his lunch break, he delivered the rendering. "Nice work," Tom said and wrote him a check before pressing him with another project, a split-level on Hertford Road. "We're under the gun on this one. The sooner the better." Tacker promised to have it Monday morning, which shouldn't be a problem. He had all of Sunday. But then Kate asked him to take her to the beach.

They took her car, heading out on 70: to Raleigh, Goldsboro, Kinston, and New Bern, and finally Morehead City, where they would cross on the drawbridge into Atlantic Beach. The land leveled out the farther they went, trees changing from deciduous to white pine to loblolly pine. Skirting Kinston, they pulled over and ate pimento cheese sandwiches. In Morehead City the gulls appeared, and blue water. They spotted a yellow cinderblock house in Atlantic Beach with a ROOMS FOR RENT sign planted in a garden.

Mrs. Johnson, the proprietor, placed them in rooms on opposite sides of the house. "We have one other guest," she said, peering at Kate as she spoke. "A nice lady who comes every spring for the air. She had polio as a child but she gets around pretty well. I offer breakfast but not dinner. You'll need to eat at one of the restaurants. Rainey's Market makes sandwiches."

IT WAS TWO o'clock in the afternoon. In an hour, they were on the beach. Kate kept on her short cover-up and they walked away from the populated area of mothers with children and fathers fishing. Tacker figured they had gone two miles when Kate said she wanted to sit down. They watched waves rushing in, slipping away, always the same, every time different. An ibis landed, studied them awhile, decided they were safe enough, and began to fish. Out over the water, five pelicans flew low and steady, as perfect as a line drawn against a ruler.

"It's going to be cold," Kate said.

"Race you to the water," Tacker said.

They fell together into the sea and rode the waves in. Kate climbed onto Tacker's back and he turned them in circles and then they swam up and down the shoreline, keeping to regions where their feet could touch the sandbar beneath them. Warmed to the water, they stopped and kissed, bobbing in the waves beyond the breakers.

"Let's go in and get dressed and find dinner," Tacker said.

Their clothes were damp and they held them aloft to dry as they walked back toward the pier, the sun blazing down.

AT THE FISH House, they sat next to each other in the booth. After dinner, Tacker scribbled circles on his napkin.

"What?" Kate said, glancing at him sideways.

"Make a hut round and it's a nest. My friend Samuel said that. An octagonal house has the most wall space," he added.

Kate tipped her head until it rested on his shoulder.

"You tired?"

"Very," she said. "Maybe we could take a nap."

"At seven o'clock?" Tacker said.

"If I try to sit in Mrs. Johnson's living room and read a book, I'll fall asleep," Kate said.

"Let's go," he said.

Outside, a handful of people gathered around an ice-cream vendor. Tacker claimed Kate's hand. He led and soon they were alone, the wooden pier sounding faintly with their footsteps.

"I wonder what it's like here when it snows. If it ever snows," Kate said.

"It probably does sometimes," Tacker said. He thought of his bed in the foursquare, topped with a blue quilt his grandmother had made. He thought of Kate in the bed. He tried to count the months they had known each other, really known each other. But there were the on-and-off times and it was hard to figure.

"I think it would all fly away," Kate said.

"What would fly away?"

"The snow. What are you thinking about?"

"You," he said.

"Ha!" she said. "You were not. You were thinking of triangular houses. If we had a blizzard in Winston and the electricity went out, would you come rescue me?"

"Of course."

He could see the snow falling slantwise, filling West End Boulevard and Glade Street, filling up parking lots. Snow followed by ice. So they must stay in the house an entire week.

They reached a bench at the end of the pier and sat down. An austerity seemed to envelop Kate. Perhaps she thought of her father. The wind was mild with only a hint of chill to come late in the night. Fishing boats bobbed and rocked. Occasionally Tacker heard a wave smack a hull. Kate sat silently next to him. "What are you thinking?" he said.

"I'm trying to remember a poem by Robert Frost," she said, "a snow poem. We read it in high school. I can't remember how it begins. There's some question." She closed her eyes. "'The woods are lovely, dark and deep.' I remember that. 'And miles to go before I sleep.'"

She spoke as if she were uncovering all she had been lonely for, all she had held inside. He wondered if she had carried these thoughts for years, unwrapping them and laying them before him, in this talk of winter and woods and miles to go, as they sat before boats bobbing at the pier on a May evening. He pulled her to him and her hair smelled of salt. He felt the sun still in it and kissed her and tasted sun and salt in her mouth and listened to the surf and wind, his hands tight around Kate's waist. Somewhere a bell sounded.

They found their way back to their rooms, tiptoeing into the living room around ten thirty. Sounds came from the kitchen and soon Mrs. Johnson's voice. "You lovebirds want some chamomile tea? I'm just fixing some myself."

"That sounds lovely," Kate said.

Her eyes were wide and Tacker thought she was going to laugh.

They sat in the kitchen and drank their tea and said good night and Tacker headed to the once-garage, which had been converted to an extra room, while Kate headed down the hallway to her room at the opposite end of the house.

AT MIDNIGHT, TACKER slipped out a door of his room that led directly outside. The moon was up and the low, sweet smell of early gardenias filled the air, the scent as sweet as frangipani blossoms in Nigeria. He headed toward town. Only at the service station did he see another soul, someone at a phone booth. He took the boardwalk and the stairs leading down to the beach. Tacker walked in the opposite direction from the one he and Kate had taken in the afternoon. He could see everything, the lull and fall of waves farther out, even shells tumbling in and falling back. He found a high reef of sand cut earlier in the day by the incoming tide and he sat. In the dark of one o'clock, he watched a sea turtle come in with the tide. It was huge and took some time to maneuver the dunes. An hour later, she had found her nest. She would lay her eggs. He had learned about the habits of the sea turtle in sixth grade. She returned to the same nest every two or three years. Only a few of her hatchlings would survive. Those that did would spend up to ten years in an ocean current far from shore, maturing.

Should he go back to Nigeria, the place he had left, and to his place in it? He could get on with the company that had hired Samuel. There was all kinds of building going on over there. He would marry Kate. They would go together. A return wouldn't be about confronting Joshua. It would be about his own soul. He had been unjustly treated, wounded. Gaines would laugh. *Wounded? You, wounded? Let me tell you about wounded.* And he would go on about someone whose father had been hung in a tree and he would be right of course.

Yet there was some irreconcilable dislocation even if it wasn't an issue of justice. He could not get entirely into one life or the other, here or there. Gaines was all the way in. So was Samuel. The last time he had run the track in Hanes Park, a crew was laying tile on the upper surround of the pool, blue and white, the colors that dominated Kate's mother's book on Greece. How was he to reconcile a swimming pool in Winston with the Osun River in Osogbo? The moon was in its descent. Tacker headed back to his room, thinking of Kate asleep at the other end of the house.

"Mrs. Johnson took her other guest to visit a friend." Kate was in the kitchen eating toast with grape jelly. "She told me we should help ourselves to breakfast. When did you get in?"

"How did you know?"

"A woman knows," she said, her eyes bright.

"Two o'clock?"

"You want to rent some bikes? Mrs. Johnson said the grocery rents bikes."

"Sure," Tacker said. "But right now you better make way or I may have to eat you. I'm starving."

"Not so fast, Mr. Wolf," Kate said. "I want more toast."

They bantered and teased and ate and cleaned up the kitchen. It was almost too easy and delightful and Tacker felt a bit frightened as he brushed his teeth. They got to the grocery before it was crowded. "I'll buy the sandwiches since you made yesterday's for the trip," he said.

"Suits me, but how will we carry them?"

"Some of those bikes have a basket," the proprietor said.

But none did. "I guess they're already rented," Tacker said.

"I've got an old haversack," the man said. "I'll fix it up for you."

As they waited for their lunch, Tacker felt a wave of doubt pass through him. He ought to be back in Winston working on the rendering for the split-level.

"Hey, mister," Kate said. "You ready?"

Tacker reeled himself in.

They rode through town to admire the houses and streets and then headed out onto a road along the shore, moving west in the direction of Salter Path. They had no plan except to ride, keeping as close as possible to the shore. It was easy going.

"A white ibis," Kate said as they rounded a turn and came into full view of the sound on their left. The bird turned into the wind and coasted downward until it landed just out of their sight. They rode so for an hour, until they were met by a high crest of dunes on their right.

"Here!" Kate said. "The beach is just on the other side."

They banked the bikes, and, Kate leading, they found a lesser dune to cross. The Atlantic stretched out forever and away, like a grand carpet leading to the heart of the world.

"Over there is your Africa," she said.

Then she took off down the other side of the dune. Tacker followed but had to be careful of the haversack. *She doesn't understand anything about Africa,* he thought. Yet her unawareness caused him to love her more. Kate spread a yellow cloth. They anchored it with their shoes. Tacker popped off the Coke caps. Salami and American cheese never tasted so good.

"We should have gotten in the water first," Kate said.

"I was famished."

"Now we have to wait thirty minutes."

"I can think of worse things," he said.

A flock of plovers landed and walked sideways against the wind down to the water.

WHEN TACKER STARTED digging, Kate joined in.

"What are you doing?" she said.

"I'll show you."

They made the hole wide enough to lie in. When they were through, Tacker placed their towels next to each other in the interior.

"A round house is a bowl, a nest," Kate said, standing as if reciting a poem before tumbling in. They wound themselves together and he kissed her and pulled away and looked at her face and did it again many times. They swam and rested again.

"I used to think of my backbone as a blade. I had to be so strong with my mother. It doesn't seem so anymore," she said, and he didn't know if the "it" was her backbone or having to be strong. It was both, he assumed, and held her close.

The tops of their feet were sunburned and they spent the evening in Mrs. Johnson's living room, a secret between them like a child, but it was their own selves they tendered and loved. That night Tacker woke, thinking about the split-level. He should have brought some drafting paper. He could have worked on sketches sitting with Kate. Now he was going to have to rush home and probably stay up all night. Still, when he saw Kate in the kitchen early Sunday morning and she looked at him with her large lavender eyes, he followed her barefoot on the cool morning lanes down to the open pavilion by the ocean, where they danced on the broad wooden floor without music until the sun blazed in through the windows.

"We have to go, honey," Tacker said.

"One more swim," she said.

"I have to do a rendering when I get back. I promised Tom I'd have it tomorrow."

Tacker had forgotten to fill the car on Saturday; it was a little under half-full and he was anxious about that too. They didn't stop but drove all the way back to Winston with the windows down, pulling into town just as the arrow reached empty.

He was up half the night working on the split-level. It wasn't as inspiring as the Firestone: a low-pitched roofline, three windows across the third level, a central chimney. The bay window in the living room was the most interesting feature and there was nothing especially novel about it. He embellished the design with a blooming forsythia in the left corner of the lot and pine trees behind, gently greened, and a pale blue sky. And then he slept for three hours before his alarm went off.

Chapter Twenty-seven

GAINES WAS SKY-HIGH at the store, a hat cocked back on his head. "The Nashville sit-ins are over, man." He waved a newspaper. "Negroes sitting at the counter and ordering their lunch. Dinner, too. Getting their Pepsi refilled. One turkey dinner, coming right up. Sixty-five cents. Soup of the day. Yes, ma'am. Cherry pie. Fifteen cents. You got it on a plate. Say you want a hot dog with all the fixings. Be out directly."

Tacker still had sand in his loafers.

"Look right here, brother. Read it."

Gaines handed him the paper. It wasn't the *Winston-Salem Journal* or any newspaper Tacker had ever seen. He looked at the grainy black-and-white photograph and scanned the story.

"What did I tell you?" Gaines said.

Tacker leafed through the paper. The *Carolina Times*, probably the same paper Gaines had shown him when his picture was in it from that early sit-in at Kress. "Where's this paper from?"

"Durham," Gaines said.

"How'd you get it?"

"Aunt Frances has subscribed to the paper for years. We got to sit tight, baby. Keep filling those beautiful seats. I can taste it," Gaines said.

"What's that?" Tacker said.

"The club sandwich I'm going to order at Woolworth's. Crispy bacon. Yes, sir. Nice thin-sliced turkey. A sweet tomato. Leaf of lettuce. Duke's May-o-nnaise. On toasted white bread. With potato chips on the side. And a foot-long dill pickle. My mouth is watering already. What are you having?"

Without thinking, Tacker said, "The same," though it had always been possible for him to order whatever he wanted at any Woolworth's in the country as long as he wasn't with a Negro.

Gaines took his hat off and hung it on the coatrack. A spot on the back of his head was bandaged.

"Hey. What's that?" Tacker said.

"Nothing much. Some fellow decided to see if he could break a stick over my head."

"Who was it? You see a doctor?"

"Didn't bother to introduce myself. Used iodine."

"What were you doing?"

"Sitting at a diner."

"Maybe you should pull back. You've got Valentine to think about."

"I am thinking about her. And my mom."

"I know. I know." In Nigeria, Tacker had once witnessed a man being flogged over the head for theft. The cane created a gash on his head. That image haunted him the rest of the morning.

During his lunch break he called Tom. "I have the split-level but I can't get it to you until this evening."

"That'll be fine," Tom said.

Tacker hung up the phone. "I've got to lie down for thirty minutes," he said to Connie. "I'll be in the lounge if you need me."

ON THURSDAY, TOM called in the early morning before Tacker left for work. "Come over tomorrow evening. I've got something I want to propose."

Tacker had promised Kate a night at the ballpark. "That should work," he said, though as soon as he hung up it needled him.

"I guess we could go to the movies Saturday night," Kate said when he called.

"I'll make it up to you next weekend."

"It's fine. Really. What if you drop by Friday night after you see Tom and let me know what he says?"

THE DOOR TO Tom's studio stood ajar and Tacker stood at the threshold until the man looked up.

"We got lucky," he said, his hair awry, the studio messier than it had been last time.

"Great," Tacker said.

"Fred Hammond called this morning."

Tacker's mind went blank.

"Hammond and Smith, the firm I'm joining."

"Right."

"The architect who was hired to design the bathhouse at Hanes Park had to pull out and Hammond landed it. But he's got bigger fish to fry. He wondered if I'd like it."

"You want me to do a rendering for a bathhouse?" An odd taste came to Tacker's mouth.

"Actually I want you to work for me. We'll collaborate.

There's not even an initial sketch yet." The man smiled as if they were planning a road trip to Mexico.

"A bathhouse?" Tacker said again.

"There are other things I can give you a crack at. But this would make a good platform. That park has been waiting for years for a pool. It'll revive the neighborhood. It's where your heart is, right?" He leaned toward Tacker. "I'd like another State alum in the office. My new colleagues both went to Virginia Tech."

"Wow. I'd have to think about it, talk with my father." Tacker put a hand to his forehead.

"What if you started half-time?" Roberts said.

Tacker hadn't even sat down. "I'd love to do it. All of it. I just don't know how soon we can find someone to take over the store."

"Tell you the truth, the bathhouse is a plum for me. The mayor's in on it. I'd like to showcase our talent."

"Like I said . . ."

"Why don't you sit down? We're going to grill some burgers. Can you stay for supper?"

Tacker looked at his watch.

"Here's the pool design. No doubt you've been watching it go in. Look it over. Let me run and tell Kathy you're staying for supper."

Tacker knew the park like the back of his hand. But looking at the rendering of the pool with the designer's embellishments was surreal, like looking at an old-timey tinted photograph of an uncle he resembled, the same but not the same. He thought of Bobby Ransom and his bullshit response about integration, of Gaines that day at Woolworth's, the way he smiled when the arrests were made, of Samuel and Chukwu at the Lebanese restaurant. He couldn't work on the bathhouse for a whites-only pool. It would be a complete sellout. He gazed out the window at the goldfish pond. What sorry good luck to have this gift dangled in front of him. He cracked his knuckles and looked at his hands. Then he picked up the design and took it over to Tom's drafting table to get a better look. Further study did not relieve his sense of the quagmire he was in, a man in a bog with a beautiful bride onshore he would never reach.

Tacker got to Kate's at nine o'clock.

"I was about to give up on you," she said, opening the door.

"Yeah, sorry. Tom invited me to supper and I couldn't really say no. He likes to talk."

"So what was his big idea?" she said, taking his hand and leading him into the library.

"He wants me to come work with him."

"That's wonderful!" She bounced up and down on her toes.

"I can't just drop the store," he said, plopping himself on the couch.

"Of course not. Did he give you a deadline?"

"Not really."

She leaned down to give him a kiss; her blouse dipped open and he could see where her suntan ended going into her bra. He didn't tell her about the bathhouse. She would be entirely for it.

MIDDAY MONDAY TOM called Tacker at the store. "Any breakthrough on your end? Fred and I took inventory of our current projects. We're going to have to hire someone. I'd like for it to be you."

Tacker hadn't said anything to his father yet. "Can I have until next week?"

"That'll do," Tom said. "But I really need to know by then."

TACKER JERKED THE Indian from its stand. He swerved out into the road. An oncoming car barely missed him, the horn echoing in his ears as he headed out Reynolda toward Wake Forest College and beyond. He laughed into the air, his head back. Of all the dumb luck. He charged the engine. Ten miles out, he pulled onto a meandering dirt road that bordered fields, skirted a pond and a forsaken barn, then zigzagged, bringing Tacker to a stand of pines and an old sharecropper's house. He parked the bike and entered the old yard. An ancient pump. Chimney straight but the house tilted away from it. He looked in a window. An old table and a tin pail. Fragment of flour-sack curtains. The scent of moisture prevailed and it filled Tacker with immense sadness, as if his parents were already dead and he were forty years old. They would never understand that there was no way he could design the bathhouse. Tom wouldn't understand either. Turning it down would appear ungrateful. Worse than that, stupid.

Frogs chorused.

Kate might understand and even be sympathetic to his dilemma. But she would still want him to do it. His hands itched as they used to before a game. He felt a cold pity for the world, for himself. With this project he could launch his career.

The smell of water and rock and a whiff of ginger.

What you go to Africa for and come back here same as always.

"DAD?" TACKER SPOKE over the phone. "I need to talk."

Early the next morning they met at Krispy Kreme on Stratford.

"You know I've been doing renderings for Tom Driskell. He's hooked up with two other architects. The thing is, he'd like to hire me half-time."

His dad set his doughnut aside and took a sip of his coffee. "I said at the beginning I didn't want to stand in your way. How soon does he need to know something?"

"Next week."

They were silent for a moment.

"Well, let's think about it," his father said.

They stared out the glass wall at the street.

"Theoretically: what would we do if you were sick for a week?"

"I guess Connie could manage until I got back—if you could check in now and then."

His dad finished his doughnut and wiped his mouth and sipped his black coffee.

"You think she could manage mornings if you came in at one? You could put in orders on Saturdays."

"Connie could run that store by herself. I just never thought you would consider it."

"Well, why not? How does she get along with Gaines?"

"Fine. They get along fine."

"Okay by you if I make her assistant manager?"

"Fine by me."

Everything was fine except that he was going to work for Tom—who wanted him on a bathhouse, who believed he was doing Tacker a favor. He felt as alone as he had when he first got home from Nigeria and had not a soul to talk with. Was it too late to learn how to pray?

Riding the Indian back to the store, heading up Stratford, he sensed a deep splitting, his heart in two places. He could almost hear the crack. He loved Kate. He wanted to be in Winston. But he also wanted to be somewhere else. Part of him might never get home.

Chapter Twenty-eight

THURSDAY MORNING, JANET, Kate's Agnes Scott roommate, called to say she was engaged. Would Kate be her maid of honor? The wedding was being rushed because she and her fiancé were moving to California. He had a job offer with what Janet called "the aerospace electronics industry." They had met on a blind date and his name was Bo Foster—Bo went to Clemson. "We just hit it off. He's perfect for me. You'll see," Janet said.

Kate wasn't so sure. "Aerospace electronics industry" sounded like war machinery. Janet had railed against Korea and the waste of it. And against McCarthy. Alone, she had stood on the front steps of the administration building at Agnes Scott and protested Senator McCarthy. Janet feared nothing. Apparently not even moving to California, where who knew what her new husband, a man she had known two months at the most, would be doing. Kate said yes; she would love to be Janet's maid of honor.

"Katie, I know this is last minute, but can you come to Greenville tomorrow? I'd like to pick out the dresses."

Kate dreaded the idea of driving to Greenville to pick out a dress. Well, she'd take her camera. That would give her something better to do than look at dresses. She called Tacker at the store. "I have to go to Greenville, South Carolina, tomorrow."

"You feel safe driving that far?" he said, not yet perceiving that he should drop by to see her tonight.

"Of course. I just thought you might want to see me before I leave." Where was his mind these days?

"I do, baby. I'll be over around seven."

In her backyard the azaleas were riotous in deep pink and purple. Objective truth: *azalea* is Latin, from Greek, feminine of *azaleos*, "dry," because the shrub flourishes in dry soil. Kate spent some time cleaning out the summer beds, getting them ready for the few annuals she hoped to plant. Turning the soil up lifted her spirits. Subjective truth: "Everything will work out." It was herself speaking in her mother's voice. Late in the afternoon she remembered that she had not been to see Mr. Fitzgerald in almost a month. She selected a few long stems of azalea and walked across the park to his house, but he wasn't home. She had wrapped the stems in newspaper, so she wetted the paper with the garden hose and left them tilted up against Mr. Fitzgerald's door. It was almost dark as she headed home, entering the back door, pulling off her Keds. As soon as she had showered, the doorbell rang. It was Tacker. She could see him through the glass by the door and she skated down the hallway.

HE LOOKED TALLER.

"Hey," he said.

"Hello," she said.

She sensed he had something to say but she wouldn't let him start. She leaned out the door and into his arms and kissed him. Something in him seemed to retreat, and her heart sank.

"What can I get you to drink?" she said. Was he going to break up with her? He'd been preoccupied since the beach.

"Whiskey," he said.

"You're kidding," she said. Tacker only drank an occasional beer.

"Not really," he said.

"I don't know," she said, rummaging around in the liquor cabinet. She didn't drink hard liquor and had hardly glanced at the cabinet since she had come home from college.

"Looky here," she said in pretend cheer. "Calvert Reserve." She fumbled with the shot glasses. Any moment she would weep. "You're feeling down," she said.

"Oh, not really. A lot on my mind."

She was next to him now, her knees close to his leg, but he didn't reach for her.

"Maybe I'll have one too," she said.

"Why not?" he said.

"Something's wrong," she said. "Tell me." *Don't tell me.*

"It's just the week catching up with me," he said. "What's this about going to Greenville?"

For her sake, she thought, he managed a smile.

"Yeah. My roommate is getting married. I have to go try on a dress for her wedding."

Tacker gulped the whiskey.

"Is that how you drink it?" Kate said.

"Pretty much," he said. "I'll get your car filled up and check the oil."

Thank goodness. "It's only four hours," she said.

"That's a long drive. You should break it up. At least stop at a filling station and get a Coke."

She drank the whiskey as he had; two gulps, not stopping in the middle to breathe. Her body filled with warmth, everything bright and hazy at the same time. "I think I can hear my heartbeat."

"Kate, baby. You're going to Greenville tomorrow. No more whiskey for you."

KATE WAS THE only bridesmaid, and the dress Janet wanted her to wear was avocado green with an orange sash. They were standing in Belk department store downtown.

"We could save some money," Kate said, telling it slant, as Emily Dickinson would say, because the dress was awful. "I could make a dress."

"No, honey," Janet said. "I want to buy you a dress."

There wasn't anything Kate could do but be fitted.

Kate had always imagined Janet marrying in a white eyelet dress in a garden. Instead, she chose a long-sleeved design with a V-neck and an oversize collar, a voluminous skirt, and a swag—like a curtain—across her backside. The veil would trail her by twelve feet.

That afternoon there was a shower to endure and tea and petit fours and cucumber sandwiches. Kate couldn't believe this was Janet, submitting to the rituals of china and crystal and silver. A sixteen-place setting of silver. The Janet Kate knew at Agnes Scott liked beer, not tea. Janet had threatened to get a tattoo. Janet read the Beat poets. She went into hysterics when Buddy Holly died. She went to New York City once and saw *A Raisin in the Sun*, a play written by a Negro woman about housing and segregation. She came back to Atlanta and made Kate walk with her around Decatur so she could see for herself exactly where the neighborhoods divided. "Georgia will never change," she had said, stomping her foot. "Maybe there's hope for North Carolina."

Now here Janet was being an old-fashioned girl marrying a man who might be designing bombs. It was easy for Kate to feel smug. But at night in the guest bedroom, her hands pressed between her legs, she wondered if she was jealous. Sunday morning before she left, she took some pictures of Janet in her wedding dress. A playful picture of Janet leaning out her second-story window, holding her veil, one leg over the windowsill, as if she would leap. And a few sexy ones, not the kind a local photographer would take for the paper.

Sunday it rained as Kate drove back to Winston. Though she had given Tacker Janet's home number before she left—"just in case"—he had not called. He didn't call the night she was back. Finally she called him Monday after a supper of cottage cheese and canned peaches and potato chips. He seemed distracted and she felt herself in the tenth grade again, hoping he would smile at her when they passed in the hall.

"Valentine's here," he said. "Gaines asked me to keep her until nine tonight."

Kate had just come from a world of riotous wedding gowns and orange sashes and tea sandwiches, a world that would not in the least interest Tacker and which she could not bring up because it would seem like a hint.

"When will I see you?" she said.

"We might have to wait for the weekend."

They were only blocks apart. Anger flared in her, but it died easily when he said, "I dream about you."

KATE WOKE EARLY and couldn't go back to sleep. She sat in the window seat and waited for the sun to rise, reading this completely wild story titled "You Can't Be Any Poorer Than Dead" from an old literary journal she had nearly tossed out. It was by some writer in Georgia named Flannery O'Connor whom she had never heard of even though she'd gone to college there. The story was so frighteningly odd that Kate imagined the writer to be some brilliant dwarf-man who lived in a tumbledown house out in the piney woods and survived on moonshine and cured pork. She looked up to see first light breaking through the trees. On her way to the kitchen to brew tea—for she meant to come back and finish the story—she went to the front door to retrieve the morning paper. Her father always fetched the paper just as the sun rose and then brewed coffee and sat at the kitchen table to read it, and by the time Kate and Brian came downstairs for breakfast, he had finished and was folding it up so he could talk with them before he left for work.

When Kate opened the door she found a large package wrapped in butcher paper and tied with string. She picked it up and brought it in, carrying it to the kitchen, where she cut the cord with her mother's kitchen scissors and pressed back the paper. It was a stack of *Life* magazines, twenty at least. A note written on the back of a blank invoice was lightly taped to the first magazine.

> *Dear Kate,*
>
> *These are for you—*
>
> *Love,*
> *Tacker*

She leafed through the stack. Every cover featured a photograph by Margaret Bourke-White, who snapped pictures of ballerinas and the great migration in India and survivors of the

Holocaust—and Winston Churchill, and Marilyn Monroe, and even Joseph Stalin.

Coming out of "You Can't Be Any Poorer Than Dead," the gift was roses. She could smell the greening. Kate was still at the table, looking at *Life*, when the sun started coming in the back windows, which meant it was almost noon. She had eaten two apples with her tea and a handful of roasted nuts and now she was starving. What she wanted was a hamburger and a strawberry shake. She threw on a skirt and sweater, pulled her hair back, and applied lipstick. Summit Street Pharmacy was a short walk. She was out the door in ten minutes.

She passed Miss Mary's house, where she had taken piano lessons for years on end. The house still looked good, all the hedges pruned and a pot of annuals on the porch steps. Kate was reminiscing about how Miss Mary would place her hands atop hers and push the keys as Kate learned the C scale, so she did not notice until she was right at the pharmacy that a group of five Negro boys holding placards were walking in a circle on the sidewalk. She tried to duck in, but someone called. She turned to see Gaines from Tacker's store.

"Oh, hello," she said, hoping to sound casual, the sun hot on her back. She was so hungry she thought she might faint, and there was no place out here to sit.

"How are you this lovely afternoon?" Gaines said.

"I'm just fine, thank you. Yes. And how are you?"

"Me? I'm okay. Thanks for asking." He took his hat off and fanned his face. The four other men kept circling. Kate could see that their signs had to do with the sit-ins. Margaret Bourke-White would have her camera and take pictures and in such a way negotiate this difficult situation just as she had negotiated situations far more daunting.

"You're not working today?" she said to Gaines. It was all she could think of. She might be seeing spots. Was she really going to faint?

"Just down here to support my brothers for an hour during my lunch break."

"I see," she said, feeling dangerously light-headed.

"You okay?" he said.

"I think I may need a drink."

"Let me help you inside," he said, holding the door and taking her elbow.

She nearly stumbled into the dark interior.

"Easy does it," Gaines said. "Just come on this way."

She let him lead. Dinette tables and chairs came into view like a rest stop in heaven. Gaines pulled a chair out for her. "Now all you have to do is order," he said.

"Thank you. Thank you so much," she said, smiling weakly.

Gaines tipped his hat and headed back outside.

"I hope that man wasn't bothering you," the grill cook said.

"Oh my goodness no," Kate said. "He works for a friend of mine." She knew that sentence would convey all the meanings necessary to keep anyone from being alarmed. She ate all of her hamburger and dill pickle and drank two Coca-Colas, and when she left the four picketers were still there but not Gaines, and she was too mortified to talk with the others.

As a young girl in that swimming pool with Brian, she had seen the black children and known they were hot, but she imagined there must be a creek somewhere they could jump in or a landing at a river. There were separate water fountains, but there *were* water fountains for Negroes, and separate entrances at the doctor's office where they could go in and wait to see the doctor just as she could. But no lunch counters where they could sit.

She developed her pictures of Janet. Awfully, she saw that in every one there were sweat stains on the fabric, at her armpits. Kate knew with a sudden clarity that Janet was being forced to marry. She must be pregnant. It was too horrible.

THAT EVENING, TACKER showed up around nine. "Sorry. Gaines was late picking up Valentine."

"I found your gift," she said. "Thank you. It's perfect." She kissed him and took his hand and led him into the library.

He paused before sitting and she thought he was going to say something about himself and Tom and the offer to work for him. But instead he brought up Gaines. "He told me he ran into you today, or, as he put it, you nearly ran into him. He said you looked—I'm not sure what he said—overextended."

"It seemed awfully warm today. I think I waited too long to eat. He was very kind. Sit down."

"Good," Tacker said and sat beside her.

She hadn't meant to say anything because she wasn't sure yet how she felt, but it just came out. "I think I get the point."

"What point?"

"About lunch counters. I would have passed out on the sidewalk today if I couldn't go in and get a cold drink and sit down. I was actually afraid." *I'm also afraid for Janet and why is all of this turmoil converging at once?*

"Are you okay? Why didn't you call me?"

"Did you hear what I said? I think I see the point. It hit me first when the boy asked for a book." She pressed a hand against his shoulder.

"I did hear you. I was beginning to think I had asked too much of you. . . ." His eyes looked dark and full. He hesitated and Kate felt it was one hesitation too many.

"Have you got another girlfriend?" It was a ludicrous thing to say. Janet's situation was making her nervous. Tacker had just given her the nicest gift she'd ever received.

"You know I don't. Listen to me." He reached for her hand.

"You've seemed distant," she interrupted, not wanting to listen because she was afraid of what he might say.

"I'm proud of you, except that I have no right to be proud of you. You came to your own conclusions. You're getting so advanced I may be the one left behind."

He paused and she said nothing, still fearful. He talked as if he had reached some peak and was looking out a far distance.

"I'm trying to work things out with my dad and Tom's offer," he said.

So his thought wasn't quite so lofty. But still she was on edge. "I feel like you're keeping something from me."

"Let me work it out."

"Okay, then," she said and teared up, and he kissed her eyes and then her mouth and held her for a long time.

Chapter Twenty-nine

MAY 25. NEWS came over the local station early Tuesday as Tacker was scrambling his eggs: late yesterday, city officials announced that all lunch counters in the city of Winston-Salem *shall be integrated*. The manager of Woolworth's at Fourth and Liberty threatened to resign at the announcement. The mayor expressed admiration for all sides. *Winston-Salem,* he said, *has peacefully resolved a major point of conflict among its citizens and moved forward into the coming decade a stronger community. So far no disturbance has been reported, though a number of block parties have been reported in Negro neighborhoods.*

Tacker pumped his arm up and down. "Score!" he cried, his voice still morning croaky. Da Vinci skittered against the cabinet. Tacker could see the plate the waitress had thrown into the trash after Gaines had eaten from it. Not anymore. He wasn't watching the oven and his toast burned, the smell almost sweet. From the back porch, he launched torn bits into the yard for birds. Sunlight fell through the trees. If only the pool could be integrated. A car headed down Jarvis. Tacker started to laugh, the doomed laugh of a lost battle just before dawn. His head seemed full of bees.

Two loud knocks sounded on his front door. It was Gaines. He smiled like the sun of a thousand days. "We did it," he said.

"I just heard. Come in. It's fantastic. Unbelievable." The foursquare seemed to rock sideways like a boat foundering on a glacier.

Gaines was six inches off the floor. Standing on the porch was Valentine, wearing a pale summer dress and sandals. She had lost a lower tooth. Gaines started into the house but Valentine appeared rooted in place. Gaines went back and picked her up, her long legs dangling down. She started crying.

"What's wrong, baby?" he said.

"I don't want to go to the Woolworth's," she said. "Someone might break my arm."

"Where'd you hear that?" Tacker said.

"A boy on a bicycle said it."

"No one's going to hurt you," Tacker said.

"You promise?"

"I promise."

WEDNESDAY NIGHT AND Tacker had not figured out what he would say to Tom when he called to take the job.

I've worked things out and I'm ready to take your offer. Only I can't accept the one assignment you have that precisely fits what I told you I wanted.

I'm ready to take your offer. I don't feel I'm ready for the bathhouse. How about another split-level?

I'm ready to take your offer. Let me tell you a story about swimming in paradise.

If he wasn't careful, he was going to blow it with Kate too. "What about it, da Vinci?"

The cat lifted his head when he heard his name and trundled his front paws. Tacker scratched him around the ears. "In the old days, you were just drawn and quartered and then it was over. Now you get to torture yourself with infinite doubt." Even if Kate saw the point about lunch counters, he didn't believe she would approve a second screwup of his career.

He'd had a letter from Samuel telling him about Chukwu, who had written from London, where he had caused a ruckus about being relegated to a less prestigious campus dorm *because I am an African*, he had written. He'd demanded a room in a newer block near the center of campus. What Tacker needed was a little of Chukwu's attitude. Actually, no. What he needed was to sleep and get up early and take a run.

Up before daylight, he took West End to Reynolda, crossed Northwest, and started uphill. It was a grueling climb, but he kept going. About the time he got to Robinhood Road, he felt the stirrings of an idea. He kept going until he could curl around on Buena Vista, and by the time he was sprinting down Reynolda back to the foursquare, the thought began to materialize. As he bolted up his front stairs, he understood it might work.

He'd get himself hired, and then, without Tom's asking for it, he'd do an initial drawing of the bathhouse. And make it pure African. Of course he'd be shooting himself in the foot because he'd get reduced to renderings of carports, additions, and filling stations for a few months. But Tom wouldn't fire him because they knew the same people and were alums of the same college. The bathhouse project would pass and he'd be clear of it.

In the bathroom, he threw cold water on his face. No time like the present. He rustled around in the music room until he found—

under a stack of records—the sketch he had begun in a trance, the sketch inspired by Alan Vaughan-Richards. Loops, circles overlapping at the edges. It still looked like segments of a short, fat caterpillar with a big head. Then there was that rectangle he had sketched, wondering if it might be a veranda, only it was cantilevered in his imagination, and then he had thought *lagoon*, which had sent him searching through his brain until it had dawned on him on the back porch in the dark of night that it was Vaughan-Richards's house. Tacker turned the page upside down to see if it looked more promising that way. He started with a clean sheet of paper, drawing first the main circular room, the lobby swimmers would enter before going left to the men's dressing room or right to the ladies' or straight ahead to enter the pool area. Tom's Carnegie Mellon associates, Hammond and Smith, would hate it.

He decided against Vaughan-Richards's idea of one room abutting directly against the next and instead sketched hallways leading to the dressing rooms. They would feature the decorative cinder block used on so many Ibadan buildings. Without thinking, he sketched the first dressing room elbowing at the center. When he drew the second, he saw they would encompass the entryway courtyard like arms. Looking down on his sketch, it appeared like an airplane if you were facing it and it was coming straight at you: the fuselage with wings cocked downward. *I might as well go for broke.* He made the windows of the central room tall and conical.

His first Christmas in Nigeria, he and Samuel had taken a twin-engine propeller plane up to Kano to pay respects to Samuel's uncle. Tacker had sketched the old wall of the city, an astonishingly tall mud structure with immense conical gates, the gates and the wall decorated with small windows at the top. According to Samuel, they were battlements for the frequent wars of the seventeenth and eighteenth centuries.

Tacker got up and drank a glass of water. It was seven thirty. He had thirty more minutes before he needed to leave for work. Back in his living room, he started a separate sketch of the roof. It would come way out over the broad veranda of the round central room. If only it could be thatch. He wished he could import some goats to hover in that deep shade while swimmers filled the pool. He wasn't in South Carolina, so palm trees were out of the question. Instead he roughed out a pod of circular tables with metal roofs for lounging swimmers.

"This might go over in Disneyland," he said, petting da Vinci.

A sense of violent hilarity kept him alert until he packed it in at the store that evening. Fortunately he wasn't keeping Valentine. He fed the cat and fell asleep on the sofa.

The next morning he called Tom and took the job. He would start in two weeks, allowing enough time to get things squared away with Connie.

Kate dropped by the store. "A movie?" he said.

"You have time for a movie?" she said, either lightheartedly or with a skim of sarcasm in her voice.

"It's been a rough stretch. Let me make it up to you."

"How about bowling?" She said it a little wickedly, like *Go directly to jail. Do not pass Go. Do not collect two hundred dollars.*

"Sure," he said.

KATE WAS AN ace at bowling.

"You never told me," he said.

"You didn't ask," she said. She held the ball at her chin, considered her object, and started her approach, her arm gliding back before releasing the ball like a cannon. Nine pins. The last one wobbled and fell.

"Strike," she said, swirling around in her skirt, displaying her legs, more toned than Tacker had noticed before, even at the beach.

Tacker sipped on his Pepsi. "Why don't I just watch you play?" he said.

She swirled one more time. "I'll be right back," she said and skipped off.

The bathhouse descended into his brain like a swamped vessel and he had a vision of himself locked beneath it at the bottom of the sea. When the reverie broke, he glimpsed a girl two lanes over giving him a look. Then Kate was back, slipping into the chair beside him.

"Your turn," she said.

"You bowl again. We don't have to play a real game," he said.

"Yes, we do," she said. "Go."

They played three games and he won two of them, but it was close and he wished more than anything that he could go home with Kate and fall into her bed. Back at the foursquare alone he couldn't sleep.

Outside the night was dry as stone, the smell of tobacco high and tight. Tacker wondered if the air in the desert felt like this and then he wondered if it was true that you could wash your hands with sand. He watched from his front porch as a DeSoto barreled down the street, windows down, music blaring. Street light scissored through the leaves.

From some other time-space continuum a single line of song wavered: *Who do you love?*

TACKER WAS BEGINNING to enjoy the nihilism he felt. A desert-like existence might be just the thing. As long as he had water, so little else was necessary: a table, his drafting tools, paper, beans, and rice. He could hear his breathing as he moved about the house. Hovering somewhere in North Africa, he transferred his sketch onto drafting paper. He laid it out carefully, more carefully than he'd ever done anything in his life.

His instruments guided him. The central building wasn't in the center at all. It was off to the left on the field. As if by divination, he comprehended the curving path that would lead up to it, with a decorative wall of cinder block four feet high. Kate's hair cascaded down before him. His vision coalesced: the central room, which would, in swimming season, remain open all day; on either side of the room, curvilinear benches flanking the walls; the center of the room large enough for dancing. A great energy filled his arms. He was an architectural outlaw. To each side of the front door, he added a decorative cone-shaped battlement. Lunacy. He repeated the cone shape in the windows, elongated rectangles with half-moon panes above each one. *Who can see out of them? They're too thin,* said Tom or one of his associates in a future conversation behind his back. Tacker ignored them.

He worked into Saturday dawn.

On the front porch, the floor felt keen beneath his bare feet. He sat in the swing and it let out a little bumpy cry, like an animal. He smelled the cedars in the yard. In the morning, he would finish up the design and drop it off at Tom's house. It was a hard call as to whether planning to fail was better than failing unintentionally.

ELEVEN O'CLOCK SUNDAY morning he took a shower and slipped the design into a paper portfolio. He pulled on jeans and a white shirt and loafers. The Indian idled where West End entered First. Blue jays called in their flagrant gibberish. One swooped over the road. The sun was already high. Tom's car was gone—probably he and his wife were at church. Tacker slipped the envelope into his mailbox.

❧

HE TOOK THE Indian to Kate's but her car wasn't there. She sometimes went to Saint Paul's Episcopal on Sundays. He left a note on her front porch. *Going for a ride. Call me later. Love, Tacker.*

He rode out toward Clemmons. Fields were flush with young tobacco plants, gas stations shuttered. It felt good to put miles behind him. For the first time since coming home, he wondered if he might like to move out of the state. Florida, Colorado, New Mexico. When would Gaines get back to Nashville and finish his degree? Was he going to have to wait for his mother to die? Maybe he could transfer to Winston-Salem State. Tacker turned onto a side road, and before long it petered out to dirt. The air turned cool and he knew there was water somewhere. Before long, he came to a pond. He turned the bike off and settled it onto the stand. A blue heron lifted off from the bank. Tacker took the circumference of the water before selecting a seat beneath a stand of cedars. He pulled off his shoes, lying back into the grass, and slept almost instantly. In his dream, he walked into a room and someone grabbed him. He couldn't see a thing. For some reason he held a small potted palm tree in his arms, and he tried to hit his assailant but the darkness was too thick. His swipes with the palm were ineffective and his ensnarement became more certain with each attempt to free himself. The darkness was everything. At the end of the dream he touched his front teeth with his tongue and understood that they were falling out.

Tacker opened his eyes, astonished by the blue sky through the cedar limbs, the green of the cedars. He moved to the place near the edge of the pond where the heron had been. Why did he care so much? Life would be so much easier if he could just forget about fairness. What was justice anyway? You couldn't quantify suffering or pleasure. The sun was full up over the treetops, sending inflamed shafts of sunlight onto the pond. Rather than illuminating the surface, the harsh light turned it gunmetal gray. Tacker began to sob. Finally he let out a deep sigh.

Riding back, he stopped at a filling station with a Coca-Cola machine and bought one and sat in the hot sun and drank it and left the bottle in the crate. There wasn't anyplace on a Sunday to buy a bouquet of flowers to take to Kate so he stopped at his parents' house, where the first heads of hydrangea were turning blue. His mother cut six.

TACKER HELD THE bouquet and a record under his arm and rang Kate's doorbell, a man in search of comfort.

"Thank you," she said. And in an apparent spasm of madness added, "You know, flowers are actually sex organs. That's why they're associated with romance."

"Wow," he said.

Kate's face reddened.

Tacker pulled her close and held her face and kissed her.

"What have you been doing? You've got a blue streak in your hair."

"Painting," she said. "Sometimes I play with Mom's paints."

"I kind of like it," he said.

She darted to a mirror, maybe to distract him from her impulsive comment.

"Mind if I put this on?" Tacker said, showing the record.

"Go ahead."

He did and then he held his hand out and she went to him and they settled on the floor in front of the couch in the library. The sound of the music was vitally sad.

"It's how I've felt today," he said.

Only the lonely.

"I've never heard this song. Who is this guy?" Kate said.

"Roy Orbison."

"It's so sad," she said.

"It seems that way," Tacker said. "But the sadness goes away when you listen. I think it's the high notes."

He started the record again. The music came out of the black disc distilled as wine. The turntable arm lifted, moved slightly forward and then back before settling into the armrest.

"That song tastes like your skin," Tacker said.

"Your shirt smells like lemons," she said.

A round house is a bowl, a nest, a den.

Chapter Thirty

꧁ KATE FILLED HIS mind like sunlight piercing water.

He and Connie figured out a schedule.

Gaines came in every day with an update on the movement. "Looking good, looking good." Tacker worried that his high spirits might attract attention. Black fellows weren't supposed to look too pleased with things, at least not in white parts of town. But Gaines kept doing his job in the same methodical way. "Yes, ma'am. No, sir." Carried out groceries, dusted shelves, threw out spent produce, emptied the trash. With Connie taking over some of the management, Tacker wanted to offer to let him run the cash register, but it would be too much, not for his dad maybe, but for customers.

Tacker recalled his own surprise the first time he glanced in the windows of the First Bank of Nigeria and saw Nigerian tellers, all men, sitting in the booths, counting out money. Then he got used to it and looked forward to going in. He loved their smart attire and the way they wrote out receipts. Their penmanship was immaculate, everyone's similar—a particular hybrid of longhand and print.

Tacker forgot to check his mail. When he did, the mailbox was stuffed. A black ant raced nervously along the edge of an envelope. Tacker flicked him into the grass. His mother had taken to writing him letters, a holdover from Nigeria perhaps. Aside from her letter, there was the usual: the electric bill, a free weekly paper, something from the NC State College alumni office, other odds and ends, including the most recent issue of *Motorcyclist* magazine. And at the bottom of the stack, so that it must have been delivered three days ago, a letter from Tom Driskell. A rockslide of embarrassment fell onto Tacker's shoulders and slid down his back.

He spotted da Vinci through the screen of the front door. "Hey, fella, your human just failed famously. Again." Pray to God Kate wouldn't learn about the design stunt. He'd probably gotten himself fired before he was even hired.

In the living room, he dropped the mail on the coffee table. To delay the inevitable he went to the kitchen and made a pot of coffee. The smell was enticing and for a moment he forgot about the letter. He remembered and the rockslide came back. Might as well get it over with. Da Vinci had settled himself and only twitched his nose at his master's voice.

Tacker tore off the slender end of the envelope, pressed it so it yawned, held it upside down, and let the letter slide into his palm. The folded paper was tattooed with typewritten indentions. Apparently Tom had needed more than a dozen words to tell Tacker what a fool he was. He took a sip of his coffee and read the first paragraph: *looking forward to having you join the firm on North Cherry . . . client happy with the Firestone rendering.* And then the letter veered into absurdity.

*I shared your bathhouse sketch with the head of Parks
and Recreation and he likes it (most of it). The
complementarity of garden elements with the building, the curvature of the walls and path, the use of
open space, the round center with rectangular
projections . . . the new Winston-Salem . . . the future.*

Tacker looked across the room at the hearth, devoid of fire in
the summer. A cool tide of air rode across his forehead.

*You seem to understand fundamental rules of
architecture that apply regardless of the age: one, that
a building should suggest durability, and yet, that it
should also communicate the very movement of time.*

This had to be a joke. Tom was getting back at him for submitting such a ridiculous design. He was going to wax eloquent
and at the end offer a flamboyant rejection. Tacker's ears burned.
He wanted to rip the letter in two, but he continued to the astonishing end.

*Come by one evening and let's discuss a few details.
We'll need to know whether you want to draft
copies for the building committee or have someone
else do that.*

At the very bottom of the page, there was a penciled note:

*I wonder if you studied Oscar Stonorov or had an
opportunity to visit his house in Pennsylvania. I see
the influence of his work in your design.*

No, you don't, Tacker thought. *I studied the sculpture of Anna Becker along the banks of the Osun River and the round houses at Samuel Adeniji's mother's compound north of Ilorin and the king's palace in Kano and practically copied Alan Vaughan-Richards's house on the Lagos lagoon.*

He wandered into his mostly vacant music room, where he had placed a copy of the design in a folder. He opened it up. It looked like an octopus in a sea garden. Yet something in it was mysteriously beautiful. It appeared to levitate over the ground like a foreign god taking note of its new surroundings.

What in the hell was he going to do? Hope Gaines wouldn't learn about it? Who could he tell any of this to? It was a stupid joke and now here he was holding his winnings. It would be a catastrophe in his parents' eyes for him to turn it down. Kate might stand by him but it would strain what they had together and he wasn't sure they would make it through. He thought about Billy Cyrus sausaged in his banking suit. He would love for Billy to know that one of his designs would soon be realized in Hanes Park. Maybe he just wanted to feel like a success again. What was so wrong with that?

There was nothing but to go through with it. He'd submitted the design. Though he'd intended to fail, he had succeeded. Could anything be more idiotic? *I'll never swim in the pool,* he promised whatever gods were listening.

He woke in the middle of the night, drenched in sweat, trailing the nightmare he'd had under the cedars. All he had was a sense of hemorrhaging, losing something as holy as blood. He would go to Tom like a man. Withdraw the bathhouse design. Explain that it was a big mistake. He'd realized that the pool would be segregated and he couldn't be part of it. He wouldn't act holier-than-thou. He'd just say it, matter-of-fact. "You know I participated in the protests. I think it's right what they're doing. We need to integrate. That's the new Winston I see." He would memorize the words so they would be right there when he needed them.

TACKER WAITED BY the goldfish pond beside Tom's studio until the man came out his front door, then stepped forward to greet him.

"Winston's up-and-coming architect," Tom said. "Eager to get started, I see."

"Good morning," Tacker said. "Actually, I need to talk this thing over with you."

"Sure thing. Come on in."

Inside, the studio was just as Tacker remembered: the drafting table in front of the window; the long table stacked with papers; trailing philodendron on high bookcases.

"Let me clear a spot for us," Tom said.

"This won't take long," Tacker said, taking the proffered seat. "What I want to say," he began.

"By the way, did I mention that the director of Parks and Recreation, Ron Mastick, is a graduate of State College too? College of Agriculture."

"I don't think you did," Tacker said, his mind beginning to freeze.

"So, what's up?" Tom said.

Tacker looked out the window. He knew the sentences. Now was the time to say them. *I made a mistake. I realized after turning in the design that I shouldn't have. The pool will be segregated. I've been to the sit-ins. I agree with them. We need to integrate. That's the new Winston I see.*

"Don't know if I'll actually be able to make the copies," he said. It sounded lame, like some kid saying he had a new BB gun but wasn't going to let anyone else try it.

"Well, that's up to you," Tom said, unfazed. He looked at his watch. "By the way, the outdoor showers are going in week after next. The pool will be done and we can start on the bathhouse. A bit of a celebration. Just a few people. Bring a girl."

TACKER HAD HAD malaria once. First it was a cool sensation in his chest. Then there was heat in his throat and he carried a stone on his back. He had left Samuel in the cafeteria and gone to the dormitory because by then he only went up to the faculty house to pick up his laundry. He lay down and pulled a sheet up and fell asleep and he was dead until he woke burning just as the sun tilted red through the window. He flapped his hand, trying to move the sheet. "Lazarus," someone said from a mile away. "He has come back from the dead. Go fetch Samuel." Tacker felt the cover lift off like a sheet of steel. Someone palmed his forehead. Samuel was there holding a glass and a pill. "Take it," he said. Tacker took the pill and closed his eyes and everything was long yellow stripes. He felt a wave break and he slept. When he woke, he was in an ice chest and his teeth rattled until he believed they would crack. *I need my fingers,* he thought, and someone moved his hair out of his eyes. When he opened his eyes next it was dark and he could make out the shape of the window and hear a drum and the drip of water somewhere. Tacker's mother walked into the room. "I'll take over from here," she said. Her nylon dress waved in the gray light but her face shone. She sat next to Tacker and read the story of Wee Willie Winkie. His groin tightened and collapsed. "That's not nice, Tacker," she said.

O say can you see, by the dawn's early light.

When Tacker was well, he counted the paces to the dining hall. Thirty-five. To the classroom, seventy. To the street. One hundred two. He ate bananas and mangos. Then fried okra. Plantain.

I'm alive, he thought. *Nothing can ever go wrong again. Look how alive I am.*

Chapter Thirty-one

KATE LEFT THURSDAY morning for Janet's wedding. Tacker was tied up at the store with the transition and so they made a date for Saturday night when she was back. She took off early, in time to eat lunch with Janet and her mother, a repast of cantaloupe and egg salad sandwiches and Fritos. Because the wedding party was small, one groomsman and one bridesmaid, there was not going to be a rehearsal, but there would be a dinner at the house that evening, so Kate and Janet got busy setting up extra tables, ironing table linens, and polishing the silver. Janet's wedding gifts were on display in the sunroom, gobs of china and crystal and her sixteen-place setting of silver, still virginal though the bride was not. Janet had told Kate after lunch that she was pregnant. "Oh my God," Kate had said. "Oh, sweetie. Are you okay? Is it—? Who's the father?" "Bo, of course," Janet had said. "You're sure?" Katie had said. "Of course I'm sure," Janet had said, before sashaying out the back door in her housecoat and rollers, where she lit up a cigarette. Kate went to her. "I'm so sorry, honey." "It's okay," Janet said. "We're going to be just fine." But her face looked bloated in the afternoon sun. The ring on her finger—white gold with an opal rather than a diamond—already looked tight.

Guests began to arrive at six thirty. Bo was among the last to show up. Kate was aghast at his appearance. He was the size of a refrigerator, burr haircut, paws for hands, a cigar dangling from his mouth even when he talked. He looked thirty-five at least, maybe forty. He kissed the top of Janet's head and pulled her to him like a stuffed animal he might win at the fair. Then he dragged her around as he made the rounds of the room. When they got to Kate, he let go of Janet for a moment, took Kate's hand, and kissed it, and she could smell alcohol on his breath. Janet's lovely upswept hair was beginning to fall. Kate sat at the table with Janet and Bo and his groomsman, whose head looked as if it had been pressed between heavy metal bookends so it was narrow and pointed at the top. Bo dominated the conversation as Janet smiled weakly. What was she thinking? They were as well fitted as an egg and a boulder. He was going to crush her. Anything would be better than this: having the baby, giving up the baby, even that other option no one spoke of but many girls did.

The next morning, Janet appeared to sleepwalk through the ceremony at the small Methodist church. There were only about twenty people and the minister, a young man so young Kate wondered if he'd been to college. Kate insisted that Janet give her her California address and promised to write every week. Early afternoon she started home and was back on Glade at four. When she opened the door to her house, she felt she was walking into a sanctuary. Light fell through the library window and into the hallway. The rooms were quiet and perfect as new candles, lit once and snuffed and waiting.

She wasn't sleepy but her bones felt tired from holding herself stiff for three days. She opened the windows and lay down on her bed. The breeze was refreshing, but she couldn't sleep. She and Tacker were going to dinner at the Robert E. Lee Hotel, to celebrate his new job with Tom Driskell. She wished they were going for a walk in the park and hot dogs at Howard Johnson's instead. Around four the phone rang. It was Mrs. McCall wanting to know if Kate could help with a fund-raiser in July and if so, could she come to a meeting Tuesday afternoon at the library. "Yes," Kate said, feeling wearied even by that bit of responsibility. She'd taken the Brick to South Carolina and snapped not a single picture of the wedding party. How could she, with Bo and his friend's pointy head and Janet's bloated face? She took the camera now and walked out her back door and down the alley. A beauteous canopy of green gave shade to the entire length of it, extending Kate's sense of the sacred that she had encountered walking through her front doorway two hours ago. A chipmunk sprinted across her path and a red cardinal swooped. The air was fresh and light. Ferns unfurled from the base of a rock wall in her neighbor's yard and she recalled what she had said to Tacker about flowers and sex organs. She lowered herself to sitting, remembering the time in the car with James. How cheap and pathetic. It made her sick to think about it.

She was heading down Forsyth when a door opened and a woman came out, waving her hands and calling. Maybe her curtains were on fire. Why wasn't she calling the fire department?

"Oh, you're just what I need," the woman said. "Your camera."

"What can I do for you?" Kate said.

"My lilacs are blooming and my son ran off with the camera. My husband is dead, you may know."

"No, but I'm so sorry." Kate was awestruck by the woman's glibness. "I'm shooting black-and-white film," she said.

"Well, just pop in some color film," the woman said.

"I can't. It'll ruin the pictures I've already taken if I open the back of the camera now."

"Well, I'll swan," the woman said. "That doesn't do me a bit of good. Who wants black-and-white pictures of a lilac bush?"

"I'm sorry you're disappointed. I could come back another day."

"My dear girl. The lilacs are at their peak, their very peak. Later won't do." She let out a sound as if she had just been punched before turning to walk back up her walkway.

"Well, goodness me," Kate whispered, and then she laughed. After a while, she came to the park. Near a bridge, she saw Tacker off to the left, kneeling in the grass not far from the new but still empty pool. What in the world was he doing? She didn't think Tacker prayed, unless it was some African ritual he had learned. He touched the grass and then moved from kneeling to a squat. She nearly called out but instead she made her way across the bridge, finding a break in the hedge. She zoomed in and focused her camera. Through the lens he looked perplexed and alert. Maybe he had dropped something, but he didn't wear a watch or a ring and he wouldn't work this hard to recover a quarter if he had dropped one; maybe a silver dollar. He stood and ran his fingers through his hair and turned in a circle, looking in every direction. She thought for sure he was going to spot her, but he didn't. She snapped several pictures, lowered her camera, punched it back into the case, and snapped it shut.

Back in her kitchen Kate examined Tacker's photograph from Nigeria, the one with Samuel that she kept in her kitchen window. Maybe the thing to do was wait several years to marry, even a decade. In college, Janet had told her that men's sex drive peaked in their early twenties but women's in their mid-thirties.

She could have a dependable man and experience immense sexual satisfaction with no regrets.

If she was honest with herself, she had loved Tacker from her perch in the tree watching him at football practice. She had loved him when they passed in the hallway at Reynolds High. She had loved him at Hart's when she was twelve buying Sugar Babies. She could call and suggest they do something informal, or she had to put on a dress and fix her hair.

She chose the most becoming dress she owned, a pink seersucker with a gathered skirt that came to her knees, a V-neck, sleeveless bodice that effected a double-breasted look, rickrack from the bodice descending into the skirt. The whole affair showed off her slender waist, which she planned to keep that way. She wore a white bangle bracelet and when Tacker rang the doorbell, she picked up a broad white hat that had belonged to her mother. To confuse everyone, including Tacker, she slung the Brick in its lovely brown case over her shoulder.

Chapter Thirty-two

Days passed and the schism in Tacker lessened. He told himself that the bathhouse was just another municipal building. He just wouldn't talk about it. Who would know? Later, if Gaines and his crowd wanted to integrate the pool, he'd stand with them. He invited Kate to go with him to the celebration Tom had mentioned.

They crossed Glade and followed a path that led them to a spot affording a view of the new pool not far from the tennis courts. Kate carried her camera, as usual. A canvas tent was up but it appeared to open in the opposite direction and they didn't see anyone. They cut down the hill and Tacker spotted the yellow stakes driven into the ground to show the general position of the bathhouse. He grabbed Kate's hand and they ran, she holding on to her summer hat. He stopped them five feet from his imagined courtyard. Holding his hand palm forward, he made a motion as if encountering a pane of glass. "This is where the decorative wall begins," he said. "It's going to skirt a path and be bordered by flower gardens. What do you think?"

"I love it," she said.

He caught her at the waist and kissed her. "Come this way," he said, and they walked the yet-to-be-laid path. He stopped again. "The double-door entrance," he said. "In the summer it's open all day." He made a motion to open the door for her. They entered the imagined bathhouse. "We're in a circular lobby, with a jukebox, of course. Over there's the ladies' dressing room. And on the left is the men's."

They heard voices.

Tacker held Kate's hand. "Tom?"

A man stepped out from the canvas tent. "Over here," he said.

Tom introduced Tacker to his new partners, Fred Hammond (tall, white-haired, cigar) and Randy Smith (forties, round face, pleasant). Tacker introduced Kate.

"You're a photographer?" Tom said to Kate, pointing to her camera.

"Kate's had some of her photographs in the *Journal*. You may have seen them. She's got a great eye," Tacker said.

"I admire a man who praises a woman," Tom said. "Let's have her take our picture."

So Tacker and Tom posed and Kate seemed immensely pleased and blushed and got flustered and recovered and Tacker thought, *This is how she would be at her wedding.* She took several shots.

"That should do," she said, and snapped the camera shut.

"My wife, Kathy, couldn't make it," Tom said to both of them. "Down with a summer cold."

"How miserable," Kate said.

There were others present—inside the tent—and Tom introduced everyone around. When the second glass of champagne was poured, the group of eight—Tacker and Kate included—sauntered to the edge of the pool. The blue tile shone like square frames of fallen sky. Kate sat at the pool's edge, took off her pumps, and pretended to dangle her feet in the water.

"You okay?" Tacker said.

"Oh yes, perfectly fine," she said.

He turned back to the men and a woman who was latched onto Fred Hammond, though neither wore a ring. The evening deepened and he imagined Gaines in the trees watching him right this minute, even Valentine with binoculars, somehow hoisted high in the crook of tree limbs, narrating his every move and Gaines writing it down to report in a Negro newspaper.

ANOTHER LETTER ARRIVED from Samuel. He asked Tacker about his family before reporting that even before opening its doors, their high school was full to capacity and needed an additional block of classrooms. Samuel had discovered that a university in Ghana offered a degree in architecture and might apply. All of Nigeria was readying for Independence Day. He hoped to go to Lagos for the ceremonies. Tacker had been too overwhelmed with Tom and the transition at Hart's and Valentine in the evenings and Kate on the weekends to keep up with the Nigerian news. He didn't feel the pull like he had even as recently as the beach trip.

Glad to hear you might be able to study in Ghana, he wrote back. *I'm doing pretty well here, getting on with a firm in my hometown.*

Meanwhile, Carl Matthews, who had started the protest at Kress, wanted to integrate bathrooms in the downtown shops.

"You know the Anchor?" Gaines said one afternoon near closing at Hart's. "You're not going to believe this. They've got a slop jar behind a curtain in the back of the store for Negro women. It's all the same," he went on. "White folks think black people carry diseases. Remember how that waitress threw away that plate after I ate a bite of pie?" He chuckled.

Tacker thought of the new swimming pool with the blue tiles like mirrors of heaven that would not be open to Valentine or Gaines because of the same idiotic idea: black people were dirty. Guilt shuttered through him.

"You okay?" Gaines said.

"Yeah. Yeah. Sure."

"Stay cool," Gaines said, taking off his apron, heading out.

IN HIS UTTER confusion, Tacker asked his mother over for dinner on a night his father worked. "I've cleaned up the old grill in the backyard," he said. "I'll fix steaks."

"That's awfully sweet of you, but why don't you just come over here?" she said.

"It's my invitation. I'm asking you over here," he said.

She arrived in slacks and a geometric-looking blouse.

"You've been shopping," Tacker said.

"Do you think it's too mod?" she said.

"Where'd you learn that word?"

"The young people have taken over the women's magazines, Tacker. All the fashions are for eighteen-year-olds. I do my best."

She followed him into the kitchen.

"You were always mod," he said. "Dad's the old fogey."

"Don't try to charm me. I'm your mother. Want me to shuck this corn?"

"That'd be great."

He opened a cabinet and stared at his odd assortment of glasses. Suddenly he wanted Kate, his own house, his own life.

"Tacker?" his mother said.

"I think I want to marry Kate," he said.

"Oh, that makes me so happy. I knew it. I just knew it."

"I didn't know it," he said, still focused on the glasses. "I didn't know for sure until just this second." And now what? Was he going to depend on Kate to drive her Nash Metropolitan on their honeymoon? Move into her house?

His mother picked at the strands of corn silk. "I'm so happy," she said again.

"I know I've worried you."

"Don't make me cry."

"BE CAREFUL COMING down the steps," Tacker said when they started out back.

"I'm not a grandmother yet," his mother said.

Tacker had already started the fire and now the coals glowed. He laid the steaks on the center of the grate, the corn on the perimeter. His mother held her arms crossed at her waist.

"When are you going to ask her?"

"Kate? I need to save up for a ring. I probably need to save up for a car."

"I have your grandmother's engagement ring. I'll show it to you Sunday. It's white gold. That used to be popular. It's yours if you want it."

DA VINCI WASN'T in the bedroom. Tacker searched the upstairs. No cat. Something felt wrong. Eleven o'clock, he grabbed his flashlight and peered beneath the back porch. Could he have gotten into the garage? No sign of him. Tacker rode the Indian around the block, down Jarvis to Sunset to First and up, hooking a left on West End, calling for da Vinci, stopping to listen, looking under bushes, sweeping his flashlight across the street, the most frightening possibility. Even more frightening: someone might have taken him. Billy the banker, taken the cat. Whoever broke the door at Hart's. Someone who would deliver da Vinci dead to his doorstep in the morning. At two o'clock Tacker gave up and went into the house and fell into bed. He dreamed of himself in Nigeria trying to piss into a Coca-Cola bottle.

Late to work and worried about da Vinci, Tacker forgot what he had said the evening before about Kate until his mother walked into Hart's midafternoon.

"You never know when you might want to pop the question," she said, slipping a slender box into his shirt pocket. "I think you'll be pleased."

In the lounge, Tacker pulled out the box. A single round diamond in a square setting, lapped by scrolling white gold that tapered to a slender band. He only vaguely remembered his grandmother. She had died when he was five. But a picture of her in a calf-length skirt and jacket, wearing a jaunty hat and standing in front of a little clapboard house, had claimed a place in his parents' living room all of his life. Only now looking at her ring did he consider how he had imagined a story about her as a daring woman with a bright mind and a sunny disposition who had perhaps not really died but only slipped away, driven out to California, escaped the rigors of rural North Carolina and a life of shelling peas.

Tacker put the ring back in the box, put the box in his pocket, tapped it, and went back to work. This week, Tom was moving from his studio to the office on North Cherry. Next week, Tacker would start part-time with Hammond, Smith, and Driskell. Maybe by August, he would have enough money to propose. He wasn't sure Kate would say yes. Right now he felt he was skating on thin ice in every direction. Just then a woman came through the checkout with several cans of cat food. Da Vinci.

SATURDAY MORNING, GAINES was late to work. "You let me down. You really let us down," he said when he pushed through the swinging doors of the lounge.

"What?" Tacker said.

"A swimming pool. You're working on that thing?"

"Well, the bathhouse, actually."

"No difference."

"A slight difference."

Tacker felt his chest tighten. You always had to pay the piper.

"My mama read it last night from the afternoon paper, nice little article in the local section about a pool in the park right over yonder. And then, lo and behold, it mentions a design by favorite son Tacker Hart. I said, 'Mama, read that back to me.' She goes to the beginning and starts over. I say, 'No. Not from the beginning. That part about the design.' So her eyes go down the page. I'm watching her. She couldn't get the guy's name right, whoever your design is reminiscent of. I say, 'Skip it. Go on.' She reads, 'Tacker Hart, a name familiar to many for his high school fame . . .' You get the picture. I say, 'His true colors come out.' And she says, 'You talking about that white boy you work for?' I say, 'Yes, ma'am. That's him in living color. White, white, white. White as snow.' Man. I thought you were with us."

"I am," Tacker said.

"You are helping to build something I can't go into. They won't let me past the gate unless I'm cleaning toilets. Or Valentine. Just like Crystal Lake."

"I'm not building it," Tacker said. "I only gave them a rendering. They're making lots of changes. The building was going to be built anyway."

"A swimming pool. I couldn't have dreamed this up," Gaines said.

"I'm not going to swim in the pool. I already decided."

"Oh. You're going to take a vow of chastity. Keep your pinkies out of the water. And that's going to make it okay for all the little Negro children who get to line up around the pool in the heat of summer and look in through some fancy wall or fence, watching the pretty white children play in the water."

"I didn't actually want them to choose my design."

"Well now, that's interesting. Your daddy send in a drawing for you?"

"Look. I'm sorry," Tacker said.

"Forget it, man."

"You think I should give it up?"

"Looks like it doesn't matter to you what I think."

Gaines kept his distance and there wasn't much Tacker could do, given how much he still had to explain to Connie, who would take over as assistant manager on Monday. She listened with what appeared to be a mix of pity and humor, as if he were still thirteen, explaining why Duke Snider was a better ballplayer than Mickey Mantle. (Tacker had turned out to be wrong.)

THAT EVENING, TACKER got home to find da Vinci on the front porch, scraggly and limping.

"Hey, fella. What happened?" A copperhead would have killed him; a trap would have left a wound. Tacker examined his front paw and found a splinter. "You get stuck in someone's basement?" Da Vinci began to purr. Tacker called Kate. "You got a pair of tweezers? I need to get a splinter out of da Vinci's paw."

She was there in ten minutes, wearing an old pair of pants, her hair tied back in a kerchief, smelling a little musty.

"I was working in the yard," she said.

They stood at the kitchen sink, where the light was good. He held the cat. Kate leaned in to press the paw. The down over her lips was darker than he remembered. He noticed an acne scar he'd never seen before.

"I got it," she said, pulling back, proffering the splinter.

Tacker put the cat down and he walked into the dining room with only a slight limp.

"Probably still sore," Kate said.

"The porch door must have been unlatched when my mom came over."

"I hadn't heard about that," Kate said.

"We cooked on the back grill. No special occasion," Tacker said, remembering the ring in his top dresser drawer.

"I'm sorry I can't stay," Kate said. "I've got to get home and clean up. Dinner with Mrs. McCall and the board."

"It's okay. Thanks." He leaned over and kissed her, her imperfections somehow sexy.

Chapter Thirty-three

MONDAY MORNING, TACKER got to the store at six. He sat long enough to drink a cup of coffee and when he stood, his vision went blurry, as if he'd been blinded by a camera flash. Gaines pushed through the delivery door not much later.

"You're not looking too good," he said, eyeing Tacker.

"Something's wrong. I feel dizzy. I keep seeing white lights," Tacker said.

"You look pasty. What have you had to eat this morning?" Gaines said.

"Nothing."

"You got low blood sugar."

"How do you know?"

"Old Daddy. I'll get you a Coca-Cola and a candy bar."

By the time he was back, Tacker felt himself shaking.

"You think I have diabetes?" he said, feeling suddenly fragile and old.

"Opposite problem," Gaines said. "You just need to eat. You and your girlfriend seem to be forgetting that."

"Thanks." He sipped on the Coca-Cola and finished the candy bar. Now he felt sweaty. "I'm really sorry about the bathhouse. I wanted the job with Tom. You wouldn't believe me if I told you what I'd done."

"Try me," Gaines said, pulling up a stool.

So he did: beginning with how Tom dangled the bathhouse in front of him; how Tacker felt boxed in; how he'd tried to kill it by turning in a rendering so bizarre he'd be hired out of pity but consigned to carports; how his plan had backfired.

"That's priceless," Gaines said, laughing, though it seemed less at Tacker than at the Fates. "White boy can't fail."

"But I did," Tacker said.

"How's that?"

"I got fired by Clintok. I haven't told anyone. Only my folks know. Not even Kate, really." Why was he telling Gaines all of this? He needed to go home and shower again. It was seven o'clock.

"You pulling my leg?"

"No. I was accused of going native, hanging out with Nigerians too much, living in the dorm with them, going to these ritual festivals and all."

"You serious?"

"Dead serious. I got put in a straitjacket and loaded onto a plane."

Gaines looked at him hard. "You are serious."

"Of course I am."

"Well, it makes more sense," Gaines said.

"What does?"

"That you've tried to help us."

"Yeah. I'm still sorry to let you down."

"I'll think of a way you can make it up to me," Gaines said.

Connie arrived at seven thirty and they had things in good enough shape for Tacker to run home and shower before heading over to his new job. Tom hadn't yet hired a secretary. Tacker spent the first week filing, cruised to Hart's for the afternoon shift, and felt pretty good that he got through his days without a catastrophe, though twice he dreamed of showing up at Tom's office and realizing too late that he was naked.

Chapter Thirty-four

AT HART'S ON Saturday, Gaines said, "We have a couple of fellows coming to Winston to talk with us about picketing Thalhimers. They're already doing it in Raleigh. Can you give them a place to stay tonight?"

Tacker was exhausted from the first week of juggling two jobs, and all he wanted to do was get through the day and spend Sunday with Kate, thinking of nothing but her pulse—in her neck, at her wrist, and anywhere else he could find it.

"I haven't got beds," he said, hoping to discourage the idea.

"They'll bring bedrolls," Gaines said, settling it, as Samuel had.

Where will you sleep?

Don't worry. I'm an African. I can sleep on the floor. I prefer it.

THEY CAME AROUND dark. Tacker was surprised that one of the men was white. They carried backpacks and sleeping bags.

Gaines came in to make the introductions. Valentine was with him, and she burst in before anyone could speak.

"Da Vinci!" she called. The cat rose and stretched and Valentine yelped as she crossed the floor, scooped up the cat, and buried her face in his fur. "May I feed him?" she said.

"Of course," Tacker said.

Gaines gestured as he spoke. "Tacker, meet Philip and Steven. Steven and Philip, Tacker."

Philip's skin was darker than Gaines's. The men took seats. Valentine settled in the music room on a cushion with da Vinci.

"Tell me what's happening in Raleigh," Tacker said.

"We're picketing in Cameron Village," Philip said. He seemed the leader. "I hear you were at State."

"Five years," Tacker said. "Couldn't afford much shopping at the time, but I took in a lot of movies in Cameron Village."

"You know the slogan for the shopping center?" Philip said.

"Can't say that I do," Tacker said.

"'Shop as you please, with the greatest of ease, in the wonderful Cameron Village!' It's a jingle on the radio."

Gaines and Steven laughed.

"We're just trying to take them up on their offer," Philip said.

When the conversation lapsed, Tacker feared Gaines would say something about the pool and the bathhouse. Steven stretched his arms overhead.

"Full day tomorrow," Philip said.

On the way out, Valentine gave Tacker a hug, and he watched as she and Gaines drove away in the borrowed car. He still didn't know whose it was. The car was like Negro newspapers and Frances's eulogy, a redolent reminder of a life he would never be part of.

People who have lived deeply in two countries always bear the awareness of both, even in their physical movement, like a twin carries his second self even when separated. Showing Philip and Steven an upstairs room, Tacker bore in muscle and bone memory of an evening in Osogbo along the Osun River, settling in to sleep beside Samuel. The front room of the foursquare was furnished with only a dresser and low table. The men opened their bedrolls. Tacker showed them the bathroom—he wanted to say the "lavatory"—but it would require explaining and in his personal reminiscence he wanted no disturbance. It seemed to him he skated rather than walked, as one apprehends oneself in dream, moving noiselessly in a world that bears the trace of others, a country that is all countries and none.

Early Sunday morning Tacker had coffee ready. The three men stood on the back porch, looking out onto the yard. Philip asked about the garage, whether it was a workshop.

"Once maybe," Tacker said. "I don't know. I keep my bike there, an Indian."

"I'd love to see it," Philip said. "Never ridden one of those."

"Of course," Tacker said.

"Maybe this afternoon," Philip said.

"Will you guys stay another night?"

"If that's all right," Steven said. "We came on the bus; probably start back tomorrow morning."

Tacker thought about the bus. The two men having to separate when they took their seats. He wondered how folks at the depot saw them: Steven, white, getting out of an old car with Philip and Gaines. In the morning light that was like a gloaming, Tacker wanted to tell them he'd been to Nigeria. But he didn't, because it would take hours and he wasn't sure himself what the relationship was between what they were doing and what he had done there.

"We'll see you tonight," Philip said.

"Right," he said. Only after they left did he consider how they had shared the upstairs bath with the claw-footed tub. At least one bathroom in Winston-Salem was now integrated.

He called Kate. "Can I come see you?" he said.

"Now?" she said, her voice unpracticed. This was how she would sound if he woke up in bed with her.

"Yes, now."

She was waiting for him, sitting on the top step of her porch. They spoke little, using instead a language of touch. At noon they took Kate's car to a family restaurant in a square white building that served a Sunday smorgasbord. They got there before the crowd.

He parked the car. A coil of hair had escaped her ponytail and he reached across the seat to stroke it. He hadn't brought the ring but he imagined that he had. What would he say? *I've never loved anyone else.* He imagined her eyes growing large and solemn. *We don't always agree,* she would say. *Which is why we'll never grow bored,* he would answer. But he felt some sadness in the daydream, some foreboding that he and Kate would never quite connect. He attributed the feeling to the general sadness he often felt on Sunday. In haste he told her instead about Philip and Steven staying overnight with him, about the new protest.

"It's okay," she said, smiling.

"It's okay with you?" he said, not sure she'd heard him.

"Yes. Are we going to eat?"

"Let's go in," he said, buoyant with joy.

WHEN TACKER GOT to the office Monday morning, the place had a new sign—HAMMOND, SMITH, AND DRISKELL ASSOCIATES, ARCHITECTS—and a secretary named Molly. Molly brought in

sandwiches at midday and the men ate sitting on stools in Fred
Hammond's office. Tom was bidding on an entire cul-de-sac in
one of the new subdivisions. Almost offhandedly, as if somehow he knew there was fire in it, he said, "We're breaking
ground for the bathhouse next week and opening the pool to the
public early August."

Tacker's mouth was full of sandwich. When he could speak, he
stuttered. "You're—you're kidding. When was that de-decided?"

"The mayor wants to open the pool. There's an election coming up this fall. The city's putting in privacy tents temporarily."

Tacker started to hiccup.

"Hope you can be there, Tacker," Tom said, eyeing him.

"I'll do my best," Tacker answered, setting the rest of his
sandwich aside.

A KNOCK ON his front door; Miss Smith from next door. She
peered into the house.

"Would you like to come in?"

"Oh no." She waved a handkerchief at the air. "I wondered if
you could fill my grocery order," she said, handing him a slip of
paper.

"Happy to," he said. "You can always call the store."

Her eyes narrowed. "Mr. Hart, do you have Negroes living
in there?"

"I live here alone, Miss Smith," he said. "I've had a Negro
guest on occasion."

She lifted her hand and appeared ready to retrieve her grocery list. "I'm an old woman. I hope you'll spare me any un-
pleasantness."

"I'll have your groceries this evening," Tacker said. "Glad to
help."

❧

Mid-July, Winston was thick green, shade beneath trees so deep it looked like water. Tacker was depositing his paychecks, spending little, working up his nerve to ask Kate to marry him. In the evenings, he rode out of town, the sky long and blue, skirts of white cloud. Heading east, he found himself amid fields of corn as tall as he was, leaves flying up to show the pale undersides. Against a stand of trees deer grazed, mothers with fawns, occasionally a second-year male, antlers not yet full. One evening, Tacker lifted Valentine onto the Indian and took her for a ride, West End to Hanes Park and around it and then Reynolda all the way out to Wake Forest College and back, and then they stopped on the bridge where Glade empties onto Hawthorne, Peters Creek flowing beneath. They picked up pebbles and threw them in, one after another. Back on the bike, they headed uphill so he could show her Kate's house. They climbed her yard steps and reached the porch and rang the doorbell, but no answer.

Tacker turned the cycle around and let the bike glide back toward West End.

"Stop!" Valentine said.

He pulled to the curb.

"What's that?" she said, pointing to the south lawn of the park.

"That's the park," he said.

"No. That." She pointed again.

The white canvas tent was still up. "It's just a tent," Tacker said.

"What's that next to it?"

"A swimming pool," Tacker said.

"Oh," she said. Her brow furrowed and she turned her head sideways. "Let's go back to your house," she said.

❦

"PHILIP AND STEVEN are back in town. Wonder if they can crash with you," Gaines said.

"You bet."

They were quiet when they came in, as though it were an evening before a solemn witnessing. They carried their placards upstairs. DON'T BUY SEGREGATION. BOYCOTT FOR FREEDOM.

In the morning, they were gone before Tacker woke up.

Chapter Thirty-five

KATE WAS WORKING out some connection between what had happened to Janet and what happened to Negroes turned away from any town's central library. It seemed an unlikely connection, yet she knew it was there if she studied the problem long enough. Since her near fainting at Summit Street Pharmacy, she felt nervous going to Hart's, not sure exactly how to act if she saw Gaines. Should she shake his hand? Say hello and smile?

She parked her car in the parking lot and rolled down the windows to let the breeze through, then checked her image in the rearview mirror and got out. Connie greeted her when she walked in. There was Gaines in living color, loading cantaloupes into a large wooden bin. Kate pretended to study her list, composed herself, and lifted her face. "Good morning," she said.

He looked at her. "Good morning," he said, without a smile but maybe with a hint of recognition, as if they had once, ever so briefly, shared a common interest. "These are some sweet cantaloupe."

"You tried one?"

"I can smell them," he said, putting his nose to the end of one. "Here. Take this one."

"Thank you," she said.

He got back to work and she pushed her cart past him. Moments later, Tacker came out of the back room and saw her and came to where she stood.

"Hey, babe," he said.

"Hey to you, too," she said. "Although my mom always said hay was for horses."

"Good day, Miss Monroe."

"Good day, Mr. Hart." She smiled largely and finished her shopping.

"Want to come help me in my backyard on Saturday?" he said, ringing up her items.

"What are you going to do?"

"Clean it up. I invited Gaines and Valentine over next weekend. I thought Valentine would be able to play if I tidied up back there."

"Sounds like fun." She kissed his cheek. Oddly she no longer felt threatened by this business about lunch counters, and she wondered how much of it was the boy asking for the book, or Gaines helping her out, or Tacker's move into architecture, or Janet's abysmal marriage. When she got home, she picked up her camera and focused it on her image in the mirror at the end of the hall. Her backbone felt solid and strong—not a blade but the living buttress of herself—and the cool lozenge in the right chamber of her heart had vanished.

Saturday she was at Tacker's house at eight o'clock. Fortunately the backyard was shady and it was a cool morning for late July. They started raking leaves down the slope of the yard. "Later I'll move them to the other side of the garage for a mulch pile," Tacker said.

"You know about mulch piles?" Kate teased.

He lowered his chin and gazed at her as through spectacles. "Yes," he said.

A dove sang its *hoo-hoo, hoo-hoo* and a filament of light illuminated a climbing rose. "I never doubted," she said.

"Let's just rake past those trees for now," he said, gesturing.

They raked in the deep shade of the porch for a while and Kate remembered months ago raking out her father's monkey grass, she in her father's old coat, and how she had gone into Hart's after seeing Gaines pass by in the alley with that bottle of milk. They ran out of shade and worked in the sun. At ten o'clock, just as Kate was about to stop and demand a cold drink, she uncovered the edge of a mossy patch.

"Oh, look!" she said.

"What?"

"Moss," she said.

"Is that exciting?"

"I love moss." On her knees, she raked with her hands, revealing a large patch of velvet upon which she then proceeded to sit cross-legged. "I'll have a lemonade," she said.

Together they sat, admiring the emerging structure of the yard. There was the climbing rose that once had a trellis. Tacker had uncovered a slate patio in front of the old stone grill. A hedge of boxwoods defined what must have been a lawn—before the trees grew so large and the yard was left untended. High in the yard, near the house, they'd uncovered two flower beds, bordered by stone, where spring bulbs had spent themselves. "There may be enough sun for caladiums," she said.

By midafternoon they had pulled up half-buried stones and defined another garden and they were smeared with dirt.

"I can't get in my car like this," Kate said.

"You can shower in my bathroom," Tacker said. "Take off

your clothes on the screened porch. You know where the bath-room is."

"Really?"

"What else are you going to do?"

She watched Tacker sitting in the circle of moss, his back to her as she unbuttoned her blouse and pulled it off. She rocked off her tennis shoes, then pulled off her pedal pushers, then peeled off her underclothes. A breeze came through the porch and her skin prickled. Tacker kept his back turned but she still felt exposed as she tiptoed through the kitchen and into the din-ing room. Da Vinci lay in the hallway. He opened his eyes to look at her and closed them again. "Not impressed, huh?" she said. She tiptoed down the hall toward Tacker's bedroom and bath. The door squeaked as she opened it and it would not fully close. "I've never," she whispered to herself.

She used the shower, washed and scrubbed, borrowed Tack-er's Prell, and lathered her hair twice. She washed between her legs with Prell, then leaned over to scrub between her toes, the steady stream of water cascading over her. Kate hadn't thought about a clean towel. Feet on the bathmat, she reached for Tack-er's. She dried her hair and wrapped the towel around her. Nei-ther of them had thought about clean clothes. She peeked out of the bathroom. For starters, she'd have to wear her damp under-wear, maybe borrow a shirt. Tacker was still sitting on the moss, faced away from her. *Good man,* she thought, as she slipped back into her damp underclothes. In Tacker's room, she rum-maged for something to put on, finding at last a man's housecoat pressed back in a dresser drawer, an item, no doubt, his mother had given him one Christmas but that he never used.

Through the porch screen she saw clouds had gathered and a breeze poured over her. "I'm through, I guess," she called.

Tacker turned and looked toward her, though she didn't

think he could see through the screen. He ascended the steps, his gaze down until he pulled open the screen door and entered, the door slamming behind him, the little latch twinkling like a bell. It seemed he would walk past her and Kate wondered if he was blinded, coming in from the bright afternoon.

"Tacker," she said.

He hesitated and then he came to her and lifted her off her feet, cupping her behind, she locking her legs around him. He moved like a tremendous machine, pressing into her, angling her upward, one hand pulling her hair back, his mouth on her neck.

She wiggled.

"Cut it out," he said, releasing her to standing, opening the housecoat, putting both hands to her breasts.

She unbuttoned his shirt.

"You're filthy," she said.

"You're not," he said, kissing her neck again.

Kate smelled the rain before it came. The first drops hit the roof of the porch like hail.

Tacker took her hand and they were in his room and he was kissing her onto the bed.

"Wait," she said, thinking of Janet and her fast wedding.

Tacker moved to his dresser and took something out, a small square envelope. She had never seen one but knew what it was and she closed her eyes and he was back, moving over her, and this time when she went down into the deepest water, she was not drowning. She was flying.

Chapter Thirty-six

🌀 "GUESS YOU KNOW the pool is opening?" Gaines said one night when he dropped by with Valentine.

"Yeah, I heard," Tacker said.

"They having a ceremony?"

"Probably."

"So you aren't going to be there?" Gaines said.

"Not if I can find a good excuse," Tacker said.

"Maybe you ought to go."

"I thought you were against my having anything to do with all that. Make up your mind."

"I'm just saying maybe you ought to go."

A CONCESSION STAND went up where Tacker's design called for oversize double doors into the circular main room. Gravel was trucked in for a temporary walkway.

✦

SAMUEL WROTE THAT he was engaged to marry a woman who was a student at UCI and when she finished her BA they planned to go to London for further study. His brother now had three market stalls and had made enough money to build himself a house. The high school in Osogbo had dedicated the chapel building.

ON TACKER'S RADIO, Senator Kennedy: *The world is changing. The old era is ending. The old ways will not do.*

ON A THURSDAY in late July, Tacker left Hart's, took the Indian to the foursquare, fed da Vinci, showered, ironed a shirt, took his grandmother's ring in its box from his bureau drawer, put it in his pocket, and walked to Kate's. Coming around a corner, he remembered the first time he called at her house and was about to leave when she came tearing down the hall and jerked open the door and pulled him in, her hair all awry. The sky was clear. A gust of wind filled the trees and a few yellow leaves scudded down and wove along the sidewalk. He didn't have a plan exactly. Buildings you planned. Proposing seemed like something you could overplan and it would fall flat. He kept his hands in his pockets. Maybe he should plan a little. He came around the next corner and there was Kate in her front yard, watering the lawn. She wore white shorts and had her hair tied up in a ponytail. He started to run, as if she might shut off the water and disappear in a plume of vapor. He was on the second set of her yard steps when she turned and sprayed him full in the chest. Kate dropped the hose, and it flapped like a fish on a boat. Her hands went to her mouth. Tacker looked at his shirt and the front of his trousers. Soaked to the knees.

"Oh no," she said. "I didn't see you."

"I'm wash-and-wear," he said, smiling, taking five big steps toward her and pulling her to him.

"Now I'm wet," she said, looking at her damp blouse.

The afternoon throbbed with green life. Tacker turned off the water.

"Oh. What's that?" Kate tapped his pocket, the wet fabric of his shirt molded around the little box.

"Let's sit down," he said.

On the front porch of the house on Glade Street he pulled out the nondescript box. It might hold his baby teeth or a Boy Scout achievement badge or the leather bracelet from Nigeria that he kept in a cigar box with his passport and visa and some pound notes he had never exchanged.

"I want to marry you, Kate. Will you marry me?"

Her eyes were lavender again, like that first morning when he was still reeling from all that had happened in Nigeria and she had confided in him and her confidence had been a light.

"Yes. Yes."

He opened the box. "It was my grandmother's. I hope you like it."

She lifted the ring, slipped it onto her finger, and closed her hand.

He wondered if every lover is redeemed by love as he felt he was in that moment. And in love he forgave Lionel Fray and understood that Samuel had forgiven him.

August comes like an orange cat
Rain pours down in an afternoon
Your hand is a cup in the shape of a magnolia petal
And as sweet.

Chapter Thirty-seven

WHEN TACKER TOLD Kate that Philip and Steven would be back in town the night of the cookout—the two men who occasionally stayed with him when they were in town for a protest—she steadied herself and took the news in stride. But that evening at home and with more time to think, she found that this change of plans disturbed the calmer waters she had sensed herself in with the man she loved. That many people in a backyard in West End would not go unnoticed, especially when the group was this mixed and included two adult Negro men. In a compartment of her mind, she understood that she still felt vulnerable in regard to public opinion. But then she viewed the ring on her finger and Tacker's confidence in who he was and she experienced a great relief to have finally decided what side she was on. She didn't have to hover over uncertainty forever, like a bird over the ocean. And perhaps it was because of this new awareness that she had come to the certain conclusion that her father had not meant to drown himself. About one thing

Aunt Mildred was absolutely right: strong men drown. But they don't kill themselves. And, no doubt because she had come to this conclusion, she also chose to believe that her parents would have made amends. There never would have been a divorce. Her father had not left, nor had he intended to. She saw him again walking in D.C. that summer past the gardens, his hair lifted by the wind. He was as certain and straight as the levels at the hardware store she had visited with Brian, who had foreseen that she would choose Tacker Hart.

She doubled her potato salad recipe for the cookout and arrived early to hang paper lanterns. Tacker was in his backyard setting up two folding tables, and the sight of him brought a rush of affection, not only for him but for the two of them together. In her high school years and even in college, even after her mother died, it had never occurred to her that she might marry and also have a career, that she might find a man, or be found by one, who would expect her to fulfill her ambitions. "How did you get to be this way?" she had asked him the day he proposed. "I'm not sure," he had said. "No, really." "Maybe Nigeria. Women there make their own money. If they're good at something, they keep doing it. My mom once told me she wanted to be a pharmacist when she was girl."

She and Tacker pushed the tables together. Tacker took her hand and kissed it and Kate apprehended the warmth of his happiness. She covered the tables with a checkered tablecloth, then plucked flowers from the rose of Sharon blooming by the street and laid them in bowls of water and set one in the center of each table. She turned her ring.

When two men drove up and parked on Jarvis, Kate knew they must be Philip and Steven. Moments later, Tacker introduced them. Philip was very dark-skinned, large, with a round face and a few premature gray hairs along his temples, a gentle giant. Steven was fair-skinned, no taller than Kate, ears sticking out from his head. They were an odd pair and she almost laughed in relief. Their actual presence seemed entirely natural, whereas the thought of them had seemed threatening. This awareness seemed important to consider later and she made a note of it.

"You've cleaned up back here," Steven said.

"Kate helped me," Tacker said, close by now, leaning over to kiss her shoulder.

"You thought about buying this house?" Philip said.

"I hadn't yet."

No one spoke for a moment.

"Kate and I just got engaged," Tacker said.

Philip's head tilted back and he laughed as large as he was, a laugh like a conclave of silverware thrown in a basket. Kate took a step back.

"You have my congratulations," he said. "You two. But we didn't know it was an engagement party. We don't have a gift."

"Oh," Kate said, recovering. "We wouldn't expect you to."

"You can't deny it," Philip said. "You two are engaged and we're here for a party. Let's celebrate."

Steven seemed embarrassed and his ears stuck out even further. Kate wanted to reassure him, but just then Gaines and Valentine came walking up the street. The girl's face was almost plump now and her hair had grown so that her braids made a full crown on her head.

Tacker cooked the burgers. At the table, Kate passed the potato salad.

"A toast," Philip said, lifting his glass of lemonade. "To Kate and Tacker. May you never thirst again."

At the end of the evening, Tacker walked her home. The sun was setting. For a moment, a perfect arch of yellow spread out beyond the trees, pink above, and higher still, purple clouds. At her door, Tacker put his arms around her neck. He kissed her, drew back and looked at her, and kissed her again, and she knew without a doubt that he was a book she would never want to put down. It would take a lifetime to know him and to know herself with him. And she had the time.

Chapter Thirty-eight

SATURDAY. THE MORNING dawned heavy and overcast. Clouds the color of tin. Tacker took his coffee onto the front porch. No birdsong. A truck rumbled and backfired on the highway a few blocks away. In a tree across the road, a bare limb hung at an angle. The cedars shone pale blue. As he finished his coffee, a lone monarch butterfly wafted over late asters. Tacker didn't know whether to pray for the pool opening to go forward with thundershowers and a thinned crowd or whether to pray for such a downpour that it would have to be postponed.

Kate was going to take pictures for the paper. He had no right to talk her out of it. For some reason—maybe to teach him a lesson—Gaines wanted Tacker to be there, so Connie was managing the store for the day. Gaines asked if Valentine could stay at the foursquare if an older cousin came along to look after her while Tacker was out.

"I don't see why not," he said, "though I doubt I'll be gone more than thirty minutes."

Valentine and her cousin knocked at the back door at ten thirty. They had taken the bus. Tacker put out cookies and showed Valentine the milk in the fridge. The cousin, Juliette, looked familiar and Tacker wondered if she had been one of the girls from Winston-Salem State who protested that day at Woolworth's and got arrested. He was alarmed that he wasn't sure and didn't know what to say, so he said nothing. She didn't seem eager to help him out.

He could easily walk to the park, but at eleven o'clock he took the Indian down Jarvis to Sunset, left on First, right on Hawthorne, and then up Glade. The ride was just long enough for him to conjure Kate's face as she opened the little box and slid the ring on her finger and closed her hand. In that moment she had looked like a girl discovering a remedy for sorrow, not because she was marrying him but because she was claiming something for herself. And he thought if he never did anything else, he had made that moment and he loved her like a river.

Tacker parked in a grassy triangular easement at the intersection of West End and Glade, uphill from the park, where he could watch the crowd gathering. The white tents glowed in the overcast day. An abundance of white children waited in hot boredom. Tacker never would have noticed white children if he had not gone to Nigeria, where all the children were brown and to see a white one was to see an exotic species. The boys wore no cover-ups, only their suits. The girls wore skirts, and the tops of their bathing suits showed. Mothers wore shifts and something his mother called a muumuu, a large shapeless dress in loud colors, a design from the new state of Hawaii. A clique of teenage boys held themselves separately under a tree, barefoot next to their bicycles, wearing cutoff jeans. One of them was smoking. Some were as tall as Tacker and as big. They had the look of animals whose territory was shrinking. Tacker wondered if he had ever looked that way. He thought of the kid with his father who had beaten Gaines up in front of Hart's. The older girls stood thirty yards from the boys under an almost identical tree, confabbing about something, turned inward while the boys faced out. Their hair was perfectly set and Tacker wondered if they were going to ruin their coifs by swimming or if they would sit on towels applying Coppertone and conjuring indifference. It was a great relief to him that he found not one of the girls of interest. He didn't see Kate and was about to park the Indian and run up her steps to see if she was still home when he caught a whiff of popcorn from the concession stand. Something felt wrong and he couldn't remember if he had told Gaines's cousin to lock the house when he left her with Valentine. There was time. He better go back and check. Normally he wouldn't think much of it, but this was a big day. It seemed important that everything be tidy and stitched up. He got back on the Indian, made a wide turn on the street, and headed back, parking in front of the foursquare because it would only take a minute. The house was locked but he opened the door and went in. Valentine and Juliette were sitting on the couch with a book and da Vinci.

"Thought I might have left the back door unlocked," he said and moved through the house to check. It was as locked as the front door had been. Tacker made one more visit to the bathroom. "I won't be long," he said on his way out of the house. Somehow da Vinci leapt out the door behind him and Tacker had to go bounding after the cat four blocks until the animal decided to stretch out on the grass of a neighbor's yard and wait for his master to scoop him up. By the time Tacker got back to the pool, things were rolling. Dignitaries had arrived. A huge red ribbon was now strung across the gravel walkway. The mayor flourished a large set of scissors. Kate was down there, her legs splayed so she could hold the camera still. She seemed alarmingly far away. The mayor cut the ribbon. Kate got the picture. The crowd pressed in. The largest teenage boys claimed remnants of the ribbon and held them up like flags. They were the first to jump in, while all around the pool the younger children hovered like little ducks uncertain of what to do when faced with the sea.

Tacker left the bike and sauntered across the park. The gray clouds had lifted and the sky was blue enough for a postcard. The mayor had his perfect day.

"There you are," Kate said. "I'd started to think you weren't coming."

"I watched the festivities from the sidelines," he said, spotting Tom Driskell across the pool. He waved.

"No such luxury for the photographer," she said.

They sat in the grass. "Want something to drink?" Tacker said.

"I'm fine," Kate said.

A little girl stood on the side of the pool in the shallow end. Her mother was in the water coaxing her to jump. The girl wore a pink swimming suit and had a pink plastic float around her waist, but she wouldn't jump. Finally, her mother convinced her to come down one step at a time, though it took several minutes on each step.

"I should get her picture," Kate said when the little girl was in the pool in her tube.

Kate was midway down the side of the pool when Tacker heard stones crunching, then a sigh as if the earth had exhaled. Kate stopped midstride and lifted her camera toward what would one day be the entrance to the bathhouse. "Hells bells," someone yelled. "Stephanie, come right here," a mother cried. "Niggers," someone called.

Schraa schraa schraa.

Fabric and air and resistance and five dark bodies wheeled toward the pool, leaping, exploding into the water. Children screamed. Mothers snatched their youngest and headed to the shallow end, where they could exit. The older boys hoisted themselves out of the deep end like fish leaping from the sea. Kate snapped furiously.

The Negro boys breaststroked to the opposite side, leapt out, and were off in a sprint before anyone could stop them. Tom Driskell had both hands at his mouth.

"My word," a woman said.

"Jesus Christ," a man said.

"Can they be arrested, Mama?" said a young girl.

"I hope so, baby."

KATE RUSHED TOWARD Tacker and he to her. "Are you okay?" he said.

"I'm fine," she said, her eyes bright.

They stood in the midst of the confused crowd. No one knew whether it was safe to get back in the pool.

"They were only in there a few seconds. Not even a minute. I don't think that's long enough to contaminate the water," one of the high school boys said. "I'm getting back in."

The girls were still on their towels, their heads swiveling back and forth in conversation. The one who seemed in charge must have decided they should stay, because one of her lessers got up to go to the concession stand and bought a Coke.

Half the families packed up.

"I'LL MEET YOU at your house around six?" Tacker said to Kate.

"Okay," she said and headed toward her car.

Almost to his bike, Tacker spied Valentine. She was on the

gravel, headed toward the pool. He didn't call—he ran for her. She was faster than he expected her to be. Twenty feet from the poolside, she stopped and looked around.

"Valentine," Tacker called. "Honey. Wait."

She turned to look back at Tacker, recognizing his voice, but already two of the white high school boys had latched on to her and were scrambling toward the pool.

I'm almost there, Tacker thought. *Don't let go.* But even as he ran, they swung her back and launched her over the water. Her body was a lavender arc in the air, her braids back, her shoes bravely pointed toward heaven.

Tacker leapt in after her. She was near the bottom, her eyes closed, bubbles escaping her mouth. For a horrible moment Tacker thought she was already dead but she opened her eyes and even underwater he saw her terror.

They broke the surface and it took only three strokes for Tacker to reach the side of the deep end. He held her in one arm and the poolside with the other. "I've got you. I've got you. You're okay."

Her lips trembled. She closed her eyes.

He would not look into their faces. He would get her out of the pool in perfect quiet. Tacker let go of the side and swam with Valentine toward the shallow end.

"Keep your eyes down," he said.

He lifted her out.

"Juliette went to the bathroom and locked the door," she said.

"Shhhhh," Tacker said.

He set her down and held her hand. One shoe was missing. He leaned toward her ear. "We're going to walk out of here and get on my bike and go to my house and da Vinci," he said.

She didn't say anything.

Tacker heard a chair turn over and pulled Valentine closer. She shivered and he put his hand on her head. He looked up. A wooden Coca-Cola box streaked malignantly through the air like a heavy mechanical kite and he ducked.

A locomotive hit his head just before a riot went off in his chest and he glimpsed creosote ties under the steel track. Something slackened. Then a pain like a railroad spike to his skull. Valentine's face bloomed before him, her eyes as large and round as airplane windows, and he thought he could see a whole continent there. But the clouds closed in and the spike hit again. He sought speech and heard something deep inside back up and shift gears and roll through his head.

Oh my God.

Someone get an ambulance.

Light streamed under the track down into the earth like high beams from a truck and he tumbled back and faced the sky and everything was as red as Kate's mother's skirt in her portrait, only there was a perfect circle of pink. He could smell the pink circle—like the Indian and Kate's hair. He reached toward it for Kate and she pulled him through the hidden door.

Chapter Thirty-nine

Summer 1963

KATE HAD TURNED in her key to the *Journal and Sentinel*. This morning she folded her blouses one more time and eyed her luggage. She surveyed the shoes she had selected: black pumps, white flats, two pairs of sandals, a pair of tennis shoes. Once more she sorted through the cotton skirts and shifts and reminded herself that she also had the summer suit. She glanced in the mirror at her short haircut and decided for the tenth time that it was too abrupt.

Brian would be here midafternoon. She started downstairs to make herself a tuna salad sandwich and sat at the picnic table to eat it. The first hydrangeas were blooming, small brackets turning from white to blue. A male bluebird left the bluebird house and returned with bits of food in tireless rounds. Full-leafed dogwoods threw shadow onto the deep brown mulch of the flower beds. She heard a woodpecker somewhere.

Early in February, Kate had applied for the Peace Corps, re-
questing as first choice Nigeria. For the two years she was away,
Brian would remain in her house and go to Wake Forest College.

Charges of involuntary manslaughter had been brought
against the boy who threw the Coca-Cola crate that caused
Tacker's death. Involuntary manslaughter. According to the
medical examiner, it wasn't the initial contact with the box that
had cracked Tacker's skull and flooded his brain but hitting the
concrete poolside. Tacker's parents requested the charges be
dropped, but the state still sentenced the boy to a center for ju-
venile delinquents for two years. Much later, when Kate developed her film from that morning of the pool opening, she was
startled to see a picture of the very boy, smiling in his cut-off
blue jeans. This was before: before he threw the Coca-Cola box,
before he was found guilty. And he looked like any American
boy, or any white American boy, with his youthful chest and
lean arms and upward-tilted face, as if the world were his and
more, and she wondered how such anger and even hatred could
have fomented in him at so young an age. To her he looked like
an innocent. This seemed, finally, the clear truth of the camera:
that the eye sees what it expects to see. As long ago, she had
expected that Gaines—carrying the milk bottle—was up to no
good. Unless the eye is corrected, all vision is lost.

Tacker lived for two days before his parents took him off life
support. Gaines and Valentine held vigil with Kate and Tacker's
parents through the forty-eight hours.

There was no hope, but Kate hoped. In the askewness of
Tacker's face, he must be deliberating a problem in mathematics
or in the eventual crossing of all lines. She pressed a finger to his
forehead to smooth the frown gathered there.

Don't leave me, oh God, don't leave me.

When it was over she experienced a darkness so acute she

thought she would die. Brian left the beach house and came to live with her. Still, in a month she lost fifteen pounds. Aunt Mildred took her to the doctor. She was put on a medication that made her nauseated and she lost even more weight. Her engagement ring fell off and she had to wear it on a chain around her neck.

Brian was her salvation. She wept into his arms. For him, she would eat potato soup or a BLT. He washed her hair in the large kitchen sink and when it was dry made her sit in the fall garden of the backyard and drink hot cocoa. He prodded her to walk with him. They put out chrysanthemums. Kate was surprised and laughed finally the evening he produced a lopsided meat loaf and served it up with mashed potatoes and green beans.

In the evenings he read to her. George Eliot's *Middlemarch*, which she had never gotten to, and *The Folded Leaf* by William Maxwell. By the time they picked up *The Good Earth* by Pearl S. Buck, Kate was reading to him.

Little by little she began to feel she might live.

She woke one morning with a sense more of anticipation than dread. Brian gave her the family she had not had in a very long time. Their embrace was a form of shelter, a home.

On a cold November morning when Brian was out, Gaines and Valentine showed up at Kate's back door.

"I'm here to help you with your yard," Gaines said. He wore bib overalls and an old coat.

"You don't need to do that."

"Miss Monroe, I'm asking to come onto your porch without alarming your neighbors. Understand?"

"Oh."

They carried in a Tupperware bowl of banana pudding and she invited them into the house and they sat in the library together and ate out of the bowl with three spoons until it was gone.

Before they left, Gaines invited Kate to a meeting at a church in Happy Hill.

"You'll be welcomed."

"Do you think?"

In the Negro church that was brown inside, calming light fell through yellowed glass windows. Kate heard only a hum of voices, and when the meeting was over and they adjourned to a downstairs room for refreshments, she drank milk and ate brownies and pound cake with canned peaches. She went to the church every time Gaines asked, just to be there. Mid-December she picked up her camera and walked to Tacker's foursquare—it had not been re-rented—and took pictures. The nandina berries blazed red in the corner bed and the cedars shone aqua green, though the hardwoods were bare and leaf litter covered the garden she and Tacker had revealed in their day of raking only five months ago. Before leaving, she sat in Tacker's porch swing in her heavy coat.

The foursquare was the opposite of a round house. Still it felt like a womb she had been wrenched from. She wondered if people always loved more after death and if this was the beginning of religion.

In February, she threw a birthday party for Valentine at her house on Glade, inviting Tacker's parents along with Gaines and the birthday girl. At the Negro church, talk turned to freedom rides. These would require buses full of students and activists throughout the South, traveling to various locations to test whether new integration laws were being obeyed.

"Don't go," Kate said to Gaines when the meeting broke and they had a moment alone in the hallway. "Go back to college. You'll be able to do more with a degree. If anything happened to you, it would kill Valentine."

Kate took pictures of a protest at the Winston bus depot and developed them herself before giving them to Gaines for the Negro press.

Ground for the bathhouse was cleared in March and it opened on July 4, 1962, dedicated to Tacker Hart. On the eve of its opening, the city council voted to integrate the pool. At first white families stayed away, but by August a few came and Kate believed it was because of Tacker, because they still thought of him as the football player at Reynolds High, their all-American boy.

She offered to return the engagement ring to Tacker's mother but she asked her to keep it and Kate wore it on her right hand. When Kate got her assignment to Nigeria, she called Mrs. Hart before calling Brian or Aunt Mildred. A few days later, Tacker's mother brought over two letters from Tacker's friend Samuel Ladipo.

"I thought you might like to write to him. I'm sure Tacker told you about Samuel." She started to leave. "Do you think Valentine would like to visit da Vinci? Do you think her brother would bring her over to our house?"

"Yes," Kate said. "It's a perfect idea."

Kate wrote to Samuel but he didn't write back.

KATE WAS STATIONED in the town of Akure, two hours from the town of Osogbo, three hours from Ibadan. Stationed with her was Marilyn Mayse, a nurse from Birmingham, Alabama. They shared a two-bedroom house and Kate taught English in a local school. She also rigged up a darkroom and one evening a week she taught a class in photography to a group of young men. No Nigerian women, it appeared, wished to learn photography. Kate and Marilyn's kitchen was equipped with a kerosene refrigerator and a two-burner range. The house was powered by a small generator that went on the fritz now and then, and when it did they cooked outdoors over an open fire and mixed their powdered milk in the morning and drank it lukewarm. At least there was a reliable water supply through a faucet in the kitchen, though they had to boil the water. They bathed in a large galvanized tin tub, warming the water every night. Their radio could pick up the BBC as well as the Voice of America if they happened to be up at three in the morning.

A boy named Abel served as their courier according to his own design. He was not officially hired by the Peace Corps or by Kate and Marilyn. Thus he could not be sacked. He might have been eight or he might have been twelve; it was hard to know. In his brown shorts and brown shirt, he reached Kate's shoulders. Yet his face suggested a mature awareness of life. After a few weeks, they accepted his daily delivery of town gossip, folklore, and news from the capital. He also dutifully reported on the number of baptisms that occurred each week along with the number of people who had consulted with the local herbalist about their illnesses. He was deeply disturbed that Kate and Marilyn did not attend Sunday services and prayed for them aloud in their presence. Finally Kate began attending the Anglican church, though Abel was only modestly satisfied since he attended the Baptist church. As a kind of retaining fee, he accepted a Coca-Cola on Sunday and dashes, or tips, from Kate or Marilyn when they actually asked him to perform some duty.

One day Abel arrived just as Kate and Marilyn had returned from the clinic where Marilyn cared for orphaned children.

"Please, mah," he said, pulling Kate's arm. "A man is asking for you. He will be here soon."

Kate's hands went to her hair. Who in the world?

"A Nigerian man," Abel said.

She waited on the front veranda drinking Squash cooled by two precious ice cubes when she saw a man approaching in the traditional costume of voluminous robes, the sun catching the upward-slanting scars on his face. He had a wife with him and a baby. Wives generally carried their babies on their backs but this man held the infant as if he had given birth to it. The little tot was a boy, she presumed, since he was dressed identically to the man, only a smaller version. She rose and walked to the steps and then she saw.

The photograph of Tacker with his friend that she had kept on her windowsill in her kitchen on Glade Street, with the goat in the foreground, the one she had now in a frame beside her bed. Tacker's long hair and the man beside him, his face tilted upward. Samuel.

A sudden smell of frangipani in the air and a rustling in the bamboo and she was down the stairs, running across the brown yard.

Swimming
Between Worlds

Elaine Neil Orr

DISCUSSION QUESTIONS

1. Chapter One begins with the line "Tacker Hart came home from Nigeria to discover a town he almost knew." Do you think Tacker ultimately understands the town more or less by the end of the novel? What are the factors that shape his changing consciousness?

2. Tacker and Kate meet Gaines on the same day but respond to him in very different ways. How does each character see Gaines initially, and why? How does this view of Gaines change over the course of the novel? Whose friendship surprised you the most?

3. The novel's title, *Swimming Between Worlds*, emphasizes the important role that water plays in the story. How does water shape the lives of the main characters? What significance does the act of swimming hold in relation to the novel's themes?

4. Why is a grocery store such a surprising yet likely setting for the unfolding of this particular story? How do houses and architecture play a role in all of the characters' destinies?

5. In many ways, this is a coming-of-age story—we see Tacker, Kate, and Gaines searching for their places in the world. What one thing does each character seek most dearly, and why? Has each character achieved his or her goal at the end of the novel? Did their wants and desires resonate with your own memories of being a young adult?

6. Tacker experiences the minutiae of day-to-day life in both Nigeria and North Carolina. In what ways does each place fulfill the idea of "home" for Tacker? Do you think he would be happier living in one place over the other?

7. Tacker and Kate's romantic relationship undergoes numerous ups and downs. What did you think of their courtship and its challenges? Did their romance develop the way you expected? How did each character have to grow and change to achieve a loving relationship?

8. Throughout the novel, the reader is invited back to experience the full backstory of Tacker's time in Nigeria. How does Tacker's experience in West Africa frame his perception of the emerging civil rights movement? Have you read any other work that connects West Africa and American civil rights in this way?

9. Examine the scene in which Kate nearly faints and is helped to the lunch counter by Gaines. Why do you think this is the

moment when her beliefs and perceptions truly change? What is its significance?

10. Discuss the ways in which Kate changes over the course of the novel. How does photography enable her to come to terms with the past and her choices for the future? Consider the line "This seemed, finally, the clear truth of the camera: that the eye sees what it expects to see." How is this true not only for Kate, but for other characters in the novel?

11. Tacker's choice of whether to design the bathhouse places him at the center of a difficult moral dilemma. Do you think he ultimately makes the right decision? What would you have done in his place?

12. What did you think of the novel's ending? Were you surprised by Kate's decision at the conclusion of the book? What do you think her future holds? Do you anticipate that her friendship with Gaines and Valentine will endure?

13. How would this story be different if it were set in the Winston-Salem of today? What similarities exist between then and now?

Read on for an excerpt from
Elaine Neil Orr's

A Different Sun

Available now from Berkley

Chapter One
Greensboro, Georgia

1840

IN GRAY MORNING light, Emma Davis stood before the old slave's garden at the back of his cabin, looking upon the precise rows of cabbage planted for fall. The gentleman she called Uncle Eli had taught her to count by fours and she was quick to note he had four rows, sixteen cabbages apiece. "That will be sixty-four," she whispered. When she looked up, the sky had emerged pale blue, still too early, she knew, to impose herself on the old man. Emma felt a sense of guarded expectancy, enough life behind her to know hope could lead to disappointment. She was not that old. Eight years today.

Uncle Eli's cabin stood thirty paces from her own family home, a nice big house on a corner lot, creamy white, two-storied, with stairs leading up to a broad back porch. It was built in 1832, the year Emma was born, and always she thought the house was for her. By now she knew everything it had to offer, from the bedrooms upstairs on either side of the hallway—she and Catherine each had her own—to the stairway with the landing and the picture of the wild turkey, to the downstairs hall with the parlor and the sewing room on the right and the dining room and the breakfast room with the butler's pantry on the left. Papa's library opened at the very end of the hall.

A ruffle of wind came up the hill from the creek and Emma hugged her chest. She hopscotched to the center of her backyard and turned in a circle. Now she smelled biscuits and cast her eyes toward the kitchen where Uncle Eli's daughter, Mittie Ann, was making breakfast. The windows of the small building glowed as the woodstove inside it burned, and Emma knew that when Mittie Ann opened the oven, little sparks would fly. She let her feet follow the dirt path between the kitchen and back stairs. A low stone wall ran along the perimeter of the house for flower beds, and rather than step up and into the house, Emma launched herself onto this elevated path, taking it all along the side of the house parallel with the street and to the front yard, watching her feet, her arms extended straight out at her sides. In a moment, she caught sight of her mother moving across the grass with her red scissors and a flat basket. Emma stepped down, her arms still out.

"Good morning, missy. You're mighty early. Are you warm enough?" Mama said. "Come. I'm making a nice chrysanthemum bouquet for you."

The house faced to the southeast and the sun struck here first, just as now. Emma leaned over the blooms, catching their sharp, oily scent as her mother cut the stems long, each one curved in its cutting, and laid them in the basket. They would go in the tall crystal vase at the center of the dining table.

"Quick to put them in water," Mama said, placing a hand at Emma's neck. Then she was gone, the rustle of her dress behind her.

Emma looked down the road toward the center of town two blocks away. In winter, she could see the courthouse but the September leaves were still full, just beginning to color. Half aware she was taking the full circuit of her home, she meandered into the side yard, a corridor deep shaded by pines, floored in pine straw, almost dark at this early hour. Midway in her passage she came upon a long light-colored feather—an owl's, she considered—stuck at an angle into the straw. She bent to take it like the gift she wanted. *I can make a writing pen*, she thought and slipped it into her pocket just as Mittie Ann called for breakfast. Emma skipped around to the back steps, galloped up the stairs and into the house.

"You seem in a hurry," Papa said. "Give us a kiss."

A ceremony had occurred in the breakfast room when Papa brought in a new clock and placed it on the slate mantel. "Repeating brass, eight days, clock, manufactured by Davis and Barber, Greensboro, Georgia," he read from the bottom, "warranted if well used." Emma's family was not related to the Davises of Davis and Barber, but she felt proud anyway. Her father taught her to say "warranted if well used." When she performed for him, it didn't matter that Catherine was the pretty one. Papa would tell Mama things Emma liked to hear. "She drums her fingers because she has places to go," he would tease. "Just watch when I teach her to ride."

Here came Catherine, late as usual, and they could start. The biscuit shaped like a heart was for Emma. "Thank you," she said when Mittie Ann laid it on her plate.

And then it was fully day, breakfast over, and Emma could go, as she did most every day, to call on Uncle Eli. This habit came out of her life—Catherine several years older, Mittie Ann and her husband Carl, who lived with Uncle Eli, occupied with work, task by task, day by day. "The old African," as Emma's mother called him, was favored because he was an artisan. His carpentry, carried out in the yard, allowed him sitting time; his age gained him some leisure. Emma found him a good talker. Her mother said his English was better than most because he had been for several years the companion of a well-to-do white boy in Savannah. Uncle Eli called Emma his white bird, meaning, she knew, he had chosen her as special. It was the first reason she loved him. That and the way he threw his feet out when he walked, as if clearing a path.

"One tomato two tomato three tomato four," she said, winding her steps across the same yard she had traveled at daybreak, scratching at her neck where her hair was rolled up.

The old man was settled on his bench at the stoop of his back porch, his hands busy inside a basket. But he was looking away out into the distance where the morning sun lit the hill. She stood a moment, twisting her hair roll so it began to come down.

"Morning, Miss Emma. What you bringing?" he said.

"This," she said, pulling the feather from her pocket, running her fingers against the grain. She sat next to him on the bench. She had bitten her cheek at the breakfast table and if she pressed her tongue to the sore place, she could still taste blood. After a while, she leaned right over the basket where Uncle Eli was occupied. It smelled like a cow yard. Maybe there were dried eyeballs in there. She began to see: old corncobs and something that was innards or roots, snatches of dogwood with berries. He bundled his collection this way and that until at last he took a bit of twine from his hat brim and tied it all up. "What is it?" she said, a prick in her palms.

He didn't answer.

"It's a star," she said.

"Not a star," he said.

"What's it for?"

"You still have that feather?"

"You see I do."

He stuck the silky frond into his arrangement like a last stem into a nosegay. "Keep out bad spirits," he said, his eyes opening so she could see into them. They were like a dark space in the woods.

A rush of fear came up from Emma's stomach. "Don't scare me," she said, feeling everything go slant. When she stood she fell straight over from her leg falling asleep. She waited there on the ground, smelling the earth, seeing his broad feet. Uncle Eli pulled her up and dusted her skirt. He pressed her head between his hands.

"You gonna be all right," he said.

Something steadied in her, as if her bones were now solid and she were real.

"I have to go," she said, "for my lessons."

"I'll be seeing you," Uncle Eli said.

Emma slipped into the library. Papa's large desk sat before a window and on it a brightly colored globe. She had a habit of spinning the globe to see where her finger would land. Mostly it landed in blue Africa, where the pyramids were. She loved the shape of the continent and how mysterious it seemed.

Right now she was a little sorry she had given up the owl feather. She peered back into the hall for a sign of her sister or anyone, but the house was quiet. It took no time to unstop Papa's inkwell, press her frilled sleeve back to her elbow, dip the pen, and drag the bright nib up the pale underside of her arm, leaving a brilliant black trail and sending a wave along her skin all the way to her chest. She blew quickly to dry it, replaced the pen, and stoppered the well. Emma caught a reflection of herself in a glassed picture on the wall. Then she looked at her arm, determined it dry, and pulled the sleeve down. In this cocoon of her self, she opened the text she was supposed to read, *The Girl's Own Book*, a gray volume all about correctness of principle. After a bit, she pulled out her Greek mythology. It was better, offering the story of Romulus and Remus, which made the whole world alive. Finally, she dipped into *Cousin Lucy among the Mountains*. Emma could tell it was not a very good story. It was too unlikely. She itched for her own paper.

THEN FALL CAME. Emma was in the backyard playing marbles. She looked up to see a girl from her father's plantation. Emma knew little about the farm three miles out of town and the forty slaves who worked it. She was familiar only with Carl because he lived in her yard and this one girl who came to the house on errands, riding in the back of a wagon when someone came into town. She might carry a basket of blackberries or deliver news that a baby had died.

"Watch," Emma said, as the girl stood close. "Watch how I do it."

"What your name?" the girl said.

"Emma. You call me Miss Emma."

"What it mean?"

A tightness gathered in Emma's stomach. "It doesn't mean anything. It's my name." But the girl pointed with her cinnamon fingers to the sky.

"My name Hannah. Mean Jesus loves me," she said.

Just then the back door opened and Papa came heavy down the stairs.

"What you doing here, girl?" He was talking to Hannah, who was now looking at her toes in the dirt. Emma watched her father. His hands rested on his belt. He was close enough to reach out and touch the other girl's head. Why didn't Hannah speak up?

"I was showing her marbles," Emma said in a rush. But her

father kept looking at Hannah and Hannah at the ground. What if he hit her? Emma felt wild, as if a frightening world lurked nearby that might open to things she didn't want to know.

"How old are you?" her father said.

"I'm nine year old." Hannah swayed in her hips.

"Almost like me," Emma said, trying to reach the girl and her papa, trying to stay clear of that other, scary world.

"Old enough to be in the field with your mama," her father said, ignoring Emma. "Next time you tell your folks to send a younger child. Now you go on."

Right then Emma knew there was something wrong with the way they lived: Hannah with the creamy skin whose name meant Jesus loved her wore only a shift you could see through while Emma was layered in more clothes than she cared for. The wrongness was so bad she wanted to pinch someone.

"Go on," her father said, and Hannah turned, her dress slipping down one shoulder. Something fell away. Emma wanted to cry, not weep, but cry, like the Bible says: someone crying in the wilderness. Instead, with the heel of her boot, she stomped the shooter marble into the sandy yard and then the others. "I don't care about marbles," she muttered under her breath.

The next morning when Papa came into the library, Emma was in her place, a seat at the round table in the center of the room. "I want some paper," she said.

"You use your slate for arithmetic," he said.

"I want to draw and write," she said.

"I don't know as girls write," he said. "Let's hear your multiplication tables in elevens and twelves."

Emma rolled it out. She loved her father.

"That's my girl," Papa said. "Come with me now. I need to talk with Mr. George at the bank. Get your gloves." At the front door, Emma claimed his hand. To a point, he seemed to know her worth, and beyond that, what he could not fathom, was a fault in her or a fault in him. She was not sure which.

EMMA STUDIED THE print in her dress. Papa had said he would not come to the revival. Now she pressed closer to Mama. The coal stove against the wall was not enough to warm her. Something shook in the preacher's voice although the voice was smooth. She looked up at him and felt a power coming at her. It licked her feet and rose all through her into her neck where it seemed to wait for her to remember taking up her father's pen without permission, envying Catherine, letting Hannah walk away, all her other wrongs. When the man called for them to come, to confess Jesus as Lord and Savior, she almost stumbled in her hurry, pulling her mother, or was her mother pulling her, and Catherine. They knelt and he blessed them and a hundred more, so many that the walls of the church seemed to bend out, blessed them in the light of their sin.

After the revival, Mama doubled up on the "extras" for the slave quarters: scraps of cloth for quilting, pots of molasses, and old blankets cut into pieces for newborns. She sent money to a Reverend Humphrey Posey in north Georgia, who had built an Indian church. She held devotionals for the household in the sewing room on Sunday afternoons. Uncle Eli and Mittie Ann and Carl professed Jesus as Lord. But not Papa.

Emma found it harder and harder to escape that sense of foreboding, that dark other world she had first sensed when Hannah's dress slipped off her shoulder. Papa's not being saved made it like a shadow in the house, like the black line she had drawn on her skin, there even when it was washed off.

December came wet and unseasonably warm, causing hay to rot in the barns. Emma sensed an ill mood in her father. On Christmas Eve, she and Catherine were to recite "Nativity," but as Emma entered the dining room, her mother instructed her directly to take a seat.

"Let us say grace," she said.

Emma prayed for clear skies and cold, only briefly pondering letter paper and a box of pencils. "Amen," she said, opening her napkin. Mama rang the bell and Mittie Ann came in to serve. Emma forgot about the bad weather and kept her eye on the wishbone. Papa began to talk.

"It's happened," he said.

"What's that, Charles?"

Emma sat up, alert to Mama using Papa's first name.

"Our friend Mr. Joel Early is going through with it."

Her mother said nothing. Mittie Ann was holding the chicken platter and didn't move.

"He's freeing his slaves, giving every last one a hundred dollars in silver, and sending them back to Africa."

Emma thought her mother's lips trembled. "Mr. Early was always odd," she said, "from the first day I knew him. Girls, look you don't dip your sleeve into the gravy boat."

"He's arranged passage from Norfolk," Papa went on. "Even giving them a new set of clothes." Her father dug into the rice as if it needed discipline. The platter of chicken hadn't moved, and Mittie Ann, who should be moving it, was standing like a stone.

Mr. Early was wealthier than Emma's father. He owned a new coach driven by a fine-looking Negro in a red vest. Suddenly she imagined the Negro gone, Mr. Early's coach flailing downhill, the horse wild, the whole world coming apart.

"Let Early go with them; I hope they all drown," Papa said, pounding his fist on the table.

No one looked at anyone.

"Let us keep our own dignity," Mama said finally. "Pass the chicken, Mittie Ann. It's getting cold."

"You wouldn't want to go to Africa, would you, girl?" Papa said, looking at the colored woman.

"No sir," Mittie Ann said.

Emma wished the woman had said it stronger, to make her believe. When the chicken finally arrived, she took a wing and left the wishbone, though she could imagine that tender white meat between her teeth, the coat of flour fried to a sweet crisp. In her mind floated lines from the poem she and Catherine did not recite.

> *But peaceful was the night*
> *When the Prince of light*
> *His reign of peace upon the earth began.*

Photo by Elizabeth Galecke Photography

Elaine Neil Orr is Professor of English at North Carolina State University in Raleigh, where she teaches world literature and creative writing. She also serves on the faculty of the low-residency MFA in Writing program at Spalding University in Louisville. Author of *A Different Sun*, two scholarly books, and the memoir *Gods of Noonday: A White Girl's African Life*, she has been a featured speaker and writer-in-residence at numerous universities and conferences and is a frequent fellow at the Virginia Center for the Creative Arts. She grew up in Nigeria. Visit her online at www.elaineneilorr.com.